Fabulous Beasts

a love story

W.A. Schwartz

Black Rose Writing | Texas

This is a work of fiction. Names, characters, businesses, places, events, and incidents are either the products of the author's imagination or used in a fictitious manner. Any resemblance to actual persons, living or dead, or actual events is purely coincidental.

ISBN: 978-1-68513-605-5
PUBLISHED BY BLACK ROSE WRITING
www.blackrosewriting.com

Printed in the United States of America
Suggested Retail Price (SRP) $25.95

Fabulous Beasts is printed in Garamond Premier Pro

*As a planet-friendly publisher, Black Rose Writing does its best to eliminate unnecessary waste to reduce paper usage and energy costs, while never compromising the reading experience. As a result, the final word count vs. page count may not meet common expectations.

For Olivia, Bella, and Nick
All my life's poetry

Fabulous Beasts is a work of fiction. We do not claim to be historians. While inspired by a true story, many of the characters portrayed here have some counterparts in real life, all characterizations, timelines, details, and incidents, minor and major, are products of the author's imagination. Therefore, *Fabulous Beasts* should be read entirely as a work of fiction, not as a biography of any individual.

–W.A. Schwartz May 2024

Much Madness is divinest Sense –
To a discerning Eye –
Much Sense – the starkest Madness –
'Tis the Majority
In this, as all, prevail –
Assent – and you are sane –
Demur – you're straightway dangerous –
And handled with a Chain –
–Emily Dickinson, *c. 1862.*

Out of the ash I rise with my red hair
And I eat men like air
–Sylvia Plath, *1962*

"I'm a kind of secret beatnik hiding in the suburbs."
–Anne Sexton, *Letter to a Friend, 1959*

Fabulous Beasts

FORWARD

In late 1962, my grandmother, Vivienne Holland—a writer, a mother, a wife—disappeared from her own life. A few months later, her life ended in a terrible, quiet tragedy.

By the time I was born, two decades later, her work, especially her poetry, had topped bestseller lists and become a staple in schools. Today, her writing is translated worldwide, and she's celebrated as a pioneer in feminist literature and confessional poetry. Yet, while her words resonate with readers everywhere, I doubt she would have recognized herself in these accolades. Her writing conveyed profound pain and raw emotion, but the essence of who she was—the "why" of her life—was something the world never truly understood.

As a young girl, I remember tracing my finger along the edges of tarnished silver-framed photographs in my father's quiet house. Unsmiling figures posed outside a grand, if crumbling, ivy-covered mansion—a place that seemed haunted to my young American eyes. Toddlers played in fields of wildflowers, chewing on grass stems, while others stared at the camera with implacable expressions. I'd lean in close and sometimes carefully remove a photo to read the faded ink on the back: "Beanie and Gran, '48" or "Viv and kids, '61." I recognized my father, a big-eyed, solemn boy, as he would look as a man, in those photos but no one else.

One photo captivated me: two young girls with wide grins and glossy ponytails stood together on a beach, the wild Atlantic Ocean churning gray and foreboding behind them. Overhead, dark clouds bloomed, and a fierce wind whipped around them, pushing their skirts tightly against their thighs. They held onto one another as if they'd just been laughing too hard to stand straight. *They were laughing in the face of an oncoming storm,* I thought. *A dangerous storm.* The inscription read, "Viv and Ruthie, 1945."

I finally met Ruthie Hampton, the "Ruthie" from that 1945 photo, in 2000. By then, she was a lively septuagenarian living in London. I'd been working on my graduate thesis, a comprehensive study of Vivienne's life, death, and influence, and I'd hit a wall that nearly forced me to abandon the project. Her extensive letters and many of her journals, which I'd read and reread, were often cheerful and chatty—a stark contrast to her dark poetry, belying what I suspected was a life at least punctuated by unbearable pain. Despite keeping diaries and sending letters on an almost obsessive basis, Vivienne fell silent in late 1962. There was nothing to help me understand what happened in those last tragic months. I sought out Ruthie, hoping for answers.

We spent hours over tea in her small, chintz-covered sitting room as she shared memories of my grandmother. Then, one afternoon, Ruthie led me up a narrow set of attic stairs to retrieve a box.

"I'm sorry," she said as I held it.

"Sorry? For what?"

"I wanted her to be understood. I didn't want the wrong person, or people, seeing those." She gestured at the box, and I stared down, wondering what I might be holding. "Those are her private journals and letters she never sent. Her last thoughts. I gathered them—or stole them—that final day."

What follows is the result of my lifelong fascination with my grandmother, Vivienne Holland. In telling her story, I was overcome with grief over the course her life took. While I realized there is no single answer to the question of *why,* what remains is her work, especially the pieces she created toward the end of her life, hidden for so many years. I am proud to call her my grandmother, humbled by her struggles, and left wishing I could have known her as a person.

Since completing this book, I've written novels, essays, and earned advanced degrees, but this project is my favorite—a tribute to Vivienne's life and legacy. My deepest gratitude goes to Ruthie; without her, this story would never have been told.

–Jane Irving, Author, London, 2024

LONDON
10 February 1963

Shivering in the cold, Vivienne stands outside her flat. In a dome of plum sky, the moon is a pale disc, casting an eerie glow. She feels a jolt of fear as she studies him, uncertain if she had, in fact, invited him here. His refusal to come inside only adds to her agitation.

She narrows her eyes, trying to make sure he's real. His coat bunches and strains at the underarms and side seams, his pale hands hidden behind his back. In this light, he could be wearing a straitjacket. The thought makes her smile, but the movement on her face is imperceptible to him.

"This is ridiculous, all these hysterics. I won't have it, not again," Jack says.

Vivienne thinks, yes, he's real.

He turns, as if to leave, and finally, she makes her mouth move. "I want you to give me back what you took."

She senses, rather than sees, him tense up.

"For God's sake, Vivienne, what are you talking about?"

"My life, Jack. You took everything. How can you not see it?"

She's on the verge of losing control, her throat tight with unspoken words that feel like rocks lodged inside.

"You're doing it again, Vivienne—acting crazy, trying to punish me," he says, taking a step toward her. His face glows beneath the gaslights, but his voice softens. "Look, you need rest. I can see how tired you are. Dr. H. called me. He says you're not sleeping. Go on in; I'll come round tomorrow. How's that?"

There are icy tears on her cheeks, though she doesn't feel the cold. "Just tell me something, Jack," she says.

He sighs. "What is it, Vivienne?"

"Was I wrong?"

"About what?"

"All of it."

He hesitates for a long time. Then, turning away, Vivienne catches a faint whiff of *her*—the unmistakable scent lingering on him. She can't stop herself. "Was I ever wrong? All those times you said I was."

He heads down the step, striding toward his car, and finally glances back. "No, Vivienne. You were never wrong."

Her boots crack against the iced pavement as she heads back up to the flat. Though temperatures are rising in London, the city remains coated in ice, with hills of snow everywhere. Silence wraps around her, broken only by a faint whirring that might be a distant car. A hazy mist hovers over Primrose Hill, and Vivienne feels a peculiar, settled calm.

She lets the heavy outer door swing shut behind her before making her way upstairs to her sleeping children. There is much to accomplish before morning.

PART ONE: 1940-1941

4   FABULOUS BEASTS

CHAPTER ONE

SPEAKING TO GOD

1

Daddy died in the fall of 1940, three days before Roosevelt promised not to send our boys to war. He died in Winthrop, Massachusetts, two thousand miles from the country of his birth. He fell into delirium and died babbling in German about murder and bumblebees. Mother was at his bedside with a cool cloth, whispering, *Shh now, darling, it will be alright*, and there were his long legs, gone all dried and scrawny and sticking out of the sheet-like driftwood, and Daddy died, even though he promised Vivienne he would not.

2

Afterward, they called him a *presence*, the lavender-scented ladies, who floated up and down, dabbing at their eyes with sharp red nails and clutching their kerchiefs embroidered stiff with tiny pink roses, like blisters. *He commanded a room; He was a presence.* Their whispers were like howls. *He would be so terribly missed.*

3

Vivienne wandered among the adults in the living room, feeling strangely weightless and sickishly dense, as if her body were made of solid iron yet still capable of floating free of the earth. No one noticed as she slipped between pairs of creased trousers and sleek-stockinged legs. Almost no one. Mrs.

Teasdale, an enormously fat woman who'd lost (actually lost; he'd disappeared) her husband a year earlier, caught Vivienne's eye and stuck out her bottom lip, making a creepy adult sad face. Everyone knew Mrs. Teasdale had loathed her husband—a skinny, unhappy man with a pockmarked face who worked for the government and spent weekends in his front yard drinking Coca-Cola, glaring at anyone who walked by. Vivienne suspected Mrs. Teasdale had murdered the poor man and hidden him in the basement. Mrs. Teasdale seemed much happier since he'd gone, and, after all, it only made sense. Vivienne had once suggested her theory to Mother, but Mother replied only that Vivienne ought never to say such vulgar things. Vivienne failed to see how a theory could be vulgar, but she stopped talking about it anyway. Still, she felt vindicated looking at Mrs. Teasdale now, in her low-cut dark blue dress and bright hibiscus-colored lipstick.

Vivienne ignored Mrs. Teasdale's glance and continued through the crowd. No one else acknowledged her, and she welcomed the inattention. As she moved, words hissed from mouths above her head.

"They took his leg, you know?"

"Oh, how terrible."

"Above the knee, the thigh. And gangrene. He was home for a time before he passed. An awful thing."

It was true about the leg. Daddy had gone to the hospital and come home without it—and, curiously, without a shoe. Vivienne tried to ask what happened to the black shoe he'd been wearing on his good foot when he'd been taken away—a leather Oxford, one of the nice pairs he wore for teaching at the University. She thought he ought to hold on to both of them, even though he hadn't been to the classroom in nearly a year. Mother hadn't answered. Somehow, Vivienne knew not to ask again. Now, she supposed, it didn't matter. What would he do with one shoe? *Do shoe,* she thought, *do, do, one black shoe,* repeating the words to herself several times, amused by the rhyme.

Vivienne sat in the dining room on one of the stiff-backed chairs, digging a fingernail into the cushion, trying to unravel a tiny cluster of embroidered flowers. Daddy's mother's needlework. That grandmother had died long ago, but the embroidery, thin and faded, was stubbornly resistant to final destruction; Vivienne had tried many times. The chairs were horrid and uncomfortable, yet Mother insisted that she and her brother, Beanie (his real name was Bernard, but nobody called him Bernard), sit on them exactly twice yearly for long holiday meals. Twice a year was quite enough, but Vivienne sat on one now. After today, she supposed they'd never use these chairs again. Mother hated cooking those meals, and she'd only done it for Daddy.

Friends and neighbors had piled the dining table with food: a big china platter with baked sweet rolls and slices of ham decorated with red grapes. Some kid (Vivienne decided it must have been a kid) had picked off the grapes, smashing them one by one onto the white tablecloth, leaving a row of squashy purple thumbprints. There was half a lemon pie, much of which was smeared across that end of the table, probably by the grape-smashing kid, and a pile of untouched twice-baked potatoes. Vivienne stared at the potatoes. Probably no one could figure out how to eat them since Mother hadn't put out extra forks. There were sticky casseroles, piles of crackers, and bowls of Jell-O in cheerful flavors. Vivienne thought it might be wrong to serve Jell-O when somebody was dead, but she was only eight, so she didn't know.

The whole thing made Vivienne both sick and sad. She hadn't been allowed to attend the funeral, but this—whatever it was—she'd been required to. She sat, hating everything about it. A horrible, black, miserable Jell-O-eating party. The people pretending to be sad, though they weren't. Except the small children; they weren't pretending, which was better. Instead, they played chase and hide-and-seek, running in and out of the kitchen, giggling, hands over their mouths, laughing even harder when their parents shushed and shooed them back outside.

Beanie, whom Vivienne considered lucky to be five, had been put to bed early because of his youth. He'd been spared the misery she was presently enduring. Beanie was called Beanie because his nickname, Bernie, had proved unpronounceable to three-year-old Vivienne, who squealed "Beeeenie!" at the new baby with such enthusiasm that it stuck. Beanie was never given a say in the matter.

Vivienne watched as Mother moved about the room, dipping her head, listening, smiling, conversing just the right amount of time with each guest, and moving on.

Mother isn't sad. She hasn't cried, Vivienne thought. *She'll never cry.* She studied Mother a bit longer, then pulled a large cloth napkin from the folded pile on the table before her, spread it out on her lap, picked it up, and dropped it over her head. The drape covered her face, the edge nearly brushing her shoulders—a shroud. In stillness, she sat for a long time, concentrating on her thoughts, working to increase their volume until they drowned out the adult words fluttering past the thin folds of fabric like moths.

4

Beanie was small; Vivienne was big and clever, so Daddy granted her many privileges. While her brother had his bath in the evenings, if Daddy's mood was right, Vivienne followed him into his study and curled up in the soft chair beside his desk. In the warm, dark office, she listened to the scritch-scratch of his pencil as he marked his students' papers. Sometimes, she would drift into sleep, and in her dreams, her father's red correction pencil would draw soft red Xs across her mind. On warm days, they went to the ocean to swim; on others, Daddy let her visit his bees. Vivienne loved watching him trap a bee in his big fist. He would hold it just long enough for her to hear the buzzing, then fling open his hand to let it go.

In the summer, sickness dulled the blue fire in his eyes, like a shade pulling across his insides. Some mornings, he still went to the college, but he stopped bringing home small prizes for Vivienne—a pencil, a neat pink eraser, or an apple, pulling them like secrets from his satchel after settling into his chair. Instead, he would lie on the sofa after work, waiting for Mother to bring him ice chips or cups of tomato juice. They no longer went to the ocean together. He no longer leaped through the salty, churning waves with Vivienne clinging to his back, feeling terrified and glorious with her very own Superman.

He refused to see a doctor. Mother begged him, but he refused. "The diagnosis is obvious," he said, "and I am doomed. No doctors!" And so, instead, he lay on the sofa, shouting and withering, until finally, he could only stay in bed. When he was too weak to refuse, Mother brought the doctor, and Vivienne watched them take her father away. When he returned, they had left his leg behind—his shoe and his leg.

Four days after that, he was dead.

5

Beneath the napkin, her face grew warm, then too warm. Sweat collected at her temples, trickling down her forehead, with one or two droplets threatening to leap over her brow bone unless she remained perfectly still. She braided her fingers together and squeezed, imagining herself as a statue made of wood. No, she thought, stone—she was a stone statue, harder than wood.

"Vivienne!" said a voice.

Suddenly, an artificial bluish light fell across her face, sharp and painful like a slap. She blinked and looked up. Mother loomed over her, clutching the napkin in her fist as if it possessed a life of its own.

"Vivienne! What are you doing? You look... well, never mind how you look. Just stop." Then Mother softened a bit and bent forward, cupping Vivienne's chin in her palm. Her words sounded brittle, like a slender sugar wafer that crumbles almost before it reaches your mouth. "Look," she said, "tomorrow, these people will be gone. You and Beanie will be home, and we'll all take a rest."

Vivienne stared at her, watching as Mother glanced around, as if her next words were hovering over her shoulder like little lost balloons.

"We will all go to church and then we'll rest, alright?" she said.

Vivienne nodded in silence. Mother took a step to leave, then noticed she was still holding the napkin. She stopped and folded it in half, then in quarters, and, oddly, once more, into a smaller square. Finally, she set it down on the table gently, as though it were made of glass. She smoothed her skirt, though Vivienne could see the black fabric had no wrinkles. Mother drew in a breath, straightened her shoulders, and returned to the living room.

Once Mother was out of sight, Vivienne picked up the folded napkin, shook it open, and plopped it back over her head. *You're wrong,* she thought. *Tomorrow, I won't stay home. I'll go straight to school. I won't go to church, and I'll never speak to God again.*

CHAPTER TWO

RUTHIE HAMPTON

We were close. What I mean is, we were closer than you might imagine neighbors would be in Winthrop. My mother always said Lorah, Viv's mother, seemed standoffish, but looking back, I realize complexity filled her life. Fritz Holland was not an easy man. He had a temper, even before he got sick; He wanted things just so and you know he was at least two decades Lorah's senior. So, I think that the age gap might have intimidated her. I think the families were friends because of us kids. For gosh sakes, me and Vivienne were inseparable, like two peas in a pod, and my big brother Stan, well, he had quite the crush on little Vivienne for the longest time. But, anyway, that's not what you were asking.

Yes, we all saw her, Vivienne, outside the house in that little nursing costume. One of Fritz's nurses had made it for her. It was quite a sad sight. She would sit there on the little garden wall in front of their house most afternoons after her father became ill. She seemed to wait, perhaps until someone called her back inside. She wrote poetry for him and put on little plays, trying her best to entertain and comfort him. It was all quite heart-wrenching. This would have been around 1939 or 1940, if I recall correctly.

You know later I spoke with Lorah, and she mentioned how Vivienne might have mixed up some of her memories, some of those things she wrote about later in life were a bit, let's say, questionable. It was Vivienne's grandfather who mostly took her to the beach, not her father, although I saw Fritz join them a few times. Fritz was quite a striking figure—tall, with thick hair and those forever blue eyes. To a little kid, he was scary, but in retrospect, he was a good looking man. He didn't go out much, but when he did, he certainly caught people's attention. Usually, it was just Vivienne with him; Lorah and the little brother stayed behind, probably because of the baby's allergies and asthma.

That might've been the only time I saw Fritz really smile when he was out with Viv. He was otherwise a serious man, what you might call a workaholic today. And, of course, there were his bees—he was quite famous for them, you know. He loved those bees almost as much as he loved his girl.

As he got sicker, though, everything changed. Viv said he refused to see a doctor, convinced he was dying of cancer, but it turned out to be diabetes—such a needless tragedy, everyone said afterward. The house had this terrible smell, something rotting, in those last months. I didn't go in much; we weren't allowed. And I know Viv's mother was working herself to the bone, trying to keep the kids quiet and away from Fritz since the noise bothered him so much.

It was probably a mercy when they sent Vivienne away. At first, I thought it was because she was a bit of a handful—not in a bad way, but she was fearless, a daredevil. Racing down the streets on her bike or diving headlong into the sea. Later, as a teenager, she broke her leg the first time she went skiing—just launched herself down the slope without a second thought. Back then, I thought they sent her away to keep her out of trouble, but now I think it was out of love. Lorah didn't want her daughter to watch Fritz die. So, Viv went to stay with her grandparents at Point Shirley for a year. And after Fritz passed, sending her away just seemed to become a pattern—off to grandparents, camps, and so forth.

Something in Vivienne changed after all that. She had been so much fun, and then she just... wasn't. Lorah carried a lot of guilt about it, but honestly, I think Vivienne was trying so hard to please her father, and after he was gone, she seemed lost.

I always blamed Fritz, at least partly; you know? For what happened later, after Vivienne grew up. I didn't care he'd been gone for years by then. I blamed him anyway.

Oh, don't listen to me, I'm just babbling now, a nosy Nellie. I knew Viv of course but not so much the rest of the family. No, I can't say I knew them well at all, but still, a person can sense things you know. Well, you could just tell.

CHAPTER THREE

MYTHLMROID, ENGLAND

1

The Poet squatted beside the muddy stream, reached into the water, and pulled at the dead fox until it came free of the trap. One of its legs was severely damaged (likely chewed by the fox itself). It broke loose with a snap, and the creature came away three-legged.

The year was 1938, and The Poet, a boy of not yet eight, stood tall for his age. "Sturdy," his mother called him. "Tough, curious, ready." He delighted in following his older brother, Rowdy, out onto the moor for any kind of adventure. "The Poet" was his secret name, the one he called himself on the inside, where nobody could see. He couldn't remember when he'd first received the name or from whom it had come. Perhaps someone in a dream. It didn't matter; he couldn't perceive himself any differently now.

"Rowdy!" The Poet shouted, barely able to keep the excitement out of his voice. At seventeen, his brother knew better than to be noisy and did not reply.

"I got him; I got him! Not a wee thing. He's a big one," The Poet shout-whispered as his brother approached, pushing his way between the birch trees and out of a narrow passageway in the woods.

"So, you did, Jack, so you did," said Rowdy, a huge boy, nearly a man. He held out his hand. "See here, Jack, hand 'im over."

Jack, short for Jerrick C. Welles, was the name everyone called him. It was his "outside" name, and he didn't mind; it suited him well enough. Reluctantly, The Poet stood and handed over the fox, tail first. Blood still dripped from the carcass, near the spot where the leg had come off, most of it congealed in the matted fur.

"Been dead a while," said Rowdy. "We'll have to see."

He rolled the animal around in his hands, inspecting the reddish-orange pelt.

"Nah," said The Poet. "It's a one; I'll show you."

He looked up at his brother, grinning. Rowdy smiled back.

"Yeah, yeah, right. You did good. Come on. Let's go."

Rowdy handed the animal back, and The Poet stuffed it proudly into his knapsack. Then the two of them set off across the moor toward home.

2

Mytholmroyd, nestled in the Upper Calder Valley of West Yorkshire, England, was a quaint industrial village defined by its picturesque yet rugged surroundings. Cradled between the flowing River Calder on one side and the imposing Scout Rock on the other—a massive, gray cliff that loomed over the village like a silent sentinel—it presented a challenge that The Poet and his brother, along with all the local boys, would attempt to conquer. Mytholmroyd was the sort of place where every soul was known to every other, where much of life was work and sleep, and where secrets were not kept for long.

In the Lakefield neighborhood of Mytholmroyd, rows of terraced houses stood shoulder to shoulder, their walls so tightly packed that the faintest sounds of domestic life permeated through the air. It was a place where the cries of a newborn during a midnight feeding could travel an entire block; the walls whispering each echo from home to home.

The neighborhood stretched along a narrow road, bordered on one side by a canal. Once busy with traffic, the canal had slipped into hushed disuse, now serving as a playground for the local children. They would leap over the fence to swim and fish, their imaginations transforming the stagnant waters into the vast and enigmatic depths of Scotland's Loch Morar. Rowdy, ever the storyteller, would weave tales for The Poet of the loch's thousand feet of "dead black silence," thrilling and chilling him in equal measure.

On the other ran dirt paths and scattered fields, some opening to the moors. Here was where the two brothers found themselves on this particular morning.

As they walked, The Poet listened to the sound of his wellies squelching satisfactorily into the muddy earth. The mist was grey and sheeted, the air thick with the smell of wet wool and earth. With each step, he put a bit more energy into his footfall. Slap. Slap. Slam! Muck flew into the air out the side of his boot, and a fist-sized blob hit his brother in the right cheek.

Ah, bollocks! said Rowdy, turning toward the younger boy, wiping at his face. The Poet took a step back. This, he thought, could go a few different ways, none of them especially good. The Poet held his breath, ready to turn and run. Rowdy was bigger, but The Poet thought his small size might make him faster in the mud. Abruptly Rowdy's face broke. A huge grin. Then he stooped, and before The Poet could get more than a half step, a glob of mud hit his scalp and began dripping down inside his collar. It stung, but he laughed.

They ran to the canal, scaled the crumbling brick wall, and wound up sweating and filthy, and hysterical with laughter, at the back door of Number 1, Aspinall Street. Somehow, they managed to not drop the rucksack, now blood-soaked and heavy with the body of the dead fox.

The Poet looked around, taking in the familiar sights of the old brick buildings and the narrow alleyways. The canal water was murky, reflecting the dimming sky above. The sound of their laughter echoed off the walls, mingling with the distant chatter of the neighborhood.

3

That night, The Poet dreamed of another fox. A cub orphaned by the one they'd found in the deadfall trap. An old lady he didn't recognize found the cub and brought it to his mother, laying it on the table in their tiny kitchen. The thing didn't run. It only curled itself into a scrubby little ball as if it might disappear. It might have been asleep, except that he could see its eyes were open. Watching. He noticed his mother holding an enormous butcher's knife and the blade moving down toward the little cub. As he watched, its face changed, taking on the features of a man; its lips moved like a man's lips, although The Poet could not tell what words it spoke. The blade flashed, and in a panic, he reached forward to grasp the cub out of harm's way. All at once, the cub was neither cub nor human but a full-grown fox standing erect on its hind legs, studying him. The blood, which was everywhere, came not from the fox but his own hand. When he looked down, The Poet could see that all his fingers had been neatly chopped off.

4

There sat a makeshift radio in the kitchen, cobbled together by The Poet's father from an assortment of bits and bobs, lovingly assembled over countless hours. It was no ordinary radio; it had become the crown jewel of the Welles household. The Poet's father boasted it was the "King of all Radios," with the remarkable ability to bring King George's voice right into their kitchen, as if he were sitting at the table with them. Their small, often stuffy kitchen, perpetually scented with the mingling aromas of baking grease and sweat, had transformed into the communal heart of their home. It was especially true on days like today when something significant was expected to be broadcast.

The kitchen was bustling and packed tighter than usual. The entire Welles family, along with aunts, cousins, and neighbors, had gathered, crowding around the radio. Some even spilled out the open door, straining to listen. They were all there to hear Prime Minister Neville Chamberlain speak about his recent meeting with Hitler in Munich, an event that held the world's breath in its grasp.

As the radio crackled to life, Chamberlain's voice filled the room: "My friends, for the second time in our history, a British Prime Minister has returned from Germany bringing peace with honour..." The words, intended to be reassuring, hung heavily in the air, as the gathered crowd absorbed the gravity of his statement, each person silently pondering what this supposed peace would truly mean for them.

"That's what I like to hear," howled a beefy, brutal man, a coal miner, face blackened from work. "Nowt about going to war, I say. Had enough o that, I say." He guffawed and took a long swig from the bottle he held.

"Oh, quit yer yakin, Ben," spat his wife, socking him in the back of the head.

"...peace for our time."

"I can't hear with me arsehole husband yakin, bloody gormless he is," the wife said. "What happened? I missed it."

"Nowt we didna already know, they signed," said Mother, Mrs. Welles. "That's it then; they signed it. Hitler and them. Bah on all of it. I'll be getting back."

The Poet's mother was distinctly practical, a woman defined by her pragmatism rather than idle chatter. She was not one to linger in doorways or lean against counters, trading stories and speculations with the neighbors. Instead, she moved with purpose through her days, attending to the needs of her family and her home with a no-nonsense efficiency that left little room for gossip or unnecessary frills. Her focus was always on the tangible tasks at hand, ensuring everything was as it should be, firmly grounded in the moment's reality.

"Aye, and I'll be heading down me shop," said Mr. Welles, taking his leave. According to Mrs. Welles, her husband had a nose for trouble brewin' an' he liked to stay outta its way good as any coward. She watched him narrow-eyed as he slipped toward the door.

"Well, I'll be gobsmacked," said the other woman. "Hear that, Ben?"

"Fuckin' knew it meself!" Ben whooped. "Right, time to get pissed, I says."

"Oi, stop being such an arse, Benny, some of us has work," said Ben's wife.

"Come on, time to go, all you," said Mrs. Welles.

"Our P.M. making a deal like that. Such a wanker."

Everyone turned to look. The last words had come from The Poet's older sister, Phyllis. At fifteen, Phyllis had blossomed into quite the rebel—or at least, that's how their mother described her. Despite her rebellion, she excelled academically, devoured books at an astonishing rate, and had a knack for writing. Her mind was a burgeoning repository of thoughts and convictions on a vast array of topics, including politics, which she did not shy away from discussing.

Since the onset of war had propelled the world into daily discourse about conflict and strategy, Phyllis had taken to poring over newspapers with a fervor. She meticulously clipped out articles, storing them as both knowledge and evidence of the times. Recently, her interests had coalesced around a particular figure: Mr. Winston Churchill. His speeches and leadership captivated Phyllis, viewing him as a beacon of resolve and rhetoric in tumultuous times. This newfound obsession only fueled her desire to engage more deeply with the world's unfolding events, much to the fascination—and sometimes exasperation—of her family.

"You should take a listen to Mr. Churchill," she said, unmoving, hands at her hips, eyes bright with anger. A tiny ball of sweat appeared at her left temple and rolled down the angle of her cheek.

The Poet felt a sudden lurch in his stomach—a premonition of impending trouble, and he knew his father sensed it too. This was the moment they had dreaded, where the brewing conflict would likely begin. He glanced around, searching for the reassuring presence of his brother Rowdy, but he was nowhere to be found. His absence only heightened the tension, leaving The Poet feeling both isolated and anxious as he scanned and re-scanned the surroundings for any sign of his brother.

"What are you saying?" said Ben, the skin on his face already deepening to crimson.

The girl stared at him, a half-smile turning her lips, but she said nothing.

Ben continued, "Callin' Mr. Chamberlain a wanker, are ya? Are ya mental? He just said it on the radio."

The sight of this man filled The Poet with dread; he was the father of one of his schoolmates, a figure whose reputation for cruelty preceded him. The stories his classmate had confided were grim and unsettling—tales of harsh punishments and deliberate bruises strategically placed where clothing would conceal the marks. At school, his friend's voice would tremble with fear as he whispered, begging for secrecy, terrified that any revelation would only bring about harsher retribution. The knowledge of such brutality deeply frightened The Poet, marking the man as someone to be avoided at all costs.

"Maybe if you tried reading something besides the Sportin' Life to place your bets, hmm?" said Phyllis unapologetically. Taking a step forward she set her gaze then added, "Or the girlie magazines."

In the room, there came an audible collective inhalation of breath.

"Phyllis!" cried Mrs. Welles. "Say sorry right now." Then she added, "And the language too!"

Phyllis set her mouth, hard. "I won't," she said. "He's a brute. Everyone knows it. And he just called me mental, which I ain't mental. And the P.M. is a wanker, so there. They's both right wankers."

Expecting an explosion, all the children shrank back, easing themselves out of the room. No one was breathing. The Poet felt like he might explode with pride. His sister was the bravest person on the planet, also possibly the stupidest.

The big man's face had gone the color of an eggplant, but he wasn't screaming. Instead, he was a sort of frozen statue, staring at Phyllis, who was staring straight back. It was excellent, thought The Poet. Phyllis was unafraid, or at least she was doing a good job of pretending.

Then, after a few seconds, Ben shrugged his shoulders, waved his bottle at Phyllis, and said, "Ah, the hell with ya, stupid cow. Ya daft cunt."

Without thinking, The Poet flew at the big man, screaming, fists flying.

"Don't you call my sister that, you stupid, stupid..." he was trying to think of something terrible to say and finally came up with, "Fat bastard. You take it back."

His fists flew, and punches landed on what felt like a solid rock in the man's thighs and back. But he kept going, unable to stop himself.

"Take it back, shut up, shut up!"

The man whirled around and had The Poet's narrow wrists in a grip so strong, it seemed he was losing blood flow to his fingers. The Poet felt his heart hammering in his chest and his breath coming in short, hard gasps. His legs were swinging wildly in the air as he tried to kick at the enormous man. It was becoming too difficult to breathe, and the pain in his wrists and arms was excruciating. His vision grew dim, and he thought for a moment he might die.

Suddenly, there were soft arms about his waist, then someone pulling him backward and his mother's voice crying, "Please, stop Jack, just stop it. Let him go, Ben, let him go.

The Poet was sweating and flailing, and he could not stop, and the man was not letting go. Other voices joined in, all begging for Ben to release the child.

And then, Rowdy was there, out of nowhere, his big brother, punching the bully with both his fists. Rowdy yanked The Poet free and pushed him toward his sister, who enfolded him in her arms and pressed his head down into her so that he could not watch.

When it was over, and Rowdy had beaten the bigger man down, The Poet remained wrapped in his sister's arms, where he sobbed angry tears for what seemed like hours until the first black chip of resentment lodged itself deep in his gut.

CHAPTER FOUR

LUCKY STONES

1

In Winthrop, Massachusetts, far at the end of town, the main road becomes rocky and deeply gouged, and where the vegetation thins and the marigolds drown, and there is nothing left but seagrass and bits of sandy rock, there sits a wall. It's an old wall, but very strong. Built before the Great War, it is made of cobblestone and concrete. It has endured a quarter century's hurricanes and storm surges, and there it still stands.

2

One afternoon in the autumn of 1941, Vivienne Holland, Ruthie, and Stan Hampton sat perched atop the sturdy wall in Winthrop as the sea breeze tousled their hair. The three were close in age, but their sizes varied significantly. Ruthie, the smallest of the trio, dangled her short legs over the edge of the wall, her bare heels rhythmically tapping against the cold, hard stone. Every so often, she would arch her back dramatically and fling her hands into the air, a display of youthful exuberance. Her big brother grimaced.

"Cut it out, Ruthie! You'll fall right over if you keep that up. Bang your damn head and be a damn retard."

Abruptly, she sat up, laughing. "Ooh, I'm telling. You said the word. You said the d-word."

"Oh, so what? You'll be a retard anyway. So, nobody will listen to you."

Ruthie's laugh faded, but her eyes sparkled with mischief, clearly undeterred by the harsh words.

Ruthie stuck out her tongue and blew her brother a raspberry and resumed swinging dangerously back and forth. In truth, the wall was only a few feet above the sand. Unless she fell straight onto her head, at a particularly awkward angle, she'd probably not end up a retard. However, Vivienne, the middle-sized child of the group and the one expected to referee the arguments, agreed with Stan that Ruthie should cut it out. However, she said nothing. Instead, she sat quietly, both hands gripping the wall on either side of her thighs, staring out to sea. She was squinting through the mist and swirl of the waves, trying to get a glimpse beyond the edge of everything. A storm was coming; that's what Grammy had said. Vivienne wanted to see not just its arrival but its *coming. Where did it come from?* Now, nothing appeared on the horizon but a vague blue-gray mist. No foreboding clouds, no thickening of the air, no wetness. Nothing to suggest the constantly anticipated *Big One* for which Grammy and Grampy had been preparing all day.

Earlier, Vivienne and the Hampton kids had been down on the sand, ignoring Grammy's warnings to stay clear of the water. The air was salty, thick, and the beach hard-packed, littered with polished stones, glittering bits of seaweed, mussel shells, their pearly interiors glinting blue and pink in the sunlight. All of it dragged forward by the tide and soon to be pulled back out to sea. Temporary treasure. They'd collected a bit, then, bored, they'd pitched it all back and sat down at the edge of the tide, waiting, watching for something to happen. Finally, when they'd accomplished nothing more than getting their bottoms soaked in the freezing saltwater, they'd retreated to a sunny spot on the wall.

"Mother says it'll be a big one," said Stan.

"Phooey," said Ruthie. "She always says that."

She slammed her feet harder, bouncing up a little; she eyed her brother for a response. Ruthie was a cynic. Vivienne wasn't sure what that word meant, but she knew Ruthie was one because Grampy said, "Little Ruthie is already a cynic."

"Quit it. And put your shoes back on," said Stan, irritation lacing his words. "Why'd you take 'em off for anyway? It's cold out here."

"Will not. Can't make me."

"Anyway, we should go soon. Wind's picking up."

He looked at the sky, which was, finally, changing. Going an odd yellowy shade.

"I want to be here when it gets here," Vivienne said without taking her eyes off the water.

"What? Are you nuts?" said Stan. "We can't be here. You know those waves. They'll be right up over this wall. They might come up Waterside Drive and your front porch, Viv. Besides, it'll be dark down here soon. Blackouts, remember? No way are we staying here."

"It'll be something, won't it, Stan?" she said without turning away from the water, without looking at him.

Stan stared at her. He was both in love with Vivienne and a little terrified of her. He thought perhaps someday he'd marry her, but, in the end, Stan was the boy who would grow up to be a fine physician. He would marry a sensible woman and become a practicing Quaker. He was that sort of boy.

"No," he said. "No, it will be dangerous and foolish." He said this in his most grown-up, eleven-year-old voice. "Foolish," he repeated the word as if he were convincing himself, or maybe he liked the sound of his voice saying it.

"You know?" Vivienne began sheepishly. "I could crawl straight into it, the green of it, maybe become a fish, or one of those purple rocks swishing in and out with the tide." Vivienne pointed at the hillocks of small stones on the sand below and laughed. Beach glass, copper-colored, a few red or blue, glinted between the rocks. "I'd be like pirate treasure, and I could see everything," she added. Lucky stones, Vivienne thought, a gigantic pile of lucky stones. She kept that part to herself.

Ruthie, who had been silent so far, watching Vivienne, said, "I want to go, Vivienne. I..." want to go into the sea with you.

3

The storm that Grammy had warned about was now unmistakably rolling in. It started with an almost imperceptible shift in the atmosphere—a slight drop in temperature and a sudden stillness that made the hairs on Vivienne's arms stand up. The previously blue-gray mist on the horizon had thickened, darkening into a menacing wall of clouds that seemed to swallow the sky.

The sea, which had been a restless mass of swirling waves, churned more violently, its surface turning a tumultuous slate gray. Each wave grew larger and more aggressive, crashing against the shore with a force that sent spray high into the air.

As the storm approached, the sky transformed into a chaotic canvas of swirling dark clouds, some tinged with an eerie green hue. Thunder rumbled in the distance, a low growl that grew louder with each passing moment. Jagged streaks of lightning occasionally split the sky, illuminating the roiling clouds in stark, momentary flashes.

The air grew humid, thick and oppressive, and the scent of rain was unmistakable. When the first drops fell, they were large and cold, splattering on the ground with a sound like muted applause. Within moments, the drizzle intensified into a downpour; the rain falling in sheets that obscured the view and soaked everything in an instant.

In their respective homes, Vivienne, and the other children curled in their beds. All night they listened to the screams and howls, threatening bangs and bumps of the storm raging just outside. They could hear the splintering of wood slats and the whirring of debris as it sped past their windows and the roof overhead. Vivienne's heart thudded, not with fear but anticipation, excitement, privilege. If she pulled the blinds and looked through the glass, she would see the eye of the hurricane.

The following day, a dead shark lay sprawled across the four feet of Grammy's geranium bed. The stench was overpowering, a putrid mix of decaying fish and seaweed, so strong that Grammy refused to open the front door. It wasn't until Grampy and a few neighbors came to help that the carcass was removed. They used slings and hooks to dig the shark out from the sand and debris, heaving it away while Vivienne watched, fascinated and horrified.

The shark wasn't the only evidence of the storm's wrath. The landscape was a mess of destruction: overthrown telephone poles, trees torn up by their roots, and fishing vessels capsized and scattered. Entire cottages had been lifted and displaced by the fierce winds, with some now floating out at sea, broken and abandoned.

Overall, Vivienne, and the Hampton children judged the hurricane to be a marvelous success.

And so went Vivienne Holland's love affair with the sea. Her sanctuary, her lover, mother, father, spirit, sustenance, and god. As for hurricanes, they held no threat. Throughout her life, Vivienne would stare down into the whirling liquid blackness without blinking.

PART TWO: 1942-1950

CHAPTER 5

ROWDY

1

On a windless summer day, The Poet sat beneath a holly tree, clutching a notebook and a stub of a pencil. He was attempting to compose a few verses for a girl in his class with whom he had fallen in love. At just twelve years old, love was not something he had expected. However, Harriet, who had joined the grammar school only a week prior, was beautiful and endearingly shy, making her an irresistible muse for his poetic endeavors.

Thus far, he'd written two words.

Your eyes...

The girl had enchanting eyes, a rich chocolate hue that was far more decadent than ordinary brown, yet not so dark as to be black. Tiny green flecks danced within them, something he had noticed only when he stood very close to her on a sunny day. She was smaller than most of the other girls, with delicate, almost elfin features that made her seem magical. He often imagined them wandering into the woods together, uncovering its secrets, creatures, and monsters. Perhaps they would sit by the pond, and he would read his poetry to her. But first, he mused, he needed to get her to say hello. With a sigh, he crossed out what he had written and started anew.

Those eyes...

No, that was also wrong.

He glanced up from his work, his eyes drifting across the moor to where his house stood. It was distinguishable from the other homes only by the crumbling corner of one side of the chimney. From this distance, they all appeared tiny and dingy—identical, depressing shacks. He heard a sound. His name, perhaps? Could it be possible from this far away? He always ensured he wandered out far enough so no one could call to him. But there it was again. Someone was calling his name. It was his sister, Phyllis. Screaming, not angry, not frantic, but something else, something much worse.

"Jack Welles, Jack! We need ye home, now! Where are ye?"

2

Rowdy joined up in early 1940. Posted to the continent, he became part of the British Expeditionary Force. For the rest of the Welles family, life continued, though against the peculiar new backdrop of rationing, periodic blackouts, and the frequent sight of bombers overhead. And there was, of course, the waiting—always waiting for word from Rowdy. But to The Poet, it was a war of newsreels, a war of heroes. He imagined his handsome brother in dramatic flights, bloodless battles, and crushing victories. His only worry was that the fight would end before he was old enough to join. Meanwhile, his boyhood life carried on: catching mice, shooting rabbits, fishing in the pond, mapping rivers, doing schoolwork—but only the parts he enjoyed— and writing poems.

Until now.

Phyllis was crying, tears streaking her swollen face.

"What—" The Poet began, but she silenced him, grabbing his arm and yanking him along.

Before they pushed open the back door, The Poet heard it—the loud, animal keening. Inside, his parents huddled together at the table. His mother buried her head against his father's chest, repeatedly banging her forehead against him. She wailed, screamed, and clawed at her clothing while he desperately tried to hold her.

A telegram lay on the kitchen table, the paper crinkled, its edges curled up as if it had been smashed into a ball and then opened again and smoothed out to be read.

DEEPLY REGRET TO INFORM YOU THAT YOUR SON CORPORAL ROLAND K. WELLES WAS OFFICIALLY REPORTED DIED OF WOUNDS IN FRANCE 3rd JUNE 1942 LETTER FOLLOWS

The Poet's world shattered in an instant. The idealized vision of war, the heroic tales he had spun in his mind, all dissolved into the harsh reality of loss. He stared at the telegram; the words blurring as tears filled his eyes. His brother, his hero, was gone. The Poet felt a crushing weight on his chest, a sorrow so profound it left him breathless.

Phyllis squeezed his arm, her own grief mirrored in his eyes. The Poet glanced at his parents, seeing them not as the strong pillars of his childhood but as broken, grieving individuals. His mother's wails pierced his heart, each cry a reminder of the finality of death.

As the reality sank in, The Poet felt a mix of emotions—grief, anger, confusion. He had always seen Rowdy as invincible, a hero who would return home with tales of bravery. Now, he faced the stark truth that war was not a grand adventure, but a brutal, unforgiving force.

He looked at the telegram again, his vision clearing. The words were permanent, unchangeable. Rowdy was gone, and their lives would never be the same.

3

The Poet dreamed he was a soldier stumbling through the early morning twilight, lost in the streets of an unfamiliar city. As the sun rose, the surrounding shapes became clearer. Gradually, he realized they were human figures, but lifeless. They were corpses. He was in a city of the dead. He ran. He sprinted faster and faster, but the bodies only grew more numerous. Eventually, he became too exhausted to continue and collapsed, kneeling beside a large puddle of rainwater among the broken cobblestones. A fishing rod lay next to the puddle, and he picked it up, casting a line into the mysterious depths. He dropped to his knees. Mud seeped through his trousers and dried as the morning turned into early afternoon. Yet, he remained kneeling by the puddle. His knees ached, his back ached, his arms ached. Still, he held onto the fishing rod, his fingers sensitive to the slightest change in tension on the line, watching, waiting. Motionless. He stared into the murky water. Down, down for what seemed like an eternity.

CHAPTER 6

AMERICAN WAR

1

It was Walt Disney who taught them about the war. Until then, the war in Europe had seemed like a distant, grand event, something abstract and far away, like imagining a New York City skyscraper you had never seen, perhaps the Empire State Building. But Walt Disney and his propaganda films brought it close. He forced them to confront it, to scale its facade, scrape bird droppings off the stone walls, and press their faces into the rough masonry, filled with the terrifying realization that they might fall to their deaths. For children, Walt Disney made it an American war.

2

By early 1942, three fully operational military forts lined the shore near Winthrop, Massachusetts. They carried out, among other things, nighttime target practice requiring the children of Winthrop to stay away from the beach and seawall and find different ways to occupy their time.

"It's not fair," complained Ruthie. "I wanna go to the beach. Stupid war."

"You're stupid," said Stan.

"Am not."

Ruthie smacked Stan's forearm hard enough to raise a pale pink mark. Stan, twice his sister's size, pulled his arm back and growled, but did not retaliate. Ruthie was lucky Stan was a gentle giant. She was right, though. It was stupid. The smell of salt and seawater was intoxicating, and you could nearly feel the coolness of the waves splashing at your ankles and the soft grainy rub of sand under the soles of your feet. It was maddening.

The three children shuffled down the sidewalk in front of Grammy's house, sucking homemade lime popsicles and looking for something to do. The tart taste made Vivienne's cheeks pucker. She wasn't sure if she liked lime popsicles yet—they were odd, like meringue or mint jelly. You had to decide about them. They had spent the morning building a hut in the woods behind the Hampton house with cardboard, scrap lumber, and twigs. By noon, it was done, but it was too hot for all three to fit inside, so they left it for another day. Now, they wandered around, bored, waiting for three o'clock when Mrs. Kent's station wagon would take them and three other kids into town for the new Walt Disney movie.

"Hey, you two. Cut it out. We're going to the movies, remember?" said Vivienne.

"Yay!" said Ruthie. Jumping up and down, she hopped off the sidewalk into the street and dropped her popsicle. She bent and plucked it off the macadam, used an index finger to rub it clean, then popped it back into her mouth. Stan tried to snatch it away from her, but she was too quick.

"You'll get sick. Poisoned. You'll probably die," he said, pursing his lips.

"She will not die, Stan. She's fine," said Vivienne, looking at Ruthie, who was small and sickly already. "Maybe you shouldn't eat that," Vivienne added, scrunching her nose.

Challenging Ruthie never went well. The popsicle, already melted to a nub, now disappeared inside the child's mouth entirely with a huge smack. She pulled out the stick and held it up, grinning.

"Too late!" Ruthie squealed.

And so, at first, the war didn't seem frightening to these American children. Safely ensconced in middle class American life and separated by thousands of miles of ocean, they were visited by ghosts in the night— superheroes, fairy godmothers, protectors, the president, and the FBI. For a while, life carried on as usual.

3

All the children adored Bambi, along with Thumper, Flower, and all the woodland creatures. Then the screen dimmed, but the lights stayed off. The children sat silently, waiting. Suddenly, a different film played. It was a combat scene, or perhaps a post-combat scene. The enemies were portrayed as small, ugly men with narrow eyes and cruel expressions. They had captured handsome Americans, shoving them towards a ditch, their small hands pushing against the broad shoulders and backs of the unarmed American soldiers. Without warning, the small men began shooting the American Marines one by one, laughing and kicking the dead bodies into the ditch. Each body fell, limp and bloodied, like roadkill.

Vivienne slid down beneath her theater chair and covered both ears to muffle the sounds of groans and screams and gunshots. The film ended, but the cries continued. Three children vomited. Two more burst into tears. One peculiar boy, who would later develop a tendency for harming others and eventually join the military only to be dishonorably discharged for malicious and unnecessary use of force, found the film fascinating.

4

All year at school, they had bell drills. A howling bell, much louder than the regular school bell. The children would grab their coats and pencils, line up, and wait for the teacher before heading into the hallways and filing down to the cellar. Some of the littler kids cried, frightened by the dark and the cold in the basement. All the children sat with pencils clenched between their teeth to prevent biting their tongues if bombs went off. After a while, the taste of pencil lead could make a person feel sick.

A few weeks after the terrible film, the bell sounded again. Vivienne noticed the cellar smelled like rotting leaves, and she had to concentrate on not vomiting. She didn't throw up, but the whole time, she gagged around the pencil in her mouth.

5

Grampy was German, or he used to be before he became an American. He wore his "Go 4th To Win the War" FDR re-election campaign button nearly every day and loved America. He had worked for over twenty years as a manager at Madison Engine Plant, but one day, they let him go for being

German. That's what Grammy said. Grampy said nothing, though the lines on his face seemed to deepen each day.

Mother said it was luck that Ruthie's father, a history professor at Browning College and friend of Daddy's, had introduced Mother to the right people through various connections. As a result, she got a job teaching Business Skills at the college, a better-paid, more prestigious position than she had at the high school.

"Moving can be a healthy thing," Mother said. "Besides, in Wellesley, the schools are excellent, and there will be much greater opportunities for you and Beanie. Think of the libraries, the universities, the theater, the parks." And, Mother said, beyond all that, there is the war.

They all had to understand that things were different because of the war.

So, they moved to Wellesley, all of them together, into a small three-bedroom New England cottage on a tree-shaded corner lot. But that wasn't true. Because Beanie was a boy, he would attend a private boarding school. Grampy, whose age and narrow skill set left him with few professional options, would find work as a night manager at a hotel some miles away, coming home only on weekends. So, the house on Amelia Street would be a woman's house, filled with womanly scents: talc, glycerin, and rose water.

Mother would say, "Do you see what happens? How the men leave, how they die, how they abandon us? But we carry on. We sacrifice for our children. We always put our children first so that they will have the happiness we have gone without."

Vivienne listened to her mother's words, feeling the weight of the extra responsibilities and the unspoken fears that came with the move. She wondered about Grampy's silence, his eyes that seemed to carry the burden of lost dignity. The war had changed everything, and she couldn't help but feel a mix of resentment and determination. She promised herself that she would make the most of the opportunities in Wellesley, for Beanie, for Grampy, and for herself.

6

After the move, Vivienne got a new bike. It was a fat Schwinn with yellow streamers on the handles and a white plastic basket she had attached herself using rope she found at the Amelia house after they moved in. It wasn't exactly new—an ancient bike, really—but they fixed it up. She and Grampy painted it a deep forest green, swapped out the tires and chain, and it rode well, even if it was a little too big.

Vivienne spent a lot of time riding around the neighborhood, her pigtails flying and her long, bare legs pedaling furiously. "I am being nice to everyone and making sure people do not think I am stuck up," she explained to Mother. The strategy seemed to work. Folks smiled and waved, and she was making friends quickly.

She felt a mix of excitement and nostalgia as she rode through the tree-lined streets. Wellesley was different from Winthrop, but she was determined to make the best of it. She missed Ruthie and Stan, their adventures by the beach, and their endless summer days. But there was something exhilarating about starting fresh, about the possibility of new friendships and experiences.

Mother took over Sunday School classes at the Unitarian Church, which gave Vivienne an instant connection to other children in the community. She missed her Winthrop friends, especially Ruthie and Stan, but lots of girls, and some boys, enjoyed being around Vivienne. "You have flair," one of her new girlfriends told her.

Mother had been right about the schools and the libraries. Vivienne was an excellent student, a conscientious and enthusiastic member of the school community, an avid reader, and writer, and an inspiration to her classmates. She amassed an impressive collection of used books and read them all. She won every library contest for the number of books read by a child, and she published her first story in The Wellesley Spokesman in January 1945. It was titled "Lucky Stones and The Hurricane."

7

Lorah Holland continued to worry, despite the success of her children. In the house on Amelia Street, she felt overwhelmed by the burden of being both father and mother. The stress was so intense that she developed ulcers and required medical hospitalization three times before Vivienne graduated high school. For Vivienne, this planted the seeds of tremendous guilt. The outstanding debt she felt she owed to her mother would grow into a tree of such enormous proportions that Vivienne could have spent her entire life climbing it without ever reaching the top.

CHAPTER 7

GODDESS

As the late dusk settled over the moor, the houses cast long, slender shadows across the landscape, and the breeze dwindled to an icy whisper that seemed to seek every exposed inch of skin. It crept up the sleeves of The Poet's rough woolen jumper and seeped through the leather soles of his shoes, numbing his toes with its chill. Yet, The Poet shrugged off the growing discomfort. Leaning back against the rough bark of a tree, he stretched his long legs out in front of him and buried his face deeper into the book cradled in his hands.

Absorbed in the world woven by Robert Graves, he was too engrossed to mind the creeping cold or the advancing hour. The words on the page consumed him, offering a refuge and igniting his imagination, more vivid and enveloping than the dimming light and the cold air around him. His connection with the text was a vivid escape, transporting him far beyond the moor's encroaching darkness.

Poet, never chase the dream. Laugh yourself and turn away.
Mask your hunger, let it seem, small matter if he come or stay.

After completing the book, The Poet flipped back to the first page. This time, he read the poetry aloud, slowly and cherishing each line. As darkness enveloped the moor, he squinted to make out the words, his voice blending with the evening's hush. Finishing the book a second time, he closed it with a gentle thud, aware of the biting cold that had seeped into his bones.

He stood up, sliding the volume of Robert Graves into the pocket of his baggy trousers. Rubbing his arms for warmth, he looked towards the twinkling lights of the town in the distance. Estimating the distance—a half mile, perhaps a mile? — he jogged, hoping to make it back in a matter of minutes. His stomach growled, reminding him of the missed supper, as he began his trek back.

The Poet's mind buzzed with the fresh poetic insights from Graves's writings. Graves's radical embrace of a life devoted to poetry—abandoning home, family, and conventional stability for the raw pursuit of art in Spain with his muse—struck a deep chord in him. This was not just inspiration; it was a call to live out his poetry in full, without reservation.

As he jogged, the chilly wind carried scents of chimney smoke and roasting fish, and hunger accelerated his pace. Smiling against the gusts, he felt a surge of anticipation for his own future. With every step, his vision became clearer-he would write and love and some day he could go in search of his very own goddess.

CHAPTER 8

WRITER, WRITER, WRITER

1

Vivienne's eyelids fluttered open reluctantly, the warmth and stuffiness of the room pressing down on her like a heavy blanket. She closed them again briefly, seeking refuge in the darkness, but the sense of daylight tugging at her consciousness was persistent. With a soft sigh, she lifted her lids halfway and propped herself up into a sitting position, her muscles groaning softly at the effort.

Peering outside, she noticed the curtains drawn back fully. Grammy did that when Vivienne seemed in danger of sleeping the whole day away. She'd been doing this lately. Sleeping far too much.

Outside, the snow lay thick on bare tree branches and stippling white across their small patch of lawn. The street was empty, plowed already, and the sun was shining. She checked the clock. It was after seven, and still, she wasn't ready to get up.

It had begun slowly, almost imperceptibly. Vivienne noticed a general sense of fatigue that crept over her, slowly dimming the vibrant energy she had felt during her early days in Wellesley. It was akin to retreating into a lengthy tunnel, each step backwards, appearing smaller and smaller, until the bright world outside reduced to a mere pinpoint of light, distant and detached.

Then had come her thirteenth birthday, about which she'd been as eager as a dead fish. All she'd been able to think about was Mother cheerfully repeating, "You're growing up now; you are a Young Lady."

Young Ladies did not hang from trees or ride bikes or delight in the feel of cool mud between their fingers. Instead, Young Ladies curled their hair into merciless bobs and wore ridiculous underthings and talked about the shape of their noses and the size of their feet. From what Vivienne had observed, Young Ladies appeared to have very limited life horizons.

By January, what had started as general fatigue transformed into a deeper, more troubling malaise for Vivienne. She felt an inexplicable languor enveloping her entire being, a sort of internal sickness that sapped her of vitality. Her body seemed to demand stillness, an overwhelming urge to sprawl across her bed, motionless, her eyes fixed on nothing, avoiding even the slightest movement if she could help it.

In this state, Vivienne devised a solitary, macabre game she dubbed "corpse." The rules were simple and somber: she would lie on her back, her arms pinned tightly to her sides, her eyes wide open yet unfocused, as if staring into oblivion. She would then pull a sheet over her body and face, mimicking the stark, eerie stillness of a body laid out in a morgue. The aim was to remain as motionless as possible, enduring the chill of the frigid mornings that penetrated her room.

"Vivienne! Vivvie!" came a voice.

Grammy was there in the room, where two seconds before she'd not been. Grammy was that way. Here, gone, here again, moving with the quick, assertive power of a tomcat. She was, by far, the hardest working adult in the house. First up, last to bed, Vivienne could not remember seeing her relax. At supper, she was out of her chair more than sitting, shuttling dishes back and forth to the kitchen. In the evenings, she always had something in her hands: mending, knitting, ironing.

"It's past seven, dear. Are you alright?" said Grammy, light concern in her voice.

Grammy sat down gently on the edge of the bed and pulled back the sheet, exposing Vivienne's face. She ran a palm over the child's forehead. Her hand was soft and dry and smelled like baking flour.

"What is it, Vivvie?"

Vivienne shrugged.

"Sick?" Vivienne said it as a question. She wasn't lying. She was sick, or at least something all around her was sick.

Grammy tilted her head. "Shall we check you for a fever?" she asked.

Another shrug. "Dunno," answered Vivienne.

"Well, let's see, your mother has gone to work, so we cannot ask her."

Grammy squinted, thousands of lines appeared around the corners of her eyes and mouth, then she raised one finger in the air, "Aha!"

"I know what we will do."

Grammy spoke with a heavy Austrian accent, pronouncing all her w's as v's. ("I know vat ve vill do!"). To Vivienne, this gave Grammy's words an ultimate authority.

"How about I check in a few hours. We will see if you are better, and then I take you to school?"

Vivienne agreed that made the most sense. She was struggling to hold back tears of relief. If Mother had been home, she would have sent Vivienne to school. Mother did not believe in sick days.

After Grammy left, Vivienne pulled the covers over her head and lay perfectly still. Then, she practiced not moving while listening to the day getting started all around her.

2

The enigmatic ailment clung to Vivienne through the tail end of winter, her days blurring into a monotonous gray. March and April were fraught with restless nights and dreary days, her body moving through the motions of school and daily activities without enthusiasm, feeling detached and numb. A silent question echoing in her mind constantly plagued Vivienne: What could be wrong with her? Internally, she felt as isolated as she imagined a blind and deaf person might feel amid a bustling, lively circus—surrounded by activity yet profoundly disconnected.

During this time, she often stared at her schoolwork, unable to muster the energy to care. Friends' voices seemed distant, their laughter like echoes from another world. Her once-bright eyes dulled, reflecting the overcast skies that seemed to mirror her internal gloom.

Then, as if nature itself intervened, a transformation occurred on a cloudless day in late April. The sun broke through the lingering gloom with such intensity that it seemed to paint the world around her in vibrant, almost fluorescent colors. The fresh green of the budding leaves, the bright blue of the sky, and the golden light bathing everything in warmth—it was as if she was seeing the world anew. In that radiant moment, the weight that had oppressed her lifted as suddenly as it had descended. She felt a rush of energy and clarity, the fog inside her mind dissipating.

By the end of the week, the dark period of the previous months felt like a distant memory, a dream from which she had awakened. She laughed with friends again, her schoolwork no longer a burdensome chore but a challenge she was eager to meet.

From that brilliant April day forward, Vivienne held a steadfast belief in the restorative power of sunlight. It had chased away her shadows, filling her with warmth and color again. For the rest of her life, she would regard sunshine as her personal elixir, a natural tonic capable of reviving her spirit and dispelling the inner darkness whenever it dared to encroach again.

3

Vivienne licked the pad of her middle finger and flicked through the glossy pages. One, then another, and another, until she found the one she was looking for. Pressing her left palm down on the magazine, she carefully removed the page, taking care not to tear the edges. This advertisement she wanted to keep.

It was Saturday morning, and she sat at the small white vanity table she shared with Mother. They shared the entire bedroom now that Beanie was home from Exeter for the summer. At fifteen, Vivienne hated sharing with her mother, of course, but what choice did they have? She only wished Mother would stop apologizing about it. *I'm so sorry it has to be this way, Viv. I know you'd rather have your privacy.* When she wasn't apologizing,

Mother was trying to make herself invisible. The whole situation made Vivienne feel too big for her own life.

Using a bit of Scotch tape, she stuck the page from *Teen Time Magazine* to the mirror and studied it. Three young girls in cap and gown, but only two beamed happily. The third girl, subtly less attractive, appeared sullen, distracted. The smiling girls displayed glittering engagement rings, with twinkling bottles of Listermint mouthwash floating above their heads. The frowning girl, clearly cursed by halitosis, had no engagement ring. The caption read: *"One Course They Didn't Teach Her."*

Vivienne knew, of course, that minty breath did not lead directly to matrimony, nor did a lack of mouthwash preclude it. However, she subscribed to the fundamental belief that, for a woman, there was nothing to life without a man. A career could be had, but it must be in combination with, not to the exclusion of, a successful marriage. She had to look no further than her mother to know this was so. Marrying an older man she did not love—a man who died and left her to work and work and come home each night too tired to do more than eat, help with dishes, and lie down— had led to nothing but misery for Lorah Holland. Vivienne swore she would die before allowing her life to follow the same disastrous course.

The advertisement would be her reminder.

To have it all. But first, to establish the foundation. *A boy. A boy. A boy.*

The torn page remained Scotch-taped to the vanity until, after dozens of dates, more than a few romantic disappointments, and at least one broken heart, it mysteriously disappeared one afternoon in the spring of Vivienne's junior year.

Later, she would suspect Mother had removed it. But by then, she no longer needed the reminder; she'd learned the message by heart.

4

Mr. T. was a lanky, middle-aged man with thick, roundish glasses and slightly shaggier hair than most of the faculty. He encouraged his English students to read widely, assigning works by Joseph Conrad, Virginia Woolf, James Joyce, W. H. Auden, Dylan Thomas, Shakespeare, Tolstoy, and

Tennessee Williams. His intense intellectualism and blatant pacifism—marked by his open criticism of American materialism, celebrity worship, and even sacred pastimes like spectator sports and Miss America—earned him tremendous respect from his politically rebellious honors English students, Vivienne included. However, many of their parents did not share this admiration. A few years after Vivienne's graduation, Mr. T would be called before Wellesley's town board regarding his political beliefs, on the grounds that he might be a communist. Wellesley was not remarkably tolerant of views such as Mr. T's.

Mr. T's request that she visit him in the classroom after school both surprised and concerned Vivienne. Her stomach churned as she entered and found him at his desk, shuffling through a stack of papers. He looked up as she came in. The room smelled of chalk dust, pencil lead, and books. Vivienne felt her heartbeat slow, and her anxiety dissipate with the familiar feeling of the room. This was her favorite place on campus, and Mr. T was her favorite teacher.

"Have a seat," he said, pointing at the hard wooden chair beside his desk.

She sat, chewing on her bottom lip, nervousness returning. She'd never been called in to speak with Mr. T, and this might be terrible. Vivienne expected the worst, even planned for it, in all situations. She ascribed to the theory that anticipation could ward off or at least mitigate disaster. Often it worked. Once in her life, it had failed disastrously.

"Thank you for coming by," he began, pushing his papers to the side and turning towards her. He leaned back in his chair and smiled. "You're enjoying the class?" he asked.

She nodded, too vigorously, looking idiotic, she was sure. She tried to slow the movement of her head; now, she looked even dumber.

"I love the class. It's my favorite."

She told herself to calm down and gazed out the window beyond Mr. T's head. Two younger kids were unlocking their bicycles. The early spring day was gorgeous, pale green, glittery with pink blossoms.

"I can tell," he said. "I wanted to talk to you about this last story you submitted."

Her mouth went dry. He was about to tell her it made little sense. He didn't get it. Why would she write about a girl and a snowsuit? Oh God, why had she written that?

She began, "I can—"

"It's remarkable. Truly outstanding."

"Oh," she said, peering at him.

He grinned. There were deep crow's feet around his eyes, tan lines where the wrinkles blocked the sun.

"I think you should consider this," Mr. T said, pushing a paper toward her.

She picked up the page torn from a magazine. "What is it?"

"Look at the bottom, the ad."

When she finished reading, she looked at him. "You think I should send it to this contest?"

"Sure. And more than that. I think you should start sending your work to many magazines and journals."

"Really?"

"I mean, you'll get rejected, certainly."

She blinked, confused. "Uh, then why send it?"

He shrugged. "Everyone gets rejected. That's the deal. Think of rejections as battle scars. Save them. Keep track of them. Take special care of the ones with comments. Those are wins. You won't get a serious publication until you have lots of rejections. That's just how it works. But you must start somewhere, and the thing is," he paused and made sure she was looking at him. "You are good, Vivienne. Superb."

Vivienne tried to inhale, but her breath caught, and for a moment, she couldn't move. The room seemed brighter somehow, warmer, fuller. Had anyone ever said that before? Mother, of course. Although what Mother said was, "I like this," or "This is good," or "This is terrific." That wasn't exactly the same. She played Mr. T's words back in her mind once more: You are good, superb.

"Ok," she said. "Ok, I'll send the story in, and I'll send others too."

Vivienne was not the sort for false modesty. She would take the compliment and do what Mr. T advised. He was right. She was good.

Mr. T nodded with approval. "And, by the way, I met with your mother last week."

Vivienne knew about the meeting. They'd had parent conferences, but she never asked Mother how they went. Vivienne was a straight-A student. It didn't matter how those stupid meetings went.

"Do you want to know what I told her?"

Vivienne shrugged; she didn't want to know. "I guess," she said.

"I told her you would make a living at writing. That's a rare thing. But in your case, I think it's true. You are a writer, and that's a fact."

Vivienne nearly floated out of the classroom, down the hallway, and out the school's front doors. Now that was something. As she rode her bicycle home, she barely noticed the pleasantly green streets of Wellesley, the pink crabapple blossoms, or the heady smell of sweet alyssum. Instead, her entire brain glittered with the thin gold stream of Mr. T's words: A writer. A writer. A writer. A writer. A writer. A writer. A writer. A writer. A writer. A writer. A writer. A writer. A writer. A writer. A writer.

5

By the time she graduated high school, Vivienne had submitted nearly one hundred stories and poems, most of which had been rejected. She wrote tales that often contradicted her own life. Vivienne, the Girl, flirted with boys, went on dates, danced at parties, studied, helped at home, respected her elders, shopped and laughed, and, of course, demurred. Instead, Vivienne, the Writer, penned stories about lonely women struggling with betrayal, adultery, single parenthood, illness, depression, alcohol, and social constraints. She was always writing about Mother. Her stories and poems were nonconformist, brutally honest, and not what 1940s post-war America expected from a young lady. Particularly not what women's magazines—and women's magazines were a young lady's only publishing option—were willing to publish.

"You'll need to give them a bit of what they want," said Mr. T., dropping a sheaf of paper onto his desk. "These are terrific, but the magazines won't publish them, and you know it, Viv."

The day outside had been icy, bone chilling and Vivienne was wearing multiple layers to protect her against the cold. Suddenly, the heat of the classroom felt overwhelming, everything was too close. But she watched her teacher's face as he spoke. He was trying to help her and in the end she knew he was right.

Gritting her teeth, Vivienne created characters and a narrative that carefully conformed to traditional gender roles and upheld the sexual standards of mid-twentieth-century America. She submitted a clean, hopeful story about a young girl's first experience with love.

Finally, in September 1949, Vivienne Holland received her first national publication. She was sixteen years old.

Vivienne held the magazine in her hands, feeling a strange mix of triumph and bitterness. She had done it. Her name was in print. But the story was not hers; it was what they wanted, not what she wanted to tell. Still, she smiled, a determined glint in her eye. This was just the beginning. One step closer to being able to tell the stories she needed to tell.

CHAPTER 9

JAGUAR

1

They squeezed into The Poet's room, all sitting cross-legged on the floor, squashed up against one another, five of them surrounding a makeshift Ouija Board. The two girls sat beside each other, so The Poet, by default, ended up between the two men. Both blokes stank of old sweat and unwashed button-downs. The skinny lad from Devon drew the short straw; he would ask the first question. He hesitated, and for a moment, The Poet thought the poor chap might be too drunk to sort out what was going on.

"Go on, don't be frightened," The Poet nudged with an elbow grinning widely. "It's just ghosts."

What was his name, this Devon chap? They'd been drinking since noon; it was a wonder The Poet could remember anyone's name. He winked across the board at one of the girls they'd invited up. One of them, the one with the green eyes and the very round bottom—he'd need to remember her name.

"Uh, let's see," said the lad, hands shaking over the makeshift Ouija board. "When will Professor Leavitt stop being such a twat?"

Everyone roared at that, but The Poet told him it didn't count.

"No, no," said The Poet. "Think of something that means something. It must be personal."

"Ask about love," said the green-eyed girl.

The boy looked trembly at that. "Ah. Ok," he said.

When there was no follow-up, the girl added, "Ask if your true love is on her way to find you at this very moment!"

"That's specific, don't you think?" said the lad.

She shrugged. She was flirting.

"Alright then," he said, taking a deep breath. "My true love," he murmured, looking at the board. Then he cleared his throat and started over. "Is my love on her way to my loving arms before the next moon is up?"

They waited, hands on the overturned glass, and for a moment, nothing happened. Then, slowly, the glass moved. Shakily at first, then a little faster. Finally, it slid, spelling out Y... E... S.

"Ha!" said the boy, leaping to his feet before stumbling and falling backward.

He was very drunk. Before he could crumple to the floor, the green-eyed girl caught him, and soon they were wrapped up in one another, and The Poet's romantic fantasies dissolved in a beery cloud of disappointment. Ah well, he had an essay due tomorrow, and so far, he'd written none of it. He disliked the subject (and the teacher) so much, he'd considered not turning it in, succumbing to whatever the consequences might be, a seriously unpleasant prospect at the very least. But now, it seemed the Ouija had done him a favor.

"Ok," said The Poet, pulling himself to his feet. "Everybody out. Out, work to do."

A few grumblings, gatherings, and wobbling toward the door, but nobody was shocked. The Poet was that way. Full of surprises and contradictions.

2

The Poet's room at Pembroke College was tiny and dark, on the third floor of a stone building so old he couldn't imagine its age. At night, the mice made scritch-scratching sounds inside the walls, and the place carried a perpetual smell of something long buried. But he loved it. Everything about Cambridge felt like a gift.

Indeed, it was a gift. Although confident he deserved to be there, the truth was, The Poet had gained admittance to Pembroke by a narrow margin. Squeaking past his exams, he'd won a place to read English Literature at the esteemed institution based on his historic achievements as a junior writer and literary critic. These accomplishments, however impressive, would have remained unknown to Pembroke had his lower schoolteachers not submitted his work to the Master of College. The Poet had been lucky. Perhaps more than lucky.

When he was alone, he sat down at the typewriter, rolled on a blank sheet of paper, and wrote three terrible sentences. Then he waited and waited some more; he wrote nothing. He sat there throughout the night. Possibly he slept. He couldn't be sure.

In the night, there came a green-eyed goddess. Beautiful and pale with a long, hooked nose, and translucent skin, she entered the room and approached his desk, placing a hand across the half-blank page.

"This is not you," she said. "It's time to stop now."

When she removed her hand, the essay had disappeared, leaving in its place a poem.

3

The Poet submitted the poem as his assignment and promptly failed. He never completed a degree in English Literature. Instead, he studied philosophy, writing many fine poems, and graduating from the university with no particular distinctions.

He never saw the green-eyed goddess again, but he never forgot what he'd learned. The verse she'd left on the page—the one about the jaguar, imprisoned, enraged, and wild—would become the most famous poem he would ever write.

CHAPTER 10

BITTER STRAWBERRIES

1

All day long, Vivienne, and the others worked the strawberry fields at Klausen Farm. They crouched before the endless rows, their hands weaving through fat green leaves to pinch ripe berries free from their stems. The labor was grueling; their backs ached, and by day's end, their hands, and faces were stained with the sticky red juice of strawberries. Despite the hardship, the summer job had been a fortunate find.

Vivienne's scholarship to Talbot College, generous though it was, only covered half of her necessary expenses. Talbot was a school designed for girls accustomed to vacations abroad, girls who switched between French and English, who skied in the winters and sailed in the summers. It was a school for girls with sprawling homes and intact families. Vivienne had applied on a whim, not expecting to be accepted. Yet, the acceptance letter had come, glowing with potential: *We are pleased to inform you...*

Her mother had immediately offered to take on more work, to pick up night shifts, anything to make it possible. This was although Vivienne could have attended Wellesley College with a full scholarship, based on her academic merit and local residency. But taking more money from her mother wasn't an option. Lorah already endured twelve-hour workdays and had suffered through gallstone episodes, worsened by stress. Besides, after her own recurrent dips into psychological struggles, Vivienne knew she needed a change, a chance to start anew somewhere far from the familiarity of Wellesley's expectations. If Vivienne wanted Talbot, she'd need money.

If she needed money, she would have to find it on her own. And that meant work that paid better than babysitting and cleaning for local housewives.

It was Beanie who had noticed the flyer posted near the high school. Klausen Farm needed young workers for the summer—hard labor, yes, but it paid better than any babysitting or house cleaning job. The physical work proved more demanding than Vivienne had expected, yet there was something satisfying about it. The daily routine of cycling eight miles to the farm, working under the sun for eight hours, then riding back, left her spent but rejuvenated.

And there was Liam, an unexpected bonus of her new job. Liam was twenty-five, a former citizen of a tiny village deep inside his vaguely blonde and Scandinavian country in Europe. His past was shaded with vague mentions of some incident that had led to his departure from his homeland. He'd been at the farm for five years, long enough to become part of its fabric. Eight years Vivienne's senior, old enough to be mysterious but not so old as to be repulsive.

"You like music?" he asked.

Vivienne, flustered, tried to match his casual tone. "Yes, I... I suppose I do. I love Bach, Mozart. The piano concertos especially." God, she sounded pretentious. Shut up, Viv, she told herself. Just shut up. They were taking a break, sitting together, sipping water from paper cups, and looking down the strawberry fields that stretched like red-fringed Christmas scarves to a line of evergreens in the distance. The air was sharp with the smell of fruit; their fingers stained purple with the juice.

"I have a few records, you know?"

Vivienne rubbed sticky fingers on her dungarees. She nodded and answered, "Yes?"

The simplicity of the moment, the sharp smell of strawberries in the air, and Liam's calm presence—something about it all felt right. As Liam stood and stretched, revealing a sliver of his toned abdomen, Vivienne averted her gaze. He noticed, but only smiled, suggesting they listen to the records after work. Vivienne, her fingers still stained with strawberry juice, agreed, feeling a flicker of anticipation for the evening ahead. This summer job, intended just to fund her college dreams, might just be shaping up to offer so much more.

2

Vivienne wrestled with her nerves as she waited for the day's work to end, anticipating spending time with Liam and stirring a mix of excitement and apprehension within her. She chided herself for feeling jittery; at seventeen, she wasn't a novice in matters of the heart. In fact, there were moments when she worried her experiences might be too extensive for her age. During senior year, she'd been more careful to space her dates out for fear that dating more than one boy at a time or even two boys too close together could get a girl labeled fast or worse, easy. She'd felt sex close to the surface this past year.

Her experiences were limited to awkward late night encounters in the back seat, many of which she found unappealing. However, there were a few moments, one in particular, that stood out as different.

There had been Bill. She liked the way he looked straight at her when she spoke, the way he listened, the things he said. Bill was smart and funny. He had nice cheekbones and the sort of laugh that made you feel both witty and pretty. She'd let him unfasten her bra, but within minutes, things had gone sideways. He was pushing her down, his weight on her, his bulk frightening her in the dark. He morphed into something inhuman, making moans and strange sounds. She'd used her fingernails to scratch his face, and he'd been furious. He'd rolled away and cursed at her, gripping his cheek, which she could see was not injured.

"I'm sorry, I'm so sorry," she'd said. It was like a reflex, she tried to explain.

He'd pushed her away.

"Damnit, what's wrong with you?"

He'd started the car and driven her home, taking the turns way too fast, her bottom bumping hard into the seat. He didn't get out to open her door.

"I'm sorry," she said again.

"Such a bitch, Viv, I didn't know you were like this."

Getting ready for bed, she fumed with anger. She'd apologized right away, but he'd still been furious. Why had she apologized? Wasn't he the one who attacked her? She had encouraged him. That's what he said, anyway. In the mirror, she noticed a slight bruise on her hipbone, about the size of a quarter. She pressed her finger into it, surprised by how much it hurt. But she loved him, didn't she? After all that, she had encouraged him. He was right about that. In the end, it was Bill who lost interest first. Vivienne wasn't sure what to think about that.

3

Liam was waiting for her when she exited the women's locker room, leaning against an enormous hay bale, chewing on a stalk. A couple of village girls watched them as they headed toward Liam's small apartment over the hayloft. Vivienne flushed under the weight of the girls' stares.

The room was small and dimly lit, the smell of hay and horses so thick it made her eyes water. Looking around, she saw it was furnished with only a mattress on the floor, a second-hand table, one chair, and a small sofa. The sofa was fractured. It looked as if two people sitting together might cause it to splinter through. Besides this, he had a record player and a few books, and very little else; the most depressing room Vivienne had ever seen. No photos, no flowers, not even a poster on the wall.

They sat on the floor and played a few records, but Vivienne's attention drifted, and she lost interest. She wanted to go home, take a bath, slip into her bed, and feel the clean, cool sheets on her skin.

"I need to go now, Liam. Thank you." Vivienne pushed herself to stand.

He stood, and she felt him looming over her, too close. He seemed huge now. Fear coursed through her. Then, without warning, he was kissing her. His mouth pressed hard to hers, one big hand around the back of her neck and the other laid flat against her stomach, moving upward. She tried to pull away, but he was pushing her back against the wall. He pressed his mouth to hers, then moved to her cheek and down to her neck. His breath was stale, and she could feel the outline of his penis pressing into her hip. She felt sick.

"Stop it!" she said, but her throat was tight, and her voice came out whispery.

He seemed not to hear. He moved his hand up and over her breast. She let out a small shriek, fear escalating to terror.

"Please," she begged. Still, he didn't stop. She pushed her hands against his chest. "My mother will worry," she squeaked.

Abruptly, he let her go and stepped back. He was grinning, almost laughing. She wiped at her mouth. It felt bruised. Her left breast burned where he'd put his hand. She wanted to tear at her clothes, to get him off her. Vivienne stared at him, at his blue eyes and the glint of white teeth between his lips. There was nothing angry or malicious there, but also nothing apologetic. Did he not understand?

He moved out of the way and opened the door for her, standing back to let her pass.

Then, she was out and walking. The sunlight was blinding as she stumbled from the barn. Her lips ached. Her body ached, and somewhere inside the ache was a longing that shamed her. And the village girls were still standing in the same spot, dark-eyed and waiting. Knowing. Knowing. Knowing.

PART THREE: 1951-1955

CHAPTER 11

TALBOT COLLEGE
1951

1

Ruthie Hampton arrived at Talbot College after the Christmas holiday, bringing a sense of comfort to Vivienne who had already been there three months. In Ruthie's presence, Vivienne stopped feeling like some three-legged, one-eyed creature transplanted from outer space and plopped into a New York penthouse to live alongside the Pekinese and Miniature Poodles. At least now there were two of them. Vivienne supposed that was a little unfair. The girls at Talbot College in Northampton were not poodles. They were more like disciplined, well-bred collies: smart, fresh-faced, energetic, conformist, selfless, committed helpers. They were active members of clubs and foundations; girls fervid in their preparation to channel all their intelligence, talent, and ambition into family, community, and eventually husbands and children.

Three months into her time at the school, Vivienne had yet to meet a girl who planned on having an actual career once she was married. It was sad, all this female potential wasted on a life of pot roasts and diaper changing. Vivienne might have felt sorry for them had all of them not come from families backed by bank accounts the size of a small country's gross domestic product. So, in truth, they would be more likely to supervise the pot roasts and diaper changing. Still, it was dismal.

Vivienne figured the college needed a shot of something different to mess up its hair and put a few fingerprints on its smooth-as-glass surface. In January 1951, that shot came in the form of Ruthie Hampton.

Ruthie cursed like a sailor, horrifying everyone, and waved a cigarette around, held between thumb and forefinger like a man. Most astonishingly, she wore slacks; exclusively slacks. Ruthie also refused to explain her sudden, mid-year arrival at a school she'd sworn all her life she'd rather die than attend.

"I went abroad," she told Vivienne, offering no additional details.

That Ruthie had also missed the last half of her senior year, and her high school graduation, had not gone unnoticed. Stan had been mum about the whole thing, but Vivienne had her suspicions. Of course, Ruthie would tell in her own time. Or not. Vivienne would never ask.

At Talbot, no one knew about that. But there were rumors. At Talbot, there were always rumors, and the mid-year arrival of a cursing, smoking, pants-wearing girl was just beyond delicious.

Isn't she just too short, too bold, and much too loud to be so mysterious? A woman of mystery should be, well, you know, beautiful. She should be Lana Turner or Rita Hayworth, not this girl.

In the end, most of the girls who knew her just decided Ruthie Hampton was a lesbian.

2

They sat together on Ruthie's bed, Vivienne leaning back against the headboard as she listened to Ruthie read.

"...he finished the last of his cigarette, dropped the butt to the sidewalk, and walked away."

Ruthie set the paper down beside her and looked up. The room was stuffy, overheated, and smoky. Vivienne felt stickiness under her arms and wondered if she smelled. It was strange that it didn't matter. Ruthie was maybe the only person in the world with whom that was true.

"Straight on, Ruthie," said Vivienne with a smile. "That's what you do. Plain and straight at them whether they like it or not."

Vivienne didn't add "like a man," but the phrase popped into her mind. Between them, Ruthie was the better writer. It was her fearlessness. It was tangible, something with shape and texture. Ruthie could write the hell out of sex and love, but it was her gritty language, her sly, edgy phrasing, and the dark places she'd go without so much as a glance back. That's what fascinated Vivienne.

"But the thing is," Vivienne paused.

"Yeah?" Ruthie narrowed her eyes. "Spit it out."

"The thing is, who's going to publish it? I love it. You know I do. But dammit, Ruth, you know who buys what. So, you just have to reign it in, right?"

Vivienne hated the words as soon as she said them.

Ruthie ignored the comment. She pulled open the dresser drawer behind her and took out a crushed pack of cigarettes. She offered one to Vivienne, who shook her head.

"You really should smoke," said Ruthie. "With your height, it would look good on you. Sort of Bacall, you know?"

She lit the cigarette with a gold lighter; the initials LL engraved into the metal. She stood, leaning against the bureau, smoking, one arm across her stomach, the other bent, elbow in the crook of her waist.

"Who would you be?" asked Ruthie. "I mean, if you could be anyone? Living or dead, man, or woman. Who would you be?"

"Where did you get that?" asked Vivienne.

"Get what?"

"That," Vivienne pointed at the lighter, still in Ruthie's left hand.

"Oh, come on. She didn't need it. She's got like twenty of these."

"Oh hell, Ruthie. She doesn't have twenty and I think those might be solid gold, and besides, is that the point? You stole it. You can't go around doing that. You know they'll kick you out."

The previous owner of the gilded lighter was Lacy Longacre, a pale-haired, squeaky-voiced girl, not likable and backed by an obscene family fortune. Vivienne didn't care about the stolen lighter. The girl probably had nineteen others. But she worried about Ruthie. The lighter was not Ruthie's only loot, nor was Lacy the only victim. Ruthie's penchant for stealing had resulted in piles of objects stuffed into corners and drawers around her room. Some valuable. Some worthless. Combs, earrings, plastic compacts, bookmarks, playing cards, broken pens, sunglasses, even a fake silver-plated salt and pepper set lifted surreptitiously from the dining commons.

Ruthie shrugged. "Who cares. Anyway, who would you be? Come on." She stretched out on the floor and blew smoke into the air. The pale smoke twirled upward until it disappeared into nothing.

"Ok, I'll play. Let's see. How about Eleanor Roosevelt?" said Vivienne.

Ruthie rolled her eyes. "Yuck. You would not. Try again."

"Ok, um, maybe Marianne Moore?"

"Oh God, she's like a hundred."

"Marianne Moore when she was young. Your turn."

"Oh, I have no idea. It was a game for you. Ha!"

Ruthie lifted her wrist and checked her watch. Then she pulled herself to a standing position, brushed lint from her slacks, and slipped into her shoes. She made a striking impression. Shorter than Vivienne, strong-limbed with dark red hair and a smattering of freckles that spread across her cheekbones, she looked a bit more Irish than the Eastern European ancestry she claimed.

"Let's go somewhere," said Ruthie. "Get out of this room. It's so stuffy."

Vivienne hadn't noticed the time. Outside, the afternoon had grown dim. It was Friday, and they both had dates. Even Ruthie had succumbed to the tradition of dating. Everyone had dates on Friday. If you didn't have a date, you found a date or someone, a friend, set you up with a date. Dates, it seemed, were the name of the game at Talbot, and not having one was worse than failing your courses. Worse than death. Worse than anything.

"It's late," said Vivienne. "We have to go."

Vivienne watched Ruthie's face change; the skin seemed to sag, and she aged five years in one second.

"Noooo. Let's beg off. Steal a bottle of something and hide out somewhere!"

But Vivienne knew they wouldn't do that. It wasn't normal, and everyone would know and ask questions, and the aftermath would be far worse than suffering through the double date they'd already agreed to. It was a blind double date. Two boys from Dartmouth Vivienne had never met were meeting them on behalf of the boys' mothers, who were both friends with Ruthie's mother. It promised to be a depressing affair.

"You never know; this could be fun," said Vivienne with mock cheerfulness.

"No, we do know. One of these guys is a drip. I remember him from when I was seven. He came to my house and made me lick a cricket. He told me I couldn't leave the garden until I licked the cricket. I wonder if he remembers?"

They both laughed.

"Oh god, well, maybe he's changed," said Vivienne.

To that, Ruthie only laughed harder.

3

And so, the trees turned, a soft wind blew, and the young women of Talbot College settled into their predictable, respectable rhythms. Books and gossip during the week with weekends reserved for what sounded like dates with universities rather than young men: "I'm off to Yale on Saturday," or "I absolutely must go down to Dartmouth," or "Harvard better call or else."

Vivienne made more friends that fall. She went out, sometimes doubled with Ruthie or with other girls, always wishing those girls were Ruthie. Stan Hampton came down from Yale, and they went out, but not exclusively. At least not exclusively for Vivienne. She could tell he was getting serious and dreaded the day she'd have to cut him off. She kept hoping something, anything, would change. In the meantime, they attended dances and parties and sometimes had fun. The after-party necking sessions were a requirement. Premature arrival home meant the inevitable and interminable query from other girls: "Oh no, was it awful? Was he terrible? Was he fresh?" Such interludes always left Vivienne with ill-defined nausea requiring several cups of tea and a long session with the poetry of Dylan Thomas before she could get to sleep. She had trouble sorting out the line where a girl was supposed to demur, especially when she did not want to demur. It seemed an awful lot easier for boys who only had to go, go, go until the girl said stop.

The 1951-1952 school year was not unpleasant; Vivienne worked hard at her studies and did well. A few of her friendships deepened, and the time passed as time will do.

CHAPTER 12

UGLINESS
1952

1

Ruthie was leaving for good. Just two weeks into fall semester of second year, and she was going away. She'd told no one, not even her brother Stan, who'd already come down twice to visit. She was off to New York City, and then maybe Paris if she could get the money together.

Conversations between Vivienne and Ruthie went in circles:

"Why?"

"To write, of course. Why did Hemingway go to Paris, silly? Or Joyce, or Turgenev?"

"You're going to write books?"

"Of course, I'll write books. What else would I write?"

"But you can write here."

"No I have to leave."

"But, why?" No answer would have satisfied Vivienne. She desperately did not want her friend to go. And, of course, there was the question of money which Ruthie dodged every time Viv brought it up. "What will you do to support yourself, you'll have to find a job, perhaps work for an editor first, or maybe at a newspaper."

Shrug, "Dunno, not worried. I have to get out of here."

Vivienne and Ruthie stood in the rain under a small portico at the Northampton train station. Rain like this was peculiar for late September, but the drizzle suited Vivienne's mood. They had maybe five minutes before Ruthie's train arrived, and Vivienne was foolishly trying to think of a way to convince her friend to stay.

"I don't understand why you have to go," Vivienne had asked. "Why can't you just stay and write here? And why can't you finish school first?"

"It's not for me. This place."

Ruthie's answer was pregnant with all the unspoken words. She would acknowledge only that it was the governor's graduation speech that pushed Ruthie over the edge.

"And everyone applauding, grinning like goddamn idiots. As if he wasn't saying what he was saying. I couldn't stand it."

The governor had droned on for over an hour with inane comments like: "Once you read Baudelaire, now it is the Consumer's Guide. Once you wrote poetry. Now you are so tired you fall asleep as soon as the dishes are finished."

Presumably the governor (or his speech writers) had meant to encourage the group of young, educated women to let go of their fanciful dreams and learn to take pride in their domestic duties, in their roles as mothers and wives. Ruthie was having none of it.

"So what?" argued Vivienne. "He just said out loud what they all think. You know that. Just ignore him. I am. I don't plan to give up. I'll have my career. I'll be a mother, a wife. You watch."

"I know you believe that Viv, but I can't do it. Me? I'd just become my mother."

Vivienne thought about Mrs. Hampton with her thick waist and fruit pies. The thought of her independent friend's unregimented personality being harnessed and restricted that way made her wince.

"I'm already starting to look like her a little," continued Ruthie, patting her stomach. "I noticed it this summer when I was home. So, anyway, I thought I could come back here, and it would be alright, but it's not. Do you understand?"

Vivienne nodded. "Yeah, yes, I understand, Ruthie, I do."

Ruthie swiped at her eyes. She wasn't sentimental. "Robert Graves," she mumbled.

"What?"

"That's who I'd be, the poet. Robert Graves. You know: *The White Goddess* and all that. You'd be young Marianne Moore, which I still don't believe, and me? I'd be Robert Graves."

"But, why?" asked Vivienne startled. "He's a man."

Ruthie's eyes widened as if the answer was obvious. "Sure, and that's exactly why. Only a man has the sort of freedom I want. Can you imagine if Mrs. Graves had run off to Spain like that? Just leave four children behind and start over for her art?" Ruthie shook her head. "That's what I want. But, of course, he's a right bastard, and I wouldn't say I like his writing that much. But I want the other thing. Whatever it is."

2

The Thanksgiving holiday had been disappointing. First, Beanie had visited his girlfriend's house for the weekend, leaving Vivienne alone with Mother, Grammy, and Grampy. Second, the weather had turned gray and frozen the moment she'd arrived back in Wellesley. Then, there'd been Ruthie deciding to stay in Paris for the holidays, which had made Vivienne angry. Finally, she'd gotten the news that poor Stanley had contracted TB during his first-year medical studies and had been admitted to a sanatorium upstate. However, if she were honest, that had been more of a relief than anything else.

Back in September, after Ruthie jumped ship, leaving Vivienne alone at Talbot, Vivienne had impulsively agreed to go steady with Stan. Vivienne was fond of Stan, but they'd been going steady for less than three months, and the arrangement was already becoming tiresome. It grew more so after he told her about the sex he'd had with some slutty librarian the summer before last. All this time, Stan had been pretending to be pure and innocent. He'd made Vivienne feel as if she were the one with all the sexy experiences because she'd gone on so many dates. The truth of the matter was that he'd slept with this full-grown woman over twenty times! At least that's what she calculated when he said, "a couple of times a week all summer." A couple multiplied by nine or ten was twenty. Vivienne couldn't get over the hypocrisy of the whole thing. She didn't care that he'd done it, although she thought it might be a problem that she didn't care. Wasn't a girl supposed to feel jealous about that sort of thing? What bothered her was that he was such a liar. Now she would have to go out and sleep with someone to even the score and so on. Only it couldn't be Stan. She went around in her head so many times that her eyes went crossed and finally decided she'd just have to break up with him. Or lie about still going steady but not go steady.

To be fair, Vivienne suspected her poorly considered decision to commit to Ruthie's older brother had more to do with a desire to stay close to Ruth than any sort of romantic feelings she might have harbored for Stan Hampton. She had decided—she would break up with him. Straight out. Simple. But then Stan got sick, and Vivienne was back to square one.

Thanksgiving weekend was lonely and dull. Still, Vivienne had enjoyed cooking turkey and baking meringue pies with Grammy. They made gift baskets for the Hamptons and batches of cookies for Stanley, although twice she'd forgotten what she was doing and wandered off in the middle. And once, she'd pushed her fingers very near the eggbeaters, daring them to chop a few right off. Mesmerized until Mother started screaming, "Vivienne, Vivienne, what in the world are you doing? You have just got to be more careful, Vivienne!" Grammy had to bring Mother a cup of tea to calm her down. It was all so silly. It wasn't like she'd have done it. After all, a finger in the batter would have ruined the cookies.

3

On Saturday, it came back again, but this time all at once, full force; the sense of impending doom, the overwhelming lethargy, and the fat tears she struggled to swallow. When the opportunity came to return to Talbot early, she took it. Hiding her hovering depression from Mother was worse than spending a few days alone in the residence hall. She got a ride with Tookie and Sam, two Harvard boys she knew who lived in Wellesley.

She squeezed into the back seat between a girl she'd never met and Leland, a friend of Tookie's she'd only met once. Vivienne was hot, silent, and self-conscious the whole way. She forced a smile as Tookie glanced at her in the rearview mirror.

"You okay back there, Viv?"

"Yeah," she lied, her throat tight with unshed tears. "Just a little tired."

The car's leather seats were warm and sticky against her skin. The smell of Tookie's cologne mixed with the girl's perfume, making her head swim. She kept catching sight of her reflection in the rearview mirror: an ugly mask, puffy and pale, her eyes flat, bleak, and dead.

4

Vivienne would have liked to blame the hollow, desolate feeling on loneliness, but it was not that. She typically enjoyed her solitude. This was something worse. She'd spied it crouching in the dark corners of her mind, perhaps as far back as October. A thick jellied ocean, pushing her down from the surface. Each time she struggled up, her limbs felt heavy and uncooperative, as if she were trying to swim through thick syrup. Her skin prickled with cold sweat, and her breath came in shallow, uneven gasps. Her head felt too big for her body, her feet weighted down, like one of those babies in a jar Stan showed her at the medical school, only wearing concrete shoes. Inside, she felt empty, without a compass.

She lay on her bed, staring at the ceiling, her mind a battleground of conflicting thoughts. *Do I need to wake up?* she wondered, but a wave of doubt drowned the thought. *What's the point?* By Sunday morning, she was stuck, frozen by indecision. Staying buried beneath the blankets felt like the only sensible option, safer than facing a day filled with choices she was certain she'd mess up. Even the thought of getting up to wash seemed pointless—she'd just get dirty again. Everything seemed futile, a cycle she couldn't escape.

5

By Monday, her mouth was parched, her skin grimy, and her muscles ached with exhaustion. By Tuesday, when her housemates returned, she was weak, dizzy, and unable to walk. Staff transferred her to the infirmary, where a zillion-year-old doctor who Vivienne thought looked suspiciously like Douglas MacArthur squinted at her for two minutes. Finally, he diagnosed a viral illness which everyone knew meant, *Girl with a lousy attitude and no vomiting or fever.* He ordered bed rest, aspirin, and fluids, then walked away without another word.

Vivienne spent a week in the infirmary recovering from her illness. After a week, she pushed herself out of bed, her legs trembling but her resolve firm. "I'm fine now," she told the nurse, more to convince herself than anyone else. "I can't afford to waste any more time."

Returning to classes, she was determined to avoid a recurrence by sheer will if necessary. She threw herself into frenetic activity. Long sessions of study, camped out in cubicle twelve at Roosevelt Library, books spread like a hard carpet around her. Frantic, last minute plans for dates. She'd go out with anyone, everyone. Anything to avoid a weekend alone in the white-gray halls of Haven House. Anything to escape that restless shudder inside.

CHAPTER 13

THE CLASSMATE

We all knew Vivienne worked too hard. She pushed herself relentlessly, barely sleeping or eating. We saw it unfolding—she was like a machine on a mission. But we didn't understand what her goal was, other than self-destruction. Many of the girls found her brash, but a lot loved her. I did. Her humor, her passion, her boundless energy, and that staggering talent of hers. No one could deny her talent. By then, she was publishing her poetry and stories. She was a mountain, a goddamn Everest of talent.

It was around then, after she returned from the infirmary in December 1952, that's when we noticed a change. She started smoking for one thing. Not like the rest of us who puffed away on dates, but as if each cigarette was a lifeline she clung to. She'd sit there with an ashtray half-full beside her typewriter, pulling one after another from a pack. Her gorgeous, long-tapered fingers, always manicured, looked elegant holding a cigarette. The smoke soon filled the room. We couldn't breathe. Then, suddenly, she quit. It was like she was punishing herself.

It was more than just a chest cold although we did not know it at the time. She was sick in a different way. It was years later that we understood. God, we were just babies then. That's all we were. Just babies.

CHAPTER 14

GETTING ON WITH IT
Spring 1953

Vivienne stood, fretful and agitated, in her bare feet, wearing only a white nylon slip and bra. Most of her clothes lay on her bed, pulled from the hangers, and thrown about in heaps and piles. She felt the coolness of the nylon slip against her skin and heard the rustle of fabric as she rifled through the clothes. She stared down at them, wondering why she'd piddled away her tiny clothing budget on bits and bobs and saved nothing to buy a suit for an important interview like this. Instead, she'd been stuck pulling various mismatched skirts and blouses off hangers all morning, rejecting one after another. Nothing worked. She owned no accessories. Nothing elegant enough to meet with a New York City fashion magazine editor.

She checked her watch again. Two hours until the luncheon. Time was slipping away. It was time to get dressed.

Still, excitement coursed through her. This was it, the opportunity for which she'd waited her whole life. Spring had come on with a bang. The sun had reemerged, the crabapple bloomed, her mood lightened, and her energy returned. In early April, she won a writing contest with American Miss magazine—a chance to visit New York as an assistant writer during the summer. New York City! The place where everything happened!

"Ahhh," she groaned, throwing herself back onto the bed. Fifteen minutes remained to sort out the dilemma and catch a cab to make it to the meeting on time. She stared at the ceiling, took a deep breath, and sat up with renewed determination. What did it matter if her clothes were old? At least they were clean. She'd already won the damn contest. They wanted her. She'd done it.

Pushing herself off the bed, Vivienne pulled her blue wool skirt off the hanger and slid it on. Loose. Pairing it with a neat, collared blouse, she checked herself in the full-length mirror. Her long, lean body wore clothes well, her skin was fresh, her hair glossy. She smiled. Get on with it, Vivienne, she told herself.

At twenty, it didn't matter if one forgot to wear diamonds and furs.

CHAPTER 15

THE SCHOOLMATE

Jack Welles was a queer fellow. I first met him at Cambridge, back in the early 1950s. We were all young men, experimenting with Victorian dress and the like. He wasn't that way. A lot of blokes at Pembroke thought he was putting it on, you know? In those old clothes and ridiculous long coats. We all had hats and pipes and the whole bit, so he more than stuck out.

He was quite something to see. Here's this huge guy stomping around in an oversized frock coat, his bushy hair and beard giving him the look of a wild prophet. He would scowl and pontificate, his deep voice filling the room. But despite his intimidating presence, he had a magnetism that drew us all in. Everyone aspired to be him. Well, not everyone, but a lot of artist types, especially the poets and writers among us. He used to hold many seances and mystical readings in his room up there at the college. I don't know if he believed in it so much as he found poetical inspiration. But we all went and looked forward to it. Of course, there was a lot of drinking, and somehow Jack smuggled in girls, strictly forbidden.

After Cambridge, once, must have been about 1953, I tried to get him a job at my firm. But he showed up in those same clothes, a little cleaner but essentially the same. I think I still could have found him a position—he was enormously talented, extraordinarily bright, and it was a publishing company. Of course, we had our share of eccentrics. But it was the way he behaved. Sitting sideways, sort of squinnying at the clients as they came and went. It upset people. You know, my secretary asked me after he'd gone. She said, 'Do you think Mr. Welles is quite right in the head?'

CHAPTER 16

NEW YORK CITY
1953

1

Manhattan. June 1953. The Astor was not an actual hotel but more like a women's boarding house with lots of rules, the main one being that men were not allowed under any circumstances. Vivienne was pretty sure they would be shot or perhaps meet an even worse fate. Many girls from all over the world stayed at the Astor; most of the ones who'd won the American Miss Magazine contest were exactly like Vivienne. At least, they were alike in the sense that they dreamed of becoming 'legitimate' writers.

They were greeted with a buffet dinner in the Swan Room on the twentieth floor of the hotel. Silver platters of shrimp and caviar, French rolls, and beef tenderloin were laid out across gorgeous pale pink and white tablecloths. Crystal bowls overflowed with peonies and roses, and the room smelled of food and flowers. The girls, each wearing the white dress they'd been asked to purchase, and which Vivienne could ill afford, sat at small tables and listened to senior editors, investors, and public officials give what amounted to self-aggrandizing speeches. As she listened to the speeches, Vivienne's mind wandered. The grand promises of the contest seemed hollow compared to the reality of her tasks. Even amidst the opulence, she felt a growing sense of disillusionment. After dinner, they posed for photographs with people whose names they would not remember.

From the moment they arrived, American Miss Magazine had unique plans for its contest winners. Instead of immersing them in the world of serious writing, they were expected to focus on marketing and publicity. Vivienne and the other young women would spend their time on marketing photo shoots, fashion shows, and publicity dinners. They would be required to hear senior editors explain the importance of 'maintaining an appropriate image' while out in New York City. The fraction left over was for writing and reviewing bubbly ad copy. The 'real' writing was left to the fiction department, staffed by men and senior female editors, all of whom were single, middle-aged, and childless. Vivienne's dreams of mixing with such luminaries as Dylan Thomas and Marianne Moore dissolved to nothing. The job Vivienne had gained access to, at least in the contest she'd won, turned out to be more akin to fashion photo prop than fashion magazine writer.

Still, it was Manhattan, and they were young.

They obfuscated authority. They snuck past the supervisors, caught cabs, went to nightclubs, met men, and some got themselves into trouble. They also found time for sightseeing between reviewing ad copy for lingerie and endless photo sessions where they sweltered in long wool kilts and penny loafers. Vivienne visited parks, roamed the spare galleries of the Museum of Modern Art, and wandered midtown's wide avenues with a sketchbook and journal in hand. She ate food from all over the world, at least to the degree her small budget would allow.

Despite the thrill of adventure, Vivienne couldn't ignore the city's hollow facade. Everything felt artificial, as if a thin, grimy layer covered not just the buildings and streets but the people too, masking them in something false and insincere. Even the moments of excitement couldn't redeem it, she thought—it just wasn't worth it.

2

"I think it's good they'll be dead," said the girl with the cat's eyeglasses. She stretched her arms and went back to flipping pages of her magazine.

It was June 19th. The headlines had loomed in Vivienne's mind for months but seeing them in print hit like a slap. *ROSENBERGS TO DIE IN ELECTRIC CHAIR.* She'd vomited that morning, once before breakfast and again after. The day was hot, more stifling than usual, a sticky heaviness clinging to the air. Her cramped, double-occupancy room on the thirteenth floor was wedged into a corner of the building, with two narrow windows facing south, giving her a view only of the blank wall of another high-rise. The lack of airflow felt suffocating. She told herself it was probably just the heat keeping her awake, making her stomach churn—but the nausea clung, persisting well into the day.

Now they were seated in the magazine's main office, awaiting the start of the daily team meeting. Vivienne held her cup of tea close, sipping cautiously, trying to calm the churn in her stomach. The room's overly chilled air, laced with the competing scents of perfume and coffee, stood in stark contrast to the sweltering heat outside.

"You what?" she blurted out, unable to contain herself. "You *think* it's good? How could it be good that someone is going to die?" Her gaze swept across the room, landing on the tired, disinterested expressions around her. On the long conference table lay a haphazard collection of newspapers and magazines, their headlines glaring back at her: *ROSENBERGS DIE TODAY.*

"Oh, Viv, calm down," one of the girls said, plucking a compact from her bag. She dabbed a finger at her lipstick, pressing it delicately onto her bottom lip before smacking her lips together. "We can't have that sort in this country," she added casually, snapping the compact shut with a click.

"That *sort*?" Vivienne's voice rose, the anger spilling over. "What on earth does that mean? Human? The human sort? They're going to electrocute them, you know. Do you even understand what that means? *Electrocution.*" The girl with the lipstick, along with another girl in green cat-eyeglasses, stared blankly, their expressions unchanging. Someone at the end of the table let out a stifled giggle. "It's like they fry you from the inside," Vivienne continued, voice thick with frustration. "Smoke actually comes out of your head."

Silence settled over the room, punctuated only by the distant hum of the air conditioning. Vivienne's words hung there, absorbed by the blank stares and detached indifference, while outside, the city sweltered under a heavy, unrelenting sky.

"Oh god, Viv, do you have to be so crass?" said another girl in disgust.

"Crass? Are you joking?" said Vivienne. "You think my language is crass? That's your worry? Our government is going to murder these people, and you think my language is crass?" Vivienne felt her frustration mounting as she looked around at the indifferent faces of her colleagues. Her heart pounded with a mix of anger and helplessness, each dismissive comment like a knife twisting in her gut.

The girl, a flat-faced, mousy-haired young woman with pale skin, pursed her lips and sucked air through her nose. "As a matter of fact, I do," she said. "And I know I'm not the only one. Also, I don't think this is the place for you to espouse your political opinions."

"This is New York! This is a literary publication! Where do you think would be more appropriate?"

Now the lipstick girl spoke. "She's right, Viv. This is a *fashion* magazine. Not the New York Times. I'm sure we all have our thoughts on the issue, but this is not the place."

Vivienne looked around the room. Some girls were munching Danish rolls, some were staring at themselves in compact mirrors, others were simply sitting slack jawed watching the drama unfold. Vivienne doubted most of them had any thoughts about the Rosenbergs at all.

Vivienne sighed and gave up, sinking back into her chair as she reached for one of the newspapers on the table. Her eyes fell on a large photograph capturing Ethel and Julius Rosenberg in handcuffs, their faces etched with terror. She swallowed, feeling a pang of nausea return as she traced the contours of their expressions.

As she unfolded the paper, her gaze drifted downward to a small print box just below the article. A three-inch square labeled *TODAY'S CHUCKLE.* Inside, bold letters spelled out a childish Knock Knock joke:

Knock, Knock...

Who's there?

Lettuce.

Lettuce who?

Lettuce in—it's cold out here.

Vivienne's stomach twisted. The joke felt absurd, glaring out from the page like a slap in the face. She stared at it, almost transfixed by the irony, as though the joke itself were mocking her and everything that hung heavy in the air.

3

Vivienne dressed with extra care for the train ride home to Wellesley. As the train swayed, Vivienne's thoughts drifted back to the letter she had sent to her brother a week earlier. In it, she'd arranged the details of her arrival and, blindly, made several regretful comments about her state of mind. Following the execution of the Rosenbergs, she hadn't been able to pull herself out of the pit. The hypocrisy of New York, the phoniness of the magazine people she'd met, the insoluble problems the world faced, and man's profound capacity for inhumanity against man felt like crushing weights on her chest. She was finding it difficult to breathe.

On her last night in New York, Vivienne had given away nearly everything she owned, keeping only one suit to wear on the trip back home. She'd lost her appetite again, couldn't sleep, and found herself restless, eventually writing a letter to her brother. She confessed her mood swings and her disappointment with the city, describing New York as grimy, suffocating, and full of people she couldn't trust. Writing it had felt like a small release, almost a kind of cleansing. She imagined it might be something like what Catholics felt after confession—though she wasn't entirely sure what that involved. Penance? Absolution?

But the letter had only stirred more trouble. Beanie and her mother had been alarmed by her words, their replies arriving almost instantly. Her mother wanted to drive up and bring Vivienne home herself, an idea Vivienne had to talk her out of. *No, no, I'm fine,* she'd insisted. *Just tired, looking forward to seeing everyone. Nothing to worry about, Mother. Headed down to the pool for a swim now.*

Now, on the train home, she felt overheated in her wool skirt and heels, her head throbbing from the tight twist of bobby pins holding her hair in place. The skirt clung to her legs uncomfortably, and the pins pinched her scalp. But she reminded herself she'd dressed this way for a reason—*to prove to Beanie and Mother that she was fine.* Especially her mother. She couldn't bear the thought of her mother hovering over her every second of the two weeks she'd be home, not with Harvard's writing course looming on the horizon.

So, she sank back against the seat, closed her eyes, and let the steady rhythm of the train lull her. The oppressive heat, the cling of her clothes, and the pulsing in her head all faded as she repeated a quiet mantra to herself: *Sun and sleep.* That's all she needed to feel like herself again. Sun and sleep.

CHAPTER 17

MOTHER
July 1953

Vivienne wasn't well. I saw it immediately when we picked her up from the train. Her hair was pinned back, but carelessly, as if she hadn't even glanced in a mirror. She looked pale, slow-moving, and drained of joy. The oppressive humidity hung over us like a wet blanket, making the moment feel even heavier. Despite her lovely outfit, she was overdressed for the weather and sweat dotted her forehead.

"Hello, Mother," she said as Beanie and I approached, her tone eerily flat. "It's good to be home." She forced a smile, but it was a hollow gesture, devoid of warmth. Beanie and I exchanged a quick glance; we both noticed the change. He reached to take the one case she was carrying, and it struck me—she'd left with two bags only a month ago. Vivienne allowed me a brief embrace, stiff and detached.

"Darling?" I ventured, restraining myself from the usual, Are you alright? She hated that question. But her state was unsettling, and I had to swallow the words back hard. Her scent was off, a stale, unwashed smell that clung to her, more than just the result of the sticky train ride. Her hair was greasy, lifeless— so unlike her. I could tell she knew what I was noticing. She managed a few words with her brother, though he was Bernard now, no longer Beanie. Sensitive as ever, he picked up on the tension and tried to lighten the mood, filling the silence with snippets about his graduation, football, his girlfriend— anything to break through the haze.

In the car, I kept an eye on Vivienne through the rearview mirror, watching as Bernard's chatter rolled over her. She nodded and murmured polite sounds—"Mm," "Ah-ha," "Oh, yes?"—her gaze drifting out the window, barely registering what he was saying.

Finally, as we neared home, I knew I had to bring up the letter. She'd pinned so much on the short story course, clinging to it as a glimmer of hope. But I couldn't avoid it any longer. I took a deep breath and told her the truth.

"Vivienne, the letter came about the writing course. Unfortunately, it's already full, and it looks like we'll have to wait until next summer." I watched her, bracing for some response, part of me fearing she'd reach for the car door and fling herself into the street. But she didn't. She only said, "Fine, that's fine, Mother." Her voice was calm, almost eerily so, and the rest of the drive passed in silence.

When we got home, she asked to see the letter, looked it over once, and then tossed it into the wastebasket without a word before disappearing upstairs to take a bath. For the next few days, she was quiet but outwardly fine, or close to it. She ate meals with us, read books on the porch, sunbathed in the garden, and slept--hours upon hours of sleep. She seemed oddly at peace. But she didn't write. Not a single word.

Then, one morning, as she reached for something in the kitchen, her robe sleeve fell back, revealing a series of raw, red gashes along her inner arm. My heart stopped. I gently pointed them out, asking what was going on, and suddenly, she unraveled in front of me.

The words poured out in a torrent. She blamed herself for everything— every failed attempt, every disappointment. New York had been a nightmare, she said, a colossal failure that had left her feeling hollow and ashamed. She believed she'd let everyone down, that she'd hurt those she cared about most. Her voice grew frantic, her reasoning tangled in self-blame that spiraled deeper with every sentence.

That afternoon, I took her to see our family doctor. He listened, concerned, and gave us a referral to a well-regarded psychiatrist. It was July 9th, 1953— the day everything changed, the beginning of our long, difficult journey into the unknown of Vivienne's mind and what lay hidden there.

CHAPTER 18

THE HANGING MAN
July 1953

1

The first time Vivienne saw a psychiatrist, it felt as uncomfortable as a trip to the dentist—only the ache was buried deep in her mind instead of her teeth. She squeezed her eyes shut, as if by doing so, she might dispel the haunting thoughts that had clung to her. The cold hard-backed, space-age sofa she sat on seemed almost hostile, discouraging any notion of comfort or lingering. Shivering in the overly air-conditioned room, she regretted not bringing the sweater she'd left in the car.

Her gaze drifted to Dr. Paul Tillosten, with his absurdly square, dimpled jaw—he looked strangely like a young Cary Grant. Who had ever heard of a psychiatrist resembling a movie star? She let out an involuntary sigh, part frustration, part disbelief.

"Something wrong?" he asked, his voice inflected with that careful, probing tone so common among doctors. She guessed he was only a few years older than her, maybe thirty. Her mother's longtime doctor had referred them here, insisting he was "wonderful" and "knowledgeable." But Vivienne had her doubts. How much could someone just a few years older than her know about anything truly important? And there was something about him—something that seemed arrogant. Or maybe it was just the way his chin jutted out. Yes, perhaps she was just judging his chin.

How was she supposed to answer his question? *Something wrong?*

Everything was wrong. That's what she wanted to scream. *Everything.* But instead, she forced a tight smile and replied, "I'm okay. I don't aspire to be here."

He nodded, tented his fingers, and leaned back in his chair. The chair's internal mechanism made a horrible squeaking sound that, to Vivienne, undermined the doctor's authority. He remained silent, probably hoping she'd fill the void with her own words. Dr. Cary Grant, Vivienne decided, had underestimated her lethargy. Silence, by default, was her forte.

Ever since returning home from New York, Vivienne had been practicing silence, imagining herself as one of those monks in a mountain cave, living alone for fifty years. Maybe there'd be a supply person who brought things on the back of a mule but never spoke. What would that be like? She imagined lying flat in the dirt, spread-eagled like making a snow angel, only there'd be no snow. Maybe it would be Tibet. Lots of sun. She'd lie there, naked, silent, and wait to die.

Vivienne folded her hands in her lap, closed her eyes, and pretended to sleep.

"Vivienne?" Dr. Cary Grant's voice broke the silence. She didn't answer. Could he not see she was asleep? "Vivienne, you are not well, do you understand that?"

She let her eyelids flutter open. She'd just listened to her mother tell him how she wasn't sleeping, had lost at least fifteen pounds, and hadn't bathed or changed clothes in three weeks. His question must be rhetorical.

"Yes, I suppose that's correct," she said, deciding that being agreeable might get her out of his office more quickly.

"I've decided we may need a more drastic course of action, Vivienne."

At that, she perked up. A drastic course of action. Might that mean help? Could she possibly be helped? "Like what?"

He flashed a big smile. "Ah, I see. I've hit a nerve with that. Perhaps you'd like to talk to me a bit?"

No, she thought. No, she didn't want to talk to him at all. "Okay," she said anyway.

"Your mother says you've not slept well and that you've been feeling irritable. Do you think that might be connected to anything?"

Connected? she thought. How? "Like thigh bone connected to the sleep bone?"

Dr. Tillosten smiled thinly, flipping through a chart that surely held her most basic details—name, age, address. "Vivienne, how old are you?"

"Twenty," she replied, "almost."

He moved through a string of questions—small, impersonal things about school, books, places she'd visited. She answered automatically, feeling a building frustration until he asked, abruptly, "Tell me about your experience with the opposite sex."

"Experience?" She blinked.

"Yes, boys. Dating. Do you have a boyfriend, that sort of thing?"

Vivienne felt her cheeks warm. *What did boys have to do with the leaden feeling in her stomach, the sleepless nights, or wanting to die?* Lately, she'd even thought about death in connection to her mother, a morbid fantasy of simply fading out of life alongside her. She muttered something vague, evasive, recoiling at the thought of discussing boys with this strange man. The stiffness of the couch was gnawing at her back, and his leather chair felt too close, his body heat an unwelcome presence in the small space.

"And dates?" he continued. "Do you go on many dates, Vivienne?"

She stammered through some response, but her thoughts grew muddled, the questions meandering into personal, irrelevant details: where she liked to go, what movies she enjoyed, and the names of any boyfriends. He barely touched on the darkness that engulfed her, her thoughts of self-harm, her despair. Instead, he seemed fixated on intimacy, probing deeper, his questions skimming over her despair and digging into her personal life. *How many times had she been touched? Where exactly? Kissed? How many times? When?*

Without warning, her emotions snapped, and she began to sob. It felt like a dam bursting, tears flooding down her cheeks, leaving her breathless. Her vision blurred, and her head swam as she tried to process the intensity of her feelings. She could vaguely hear him speaking, but his words were lost in the rush of her grief and confusion. He shifted closer, draping an arm around her shoulder, pressing a tissue into her hand. She only cried harder, feeling trapped in his unexpected embrace, too overwhelmed to pull away.

Vivienne sat there, shoulders shaking as her sobs racked her body. The rough texture of his tweed jacket scratched against her neck as he murmured softly, patting her shoulder, assuring her she'd soon be "alright." When he finally led her back to the waiting room, she was silent, unable to find her voice. He told her to sit while he took her mother back to the office. Minutes later, her mother emerged with a prescription in hand and an appointment card for the following week.

It all felt like a blur, an almost surreal, disorienting experience she couldn't quite grasp. As they left, the weight of that encounter sat heavily on her, pressing down, deepening the dark pit she'd been trying so desperately to escape.

2

Vivienne took the sleeping tablets Mother gave her. At first, they worked. She fell into a dark, dreamless sleep. Waking up wasn't refreshing, but it was amnestic, which felt like a victory compared to the torturous twisting and turning of previous nights. She practically celebrated the relief.

The same happened the next night and, to some extent, the night after that. But by the fourth and fifth nights, the tablets only worked half as well. By the second week, even a double dose had no effect.

Each night, as she lay awake, Vivienne felt the weight of disappointment pressing down. The tablets had been a brief escape, a fleeting reprieve from her relentless insomnia. Now, that small glimmer of hope was fading, leaving her stranded once more in the suffocating dark.

3

The girl sat across from the doctor, looking disheveled and blunted. Her appearance had deteriorated over their last several visits. The sleeping tablets were not helping, and she seemed resistant to analytical intervention. She was now barely moving and nearly mute. He found her distasteful to interact with and noted a mildly foul odor as she entered the office. It was such a pity. She was a pretty girl. Or she had been. He'd been up to her college during the war. They had a WAC station up there, full of cute girls. He glanced at his watch—fifty-five minutes remaining in the session. That is, if they stayed the whole hour. This time he'd asked the mother to accompany the girl rather than waiting outside. The last session had been unproductive, and it was clear the girl would not be any more interactive today.

Her diagnosis: Post-Adolescent Psychoneurosis Secondary to Female Sexual Frustration. Treatment was next to impossible without her cooperation. Besides the primary diagnosis, she suffered from a deeply ingrained delusion about becoming a writer. According to the mother, this had consumed the girl since early childhood. He was certain that outpatient therapy wouldn't handle that situation.

The doctor addressed his comments to the older woman.

"Mrs. Holland, I'm afraid we've come to a difficult juncture. Unfortunately, there isn't another option here."

"I'm not sure I understand, doctor."

"The problem, Mrs. Holland, is sexual. Typically, I would prescribe a course of analysis, but in this case, the situation is deteriorating too quickly."

The woman looked at her daughter, who hadn't moved but only sat with downcast eyes and ruined hair hanging in her gaunt, gray face.

"I'm afraid I don't understand," she said.

"I have a colleague at Silver Hills. It's all arranged. He'll administer the treatments three times a week for eight weeks on an outpatient basis. And we'll see how things go." He glanced at the girl and then back at the mother, hoping she'd understand without making him spell it out. Patients often balked at the words. They'd already discussed this possibility, so really, she ought to remember.

The woman nodded. "I understand, and yes, I agree."

"Good, that then. We'll have a few papers for you to sign. You're making the right decision, Mrs. Holland." He leaned forward and patted her hand. "The best decision. And you, dear?" The doctor leaned toward the girl, who made no sign she'd heard him. "Your mother knows what's best for you, isn't that right?" He smiled, repeated, "Isn't that always, right? We'll start Friday. Bye now."

As they left, he glanced again at his watch. The whole interaction had taken less than fifteen minutes. He would have to ask Alice to do something about airing out the office.

4

Mother and Mrs. Hampton drove Vivienne to the sessions several times a week in the back seat of Mrs. Hampton's station wagon. It was the only vehicle big enough for Vivienne to lie down in the back. Most days, Vivienne wore the same clothes she'd had on all week. Sometimes Mother washed her hair. Usually not. Vivienne didn't see the point; it would only become soiled again.

Mrs. Hampton and Mother sat waiting in the vestibule at Silver Hills Hospital while the nurse took Vivienne into the back. Thirty minutes later, she returned. Mute, confused, disoriented, shaking, and sometimes injured or unable to walk. Twice her wrists and lower back were bruised, and once, her ankle sprained.

The doctor who administered the 'therapy' was a short, grayish-skinned man with small wire-rimmed glasses and eyes set too close together, making him appear a distant relative to a rodent, possibly a beaver. Vivienne called him Bartholomew because he looked like a Bartholomew and because she couldn't remember his other name. Bartholomew did not dress like a doctor. He wore a blue smock with a Chinese collar, a blue skullcap, and long black rubber gloves. She never saw him without two enormous silver paddles. Those paddles, one in each hand, were always coming at her, never reaching but always approaching.

Week after week, Vivienne endured the sessions. Her recall of the procedures was fractured; it all came back to her in flashes, like trying to see a complete scene reflected in shards of a broken mirror. The smooth rubber sheet. The thick leather straps tight around her wrists and ankles. The sickening thud of her heart, the way her throat would swell, threatening to choke her to death. Then, two metal plates fitted to her temples, followed by a soft whoosh and click, then three seconds of pure white silence. Then smash! It was a spasm of pain so intense it was made of color: blue, purple, and white streaks. Her hair was being ripped from her skull, her back arched, and her spine was being split. It was like being squeezed forever in a vice. And then, after an eternity of agony, there was nothing. She was falling and falling through a vacuum. And the terrifying nothingness was almost worse than the pain.

In nightmares, Vivienne would recall Bartholomew as an executioner, always the hanging man.

5

The plan had been for twenty-four sessions of electroconvulsive therapy administered over eight weeks, but just after the thirteenth treatment, Vivienne disappeared.

CHAPTER 19

BALD WHITE DAYS
August 1953

1

She'd been missing for forty hours. Even the police feared the worst. Neighbors, friends, and citizens of nearby communities joined in the search, their flashlights piercing the night and their voices echoing through the woods and streets. The headlines screamed: BEAUTIFUL COLLEGE CO-ED GOES MISSING AT WELLESLEY. Television coverage and articles in the Boston Globe and the New York Times spread the news like wildfire. Nearly three hundred newspaper articles were published all over the country.

Somehow, the description of Vivienne's clothing morphed from the modest skirt and blouse she'd been wearing into a 'strapless halter and short shorts.' Regardless of the media outlet, they consistently highlighted Vivienne Holland's appearance, overshadowing the gravity of her disappearance.

Mrs. Holland clung to hope, her eyes red-rimmed from sleepless nights, sitting by the phone, willing it to ring with positive news. Her husband paced endlessly, muttering prayers under his breath. Friends remembered Vivienne's quick wit and boundless love of life, hoping against hope that she would return safely.

Police deployed bloodhounds to scour garages, abandoned structures, and the wooded areas behind Dover Road. Local Boy Scout troops joined the effort, assisting in the search and offering refreshments to the police and volunteers.

"They'll find her, don't worry," was the constant refrain, but Lorah Holland was shattered. She felt the weight of every unspoken word and unguarded moment. Her daughter. Her responsibility. She'd been told to guard the sleeping pills. There had been fifty in the bottle. She should have known. Done something.

Lorah's mind raced. Perhaps she should have mentioned Fritz's mother to the doctors—the woman's history of mental illness and her decades in an asylum. Maybe keeping the family secret had made things worse for Vivienne. Maybe this. Maybe that. None of it mattered now.

Her hands trembled as she remembered Vivienne's last words, her last smile. Tears blurred her vision, but she blinked them away. She couldn't afford to fall apart now. Not when Vivienne needed her most.

In the evening, everyone gathered at the Unitarian Church to pray. The air inside was thick with incense and the soft murmur of whispered prayers. Candles flickered, casting warm, trembling light on the worried faces of friends and neighbors. Lorah stood among them, her hands clutched tightly together, as if holding on for dear life. She could feel the supportive hands of her community on her shoulders, hear their murmured reassurances, but her mind was elsewhere, with her daughter, lost and alone somewhere in the night.

2

Time had slipped away from her, or perhaps it had never existed in this place. Vivienne's eyes opened to a darkness so complete that it swallowed her whole, her own hands invisible in the thick black. Somewhere in the distance, a low, desperate moan echoed, cutting through the silence and quickening her pulse. She felt disoriented, nauseous, a pulsing pain throbbing in her skull. An acrid smell filled her nostrils—vomit mingled with the earthy stench of rotting wood and damp decay. Where was she?

She shifted, trying to sit up, and instantly regretted it. Her head thumped against something hard above, and a sharp pang shot down her neck, ricocheting along her spine. A thin whimper escaped her cracked lips, but the sound was barely a whisper, lost in the suffocating darkness. She tried to cry out again, but her throat was raw, her mouth parched and tasting of copper. A jagged edge scraped against her cheek, and she recoiled, feeling warm liquid trickle into her eye.

Her mind clawed for answers. *How had she come to be here?* The memory danced at the edges of her mind, just out of reach. Had someone taken her? Had she been buried underground? The idea tightened her chest, squeezing until she could barely breathe. Panic clawed at her insides, the desperate urge to escape clashing with the cruel reality that she had nowhere to go.

Time became meaningless as she lay there, enveloped by the darkness. Exhaustion seeped into her bones, draining her last reserves of strength. Slowly, the sharpness of her fear dulled, giving way to a strange calm, a numbing emptiness. She felt herself slipping, teetering on the edge of consciousness once more.

Then, it came to her—a chilling realization. She was dying. No, she was already dead. *This* was death. The thought washed over her like an icy wave, numbing her from the inside out. She raised a trembling hand to her face, feeling the grime caked onto her skin, the cloying scent of decay thick around her. Perhaps she'd already been buried.

Oddly, an unfamiliar sense of relief unfurled in her chest. *This is good,* she thought. *This is what I wanted.* Oblivion. Peace.

In the end, exhaustion overcame her. She let her eyes close and surrendered to the stillness, embracing the void.

3

Ruthie and Mrs. Hampton sat with the family in the living room. Grampy, sedated to calm his hysteria, now slept in his chair. Grammy sat with her head bent, fingers flying over her knitting. She refused to speak and looked as if she might stab someone with a knitting needle if they came near. Ruthie was encouraging Lorah to sip at a cup of lukewarm tea. Outside, the sky was a deep, solemn gray, and thunder rolled ominously in the distance. If it stormed, the police would call off the search. They'd already done it once.

Two days, the continuous heat, one rainstorm. It seemed impossible that Vivienne was still alright.

Suddenly, someone was shouting. Pushing herself up, Lorah jumped at the sound of the front door slamming and Beanie's voice reverberating through the house.

"It's Viv! We've got her! She's here, Mother, she's here. Call an ambulance! It's Vivienne!"

Lorah's cup clattered to the floor as she rushed to the door, her heart pounding. Ruthie and Mrs. Hampton followed, their faces a mix of hope and fear. Grammy's knitting fell to her lap, her eyes wide with shock.

CHAPTER 20

DO NOT BLAME YOURSELF

1

The little Christmas tree looked sickly. Barely four feet tall, distorted, lacking branches on one side, it listed piteously to the left. Vivienne stood over it and tapped a fingernail at one of the six battered red Christmas balls drooping among the dry needles. Plastic. Made sense. Glass was risky. Practically everyone in here was suicidal. Or homicidal. Vivienne herself wanted to kill her mother for putting her here.

They'd overlooked the wires. Vivienne glanced over her shoulder, checking the room. No one was watching. Across the day room, a nurse wearing a bright red cardigan with HAPPY HOLIDAYS 1953 stitched across the breast was engrossed in a lively conversation, waving her hands excitedly as she chattered with another nurse. They'd be preoccupied for a while.

Her fingers traced the thin steel wire holding a garish ornament to the tree. If she wanted to, she could slip the hook off, press it hard into her wrist, right into the vein, before anyone had a chance to intervene. But she wouldn't. She knew it, and, more importantly, the staff knew it too. That's why she was allowed here, free to roam the day room, while others remained confined to their rooms.

The thought felt hollow, though. Her lack of drive to turn a Christmas decoration into a weapon wasn't due to some newfound resilience. No, she blamed it on the lethargy brought on by her treatment. The shock sessions left her drained, unwilling to expend energy on even the simplest of tasks, let alone summon the resolve for any act of "delicious violence," as she'd once thought of it. And yet, if she were honest with herself, something had shifted. She couldn't deny it, however faintly: she felt… *better*. Not a lot, just a faint glimmer, a slight lightening of the relentless weight she'd been carrying.

Four months. She'd been here at Boston Hospital for nearly four months, enduring the treatments, feeling numb and scattered most days, as if some part of her had detached and was floating above her body, watching from a distance. But now, something was changing. It wasn't happiness or hope—not yet—but the despair had started to loosen, just enough for her to recognize that there was a difference, however slight.

As she sat there, gazing absently at the wire on the ornament, Vivienne couldn't quite name what she felt. It wasn't peace. But for the first time in a long time, it also wasn't agony. She leaned back, letting her hand drop, allowing herself to feel the faintest stirrings of something else.

Vivienne found a chair and dragged it over beside the little tree, then sat down. Poor thing needed company. She leaned in and inhaled, catching, however faintly, the scent of pine and fresh air. She touched a few of its needles with the tip of her forefinger.

"It's alright," she whispered. "We will both get out of here one way or another." One of the best things about being an asylum patient was that you could talk to a tree, and nobody would look at you twice.

2

Vivienne had required three weeks on the medical unit before her transfer to psychiatric to treat, among other maladies, a badly infected facial laceration. In a drugged stupor, Vivienne had split her cheek open against a rotting beam in the crawl space where she'd hidden after overdosing on sleeping pills. In retrospect, she considered the plot to end her life rather well-conceived. Unfortunately, she'd either miscalculated the number of pills required or vomited up enough to prevent death. Instead, she ended up in a state of semi-consciousness, making involuntary noises loud enough for her brother to rescue her. By that time, the wound was maggot-infested and required surgery. She'd have a scar, they said, but she was fortunate, they said. Pretty much everyone, from doctors to neighbors, reminded Vivienne how lucky she'd been not to die.

At first, Vivienne bided her time, counting the minutes until discharge so she could hatch another plan. Climbing the Empire State Building and flying to her death was one idea. Another was secreting away more pills, but she knew Mother would be more careful. She rejected hanging due to the high likelihood of survival, and a gun was out of the question. Gas might work, but privacy was an issue. Finally, Vivienne read about the Japanese general, Imai Kanehira, who died by jumping from his horse onto a sword. Creative, but it might upset the horse.

Before she could complete a plan, Vivienne's urge to die faded. There was a new doctor. Young, stylish, brilliant. At barely thirty, Dr. B. made Vivienne think of what Mother might have been if she were a witty, self-aware film star, instead of an over-worked, over-stressed, widowed teacher. Dr. B. wore flowing skirts and peasant blouses. She smelled of flowers. She was lively, a wife, and a mother and Vivienne aspired to be just like her. She did not hate Dr. B. for the treatments, nor did she blame her. For the rest of her life, Vivienne would remain terrified of hospitalization and traumatized by the remedies, but her devotion to Dr. B. never wavered.

Because of Dr. B., Vivienne submitted to being wrapped in cold sheets, dipped in ice baths, poked with needles, doped with Thorazine, and shocked with electricity a dozen more times when she became delusional. She'd been paranoid, demanding proof of staff identities before allowing them into her room. She recalled confusion and a hideous sort of fear. It was as if her brain wasn't processing sensations, which came at her like a fire hose at full throttle. This state seemed to go on forever. She was constantly trying to find a place to hide.

Then one day, it stopped.

All at once, Vivienne could answer the doctors' questions: "How are you feeling today?" "I'm alright, how are you?" She could eat her breakfast and taste the food—the juice was watery, but the eggs were good. She wanted to go for a walk outside, to feel the sun on her skin. It was as if the world had reorganized itself while she'd been away, although she did not know where she'd gone.

3

In February 1954, Dr. B. declared Vivienne well enough for discharge and return to Talbot on special status. Her diagnosis: Delayed Adolescent Turmoil. She recommended Vivienne take on relationships, sexual encounters, and academic burdens slowly and carefully, allowing herself time to continue recovering. Vivienne would work with Dr. B. in outpatient sessions twice weekly.

Beanie drove Vivienne back to Talbot. It was a chilly Friday afternoon, with lovely monochromatic winter scapes along the highway. They'd planned to take the longer route and visit one of Beanie's school friends along the way. However, the conversation grew tense just thirty minutes out of Boston, and they cut the drive short.

Vivienne, who had been sketching and absently prattling on about her therapy sessions, made a series of unkind comments about Mother. Suddenly, Beanie stopped her, holding up a hand.

"You need to be respectful," he said, his voice sharp.

"You do not know, Bean. You've no idea what it was like. You're a boy, for one. I had to share a room with her. She was into everything, on me. Suffocating me. It was terrible. Dr. B. says it wasn't normal. It was enmeshed. She was living through me. Dr. B. says—"

"Stop," he interrupted her. "Mother loves you, Viv. That's all. She did her best, and she loves you so much."

"That's not it. Dr. B. says we were in a sort of competition."

"Oh, what the hell is that supposed to mean?"

"You know, over Daddy. We're nearly the same age, Mother and me."

Beanie looked at her incredulously, taking his eyes off the road a moment too long. He had to swerve to get back on course. "Jesus, Viv. Come on. That's just stupid."

Vivienne sucked in her breath, resisting the urge to smack her brother. He was driving, after all.

"Well, that's what I figured out. I needed to… I couldn't breathe. I was, I don't know, suffocated. Depressed."

She wished she could remember how Dr. B. explained it. It made a lot more sense when she said it.

Vivienne had stayed on two more months working with Dr. B. as an inpatient. After the additional shock treatments, Vivienne had become something of a curiosity on the ward. It was like the psychiatric equivalent of being just that close to her kidneys shutting down.

"I've seen nothing like it, a total turnaround and so quickly. It makes little sense," said Dr. B..

Other psychiatrists came to see Vivienne in little groups. They always wore long white coats and had nothing interesting to say. They entered her room and conferred together without introduction, ignoring her presence altogether. They seemed to forget or not know that she spoke English. Or perhaps they thought she was deaf. Or feeble-minded. If she'd cared, she might have felt like a zoo animal, but she found it amusing. Inevitably, their conversations were circular and pointless. They seemed to enjoy hearing their own voices.

"Clinically unique," one would say, turning to another. "It can't result from shock therapy, Doctor, do you imagine? But, perhaps it is the shock therapy, Doctor. Do you think it's shock therapy, Doctor?"

Vivienne also thought it interesting that they called each other Doctor unless, of course, they were all given the name Doctor at birth, which was possible but would have been a remarkable coincidence.

Because her case was clinically unique — she had responded remarkably, even miraculously, well to her electroconvulsive therapy sessions — Dr. B.. invited Vivienne to take part in what the doctor referred to as "analysis." Together, she and Dr. B. explored some of her issues with her mother. Dr. B. suggested that, after her father's death, Vivienne's mother had taken on an overbearing and controlling role in her life, acting as protector, provider, and jailer. Vivienne felt the only way to escape this dynamic was through psychological withdrawal, manifested as depression, or, in its most extreme form, thoughts of suicide.

"But wait," cried Vivienne. "Mother was wonderful to us, me and Beanie. She worked hard, totally self-sacrificing. Two jobs. She never even dated or remarried."

"And you felt suffocated."

"Yes."

"Sharing a room with your mother. No privacy. Your mother following all your achievements so closely, so involved in your friendships, your romantic life."

"Yes."

"Your only choice was psychological regression through depression. Even suicide."

"Yes."

"Do not blame yourself, Vivienne. I give you permission. Do not blame yourself."

"Yes."

But now, sitting in the car with Beanie, it was all mixed up in Vivienne's mind. She couldn't remember precisely, much less articulate any of it.

"You were depressed. We know that" said Beanie, "but it's not Mother's fault. You stop that. You're punishing her. Breaking her heart. She says you've barely spoken to her, Viv. You can't do that."

He was confusing her. It had seemed so clear back in Dr. B.'s office. On the sofa, Dr. B. nodding calmly as she spoke. Vivienne tried to conjure her last memory of Mother at the psychiatrist before she took the pills and crawled under the house. Mother, nodding idiotically at Dr. Tillosten, agreeing with him. Mother at Silver Hills letting them do THAT to her. Mother, emotionless, cold. No tears. It had made Vivienne so angry she'd wanted to shake Mother, scream in her face, get some kind of reaction out of her. She tried explaining this to Beanie.

"Vivienne, they told us to behave that way. They told Mother she must never allow you to see her fearful or broken or even sad. For God's sake, that's what she was doing. Pretending because that's what they told her to do. She was dying inside. She still is dying inside."

Vivienne stared out the window. The bare trees like skeletons bordered the road, the snow half-melted in brown, sludgy drifts.

"I'm sorry, Beanie. I'm so confused." Vivienne thought that was partly true. She might not have been sorry, but she was confused anyway.

They both stared ahead at the road in silence for many minutes. Finally, Vivienne felt something rise, reorganize itself, and then settle back down between them.

"Hey, how about Sunday?" said Beanie, his tone artificially light. "Can we come up for a visit? Mother wants me to drive her."

"Yeah, I'd like that." Vivienne smiled at her brother, but she wasn't sure if it was true or not. Something had seeded itself inside her like a grain of sand. She couldn't shake it loose and couldn't get a look at it, either.

4

By spring of 1954, Vivienne was fully re-enrolled at Talbot College, and her weekends filled with a revolving door of dates. She embraced her new freedom, dating multiple boys, never settling, enjoying the lightness that came from detaching herself from expectations. In May, she lost her virginity to a boy named Maury, an encounter she would later describe as "exceptionally bloody and otherwise underwhelming." When Maury nervously asked her for feedback, Vivienne, never one to soften the truth, told him plainly that the experience had been somewhere between boring and awful. Predictably, Maury lost interest and didn't call her again. Vivienne waited for the familiar pang of rejection, but it never came.

Instead, she moved on to other affairs: some with college boys, others with friends' boyfriends, and twice with professors—one of whom was married. Each encounter felt like a small rebellion, a deliberate defiance of the boundaries that had once felt so confining. It was as if her psychiatrist, Dr. B., had cut loose every restriction with one decisive snip. Whether he intended to or not, he'd granted her permission to do anything, everything. That's how it felt, anyway.

A wild, electric energy pulsed inside her, and she returned to college that year with an insatiable drive to feed the flames. Sex became more than just a distraction; it was a declaration, a way of claiming herself on her own terms. Over her senior year, her life took on a sharp, dizzying edge—the sex, the drinking, the brazen taking of whatever she wanted. Each act of defiance became its own reward, a thrill that filled the spaces where her old, stifling rules once were. She wasn't simply living anymore; she was pushing, pressing against every boundary, determined to consume every bit of life on her terms.

Vivienne resumed correspondence with Mother, although her letters were carefully constructed and minimally revealing. She wanted Mother to be happy. She'd sorted out that much. Her mood, she would have described as elated. She felt powerful, focused, eager, and well on her way to achieving all her goals. She decided that success in all spheres, professional and personal, would require getting as far away from Massachusetts as possible. Her grades were still top of the class, although she'd slightly relaxed the murderous self-imposed pressure to excel, be the best, and always win, at least regarding school.

By 1955, she'd begun applying for a Fulbright scholarship. If granted, the scholarship would take her across an ocean, three thousand miles away, to the United Kingdom.

PART FOUR: 1956

CHAPTER 21

CAMBRIDGE-THE BITE
1956

1

Vivienne folded the creamy stationery and pushed it into the matching envelope. She addressed the envelope and added a stamp, sealed it, and sat studying it for a moment. Writing Dr. B. was a risk. There was a possibility she'd get no response. Dr. B. was under no obligation to correspond with a former patient. Particularly one who had moved to England. There was no longer a doctor-patient relationship. They weren't friends or peers. So, what were they? Nothing. But she needed to know what to do, and correspondence with Dr. B. might be her only hope. Vivienne tapped the envelope against the desk a few times before gathering up the other letters she'd written and placing them all into her handbag.

Coming to Cambridge had seemed clear a few months earlier. She'd won the scholarship, made plans, and set sail without a second thought. And here she was, with a suitcase full of essays, stories, poems, and her head stuffed with unwritten words. It had been a shock to discover the place already crawling with young people who seemed startlingly bright and talented. Students with twice or three times the volume of work Vivienne had accumulated; students who never slept; students who read four languages and spoke five; students who did everything lightning fast and seemed to have time left over to be friendly and even funny.

Vivienne had written to Dr. B., sharing both her challenges and small victories as she settled into her life abroad. *"The work is intense,"* she confessed. *"We are reading plays in French, and me not knowing a word of*

French. Ha! I have hired a tutor, but I fear I have little aptitude." Despite her struggles with the language, she seemed undaunted, determined to push through.

Her tone softened as she described her new home. "*As for Cambridge, it is, without doubt, the dearest little town I've ever seen. I am passionately in love with its charming streets and shops, astounding architecture, and sweet people. Honestly, I could live here forever.*"

It was clear that, amid the rigor and unfamiliarity, Vivienne had found a place that captured her heart—a corner of the world where, for the first time, she felt she might truly belong.

Vivienne's room was perched on the top floor of a charming house shared with twelve other young women, all international graduate students. The setup suited her; the house had a sense of freedom that felt refreshing after the strictures of her past. The rules were notably relaxed, largely due to the "elderly" residents—meaning, of course, that everyone was over twenty-one. Male visitors were permitted, and there was no early curfew, which Vivienne found a welcome relief.

In the letter, she described the dreary English winter: "*The February days have been a sort of grayish miserable rain,*" she wrote, "*which I hear is typical for this time of year, although I managed a few 'punting' excursions. It's a kind of boating on a narrow river called the Cam, with lengthy poles pushed off the bottom.*" Despite the bleak weather, Vivienne seemed to be embracing her new life, finding intrigue even in the drizzle and the muddy waters of the Cam.

And, lastly, a plea for continued contact:

"*This is just a brief note to say hello and let you know I arrived safe and sound and am thoroughly installed and on my way to becoming a proper Englishwoman. I do hope we can establish a more regular correspondence. Well, Corneille's tragedies are calling, so I need to go. Please write and tell me about things.*

Love,

Viv."

It was a casual sign-off, but underneath, it was laced with an unspoken hope—a lifeline she was casting out into the world, hoping someone would reach back and tether her to something familiar.

Vivienne had the peculiar sense of becoming unmoored. Like a helium balloon with her strings cut. She could see herself floating up and up dangerously near some ill-defined point of no return. She'd begun writing Mother a few times a week, then daily, then twice or thrice daily. A habit she'd picked up as a camper when she was a child. Mother always wrote back, then and now. But it wasn't enough. Vivienne was still floating. Not depressed, lopsided, unhappy, but somehow unsettled. It was as if a piece was missing. Perhaps Dr. B. would tell her how to find it.

Vivienne yanked on her coat and checked her watch. If she hurried, she could get all these letters in the mail, and they would go out today. She had forty-five minutes to get this down to the post and get back. After that, she had to get ready for a party. She was hoping to cross paths with a handsome young poet she'd been very much wanting to meet.

2

The Poet had encountered the woman just once. There'd been something of an electric current around her, a warning to stay away. And, anyway, he should have known. His horoscope for February 10th, 1956, had predicted the evening would end only at his disastrous personal expense. And yet he'd taken the risk. Completely out of character, he'd ignored all warnings and plowed right ahead. Still, he'd never have predicted she would do what she did.

By the time he arrived at the pub, the party was already in full swing, and there she was again. Bright red hairband, red shoes, red lipstick, and a bit of silk flair the color of sticky candied apple around her neck. She was tall, blonde, and startling-looking, just as he remembered. She looked Swedish; it was the hair. That's what he'd thought when he'd first seen her at Charing Cross. He was wandering the bookstands, and they'd been arriving, the entire group of Fulbright scholars, and those two, the tall girl and her friend. They looked Scandinavian. But then he'd heard their American accents. Of course, he'd thought. The hard-edged confidence in their shoulders, their breasts, the tilt of their chins. Only American women had that. The tall one had her hair cut Veronica Lake style, heavy bangs swept over, and she looked away as The Poet walked past, but the shift in her glance was intentional, not shy. As he walked away, he felt her eyes on his back. He didn't turn around, although he'd wanted to.

Vivienne Holland. That was her name. Her eyes shone in the dim light of the pub. A crush of diamonds thought The Poet. Her pretty face was round and tight, and she was drunk and joyful, wobbling on her heels and giggling into her friend's sweatered shoulder.

"Newnham College, English Literature," she shouted at him, wide-mouthed to enunciate and waving her glass around, sloshing liquid over the edges. Certainly drunk, but to be fair, everyone was drunk. The exception was The Poet. He liked to keep in control.

"Welcome," he shouted back.

Raised voices were necessary as the pub boomed with conversation—mostly men attempting to be heard over the blaring jazz music. Suddenly Vivienne was smashed up against his chest and shouting directly into his face.

"I did it, mine..." she screamed. They were only inches apart. "I liked that part, particularly." He watched her generously painted lips form the words he'd written and felt instantly aroused. "The last most deathly jewel..." she drifted into a slurry inattention.

"You like?" he shouted back, realizing too late that the depth and resonance of his voice prevented the need for such volume.

Her eyes widened, a brief flash of surprise crossing her face before she broke into a radiant smile, her perfect American teeth gleaming. Then, with a casual shrug, she shouted back at him—a line of his own poetry, clear and confident. He raised an eyebrow, momentarily taken aback. Had she prepared for this? Had she memorized his verses with the intention of impressing him when they finally met? Other women had done that, women who didn't care much for the poems themselves but were drawn to *The Poet*. But something about Vivienne struck him as different.

As he watched her, he sensed she truly admired his work, not just the persona attached to it. She was reciting lines from a piece that hadn't appeared in the Review that day; it was published over a year ago, tucked away in an obscure journal. And it was a dark piece, a poem raw with violence, scarred by images of war and death. Yet, she spoke it with fervor, her voice carrying an edge, her teeth almost gnashing with each word.

He couldn't help but be intrigued. This girl, with her brilliant smile and unapologetic passion, loved his work—*really* loved it, even the jagged, unsettling parts. And somehow, in that moment, she fascinated him beyond words.

"More brandy?" he asked, leaning into her ear. Her blonde hair was soft, and she smelled of honey.

"Yes, yes, please," she said and held up her glass, sloshing the remaining liquid onto the front of his shirt. She grimaced, apologized, then burst into fresh gales of laughter.

3

There was a small, private bar tucked beside the pub, a cramped room reeking of stale ale, sweat, and tobacco—the unofficial sanctuary of the men's poetry club. The Poet doubted Vivienne would notice the stench in her current state. He poured her a measure of brandy, watching as she sipped some and spilled the rest. She was, indeed, quite drunk, but even in her disheveled state, she was captivating. In her heels, she was nearly as tall as his six foot two, her long, athletic legs lending her an imposing presence. Her eyes, however, were the most striking—bright but guarded, almost impenetrable, as if she held secrets behind invisible shields.

They stood close, leaning into each other to shout over the music, their heads nearly touching as they discussed poetry—his and hers—art, reviews, gossip from the literary world, anything that came to mind. When the jazz kicked up and dancing filled the room, they joined in, wild and reckless, stamping and clapping, laughing and screaming at one another. At one point, he leaned in, telling her she was beautiful. She smirked and told him he was "all there," an offhanded but strangely intimate compliment.

After some time, she gestured toward her friend, now slumped in a chair, nearly passed out, and mentioned she had "obligations." He, too, had obligations—a girlfriend, though he'd conveniently left her out of the evening's conversation. But when Vivienne pressed her body closer to his, the space between them vanished. Instead of pulling away, he leaned in, kissing her hard on the mouth as the music swelled around them, and bodies pressed in on all sides.

Without a word, he reached up, tugging the scarf from her neck and stuffing it into the pocket of his old corduroy coat. She pulled back, eyes flashing, and then lunged at him, her lips grazing his neck before she bit him—hard—on the cheek. Shocked, he drew back, his laughter mingling with the sting of the bite. He touched his face, feeling warmth trickle onto his fingertips. When he pulled his hand away, his fingers were wet with blood.

He glanced toward the doorway just in time to catch a glimpse of Vivienne and her friend slipping out into the night, her laughter echoing behind her, leaving him stunned, amused, and slightly dazed in the dim, smoky haze of the bar.

4

That night, The Poet dreamed of a swaying, slender-legged woman. She appeared as a pale and sweet-smelling spirit, her presence both enchanting and foreboding. As he approached her, he realized she was no goddess. Instead, she was made from a thousand white-hot thunderbolts, her form crackling with energy. He reached out, intending to inflict pain with a bite, but the moment his teeth met her skin, he felt the searing pain himself. The agony was overwhelming, a mirror of his own actions.

When he woke up, he felt the wetness on his cheeks, tears streaming down his face, unbidden and unexpected. The dream had been so vivid, more real than memory, and its emotional weight clung to him, refusing to dissolve with the morning light. Pain, confusion, and a strange sense of loss simmered within him, stirred up from places he hadn't realized were still raw.

He lay there, staring blankly at the ceiling, his mind sifting through fragments of the vision. Faces and voices, intense and fleeting, flashed through his mind. He tried to piece together what it all meant, but the dream eluded him, fading like smoke even as it left its mark. The tears kept falling as he searched his heart for some understanding, some explanation for why this vision, above all others, had shaken him so deeply.

CHAPTER 22

PURSUIT

1

Determined not to appear overeager, The Poet let two days pass before dragging his mate, Peter Boris, over to Halsey House, hoping to see her. Together they stood beneath her window, or what they surmised was her window, and threw dirt clods at the glass. The bite she'd left on his cheek still ached, and indeed she'd left quite a mark, clear, and deep enough to cause many taunts and sneers among his mates.

"She's not coming, mate," said Boris, a stocky fellow with a mop of unruly hair and a perpetually skeptical expression.

"Oh, shut up, grab another one," said The Poet. He lobbed a chunk of mud upward, missing the glass entirely as it splatted against the brick side of the building.

"Christ," said Boris. "You must be drunk."

"Oh, shut it, I'm not fucking drunk, I'm in love," said The Poet, his eyes gleaming with mischief. "Go on, help me."

It was a long time before she came down, wearing a flannel robe over her modest nightgown. She told them both they were idiots, throwing mud at the wrong window, and they'd better stop it right away, or the house mother would likely have them kicked off campus for good. The Poet laughed at that. After a fiasco involving a goose and copious amounts of alcohol last year, the Dean had already forbidden him from returning to Cambridge. Since his graduation, The Poet and a few other club members had been excluded from campus more than once. They'd not listened, and now, of course, he was glad.

"Come out," he begged. "Come with us."

"You must be out of your mind. What time is it?" she asked, her eyes darting nervously.

He looked at his wrist, which was bare. Shrugged. Looked at Peter, who also shrugged. "Time to go. That's all, come along now." He grinned at her, his charm irresistible.

"I'll have to get something on," Vivienne whispered, glancing back over her shoulder. "I'll have to get past the housemother. She has ears like a bat."

"Face like one too," Peter muttered, then quickly added, "Sorry. I mean, I've heard."

"Shush," Vivienne pressed a finger to her lips, eyes sparkling with mischief. "Like a witch, you mean. She'll hear you and cast a spell. Okay, wait here."

As she slipped back inside, The Poet and Boris exchanged a triumphant glance, barely containing their excitement. The cool night air settled around them, crisp and laced with the faint sweetness of blooming flowers. Somewhere in the distance, crickets droned, an insistent hum underscoring the quiet thrill of the moment. They waited, hearts pounding with anticipation, ready for whatever reckless adventure Vivienne had in mind, as if the night itself held some promise of magic and chaos.

2

In five minutes, she was back, dressed in dungarees and a loose button-down blouse. After dropping Peter at his flat, Vivienne, and The Poet made their way to his tiny, borrowed room in a friend's flat. They lit a small stove for heat, its flickering flames casting a warm glow around the room. Sitting on the floor, side by side, leaning against the bed, they drank brandy while reading poetry to one another.

She read the one poem she'd recently published and asked him for an honest review. It was the one about the stone carvings, the one Peter had maligned badly, almost sarcastically calling it girlish and collegiate in their club's tiny but well-respected journal.

"It sounds brittle," he said, refilling her glass. She looked at him, her face still and unreadable.

"What does that mean?" she asked, voice sharp.

"Cold. It sort of leaves me with nothing, you know, here." He thumped his chest for emphasis.

She rolled her eyes. "Oh, for God's sake. Do you honestly think that"—she pointed at his chest—"is the point?"

"The point of what?" he asked, thrown off balance.

"This!" She waved her poem in the air between them. "This. What we do. The reason we write."

She drained her glass in one swift gulp and held it out for a refill. He poured her another, watching as she processed her frustration.

"Look," she said, leveling her gaze at him, "I don't know what you're doing, but if I want to feel, I'll just pat a puppy or something. That's entertainment. This is something else. Something more."

"Like?" he asked, genuinely curious.

"I don't know. The voice in my head, perhaps." She slumped back into her chair, closing her eyes. Her voice softened, almost vulnerable. "They laughed at me, Jack. In that terrible review, they laughed."

He studied her in the dim light, her features softened but still intense, her skin glowing faintly in the moonlight filtering through the window. Guilt pooled in his stomach.

"You know what they did?" he began slowly, measuring each word. "They concocted an elaborate and cruel plan because they wanted to reach you, Vivienne. Because *we* wanted to reach you. I don't think any of us knew how else to do it."

Her eyes flew open, hurt and confusion flickering across her face. "What are you saying, Jack? That review was meant to... reach me?"

"Yes," he admitted, his voice weighed down by regret. "They—or rather, we—were trying to push you, to provoke some kind of response. We didn't realize how deeply it would cut. At least, I didn't. I'm sorry."

She stared at him, his words settling over her like a cold mist. The room felt suddenly colder; the warmth from the stove seemed powerless against the chill that now separated them.

"Well," she said at last, her voice trembling, "you reached me, alright. And it hurt. It still hurts."

He reached out instinctively, but she pulled back, wrapping her arms around herself as if to shield against the lingering pain. In the silence that followed, the crackling of the stove was the only sound, a fragile warmth in the otherwise darkened room.

Technically, the scathing review had been Peter's doing; he was the editor, after all. His words were brutal: *Trite, light, obsessed, this poem is written in a style we see so often coming from the collegiate female.* The critique wasn't only unfair—it was wholly untrue, but it had effectively destroyed Vivienne's debut in one of Cambridge's most prestigious literary journals. And yet, it wasn't just Peter's fault. None of the men in their group had objected. None had stood up for her, not even *him.*

Vivienne shook her head slowly, disbelief etched across her face. "Why would they want a connection with me, especially if they hated my work?"

The Poet had the answer, but he kept it to himself. Instead, he said, "I'm sorry, Vivienne. We were all cowards. Every one of us."

For a moment, they sat in silence, close enough that their arms brushed from elbow to shoulder, their thighs radiating heat against each other. The air between them was thick with unspoken emotions, a tense quiet that neither dared to break. Then, without any warning, as if a frame had skipped, they were on each other—arms and legs entwined, pressing, pulling, collapsing back onto the bed. Buttons popped, zippers tore, each piece of clothing shed in their shared urgency. They were both strong, physical, neither holding back. By the end, they lay panting, bodies marked with small bruises and bites, marks that would continue to bloom in mysterious hues over the coming days.

Eventually, they settled under the quilt, Vivienne resting her head on his chest, already asleep. The Poet lay there, looking down at her, feeling a mixture of admiration and guilt. She was unlike anyone he'd ever known— a creature of contradictions, brash yet vulnerable, brilliant yet fragile. In her, he saw something dangerous, an inspiration that pulled at him the way the edge of a cliff tempts one to look over, to dangle precariously in the face of the vast, roaring sea.

Unable to sleep, he slid to the edge of the bed, watching the embers in the hearth. The fire they'd lit hours before was now a collection of sputtering coals, casting faint shadows that danced along the walls. He felt suspended in that moment, caught between the beauty of their shared passion and the turmoil he'd helped create, aware that both were destined to leave scars.

CHAPTER 23

AMERICAN BIRD

1

Vivienne was drinking too much. Losing count of the evenings, the episodes, and worst of all, the men. She'd seen Jack Welles but a handful of times since the party. Each time she wrote in her calendar, the words *Jack with passionate abandon*. Every time he'd overwhelmed her with his blasting presence, violent, virile body, and his poems which he read to her in an unapologetic Yorkshire accent. But every time, too, he'd left her with a terrible emptiness. Their separations were perfectly understandable but terribly frequent between his bizarre living arrangements (he camped in various friends' flats around London and Cambridge), and Vivienne's Spring travel schedule. And yet Vivienne knew his type and felt deeply insecure about the relationship. 'I make better love the more love I make,' he'd said, as if that justified his reputation for womanizing. She'd nearly slapped him for saying that. But she'd remained silent.

So, let him go, she told herself. *Let him run, let him drift away, or lose him entirely. Fill the empty spaces he leaves behind. Occupy yourself. Write fiercely, cook elaborate meals, study harder, read until your eyes blur. Pour yourself into everything else. Never nag, never chase.* She laughed bitterly, shaking her head. *Ha! You knew this would happen, didn't you?*

The warning signs had always been there, but she'd chosen to ignore them, chosen to dive headfirst into the fire, thinking she could hold on to something that was never truly hers to keep. And now, here she was, talking herself out of heartache, determined to reclaim all the pieces she'd given away, to fill the silence he left with her own defiant, furious drive.

To Vivienne, Jack grew more perfect with each encounter, as if he were crafted from the best parts of every man she'd ever loved or even admired. And so, despite her reservations, she threw her heart at him, hating herself for the vulnerability it exposed. She filled her evenings as best she could, balancing her time between late nights at the library and drinks with friends, male company that was mostly platonic—though, occasionally, it strayed from that boundary.

One evening, Jack returned to Cambridge, eager to see her, only to find that she was out with Angus Mayberry, a boy for whom she felt a genuine fondness but no romantic fire. Her absence grated on him; he left in a fury, charging into the night, swearing he'd wash his hands of her, never see her again. But as the hours wore on, his anger waned, morphing into a yearning he couldn't quite suppress. Finally, late in the night, he sent a friend to track her down with a message to *"come quickly to the flat."*

Could he have been more arrogant? Summoning her as though he were royalty, expecting her to drop everything at his whim. Vivienne's initial reaction was to ignore him, to respond with equal indifference, to hold on to some shred of dignity. But she knew herself too well—knew she'd already surrendered. And so, swallowing her pride and casting her self-respect aside like scraps of paper, she ran to him, following his call, unable to resist the pull he had over her.

They spent the night making love, spilling secrets, and sharing dreams. His of panthers and foxes and hers of terrible things: bottomless moats and deformed humans, acid lakes, and god pulling her hair from the inside out. As they talked, she leaned her cheek against his, taking comfort in the feel of his unshaven skin. She felt a fleeting sense of peace, as if the night could hold them safe from all the chaos outside.

2

For weeks, they were inseparable, tangled in a fierce and heady romance that consumed them both. They walked through the countryside, drank wine, shared meals of cheese and boiled eggs. They read Siberian poetry to each other, punted lazily down the Cam, and made love in secret glades and fields, hidden from the rest of the world. Nights were spent in his freezing, dilapidated room, huddled together under threadbare blankets, their words and bodies intertwined as they tried to outdo one another, to become the characters in their poetry—he, the "blood-hungry beast," and she, the bird desperate to fly but irresistibly drawn back to him.

Vivienne was intoxicated by it all, euphoric in a way she hadn't thought possible. She wrote fervent letters home to her mother, to Ruthie, even to Dr. B.: *"The rest of my days will be saying poems and loving of people,"* she proclaimed. *"Please do not mind that he is poor, that his manners are rough. He does not need to impress because a lion, a panther, a god is above that. Once you know him, you see that all others are nothing compared."*

She was twenty-three, and he was twenty-five. She dreaded the idea of returning to America, to its cold and commercial demands. Meanwhile, he dreamed of adventure beyond his tiny island, of worlds yet unexplored. They devised a plan: they would travel the world together, settle in a cheap Mediterranean village, and live simply—writing, teaching English, scraping by on whatever they could earn. They convinced themselves that they needed nothing but each other and that love and poetry would be enough to sustain them.

In moments of quiet, Vivienne felt the faint stirrings of doubt. She wasn't naive; she knew how fragile and consuming love could be, how dreams often withered when faced with reality. But she pushed the worries aside. She wanted him—this intense, enigmatic, god-like man who made her feel wild and alive. And she knew he wanted her, his "American bird," the one creature who could match his hunger.

So, they fell, recklessly, impulsively, and passionately, into each other's arms and each other's lives, as though the world outside their romance did not exist. They were unbound by limits, unmoored from past or future, swept forward on the gale of their words and desires, blind to the edges and intoxicated by the fall.

CHAPTER 24

PETER BORIS
Spring 1956

You know, they used to say that Jack Welles was the biggest seducer in Cambridge, but we were terrific friends, and I never saw it, never heard it said directly. But, of course, I worked hard. Jack used to call me 'Professor' instead of Peter or even my surname Boris, because of how much time I spent studying. I was only twenty-three, mind you. Jack found it hilarious.

Anyway, I might have missed a few things, but I think it was one of those rumors he got started about himself. He had this big look, making it easy for people to believe things about him. He went round in this oversized pea-coat and black corduroys he dyed himself. Some public schoolboys thought him crude in his 'fisherman' get up, and a few girls found him intimidating. But Jack just didn't give a toss.

You know, we were all sort of obsessed with Graves and The White Goddess. Believing all that rubbish about living as a poet to be a poet, women as muses, and so on. We were young; it was the time. Understand me. Jack was in love with Vivienne. But I think love might have meant something for Jack that it didn't mean for her. He was looking for a muse. With Vivienne Holland, I think he believed he'd found her.

Jack had a way of creating his own legends. He liked to stir things up, make life a bit more dramatic. There were always rumors about him having ladies up in his room, but I saw no evidence of it. He talked a big game, though. I remember one evening in the pub, he regaled us with a story about a supposed rendezvous with a girl from Girton. The way he told it, you'd think he was

Casanova reincarnated. But then, that was Jack—always performing, always larger than life.

When it came to Vivienne, things were different. I remember the first time he saw her at a reading (or it was the first time he'd seen her when I was with him.) Anyway, she was up there, reading one of her poems—something about stone carvings. Peter, our editor, wrote a scathing review, calling it trite and light. Jack was captivated. He told me later that night, "She's got something, Boris. Something real. Not like the others."

Their relationship was intense, to say the least. They'd argue about poetry, life, everything. I'd see them in the library sometimes, their heads bent close together, deep in discussion. Other times, they'd be in the pub, laughing loudly, seemingly oblivious to everyone else. Jack was all about living in the moment, and with Vivienne, those moments were electric.

One night, after a heated argument with Peter, Jack showed up at my flat, bottle in hand. "She's something else, Peter," he said, slumping into a chair. "She's not just a muse. She's... I don't know. She's everything." He downed half the bottle in one go and just sat there, staring at the floor. I'd never seen him like that before. Vulnerable, almost.

Vivienne brought out a side of Jack that none of us had ever seen. He wrote better when he was with her, more passionately. He seemed more alive. But she also made him more reckless. Sometimes he'd disappear for days, only to return with wild stories of their escapades. They'd spent a week in a tiny cottage by the sea once, living on bread and wine, writing and making love. Jack came back looking like he'd been through a war, but his eyes were shining.

Their love was like that. All-consuming, reckless, beautiful, and terrifying. Jack was searching for something in Vivienne, something he felt was missing in himself. And for a while, it seemed like he'd found it. But, as with all things Jack, it wasn't meant to last.

We all knew it was too good to be true. Jack, with his need for drama and Vivienne, with her fierce independence. Together, they were ablaze. Eventually, they'd burn out. But for that short, wild time, they were everything to each other. And Jack Welles, the biggest seducer in Cambridge, was well and truly seduced.

CHAPTER 25

IN THE STARS
Spring 1956

1

The Poet pedaled along the narrow path tracing the River Cam, grinning like a schoolboy as he waved to the Sunday punters drifting by. Sunlight danced across the water, turning it a rich emerald green, and the ancient bridges with their golden arches cast perfect circles in their reflections, as if someone had painted them there in soft, blurred strokes. The air was thick with the scents of spring—fresh rain mingling with the sweet perfume of dogwood, yellow dahlias, and the roses that seemed to bloom in every garden, as if all of Cambridge had decided to embrace life anew.

Just months before, the city had felt gray and lifeless, draped in the heaviness of winter, but now it had shaken off the chill and opened itself to the warmth. And Vivienne—Vivienne was the embodiment of this transformation. She was wild and serene, both outrageous and wonderfully ordinary, a living, breathing poem. To him, she was everything he had ever written and everything he had ever hoped to write.

This early morning ride, this heady freedom, was merely the prelude to seeing her again. His pulse quickened at the thought. Reaching his lodgings, he leapt off his bike, barely bothering to lock it, propping it haphazardly against the weathered stone wall as he raced inside. He was still smiling, half-laughing to himself, caught up in the joy of spring, in the thrill of her, as if the whole world had unfolded just for them.

He'd only left her an hour ago, and yet the pull to return to her was insistent, almost unbearable. Had he ever felt this way about a woman? Yes, surely—no, no, not like this. And did it even matter? What mattered now was the urgency that had settled in his bones, the restless ache to be near her again. He needed to clear his head, to steady himself.

In his small, dim room, he stripped off his clothes, threw open the window to let in the fresh spring air, and filled the old bathtub. As he sank into the warm water, he replayed fragments of their conversations, her laughter, the spark in her eyes when she challenged him, her brilliant mind that seemed to catch fire every time they spoke. She was like no one he'd ever met, and each moment with her left him craving more.

Drying off, he pulled on a clean shirt and settled at his desk. With a deep breath, he reached for a sheet of crisp, white paper, and the sound of his pen scratching across the page filled the quiet room as he began his letter to Phyllis.

Dear Phyllis,

I hope this letter finds you well and thriving. I have met someone extraordinary, an American woman named Vivienne. Her presence is a force, her intellect sharp, and she brings a vitality into my life I hadn't realized I was missing. Our conversations are like matches striking flint, igniting ideas and passions I'd only dreamed of before.

You'd love her, Phyllis. Her Mars is smack dab on my Sun, astrologically speaking. You'd probably say she's exactly what I need, and I think you'd be right. She's a writer too, and her work is stunning—brave and unflinchingly honest.

I feel as if I'm living inside one of our favorite poems, each day a new stanza, each moment a line break. She sees through me in a way no one else does, cutting past my defenses with an almost terrifying clarity. She is the muse I didn't know I was seeking.

I can't wait for you to meet her. I know you'll understand when I say she's changed everything.

With all my love,

Jack

He put down the pen, re-reading his words with a mixture of excitement and a faint pang of guilt. Phyllis had been his confidante, his touchstone, for so long. But this—*this* was different. Vivienne was a hurricane, a fire, a living poem, and he was caught in her storm. He folded the letter, sealed it, and placed it on the corner of his desk. In the quiet of the room, the certainty of his words settled around him.

For now, he would go back to Vivienne.

2

The Poet lay down on the bed, though it was hardly a bed at all—just a thin mattress on the floor. He only meant to rest for a few minutes before cycling back to Vivienne's. He draped his forearm over his eyes, intending just to close them for a moment. But before he even had the chance to think, *I've met an American,* he slipped into sleep.

In his dreams, he wasn't with a woman but instead drifted toward a continent. It was beautiful, long-limbed, with clear skies and unyielding self-assurance, a land both seductive and formidable. This vision had a kind of self-confidence born of its size, wealth, the geographical gift of being nestled between two vast oceans, and an unshakable belief in its own luck—mistaken, perhaps, for character. Lying in his dream bed, The Poet watched as the country approached him, floating toward him, hovering just above, like a presence near the ceiling. Though it wasn't a woman, he couldn't help himself. He fell in love, drawn to it in a way that made no sense, yet he went along willingly, helpless in its pull.

When he woke, the dream lingered, ghost-like, even as he prepared to leave. He mounted his bicycle and pedaled along the Cam, his thoughts filled not with a country but with Vivienne. The day was impossibly bright; the sky stretched vast and blue above him, the edges of the world sharper, more vivid, as if everything had taken on a richer hue. He reached the little flat they'd shared the night before and bounded up the steps two at a time, barely able to contain his eagerness.

He knocked, breath held, anticipation humming through him. When the door swung open, there she stood, her hair wild, a mischievous smile playing on her lips. Without a word, she reached for him, pulled him inside, and they collapsed into each other's arms, picking up right where they'd left off.

In that moment, time ceased to exist. There was only this, only her— her laughter, her touch, the thrill of losing himself in her. Nothing else mattered. The Poet surrendered, forgetting the dream, the world outside, and even the contours of his own identity. All that remained was Vivienne.

3

His genius distracted him. Vivienne saw it. Jack could not get himself published because he did not have the skills to type, revise, organize, and submit his work. So, Vivienne happily typed Jack's manuscripts, polished his verses, and ensured his work reached the right publishers. She managed the practical aspects of their life, allowing Jack the freedom to immerse himself fully in his creative endeavors. She knew his poems would shock the world; He was better than Yeats. Better than anyone. And besides, she loved him. She guessed she'd loved him since that night at the pub when he'd stolen her scarf.

It was as if the universe had created Jack Welles specifically for her. Since meeting him, everyone else paled in comparison. Jack was a beautiful, powerful, artistic genius, and he was the first man Vivienne had ever met with whom she could easily visualize having the sort of life she wanted. Jack didn't care about a traditional domestic existence. He didn't care if she cooked or cleaned or mended. He loved her writing. So, when she visited Jack in London at 112 Sidney Street and cleaned his greasy, soot-stained flat and cooked him a meal that came as close to real food as she could muster given the limited kitchen access, he was so grateful that afterward, he lay on the bare floor, and groaned in ecstasies like some sated, mythic beast. She laughed and laughed. She would never lose her writing to domestic duty with Jack, nor would she become what she feared most, her mother.

Vivienne's heart soared. In that moment, she felt an exhilarating sense of liberation and possibility. Here was a man who understood her, who saw her not as a helpmate or a housewife but as an equal, a partner in the grand adventure of life. Jack's acceptance of her proposal was not just affirming their love but validating her dreams and aspirations.

The following days were a whirlwind of plans and dreams. They spoke of their future in vibrant hues, painting a picture of a life filled with poetry, travel, and unbridled creativity. They would live in sun-drenched places, write side by side, and support each other in their artistic pursuits.

Jack's enthusiasm was contagious. His intense focus and dedication to his work made her believe they could conquer any obstacle together. She admired his rebellious spirit, his disdain for conventional norms, and his refusal to conform to society's expectations. He was everything she ever wanted. He was more.

In May, she proposed. They were sitting together on a makeshift sofa in the steamy heat of his borrowed flat. She curled against him with a book; he sat turning pages of manuscript.

"Jack," she said.

"Hmm," he said, still looking at the typed page he was holding.

"Marry me."

He set down the paper and turned his head. Their noses were now almost touching. She could smell on his breath the cheap wine they'd been drinking the night before. There were craggy marks around his eyes, where he squinted into the sun on his long walks across the moor.

"The girl wants to marry me?" A small smile curled his upper lip.

"Yes, marry me."

They'd known each other for less than three months, dated barely four weeks. And yet, in that fleeting time, Vivienne felt herself plunging deeper than she'd ever thought possible. Even now, though, a small, persistent doubt crept into her mind, a whisper of caution amid the rush of her feelings.

Before she could think, the words slipped out of her mouth, almost against her will: "Let's get married."

He didn't hesitate. Jack never did anything meekly, and she knew he'd be decisive, one way or the other. He nodded, his voice steady, "Yeah."

The firmness of his answer left no room for uncertainty. He took her face in his hands, looking into her eyes with a warmth that chased away her doubts. "Let's do it, my wild American bird," he said, his lips brushing hers in a gentle kiss. Then, in a whisper that felt like a promise and a declaration all at once, he murmured, "My America."

In that moment, she felt as if they were suspended in time, standing on the edge of something vast and terrifying and thrilling. Whatever lay ahead, she was ready to leap, and she knew he would be there, leaping with her.

CHAPTER 26

RUTHIE
Spring 1956

I visited her in Cambridge that spring she met Jack. From the moment she picked me up at the station, I knew something was off. Vivienne couldn't sit still, her hands never resting, fiddling with the saltshakers and silverware as we waited for Jack at the café. She was eager, almost too happy, but there was an edge to it, like she was teetering on the brink of something.

As she recounted her relationship with Jack, Vivienne suddenly blurted out, "He can be sadistic." The words came out with a mix of awe and resignation, as if she was half-proud, half-accepting of the fact. She repeated it, almost like she was trying to convince herself it was alright. "But it's alright. I'm teaching him, Ruthie. He's so much better already." She spoke with the tragic optimism of a heroine in a novel, someone who believes they're destined to save a tortured soul. She even compared their relationship to being married to Dylan Thomas—Dylan Thomas, for God's sake. I was horrified.

When I finally met Jack that afternoon, I began to understand her obsession. He was the most physically intimidating man I'd ever encountered—tall, broad-shouldered, with a voice that crashed into you like a wave. Jack Welles didn't just enter a room; he took it over, filling every corner with his presence. His insensitivity was startling, especially for a poet. He seemed unaware of—or indifferent to—the effect he had on others. Or maybe he did know and simply didn't care. Yet, there was a magnetism about him, a raw, untamed energy that drew you in even as it warned you to keep your distance.

I wouldn't say he was truly sadistic, at least not in the sense that he enjoyed causing harm. He just seemed indifferent to how his words or actions affected others. But if he were in a foul mood, I could see him being intolerable, overbearing, impossible to bear. Not that Vivienne was a picnic when she was in a mood, either. Watching them together was like watching a hurricane gather strength. They were constantly touching, exchanging intense glances across the room, an electricity crackling between them that was both mesmerizing and terrifying. It was like standing on the edge of a storm, knowing you should run but unable to look away.

I made one terrible mistake, though. I was worried—confused by the intensity of their relationship and what it was doing to her. I'd always imagined Vivienne would end up with someone flexible, supportive, maybe a little modern. Not this... caveman. Jack was bright, yes, and talented, but still a brute. So, at one point, I pulled her aside, intending to snap her out of it. I asked, "What the hell, Viv? What are you doing with him? He's a bully."

The look she gave me—it was like I'd slapped her. Her eyes widened, huge and wounded, and for a brief moment, I thought she might crumble in front of me. Instead, she whispered, barely audibly, "Get out." Her voice was low, as if she didn't want him to hear. "Just get the hell out, Ruthie."

So, I left. It killed me, but I went. I never imagined it would be the end of our friendship, but I was scared for her. I thought she'd come to her senses eventually, that she'd reach out. But it was over. That was it.

I wasn't even in England when they got married. Nobody was. It all happened so fast, a rushed, quiet affair. Only Vivienne's mother, poor Lorah, was there. She loved Vivienne more than anything and did her best to be there, but it must have torn her apart. Later, people would say terrible things about Lorah, questioning her role, her choices, but she was just a mother trying to love her daughter, helpless in the face of what was coming.

Looking back, I should have seen it. We all should have. Watching Jack and Vivienne together for five minutes was enough to know they were a storm waiting to break. But maybe we were naive. Maybe I thought Vivienne would grow tired of this fantasy, drop the domestic dreams, and return to writing. But by the time I saw her again, it was far, far too late.

CHAPTER 27

BENIDORM
Summer 1956

1

This was Spain. Vivienne stood on the small iron balcony, her hands resting on its railing. Each time the breeze shifted; she could smell the sea. A poorly paved road fronted the pensione; a few men pushing donkeys, pulling wooden carts. Children ran after one another in the sunlight. Beyond the road lay the beach and the dark blue waters of the Mediterranean Sea. The sandy beach gave way to enormous cliffs to the north, and clusters of fishing boats were anchored close to shore. A fig tree had grown to the second floor; its broad leaves framed the spectacular view.

In June, they'd been married in a three hundred fifty-year-old London church, the plan for a big American wedding in Wellesley temporarily forgotten. It had been beautiful. The interior of the church was lit with candles, casting a delicate white light across the pews. It smelled of stone, dust, and centuries of worship. Vivienne held a single peony in her hand, soft pink petals like tiny shreds of velvet. She wore a summer dress of pink chiffon borrowed last minute from a friend, and she'd tied three satin ribbons into her hair, two pink and one pale peach. Jack wore his everyday jacket but found a clean shirt and a tie that looked new or newly borrowed. He was gorgeous.

There had been every reason to put off the wedding and almost no justification for doing it early. First, married women were not allowed Vivienne's current scholarship or living arrangements under university rules, so they would need to keep the marriage secret for at least a year.

Second, Vivienne's American friends and family would be terribly disappointed to find out she'd been married without them. Finally, they would have to do the whole thing again in America the following summer to avoid a serious social disaster for Mother.

Vivienne felt an urgency about the whole thing. "Mother is already here in England," Vivienne had reasoned. Jack had agreed. "We are in love," Vivienne said. "So, why not just do it now?" Jack had agreed.

And so, with only Mother as witness, they were married at St. George's Church in London on Bloomsday in 1956, a year earlier than they'd initially planned and less than four months after they'd met.

Jack emerged from their small room. "You were right," he said, slipping his arms around her waist.

"I was," she agreed.

The pensione's owner had practically kidnapped them at the train station upon their arrival from Alicante.

"Here," she'd beckoned. "Come," she'd said. They'd been drawn to her colorful clothing and queer appearance; black eyebrows painted at a slant from the bridge of her nose to her temples, her heavy cherry-colored lipstick, tawny wig, and coal-black eyes. She spoke Catalan and only very broken English. Both Jack and Vivienne understood the word "cheap." "Come, come," she repeated. And they followed.

Upon seeing the view, Vivienne immediately agreed to take the room.

"Wait, what?" Jack looked confused.

"Sí, Señora!" The old woman clapped her hands together, smiling broadly to reveal gray gums and two rows of stained teeth.

"I know," said Vivienne. "But," she gestured over the railing at the view.

Jack was shaking his head, incredulous. Had she forgotten what they had discussed before they arrived? But they were tired and hungry, and Vivienne's typewriter was heavy.

Other than the view, the so-called "villa"—as the old woman had grandly described it—was little more than a worn-out building with the barest of amenities. There was no running water, no functional kitchen, and the shared bathroom was scarcely big enough for the family living there, let alone for borders. Their room was tiny, cramped with a double bed pressed against one wall and a rough wooden bench beside it. A small gas ring sat on the table for cooking, and a handful of candles offered the only light. The single chair was dangerously undersized for Jack, but the view was breathtaking, and the price was right.

"How about this?" Vivienne had said, sweeping her arms wide as though presenting the outdoors to him for the very first time. "We'll just get two more chairs and sit out here. I'm sure we can rustle up that small table from somewhere." She flashed her most brilliant, optimistic smile.

Jack shook his head and let out a tired laugh. "I'm beat. Fine."

The old woman, who had been watching them with a mixture of suspicion and bemusement, nodded approvingly. "Ets una parella preciosa. T'encantarà aquí," she said in Catalan. She reached out with a bony, suntanned hand and touched Vivienne's cheek with surprising gentleness. Her hands were rough and calloused, deeply weathered by the sun, a striking contrast to her face, which was pale and softened with heavy makeup.

"*Preciosa*," she repeated softly, then turned and disappeared down the narrow hallway.

As they settled into the tiny room, Vivienne felt a rush of conflicting emotions—excitement and apprehension weaving together. They were in love, yes, but love wouldn't make the room any bigger or the typewriter any lighter. She glanced over at Jack, who was already rearranging their few belongings, determined to make the best of it. She smiled at him, hoping her enthusiasm would be enough to sustain them, to lift them above the limitations of the crumbling villa and into the adventure they'd dreamed of.

But even as she smiled, a flicker of doubt tugged at her. This was the life they had chosen, the life they'd envisioned—rough, raw, infused with passion and poetry. Yet she couldn't help but wonder if they were romanticizing hardship. She pushed the thought aside, resolved to believe that love and poetry would fill the cracks. For now, she had her dreams and the man she adored beside her, and she hoped that would be enough.

2

As the blazing sun beat down on Benidorm in the late afternoon, the pensione grew hot and dry as an oven. The old woman, known in the village as The Widow, brought a pitcher of water so cold and clear it sparkled in the sunlight. Her son, or a young man Vivienne assumed to be her son, carried up two wooden stools and a small table and placed them on the balcony. They feasted on sardines and cheap wine, drinking all the water from the pitcher, deciding it was the best water they'd ever tasted. They watched the people emerge from siesta hour and return to work among the town's white stucco buildings and cobblestone streets. The sounds of music—guitars, bandurrias, and castanets—drifted up from the bars and cafes. Laughter and conversation mixed with the thickening smell of cooking fish and baking bread as the evening wore on.

"We could live this way forever," said Vivienne, though she wasn't entirely sure she believed it.

The sky turned watercolor shades of pink and amethyst, then the blue of a bottomless ocean, the moon a hood of silver reflected in its surface. Finally, they retreated inside, the doors flung open to the Spanish night. They made love in the black heat, and afterward, Vivienne fell into a deep and dreamless sleep.

They spent mornings writing and afternoons sitting oceanside, the sun hot on their backs, the occasional sound of someone pouring old dishwater over the sandy cliffs. Behind them, suntanned women lugged pails full of eggshells and melon rinds to dump into the sea. And everywhere, the smell of dead fish and the feel of burning hot sand beneath their feet.

The Widow's house had only cold water. The cupboards were full of ants, and all cooking had to be done on the blue flame of one old petrol burner, shared among the seven occupants. The burner in their room worked not at all. Vivienne, who cooked, cleaned, and did the washing, was the only one who noticed these things. Jack couldn't have cared less.

One day, she and Jack were down at the beach, stretched out in the sun, when her gaze caught on an old woman sitting a few feet away, half-shaded by a ragged umbrella. The woman's skin was browned and deeply creased, hands calloused and knotted with age. She sat perfectly still, a piece of mending in her lap, eyes fixed on the fabric, unmoving. Vivienne watched her for so long, she started to wonder if the woman had passed away right there, frozen in the heat. Just as Vivienne was about to nudge Jack and point her out, the woman pulled a stitch—just one, slow and deliberate, as if there were all the time in the world. Vivienne continued to watch, mesmerized. Another five minutes passed before the old woman pulled another stitch.

Now there was a woman who could give Grammy a run for her money, she thought wryly. *"Work until you die."* That was Grammy's motto—and, Vivienne supposed, her mother's, too, though she'd never said it outright.

As she watched the woman in her strange, serene patience, Vivienne's mind drifted to a childhood memory: sitting on the old sea wall with Ruthie and Stan Hampton, listening to Stan talk about rebar. She could still picture him, hands gesturing wildly, explaining how they put rebar inside concrete to make it stronger, unbreakable, able to withstand anything thrown its way. She'd barely listened at the time, but now, watching the women of Benidorm—their tough, resilient host, The Widow, and women like this one on the beach—the idea of rebar seemed oddly fitting.

These women are made of something stronger, she thought. *Something unbreakable, buried deep inside them like reinforcement.* They were tough, unyielding, as though their very bones were made of steel. They aged with work etched into their hands and faces, each wrinkle a testament to what they'd survived. She admired them for it, even envied them in a strange way. They seemed so certain of who they were, so rooted. She had never felt that certainty.

But what was she made of? Tin foil, maybe. Something shiny and easily crumpled, not built to last. She thought of the comforts she missed back home—warm showers, a proper kitchen, fresh coffee in the mornings, things that felt almost laughably trivial now but made her feel like herself. Here, she was half-lost, floundering in this rough life she'd thought would be romantic, adventurous. Instead, it felt uncomfortable, exposed.

But I love him, she reminded herself, glancing over at Jack, who was reading with his usual intensity, oblivious to her inner turmoil. *Isn't that supposed to be enough?* That was why they'd come here, after all—to live on love and poetry and the thrill of the unknown. And he seemed perfectly content. The cramped room, the lack of running water, the endless meals of bread and cheese didn't seem to bother him at all. He thrived on this challenge, on shedding the softness of comfort.

Maybe it's just me, she thought, feeling a small pang of shame. *Maybe I'm not built for this. Maybe I'm not as free-spirited as I wanted to believe.*

She kept quiet, though. Jack had settled in so naturally, like he belonged here. She could see the satisfaction in his face whenever he looked out at the ocean, at the golden hills stretching beyond the villa. She wanted so badly to match his ease, to share in his certainty. But deep down, a voice whispered to her, a persistent tug of doubt she tried to ignore.

I don't have rebar inside me, she thought. *I don't have that strength. I'm just... me.*

She sighed, gazing out at the endless stretch of the Mediterranean. "I hope we find what we're looking for here, Jack."

He laughed, pulling her close, his arm warm around her shoulders. "We already have, Viv. We have each other. And this," he said, gesturing out to the vast, glittering sea. "What more do we need?"

She forced a smile, resting her head against his shoulder. "You're right," she whispered, more to herself than to him. *This is it. You have everything you wanted.* She repeated the words in her mind, as if willing them to take root and silence her doubts. But as they hung in the air, they felt strangely hollow, as if they might drift away with the breeze, leaving her with the uneasy feeling that love alone might not be enough.

3

In the third week, Jack was tired of the noise. His concentration was suffering, he said. They'd have to move away from the water and the crowds, into the hills.

They found an enormous country house for let. It had a spacious living room, a grand dining room, and enough space for each to write. The bedroom windows opened over the Spanish hills, lush with grapevine and dotted with white pueblos. In the evening, Vivienne watched as wrinkled, very tanned old women came to sit in chairs with their backs to the streets. They wove nets of thick rope while they talked and sat in the cooling air.

The change was remarkable. Gone were the cramped quarters and the incessant bustle of Benidorm. Now tranquility surrounded them, the sound of birds and the distant murmur of village life.

They bought produce from the local markets—squash, zucchini, potatoes, tomatoes—armfuls of colorful vegetables that Vivienne transformed into hearty, if unconventional, meals. The scent of fresh herbs and roasting garlic filled the little house, blending with the salt of the sea air wafting through open windows. They reveled in the cool tile beneath their feet, the simplicity of the white plaster walls, the sense of peace that wrapped around them. It was everything they had imagined for this extended honeymoon, and they decided to stay at the house for the remaining ten weeks. In her journal, Vivienne wrote that everything was perfect.

But as idyllic as it seemed, a subtle tension threaded through their days, something just below the surface. Jack had begun to withdraw, slipping into long silences, disappearing for solitary walks. His restlessness had become almost palpable, a need for isolation that felt like an invisible wall between them. Vivienne tried to make light of it at first, telling herself that everyone needed their own space. She loved him fiercely, but she also loved the house, the countryside, the feeling of isolation from the demands of their previous lives.

Yet, even as she tried to settle into this life, she missed the vitality of town—the local markets, the daily exchanges with shopkeepers, the hum of life by the sea. The quiet, which had once felt peaceful, began to feel stifling. She found herself lingering by the window, gazing out at the hills, wondering what Jack was thinking during his long silences, wondering if he felt this same ache for something unnamed.

She poured herself into her writing, filling pages with descriptions of the landscape, of the strange beauty of their life here, of the people they encountered on their trips into town. She tried to capture the texture of the days, the way the sunlight filtered through olive trees, the warm scent of earth and herbs. But the act of writing, once her refuge, now felt like a distraction, a way to avoid facing the quiet, persistent unease that had begun to settle in her heart.

You thought so, didn't you? she wrote in her journal, addressing herself with a hint of irony. *You thought this was the answer.* The house, the hills, Jack's presence—each part of this life seemed to hold a promise of perfection, a vision she'd clung to with all her might. And yet, she couldn't silence the small, steady voice in her mind, the voice that questioned how long this harmony would last, how long she could pretend that everything was as it should be.

The journal pages held her doubts, her fears, words she would never dare say aloud. She wrote about the little fractures she felt in their perfect life, as if the idyllic setting around her were a delicate vase perched precariously on the edge of a table. One nudge, one wrong word, and the whole illusion might shatter.

Will you look back and laugh? she wrote to her future self. *Or will you remember this as the beginning of something breaking?*

CHAPTER 28

YOU HATED SPAIN
Fall 1956

1

In retrospect, Vivienne would think the telegram arrived just in time. The weather was dreary, the Cambridge skies woolen gray and fat with rain clouds, the days so short it seemed darkness dropped again before they'd had time to finish their morning coffee. Money was a constant worry; they'd used up nearly all of Vivienne's scholarship money on the honeymoon in Spain, and there'd been no publication income since October.

Vivienne could not tolerate the stress of keeping her marriage secret and instead told the college the truth. Surprisingly, Cambridge had not removed her tuition scholarship, only her housing, expecting, of course, that her new husband would provide for the shortfall. And so, she `and Jack returned from Spain and moved onto the first floor of a charming but cramped Victorian place near the college.

Jack's patience frayed quickly, his irritation sharpening with each day. He complained about the lack of privacy, snapping about the neighbors or the thin walls, but Vivienne suspected the real source of his irritation lay elsewhere. His stack of rejection letters had grown steadily in recent weeks, each one a small blow to his pride, chipping away at his confidence bit by bit.

Not that she could blame him entirely—she, too, had to admit that the charm of their flat was beginning to wear thin. When they'd first moved in, its nineteenth-century character had felt romantic, almost poetic. But now, the tiny, perpetually damp kitchen, with its grimy windows and cluttered shelves, felt more like a cell than a space for creativity. She was tired of tiptoeing around the stale smell in the shared bathroom, a scent that reminded her disturbingly of mushrooms left to rot in the back of a refrigerator.

And then there were the neighbors: a loud, insufferable French couple who seemed to specialize in public arguments, their shrill voices and pointed insults piercing the walls and disturbing what little peace the flat offered. The spoiled pair's constant complaints—about the water, the walls, the weather—only added to the oppressive feeling of the place.

Vivienne tried to be patient, to remind herself of why they'd come here, of the passion that had led them to this city, this flat. But a nagging voice in her mind wondered if they'd romanticized hardship a little too much. She'd dreamed of a simple life of writing and love, but this... this wasn't quite what she'd pictured. Each day, she found herself struggling to muster the optimism that had once come so easily.

The tension between them grew, a quiet, simmering thing that neither of them spoke of but both felt. The small, damp corners of their life seemed to close in tighter, and Vivienne couldn't shake the feeling that something was slipping away, something essential to the vision they'd once shared.

Vivienne's work at Cambridge was rigorous, to say the least. She mostly enjoyed the seminars, reveling in the lively discussions and the intellectual camaraderie they offered. And much of the writing brought her a deep sense of satisfaction, an outlet for the thoughts that seemed to bubble endlessly within her. But the required reading was another story. The sheer volume of it weighed on her, thick academic tomes that seemed to suffocate her creativity, leaving her feeling stifled and, at times, overwhelmed.

Balancing it all—hours of dense reading, her own assignments, and, on top of that, the day-to-day grind of cooking and housework—left her with precious little time to write anything of her own. She would find herself staring at her typewriter late at night, exhausted and frustrated, her mind too foggy to compose more than a sentence or two. In those moments, a gnawing resentment began to build. She'd come here for inspiration, for growth, and yet, between the endless reading lists and domestic duties, her creative spirit felt as though it were being slowly choked.

She tried to remind herself that this was only temporary, that she'd chosen this path and wanted this education. But as the weeks wore on, the sacrifices felt heavier, her time more fragmented, and her own writing—a piece of herself—seemed to slip further out of reach.

At Halsey House, she'd had no housework or cooking to worry about, and laundry duties had been minimal, as she had only her own clothes to manage. Now she was doing everything; cooking and laundry for two people and cleaning an entire flat. It never occurred to Vivienne she might ask for Jack to help. Nor did it occur to Jack that he might offer.

Worst of all, they'd been fighting, picking at each other, and allowing the arguments to escalate to violent disagreement. Often Jack was dropping off into a silent black rage from which he might not emerge for hours. Once, it had lasted an entire day. Thinking about it now, Vivienne recalled something beginning to unravel near the end of their stay in Spain. At the time, she'd let it go, the thing with the letter. But it was important, wasn't it? It meant something, and she should have paid attention. After all, they'd cut short the trip coming home a whole month early.

2

The argument over the letter had spiraled beyond anything Vivienne had expected, erupting into a storm that left Jack stomping out into the Spanish night, his silhouette disappearing into the darkness without so much as a word about when he'd return. She stood in the doorway, peering into the empty landscape, trying to imagine where he could have gone. The pueblos around them were dark, and the nearest town was miles away—a journey too far to make on foot, especially at this hour.

Vivienne leaned against the doorframe, feeling the cool night air wrap around her as she tried to trace back to the moment it had all unraveled. She blamed herself for pushing, for letting the letter become such a flashpoint. *Why couldn't you just let it go?* she thought, self-reproach curling in her stomach. But it wasn't just the letter; it was his reaction, his sudden anger, and the familiar sting of his words.

"You're too sensitive, Viv. You're overreacting." His words echoed in her mind, sharp and dismissive, like a needle prick that turned into a dull ache. She'd heard them before, and each time they settled deeper, seeping into her, making her question her own emotions. Was she too sensitive? Did she always blow things out of proportion? The doubt crept in, uninvited, eating away at the righteousness she'd felt just moments before.

Jack had said the same thing after the awful bullfight. The horror of what they'd done to that poor creature—the screaming, the blood, and then the goring of the man who was not a man. When they carried him past, Vivienne saw he was just a boy.

"How could these people find such brutality entertaining?" she'd asked Jack, crying. She wanted to leave. He told her to open her mind and try to see the world differently. To be less *American*. "You are too sensitive," he'd said again, and they'd stayed. She could barely stop thinking about it now. She hated him for it. She hated Spain for it.

But she wasn't being too sensitive, she thought. Not with the bullfight, and not now, about the letter. She'd only wanted him to understand, to listen instead of dismissing her. And yet, here she was, standing alone in the doorway, wrapped in shadows, left to pick apart her own feelings while he was out there—*wherever*—deciding whether or not he'd come back at all.

What had Jack written precisely to his mother, sister, and father?

'Don't worry about Vivienne being a drag on me. She's quite bright and an excellent cook and homemaker. She's very supportive of my writing. It will be alright.'

It still made her cringe to think of him writing those words. Vivienne had found the letter before he'd mailed it. Why not tell them to go to hell? What exactly had they said about her, his wife, for him to respond like that?

"I can't believe it, Jack," she'd practically screamed at him. "How can you not defend me? Tell them to go to hell. Why justify whatever heinous thing they are saying with that pathetic defense? I'm a cook? What is that?"

"You are a cook."

"So what? That means I'm not a drain on you?"

"Just stop it. You're acting crazy. I was trying to be supportive. That letter is supportive, and you are acting completely insane. I'm going out."

She watched in amazement as he snatched his raincoat off the hook by the door and started putting it on. He looked at her.

"It's dark," she said. "Where will you go?"

"For a walk. It's not that dark. Full moon. I'll go, and you can calm down."

She felt a terrible wrongness in her stomach, then all around her. She shook her head. She needed the words to explain this was about him, not her. He'd done something wrong. But no words came.

"You know, Vivienne, I don't know why you always do this. It seems like every day. You come up with something to ruin everything. I don't understand it."

She stood there, feeling the floor tilt beneath her. How could he twist things so effortlessly? Make her feel like she was the one who was unreasonable, unstable? She clung to the doorframe, trying to steady herself against the onslaught of doubt.

"I just wanted you to stand up for me," she breathed, almost to herself.

But he was already gone. The door clicked shut behind him, leaving her alone with the echoes of their argument and a deepening sense of isolation.

She thought back to the bullfight, the blood, and horror, and how he'd dismissed her feelings so easily. His words replayed in her mind like a mantra designed to wear her down, to make her question her reality.

Four days later, they packed up and headed home to England. But the seed of doubt had been planted. Each time Jack dismissed her feelings, told her she was overreacting, it grew a little more. She felt herself shrinking, folding inward, questioning everything. Was she losing her mind? Or was Jack, at a measured pace, insidiously rewriting her reality?

The weight of it pressed down on her chest, making it hard to breathe. She wanted to scream, fight back, but there were no words. The growing darkness swallowed her voice inside her.

Vivienne crossed her arms, shivering slightly despite the warmth of the night. She felt small, a vulnerability creeping in that she hated acknowledging. *Is this what love is supposed to feel like?* she wondered, the question hanging bitterly in her mind. She'd always imagined love as something steady, a refuge; but now, more often than not, it felt like a constant balancing act, teetering between passion and hurt, devotion and doubt.

As the minutes slipped by and the darkness deepened, she leaned against the doorframe, staring into the night, wondering if she'd see his shape reappear on the horizon. And despite the hurt, the anger, and the doubt, she knew she'd be waiting there, hoping he'd come back, because for all her resilience, she couldn't deny that her heart was bound to him, however painfully, however imperfectly.

3

The telegram arrived on a bleak Thursday morning, its arrival unexpected and its promise unimaginable. Vivienne had just returned from a disappointing trip to the library, the weight of gray skies and the looming likelihood of yet another rejection hanging over her as she opened the door to their flat. Jack stood waiting, a faint tension in his posture, his expression unreadable as he held out a thin envelope.

She took it, her fingers trembling slightly, and tore it open. The words seemed to jump off the page:

TO: JACK WELLES. OUR CONGRATULATIONS ON ACCEPTANCE OF ... BY PUBLICATION BY H. ROWE. DETAILS TO FOLLOW BY LETTER.

She read it twice, her mind struggling to catch up, and then felt Jack lean over her shoulder, his breath warm, as he read the words with her, both of them rereading it just to be sure. The realization hit, sharp and electric, and without a word she leaped out of her chair. Jack laughed, grabbing her around the waist, lifting her off her feet as they both erupted into a frenzy of joy. They spun and laughed until their legs gave out, collapsing together in a breathless heap on the floor, staring up at the cracked ceiling with wide, giddy smiles. Vivienne rolled over, pressing her cheek against his chest, listening to his heartbeat still pounding from the excitement. In that moment, the gray of the morning, the rejections, the doubts—all of it faded away, leaving only the elation of this shared victory. She closed her eyes, breathing him in, letting herself believe, if only for a moment, that this was how things were meant to be, the two of them in sync, buoyed by the thrill of their dreams finally coming to life.

"You are magnificent. I knew it," she said.

"We did it, Viv; the book is yours," he replied, pulling her close. "Without you, it would not have come off, and you know that's true."

She did not argue. She'd edited, revised, typed, and submitted Jack's manuscript. She'd contacted magazines and publishers, written letter after letter until, finally, the world had listened. If it hadn't been for her, he'd still be fishing off a rock somewhere. She said nothing.

Vivienne felt a deep wave of relief wash over her, unexpected yet undeniable—it was his book, not hers, that had been accepted for publication first. She hadn't realized, until that moment, just how much pressure she'd been carrying, how much weight she'd put on her own shoulders. If her work had been published first, it would have complicated everything: his pride, their balance, their fragile equilibrium.

Now, with his victory leading the way, she could rejoice without reservation. She could bask in his success, cheer him on without feeling the pangs of guilt or worry. She had room to breathe, to keep working, to wait until her words were truly ready. His achievement gave her permission to take her time, to grow at her own pace, and she was grateful for it.

Vivienne leaned into his chest as they lay together on the floor, feeling the steady rise and fall of his breath, the warmth of his success filling the room. It was his moment, his dream coming true, and for the first time in a long while, she felt that it didn't matter if hers came later. She was happy just to be here, to be part of this, with him.

They celebrated with lunch at a pub and a book-buying frenzy, followed by tea and a long walk. Vivienne talked non-stop about all the publications to come. Jack was launched, and the doors, now open, would never close.

From here, the future looked clear. They would return to America in the new year. Vivienne would accept the Talbot teaching position she'd been offered. Her salary would be enough to support them so Jack could write full-time. Jack was the genius. Her own writing? Vivienne could sort that out later.

In the early evening, they strolled back to the flat, their steps leisurely as they made their way through the horse park. The air was cool, tinged with the earthy smell of damp grass and the lingering warmth of the sun fading into dusk. They walked in a comfortable silence, the energy from the morning's news still buzzing between them, a quiet contentment in each shared glance and light touch.

A few horses grazed in the field nearby, their silhouettes soft and graceful against the darkening sky their shapes still, necks bent, standing ankle-deep in the low marsh fog. Vivienne paused to watch them, captivated by the calm beauty of the scene, the gentle flick of tails, the sound of their hooves scuffing against the ground. She felt a strange sense of peace settle over her, a stillness that contrasted sharply with the tension and uncertainty that had colored so many of their recent days.

"There's some muck there," Jack said, pointing. "Watch it; stuff sticks."

She picked up her foot and waggled it. In less time than it took to shake a bit of dirt off her boot, she imagined things going sideways—her future not what she had planned, but what she feared. Then, as quickly as it had come, the doubt vanished. She smiled at Jack. "It doesn't matter. A bit of mud."

Jack wrapped his arm around her shoulders, pulling her close, and she leaned into him, absorbing the warmth and solidity of his presence. For the first time in what felt like ages, she felt fully present, here and now, without the usual worries tugging at her mind. They didn't need to say anything; the quiet spoke for them, filling the spaces where words would normally go. The future felt, for this brief, golden moment, like something they could shape together.

As they left the park and neared the flat, Vivienne couldn't help but glance back at the horses, still grazing under the deepening blue sky. She let out a small sigh of contentment, squeezing Jack's hand, savoring the rare simplicity of their happiness.

CHAPTER 29

PHYLLIS AND JEAN PAUL
December 1956

1

They came without warning, their arrival announced by a hastily scribbled postcard from Jack's sister. She'd decided, at the last minute, to pass through Cambridge on her way to Paris, where she'd be starting a new job. And, by the way, she was bringing a friend—a French friend. Vivienne read the postcard twice, feeling a knot of frustration tighten in her chest.

It couldn't have come at a worse time. She and Jack had finally settled into a rhythm, a quiet routine that felt like the first real balance they'd found since moving in together. Each morning, they woke early, shared coffee and eggs, and spent the first few hours working across from each other at the big, worn table they used for everything: eating, writing, planning. Vivienne had even labeled the ends of the table with small inked cards, one reading *Mrs. Welles* and the other *Mrs. Wells,* a little joke they shared. Jack's card had long gone missing, but he'd been touched by the gesture, calling it "a writer's tribute to a marriage of the minds." Now, he'd cluttered his side with jagged pages and pencils and crumpled sheets; Vivienne's materials, her typed manuscripts and blank pages were organized on her side in neat stacks, and the Olivetti typewriter squared off in the middle.

When they'd finished, she washed up the dishes, made the bed, and tidied the flat. In the afternoons, depending on the weather, they took walks and read to one another. Jack's interest in all things metaphysical had intensified, and he was teaching Vivienne about horoscopes and tarot. Skeptical at first, she was seeing, if not the truth of it, at least the magic.

Their routine had brought a sense of stability, a delicate peace Vivienne treasured. They had their own spaces, their own time, a quiet understanding in those early hours that they were building something together, separately but side by side. Now, she feared, that peaceful rhythm would be disrupted, filled instead with the chatter and demands of guests they hadn't invited.

Vivienne placed the postcard back on the table, trying to swallow her irritation. She knew she'd have to put on her best face, be the gracious hostess, especially in front of Jack's sister and her friend. But as she glanced around the flat, she couldn't help but feel the creeping sense that this visit would throw everything off-kilter.

"Where would Phyllis sleep?" Vivienne asked, her voice tinged with underlying worry. "Oh, wherever is fine," Jack replied nonchalantly, his eyes already drifting back to the tarot cards sprawled on the table.

"How long will they stay?"

"She didn't say."

The thing was that Jack's attitude wasn't so casual. He'd be annoyed if the visit didn't flow. He'd be embarrassed, even angered, if Phyllis was uncomfortable or put out. So 'wherever is fine' did not apply.

"You'll love her, Viv. She's magnificent."

He kissed her, his lips brushing hers with a mix of urgency and comfort. As he pulled her close, she felt both reassured and unsettled by his touch. She curled into him, inhaling his smell. Jack was so easy for her to love if only she could surgically remove the less appealing bits. His temper, his moodiness and possibly his relatives.

The morning they were to arrive, Vivienne left for the shops. She'd cook something special for Phyllis and her friend. Jack would appreciate it, and Vivienne loved to cook. The guests were due to arrive early afternoon. Still, she and Jack had not discussed the details, at least not in-depth.

Vivienne had meticulously washed and dried extra sheets and blankets at the laundry the week previously (a three-mile walk round trip), presuming the couple would stay on the sofa and floor or some combination.

Alternatively, Phyllis would sleep with her, and the two men would share the floor/sofa. That seemed most practical, although Vivienne detested the idea of sharing a room, let alone a bed, with a woman she didn't know. Women talked, and one never knew if a particular woman would be the type to talk more about books or wallpaper. If it was the latter, a night spent together could be genuinely torturous.

Stepping outside, the day was gentle, the scent of earlier rain mingling with the earthy aroma of damp soil. The skies were pale blue. The narrow road was a muddy track with puddles of water still standing. She took deliberate steps, mindful of the pitfalls between stones, and came to a half-hinged gate. Pushing it open, she walked up a path and into a brilliant green meadow. Cutting across and through the damp grass, Vivienne could hear only the occasional dog barking back near the houses and the sounds of the birds. A young robin, barely a few inches long, was fluttering between the branches of a dogwood tree. She stopped, moved in closer, squinting into the sunlight to see it more clearly. After a while, the creature alighted and sang.

A breeze picked up, pushing the bird's branch dangerously back and forth. The bird wobbled but clung on and kept singing. The breeze became wind, and Vivienne shivered. The bird's feathers ruffled, and the bird kept singing. Vivienne smiled and headed up the path on her way to the shops.

2

They ate pork loin and potatoes and fruit with bottles of brandy contributed by Phyllis's friend, Jean Paul, who was half English and half French. He was a good-humored, small man, quite a bit older than Phyllis, yet energetic and youthful in his black beret and chartreuse scarf. As Vivienne and Jack had suspected, Jean Paul was Phyllis's latest lover. Phyllis had kept this information secret until she arrived in Cambridge.

After dinner, while Vivienne cleared the dishes, Phyllis, and Jean Paul sat at the table with Jack and smoked. Phyllis was a striking woman, older than Jack by nearly six years; she looked so much like him. They might have been male and female versions of the same person. She was tall and robust, but unmistakably female. She possessed a softer version of his square chin, long nose, and deep-set, intensely intelligent eyes. She wore a black turtleneck snug across her generous breasts, fitted black trousers hemmed just above the ankles, and short, black leather boots. She'd tied her thick blonde hair back in a braid, and two bright gold hoops sparkled in her ears. Vivienne thought she looked Amazonian.

"Come sit, Viv," Jack said, patting the chair beside him.

Vivienne smiled but said nothing. He wasn't looking at her. Instead, he was entirely focused on Phyllis, gazing at the paper she'd placed on the table between them. She was pointing at a specific spot on the paper.

"If you look here," Phyllis was saying, "you can see the moon of Saturn is coming right over the house of Mars on the 23rd." It was a star chart, twice the size of any Jack had put together.

"And this?" Jack asked, reaching a finger to touch one point on the chart.

Phyllis came around to the other side of the table and took the seat he'd just tapped for Vivienne.

"Jupiter on the cusp of the fifth, moon near...." Vivienne stopped listening. Phyllis glanced up at her and then back again at the star chart. Suddenly, Vivienne felt as if a door had slammed shut, cutting her off, leaving Jack and Phyllis on the other side. Jean Paul's presence seemed superfluous, and this thing, whatever Jack and Phyllis were sharing, abruptly took on enormous significance.

Jean Paul, oblivious to it all, excused himself early and went to bed. Jack and Phyllis continued in whispery voices about moons and stars. They dealt tarot cards and drank wine, and by the time Vivienne had finished cleaning up, Jack and his sister were so deep in some weird, convoluted discussion, trying to catch up seemed pointless. So Vivienne just sat quietly, watching them, with their heads bent together, mouths full of witches and goblins, as they sketched and chattered into the night.

3

They stayed on for ten days, which in Vivienne's mind was far too long. Every night, they held seances, conjuring beasts, ghosts, spirits, goblins, and the like. Jack invited friends, even some women, from Halsey house. He'd always been fanatical about his writing schedule, insisting that missing even one session exposed them to the tragic banality of everyday middle class married life. Vivienne's argument that barely surviving on one academic scholarship in a four-pound flat without central heat or hot water hardly qualified as middle class, banal, or otherwise, had never swayed him. His retort was always the same: Americans were too rich and too ignorant to understand. Yet, with Phyllis's visit, he happily skipped their morning writing sessions altogether.

Instead of writing, Jack and Phyllis spent the mornings either sleeping off the effects of too much drink and talk or taking long mysterious walks, returning radiant and refreshed. Vivienne fumed in silence, her anger simmering beneath a facade of civility. She did all the shopping, cooking, cleaning, and laundry with no offer of help. By the time Phyllis and her lover departed England, Vivienne seethed with resentment, not just at the workload, but at Jack's blatant hypocrisy.

And yet, a grimy sense of guilt gnawed at her, sharp and insistent. *What sort of woman envies her own sister-in-law?* she chastised herself. *What sort of wife are you, Vivienne?* She felt almost ashamed at the bitterness curling within her, a bitterness that had nothing to do with Jack's sister personally. It was deeper, murkier, an envy of anyone who might disrupt the fragile bubble she and Jack had created for themselves. An ugly fear that, to Jack, she was or could easily become, invisible.

She'd felt this way before, in Yorkshire with Jack's parents. Or rather, with his mother. Watching Mrs. Welles serve Jack as he lounged on the couch, reading Shakespeare and listening to Beethoven on his ancient gramophone. During their two weeks in his childhood home, Vivienne felt herself dwindling, fading.

She'd take long, solitary walks at night, winding through the narrow streets and quiet parks, her footsteps echoing softly in the empty dark. The city had a strange beauty at this hour, but she barely noticed it. Instead, her mind drifted to a haunting thought that had started visiting her more frequently—*What if I disappeared?* The idea lingered, unsettling and yet oddly comforting, the notion that she could simply slip away, melt into the night, her absence unnoticed for days... maybe even forever.

Vivienne wondered who would miss her first. Would Jack even notice? Or would he simply assume she'd gone out for a stroll, too caught up in his own world to question her absence? She imagined her empty side of the bed, the pages of her journal left open, her cup in the sink, all signs of a life that had vanished quietly, without fanfare.

The looming threat of disappearance, she thought. It was not that Vivienne was small. It was that Jack was enormous, his presence like a planet, a giant sun, around which women orbited. Jack was only fractionally hers. The big juicy bits he reserved for others—other women, better women maybe. His mother. His sister.

4

They stood together in the frosty morning at one end of the train station. It was early. Several trains sat motionless on their tracks. Between them, slices of clear blue sky ran like ribbons beyond the train shed. Then, there came the sounds of conductors and riders shouting and the screech of wheels on tracks.

With Phyllis in Paris indefinitely and Jack and Vivienne planning to move back to America, it might be some time before they would see each other again. Awkwardly, Vivienne and Phyllis said their last goodbyes. Just before Phyllis released Vivienne from a slightly painful last embrace, she whispered something inaudible into Vivienne's ear. Before Vivienne could ask for clarification, Phyllis was boarding the train with Jean Paul right behind her.

Vivienne and Jack stood on the platform as the train pulled away from the station, Phyllis at the window, waving down to Jack, Jack looking sadly up at his sister, and Vivienne silently studying them both. The scent of Phyllis's perfume—heavy, expensive, and still lingering—felt like a symbol of something larger. *Intrusive,* Vivienne thought, as the scent clung to the air. Jack's family, his world, his legacy—they were all parts of him that she'd never fully belong to, no matter how close she stood.

"What did she say to you?" Jack asked softly, his eyes still on the disappearing train.

Vivienne just shook her head. "I couldn't quite hear," she said.

As the train disappeared, they stood in silence, the frigid air a solid barrier between them.

PART FIVE: 1957-1959

CHAPTER 30

RUTHIE
Summer 1957

They confiscated her D.H. Lawrence. Did you know that? All of them, she had several. Of course, it was ridiculous, but authorities in the US banned the book. Poor Vivienne. She'd had one hell of a time with the Atlantic crossing, seasick like crazy. So, I was at the harbor in New York to pick them both up, she and Jack, of course. Imagine, I've not seen Viv since the disaster in Cambridge a year earlier, after which she'd practically forbidden me to contact her, and there I am standing in the port watching for her up on the deck of Queen Elizabeth II. I wasn't even supposed to be there. Viv had asked Marcia, another Talbot friend of ours, to pick them up. Marcia and her new husband. But you know, they just didn't know Vivienne all that well and, of course, they'd heard about all that business when she went missing and, well, you know how people feel about that sort of thing. So, anyway, I was in town, and I'm a friend of Marcia's, and she asked me to tag along. Selfishly, I thought it would be an excellent opportunity to smooth things over with Viv and Jack. We'd exchanged a few letters but never really gotten past what had happened.

Anyway, there we were waiting when they disembarked, and Vivienne was still green with seasickness and mad as a hornet about her books. They had something like three hundred books with them. Vivienne had tried to explain she needed the Lawrence for the courses she'd be teaching at Talbot in the fall, and do you know what the official said to her? He told her she was much too young a girl to be a professor!

Luckily, the whole thing passed over quickly in their excitement at reaching America. And, after she got her color back, Vivienne looked just wonderful. She had on this bright red sundress and a big broad hat with a bit of black silk scarf, and I thought she looked like a movie star. All bubbling and talking continuously. She was so different from the last time. All that nervous agitation is gone. She was confident and really over the moon with Jack. I decided right then and there I'd been all wrong about the marriage. She was fine. In Cambridge, I had observed her quietly weeping over her pots while she cooked. I was prepared to make a big apology, but strangely Vivienne acted like nothing had ever happened between us. In fact, she never brought it up again. I kept meaning to come back to it but then, in the end, we ran out of time.

In any event, it was an enormous relief to see them get off the boat in such a happy state. I mean, except for the silly business about the books.

You know, we all went over to Marcia's townhouse in Manhattan for an early supper. Marcia was one of us schoolgirls who'd chosen a more traditional route. She married the son of a wealthy banker, had children (I think she had four in the end—I lost track). She was just this ideal wife and mother. She'd been an exceptionally talented painter, but as far as I know, she painted only portraits of her children once she was married. It was alright though; you understand. For Marcia, it worked.

Mostly, the welcome party went well. Several of Vivienne's other friends were over at Marcia's, and we were having a terrific time. Vivienne always loved a party, and I remember she'd had several cocktails and was chit-chatting happily. Sort of buzzing around. She'd borrowed from Marcia this little cap-sleeved dress the color of emeralds, and it showed off her suntanned arms and legs. But Jack sort of hung back. He seemed a bit overwhelmed. Later I heard Marcia's husband didn't like him very much. Thought he was arrogant. I think that was the word. Indeed, Jack could be glum. I think that happened when nobody paid particular attention to him, and that night we were so much more interested in Vivienne. I think Jack had become famous in England by that time. He'd won many awards; his book was about to be published. But in America, nobody knew anything about him. I think that was a hard change for him. He was a terribly handsome man, though, I must say. It seemed to me that he wouldn't have had any difficulty charming everyone if he'd just tried a little harder. But he didn't seem interested.

That's when I noticed Vivienne kept checking. You know, looking over to see how he was doing. It was bothering her. She would tense up. And after a while, they disappeared into another room, not subtle. When they reappeared, she wasn't the same. Hard to explain, but it was like there was a bit of weight on her. I could see it, although she did a good job smiling and carrying on. But Jack, it was like he didn't give a darn what you thought about him. He just didn't care. Vivienne cared loads. That was the thing about Viv, the thing that made it so hard to understand what she did in the end. I always thought of people who did that as hopeless, not invested you know. But Viv was not that way. She loved life, she loved being alive. Or at least, that's what we all thought.

CHAPTER 31

AMERICA

1

Vivienne's emotions were a turbulent mix, like waves crashing against the cliffs of her consciousness. On the surface, she radiated confidence and joy, her bright red sundress and broad hat creating an image of a woman who had everything together. But underneath, she suffered a gnawing unease.

Arriving in America should have been a triumphant return, especially with Jack by her side. He was everything she had ever dreamed of—a powerful, magnetic force of an artist, a genius whose passion and brilliance captivated her. And, somehow, he had chosen *her*. He had loved her, accepted her, and even agreed to her impulsive proposal without hesitation. Together, they had created a vision of a life filled with love and poetry, of endless adventure and artistic fulfillment. But reality was proving to be more complex.

When they disembarked from the Queen Elizabeth II, a severe case of seasickness had physically weakened Vivienne, and she'd felt unable to fight the confiscation of her D.H. Lawrence books. However, Jack's apparent indifference to her distress bothered her a great deal more. He barely noticed, turning instead to greet the welcome party, laughing, smiling, then walking several steps ahead of her, leaning close in conversation with one of the younger women in the group. A woman Vivienne did not know.

Later, at the welcome party, in Marcia's townhouse, Vivienne was in her element, surrounded by old friends, bubbling with conversation and energy. Yet she was acutely aware of Jack's growing discomfort. Despite his charm and gregariousness at the boat, he exhibited an acute inability or unwillingness to interact with Vivienne's friends at the party. She wanted her world to enchant him just as his world had mesmerized her. But he seemed distant, almost resentful.

When they disappeared into another room, the brief confrontation left a mark on her spirit.

"I'm doing nothing wrong," he bit back at her when she questioned his attitude.

"You're not being sweet Jack, I don't understand? What's wrong?"

"Nothing is wrong Vivienne. Why do you always think something is wrong? Am I supposed to put on a monkey suit and dance a jig for these people. For God's sake, get off me for once." He downed the remaining whiskey and forcefully made his way out of the room, pushing past her.

She reemerged, trying to maintain her bubbly exterior, but the weight of Jack's dissatisfaction hung over her like a storm cloud. Her excitement had dampened, and her confidence was shaken. As she looked out at the darkening sky over Manhattan, she felt a chill of foreboding, a sense that the honeymoon had already come to an end.

2

The Poet closed his eyes, dug his toes into the floury sand, and let the sunlight prickle his skin. Strange how rocky and hostile the English beaches were by comparison. This bit of America, this welcoming coastline of Cape Cod he loved. This is the America of which he'd dreamed; soft, welcoming, feminine. The blue-green waters of the Atlantic, warm by English standards, had kept them swimming much of the afternoon. Now they lay back on the beach, exhausted, panting.

They'd spent the summer on the Cape. In an isolated little cottage with a screened porch and a floor thick with pine needles. Squirrels and chipmunks scurried around the roof and through the surrounding trees. They swam and slept and made love and rode their bikes into town for groceries, from which they cooked simple meals. Mostly they wrote. They managed to write and submit (Vivienne did all the submitting) poems and stories to the Saturday Evening Post, The Spectator, The Atlantic, and The New Yorker throughout that summer. By early August, Vivienne had prepared all her lessons for her first semester at Talbot and begun the outline for what was to become one of the most important books of the twentieth century.

The cottage had come from Vivienne's mother; she'd rented it for them as a wedding present, and they had left immediately following the wedding reception. The Wellesley reception was held on June 20th, 1957, almost exactly one year after their small wedding in London and a few weeks after they arrived in America. Vivienne's mother had transformed her backyard into a wonderland with white chairs, pink tablecloths, paper lanterns, and flowing champagne. There were so many pots of carnations in shades of pink that it was impossible to walk two feet without stumbling over one.

The wedding gifts were splendid: excellent cutlery, lovely cooking pans, and cash—which shocked The Poet, but Vivienne assured him was standard in the US. The Poet stared at the small pile of bills, making a mental note to write his sister about this remarkably generous and incredibly weird tradition. He'd already written home about America's newness and opulence (enormous houses each on their own grounds, fifty-foot-long cars, and speedways crisscrossing the landscape like space highways out of a science fiction novel). Vivienne looked beautiful in a long pale blue dress; her hair done up like an English queen. Glimpsing himself in the foyer mirror, The Poet conceded he too looked quite good, possibly even handsome, in his new dark blue silk suit and tie.

Most of the guests, Vivienne explained, were friends and colleagues of her mother's. They were what Americans referred to as "great people" or even "really interesting people." They were clean; everyone was spotless, to the point of smelling antiseptic. They were polite, though not deferential, cheerful but not to the point of idiocy, articulate although not exceptionally well-read, and reasonably, but not remarkably, well-educated. Best of all, they were enthusiastic. The Poet noticed that enthusiasm for anything and everything was valued like gold in American social interaction; the words "Wow!" and "Right!" and "Exactly!" abounded. He detected little, if any, original thought. But, to a one, they knew how to consume, rearrange, and then regurgitate other people's original ideas, possibly without complete comprehension of them. It hardly seemed to matter. Listening was not required. Each person in a conversation seemed only to be waiting for the other person to stop talking so that they might resume whatever it was they were saying in the first place. It was curious how anyone learned anything from anyone else, but The Poet assumed that mystery would be revealed in time.

As a group, these people were also ambitious. The Poet thought it might be the ubiquitous presence of a blind, bland ambition that separated Americans entirely from their European counterparts. Not that the English—some of the English at least—weren't driven to achieve rank, fame, power, etc.; it was that, at least among this group of Americans, The Poet could not have guessed what they were working so hard to achieve. Worse, he was pretty sure they couldn't have imagined it either. Ambition, it seemed, was valued simply because it was ambition.

He looked around, everyone smiling, drinking, eating, talking. The Americans appeared to be entirely happy if everyone was "mixing." The Poet's problem was learning how to "mix" well. The biggest social crime one could commit in this shiny country was the crime of "not mixing." One must mix. Not mixing could be an occupational hazard. Overhearing a conversation—Cousin Barry had lost his job as an automobile salesman, apparently because he was a little "off" and did not "mix." The Poet would have to work on that.

He watched Vivienne mingling and chatting. She was happy. Thrilled. Vivienne felt everything this way. Like a piano keyboard with no middle C, all the way up to the top of the scale, then all the way down. Sometimes he envied her for it, but she paid a high price. The Poet understood melancholy. But Vivienne's darkness was different; it was a vicious, living creature. He'd seen the tender spots on her temples, the scars from her treatment. He'd heard her nightmares of amputated limbs and death machines.

He went to her, slipping his arm around her waist. He pressed his lips to the top of her head. Her dark blonde hair was soft, freshly washed, and smelled of rosewater. She looked up at him, her blue eyes shining with happiness and perhaps just a hint of relief. For a moment, everything seemed perfect, as if their love and the beauty of this American summer could protect them from the darkness within and around them.

But deep down, The Poet knew that life was never that simple. He felt the weight of his own insecurities and doubts, the pressures of their ambitious plans, and the uncertain future ahead. And he could sense, even if she didn't show it, that Vivienne felt it too. They were two dreamers, trying to hold on to a fleeting moment of happiness while the real world loomed just beyond their idyllic Cape Cod summer.

CHAPTER 32

WORDS FOR A NURSERY

1

It all started with the pregnancy scare. Until then, the summer had been going along smashingly well. Jack loved Cape Cod. He adored the little cottage Mother had rented for them and was even enjoying the very few people they'd met, most of whom Vivienne found about as interesting as the dandelions.

Smashingly well might have been an overstatement. Vivienne had a few complaints, none of which did she share with Jack. He was so happy, and he seemed not to notice the cabin's heat with its sweating walls, the spiders, the flannel sheets that never felt quite clean. The pine needles did not bother him. They were everywhere! Sticking to the bottoms of Vivienne's sandals and the backs of her thighs, impossible to keep off the floor. Then there was the constant sound of squirrels on the roof overhead. To Vivienne, they might as well have been rats, but Jack loved them. He loved all the little furry, feathered creatures.

She also disliked the isolation: they were too far from the shops and all alone. There'd been nobody around until the last week when a new couple rented the cottage just behind them. The boy brought along his radio—an enormous monster of a thing. He'd set it up at an open kitchen window and let it blast some awful noise he called music late into the night. Jack refused to go over and ask him to turn it down, so Vivienne lay awake with a pillow smashed against her ears, which did little to muffle the noise.

And the heat, oh god, it was insufferable. To escape the heat, Vivienne and Jack had to move their writing out of doors but then the biting horseflies, big as hummingbirds, seemed to multiply.

Through it all, however, had been the ocean.

Every afternoon, they rode their bicycles down to the sea. They swam in the warm water until exhaustion forced them out, and then they lay in the soft sand beneath a big, glorious sun and slept. The sea was Vivienne's reward for the rest of it. On the ride home, she licked at the saltwater on her lips and curled her toes inside her tennis shoes to feel the grains of sand rub between her toes. During those weeks, her skin stung all the time, a pleasant combination of light sunburn and saltwater and wind. It was like carrying a bit of ocean around on her body. A bit of home.

But then, everything changed.

Her period had been late. At first, she said nothing to Jack, but with each passing day, she sunk further into a desperate panic. After five days, she was so terrified she couldn't eat. She told him, and, as she expected, he wasn't worried.

"These things happen," he said, his voice calm and reassuring. "Periods are late," he said. "Try to calm down," he repeated, placing a gentle hand on her shoulder. She shrugged it away. His nearness irritated her. It felt condescending.

Vivienne did not calm down.

After a week, she could do nothing but lie in bed, terrified of the consequences of a pregnancy. First, Talbot would fire her for being pregnant. That had been specified. Talbot did not allow pregnant women, married or not. Second, without a source of regular income, they could not pay their bills. Third, they'd lose the apartment, which did not allow children, anyway. Fourth, she'd have to take on some menial job and have childcare in addition. Finally, she could not write.

But, she thought, perhaps there was an alternative. What if Jack got a job? A proper job? He had a degree from Cambridge, after all. He had publications; he was qualified. He could teach. The thought was fleeting. No, she told herself. Jack had to write, and he could not do that with a job, he wasn't Vivienne. He did not multitask and could, in fact, fall into idleness without the specific structure and support provided him by Viv. Still, if it meant a baby perhaps, he would make it possible. *Do not ask him,* she told herself. And she did not.

When nine days had passed, Vivienne and Jack rode bikes to town to see the doctor. Vivienne had the test, but the results would take several days. So, they waited. Vivienne slumped over her typewriter, trying like mad to write but coming away with only blank pages and a blinding headache. Two days later, the blood came—suddenly, in a rush. Jack more frightened by this sudden flood than by the bleak psychological void Vivienne had spiraled into during the long absence of her period.

For Vivienne, the relief was enormous, but also it came with a sharp edge of resentment. She said nothing.

2

The shops were miles away, requiring either a long bicycle ride or, if they needed groceries, catching a lift from the manager's wife, a busty forty-ish woman who talked constantly and claimed to be a distant relation to the Queen. She was generous in offering them rides, but the manager's wife was also infatuated with Jack. She'd had taken to stopping by unannounced. At first, just once a week, and she'd bring a bit of cake as an excuse, but later she'd stop around for chat more frequently, sometimes stretching the visits to teatime and once or twice all the way to supper. Jack didn't seem to mind. He was always eyeing her capris pants, which she wore with impractical, strappy little sandals. Vivienne hadn't cared. The woman was tacky and stupid and phony, and Jack could not possibly be interested in her, but he was letting her sit in their kitchen, which was annoying.

And then last night, out beyond the tree line, Vivienne had seen them. Facing one another, the alabaster skin of the woman's ankles was visible in the moonlight beneath the cuff of those stupid capris, one arm draped lazily up and over Jack's shoulder. His face bent towards hers. And suddenly, the image disappeared as the moon slipped behind the clouds. The image wiped out as quickly as it had appeared, the forest in darkness.

Of course, he denied it.

He'd been "out having a walk," he said. "But Vivienne, you know what I think of her. She's not the least bit attractive. You're crazy. Stop it now."

This morning Vivienne lay spread-eagled across the cottage bed. She was wearing a sleeveless T-shirt and underpants and nothing else, declaring it too hot to dress, too hot to move, and too hot to be in any mood except the one she was in.

"Why must you always do this?"

"Why must I always do what, Jack? What am I doing?"

"This, this, ruin everything!"

He threw his head back and spread his arms up from his sides, palms up, showing the position of her body on their bed.

"I don't feel well. I told you. I'm not doing anything."

Vivienne pushed herself up to her elbows and studied her husband. She knew he was angry. She wasn't helping the situation any, but she could not summon the energy to smooth things over. Not just now. She'd seen what she'd seen.

"I told you, you're mistaken. Completely crazy, ok? Can we just get past this?"

"It's fine. I'm tired now. Just let me rest, ok?" Vivienne said the words feeling the lie weigh on her heart. She wasn't fine. She was enraged.

She watched his back stiffen.

"Fine, suit yourself. I'm going down to the beach. But I'm telling you, Viv, I cannot keep doing this. You have to get ahold of yourself. You make these things up when you," he hesitated a few seconds, then added, "You know when you've had a difficult time."

Last night she'd let it go, accepting his explanation. He'd called her crazy and over-tired when she'd confronted him. *You're seeing things, making problems where there aren't any.*

She'd forced herself to believe him, slept badly and awoken with an anxious, nauseous feeling in her gut. She was not able to stop herself from bringing it up. Questioning, harassing, accusing. That's what he called it. *I can't stand this harassment, these untrue accusations, the constant questioning.* Now he was angry, and he would stay angry possibly all day. *Why could she not keep her mouth shut?*

Vivienne got up, then, changing her mind, flopped, fishlike, back onto the mattress. In these situations, it was always best to remain still and wait for inspiration to strike.

CHAPTER 33

THE BLUE FLANNEL SUIT
September 1957

1

"How do I look?"

Jack's eyes drifted slowly up and down her body. "Hideous."

"Thank you."

"Quite welcome," he replied, returning to his coffee and the tiny book of poems he'd been absorbed in when she entered the kitchen.

"Do me up," she said, turning her back to him.

He reached up, pulling the zipper on the back of her blue flannel skirt, then gently turned her around by the hips. "You look wonderful," he said, his tone softer now. "You're miles more qualified than all those gobs and goodles, you know that."

She laughed. Jack's words, the best words, always made her laugh.

"Not true. I haven't a Ph.D., I haven't a published book, and I have exactly zero minutes of teaching experience. I am not at all sure how that makes me qualified to be an English instructor at Talbot College."

Vivienne was right, of course. Her only qualifications were a degree from Talbot and English Department faculty members campaigning on her behalf.

"Well, yeah, that's all true," he said, nodding with a mock-serious expression on his face.

She thwacked him on the shoulder. "Oh, come on. You can do better than that."

He stood up, resting his gigantic hands on her shoulders. He leaned close to her, touching his forehead to hers. "You will be brilliant. Completely brilliant."

"Better," she said. "Thank you." She spun around. "How do I look?" He placed his hands on her waist and then gently brushed them upwards over her breasts and touched her neck. Laughing, she pushed free of him and went to the kitchen. A moment later, Vivienne set a steaming mug of tea down by Jack's elbow. He made a sound like a satisfied bear but went on writing. She ran a hand gently across his broad shoulder, the rough feel of his jumper beneath her palm comforting. She kissed the top of his head.

He was teaching her to write differently, to pull her words from a deeper, more soulful space. He said hypnosis, meditation, and even prayer were all necessary to write genuinely raw poetry. So far, Vivienne didn't think she'd gotten anywhere close to 'raw,' but her poems were better. Less rigid, more ambitious.

"Give it time," Jack said. "You will be brilliant," he said. She was miraculously qualified (even with no qualifications).

Vivienne knew it wasn't true. She was a terrible speaker and an even worse teacher. Most of the required books on her syllabus were relics from her college days, ones she'd barely skimmed and could hardly recall. And grammar? It had always been something she grasped intuitively, guided by sound rather than the exacting, labyrinthine rules of English grammar. Did she know those rules? Maybe not. Probably not. But her real worry? Nearly seventy-five students across four courses. All that prep, testing, grading—when would she have time for her own writing? The short answer was simple: she wouldn't.

Female professors didn't marry, and those who did rarely succeeded. Married or not, women in academia rarely published much. Only male professors seemed to have the privilege of writing as well, and that was largely because they had wives. Almost every one of them had a wife who took care of the cooking, cleaning, and daily support, freeing the men to write in their spare time. Many wives even acted as secretaries, as Vivienne did for Jack—typing, editing, mailing.

So, no, she didn't believe her husband's encouragement. She would not be a brilliant instructor, and there was a very real possibility that teaching would mean the end of her writing.

"Stop whining," she muttered to herself. "Anyone can do anything for two years. You'll just work harder—get up two hours earlier and use that time for writing. Discipline, focus. Make it happen. That was the plan, wasn't it?"

And so, on a crisp golden morning, in the fall of 1957, full of youthful energy and grand plans for her future, twenty-five-year-old Vivienne Holland (known on campus as Mrs. Welles) stepped into Wilomena Grimes lecture hall, took her place at the podium and began.

2

The Poet watched her go. Shutting the door behind her, he was alone in their tiny flat on Beacon Hill. It was two rooms plus a small writing alcove and a kitchen so narrow one could touch every appliance from a single spot in the middle of the floor. They had chosen it for its abundant light, thanks to its corner location. Vivienne loved the extra windows. They'd spent days polishing the old oak floors and painting the walls a warm yellow. After the dreary gray of England, the glow of their little place was refreshing. They had precious little furniture, but The Poet had fashioned a large desk from an old door and some file cabinets, and they used it for everything—from work to meals to paying bills and astrological forecasting.

He sipped his tea and, after a minute, lay aside the heavy black pencil he'd been using. Out the window, he could see Vivienne walking toward campus. That was another reason they'd taken the flat: its proximity to Talbot College. If the weather held, she could walk to campus, which she insisted on doing. From the window, Vivienne appeared slight, fragile. As he'd watched her in the kitchen, her stiffness had struck him, the way her face looked pinched and vulnerable, her summer tan faded to a weird green tinge, and her hair scraped back against her head. The scar under her eye looked lumpish, and her attempt to hide it with powder was obvious. Her blue suit looked awful, uncomfortable; it had made him think of a straitjacket. Something had gripped her. Fear of judgment, perhaps. She was going into that classroom to be assessed not only by the students but likely members of faculty sitting in the back to make certain they'd not made a mistake in hiring this youthful woman. Especially this young woman who'd had a *nervous breakdown*, or whatever they might call it.

She was his wife. The Poet ached for her, but he could do nothing. Vivienne would have balked if he'd tried to stop her. If he'd said anything other than what he'd said, she'd have been angry and insisted on doing exactly as she did, anyway. And so, The Poet watched from the window as his young wife went out to take on the world.

CHAPTER 34

THE FRESHMAN
Fall 1957

We all hated her. This was 1957. We were freshmen. This was Talbot! All girls, right? Everyone wanted male instructors. The ones you might get a crush on, of course. If not the handsome men, we wanted the young, stylish women or the older, loving female professors, like your mother. Mrs. Welles, egad, she wasn't like any of those. She was young, but not attractive or stylish at all. And, of course, we didn't know the future, didn't know she'd become, well, who she'd become or what would happen just a few years later. We just thought she was terribly tense and frightening. We were terrified of her. She was strict. She made assigned seating right away, me up front, the second seat because my last name began with an A.

Mrs. Welles had a reputation for genius, or at least successful talent. Some said she was 'up and coming,' but we mostly ignored that. KNOWN WRITERS surrounded us, all men, of course. Mrs. Welles entered class with lots of books and notes, terribly organized and on a mission. She didn't smile or joke around like other younger teachers. She just marched in, set down her things, stared us into silence, went about the business of instructing, and then marched out. You know, there were times I thought she might explode from the tension or more like shatter. She wasn't angry, just intense, and graded like a demon. Achieving anything better than a C was nearly impossible. I eventually managed a low B by nearly killing myself and talking with her frequently about my work.

I don't think anyone would deny she was an excellent teacher. She had lots of different ways of approaching the subjects. She taught TS Eliot and discussed

Tarot cards. She made up mental exercises. She walked around the hall reading aloud from a text and encouraged participation from the students. But her persona, hair pulled back severely, dour tailored clothing, strict demeanor, was just awful. Many girls complained, but I grew to admire her and enjoy her classes. Others felt like me.

Then, this thing happened, and it exploded the class, really split the class in two.

Talbot had a strict rule about missing class. Some unspeakable disaster (the details of which I cannot recall) would befall the girl who skipped class more than twice. It wasn't done. One morning, the girl in the chair next to mine was missing. Thirty minutes into class, she still hadn't shown up. It was bizarre, but I forgot about it until later. That Friday, and we were all busy getting ready for the weekend. Girls were buzzing up and down the hallways, trading clothes, making plans, you know. Then suddenly, a girl came in hysterical, screaming, "They've found her, and she's dead!"

The news of the girl's suicide at Paradise Pond shocked everyone. Most of us didn't know her well, but her death created a wave of grief and hysteria. Girls were sort of going crazy. Visiting the infirmary and all that. Nobody had dealt with death before. Other than maybe a grandparent or something and this was so unthinkable; she'd hung herself this girl, eighteen years old and hung herself down by the pond. By Monday, we expected Mrs. Welles, who never showed emotion, to address the tragedy. Instead, she continued with her lesson, starting with a quote from D.H. Lawrence chalked on the board: 'Life is only bearable when the mind and the body are in harmony, and there is a natural balance between them, and each has a natural respect for the other.'

Anyway, it upset a lot of the girls. They felt she didn't care. Some said she had no feelings at all. But I wondered if her behavior was deliberate, meant to help, not to harm. Although at the time, at eighteen, I didn't know how that might be true. Now, so many years later and, of course, knowing how tragically her life would unfold, I think it is clear.

CHAPTER 35

FAME
March 1958

1

In 1958, a car could cover the distance between The Astor Hotel on E. 63rd—where Vivienne had endured that agonizing Manhattan summer five years earlier—and the Eaton Auditorium on 19th Street in approximately ten minutes. A healthy mourning dove, if suitably motivated, might even make the journey in less than three hundred seconds. To Vivienne, however, the two locations might as well have been galaxies apart, so profoundly different was her arrival in New York on this beautiful spring evening in 1958 compared to what it had been in 1953.

Back in the city for Jack's first significant American poetry reading, they'd splurged on a cab from the train station. The city sparkled, almost winked at them—a knowing welcome, a friendly "how do you do" as they glided effortlessly through the streets. Their driver, a big man in need of a shave, leaned over and wished them luck with a broad grin. He seemed to know who Jack was, which took Vivienne by surprise. Jack was becoming a bit of a celebrity, and not just for his writing. His voice, his presence, his unique personality had gained a following here in America. His children's stories were selling, though still not well enough to guarantee a steady income, but his reputation was beginning to take on a life of its own.

This request for a reading in New York, which followed on the heels of a Christmas New York Times Book Review coverage, was a genuine breakthrough. The city remained a literary mecca in the United States, and they both knew that success here meant success period. And without New York, there was nothing.

The evening was cool, not quite dark, but windy for spring. An icy breeze whipped up the corridor of skyscrapers, beating a path straight through the thin fabric of Vivienne's coat. She'd rejected her heavier wool one; it was terribly worn and years out of style. This one, at least, was a lovely pale peach with a neat flair cut. But, God, she needed a new wardrobe. No place in the world could make a woman feel dowdy so quickly as New York. Oh well, she took Jack's hand. She was married to the most extraordinary man in the world. They were young, and this was to be their night.

2

Inside the large hall, people were still filing in and taking seats. There was a small stage up front, its wooden floor badly scratched and aged. Worn red curtains hung partially closed, and Vivienne could see stacks of cardboard boxes and what appeared to be storage cabinets behind. Despite the elegant name, Eaton Auditorium, it looked like an infrequently used community theater stage. A sturdy and nicely polished podium was set up in the front, and a cluster of middle-aged men in suits and one well-dressed older woman stood nearby. There was the clatter and scrape of folding metal chairs and the echo of muted voices all around. Vivienne tried but could not hear what they were saying.

Looking around, Vivienne noted only about half the seats were filled, and she felt a stab of anxiety. The place smelled of dust and linoleum. But, glancing at Jack, she knew he was unaware of anything negative. He was already grinning broadly and waving to someone he recognized. Center of attention. He would be in his element all evening.

They were early, Vivienne told herself. More people would come.

And so they did. The women, young and old, the students, the benefactors, and, of course, several of Vivienne's colleagues from Talbot and their spouses. Mother came, of course. She'd driven down from Wellesley, an enormous inconvenience, not to mention expensive when one considered hotels. Still, she'd insisted, and there she was in the front row, which both comforted Vivienne and made her feel as if her brain might spontaneously combust. Mother was, in one way, Jack's biggest supporter. She loved Jack. Adored him. Respected his work. But still, the support had emotional strings. Jack was not, after all, Stan Hampton. Not a successful doctor, not so many things. Mother would never understand that a man like Jack, not *like* Jack, but *exactly* Jack, was the only man with whom Vivienne would ever really be safe. So, while Mother worried incessantly that she, Vivienne, might slide back into the dreadful summer and fall of 1953, it was precisely the lack of Jack that had brought all that on. It was Jack who kept Vivienne safe from herself.

A few minutes to start, and the turnout was still a little disappointing. Both Vivienne and Jack had hoped to draw a few of the prominent writers and critics they knew were in town. But, unfortunately, both the senior editor of the English literary magazine The Observer and a legendary poet they'd invited, and his wife had sent their apologies without excuse, which Vivienne thought had a certain cruel authenticity about it.

Finally, with the hall hushed and nearly full, it began.

Jack looked like some Yorkshire god reading his poetry. Vivienne had to persuade him to have a haircut and wear the new clothes she'd bought him: a dark gray suit and a golden yellow tie. She could see a few members of the audience following along with their fingers in the books they'd bought before the reading. His voice was deeply resonant, his lines in equal parts brutal and divine. As Jack read the one war poem he'd included in the evening, she and several others in the audience were moved to tears.

After the reading, Jack signed dozens of books. "Mr. Welles, would you mind? ... Mr. Welles, I'm an absolute fan of..." "Hurrah for you..." This last comment came from an extremely young, wide-eyed, and giggly girl who, after Jack had signed using Vivienne's shoulder as a writing desk, took the book back, clutched it to her chest, and exclaimed loudly and with a little hop in the air, "Oh, gosh, Mr. Welles, I just want to say hurrah for you!"

Vivienne, who could not have been five years older than the hopping girl, felt terribly matronly. And worse, absurdly jealous. Another woman (it seemed they were nearly all women) quickly filled the first girl's spot, and Jack smiled, took her book, and held it in the air as if to ask Vivienne, would it be alright if he borrowed her shoulder once again? It was, and they continued like that for some time, laughing cheerfully about the success of the evening and his new fans, some of whom Jack said he didn't think had ever read his poetry before that night.

All jealousies forgotten; Vivienne felt giddy as they left the hall that night. It had gone well. Even Mother had been complementary and perfectly sweet. Offering nothing but positive remarks and even purchasing two additional copies of the book 'for friends,' which she had Jack sign. They'd agreed to drive over for the weekend to see her in two weeks.

In the cab, Vivienne leaned against Jack's shoulder and felt her breaths coming deep and slow for the first time in a while. It would be ok. Her poetry was winning prizes now. Her publications were adding up. Jack's book was doing well, the positive reviews coming more quickly and from more prestigious sources. With the additional income he was now earning teaching the one course at the local women's college this semester, she could undoubtedly leave Talbot in June and resume writing, and, in Vivienne's mind, more importantly, caring for Jack, full time.

By the time they arrived home the next day, Vivienne had forgotten all about the wide-eyed young girl with the giggly 'Hurrah.' Jack would not forget. He would mention the girl to his sister in a letter a few days later, referring to her as *one of an assortment of maidenly creatures* who'd accosted him after the reading that night. The star-struck girl was the first, but not the last, to show Jack Welles what fame was all about.

3

It should have been a celebration. The reading in New York was declared a grand success, and Jack's American publisher sent them two bottles of champagne, beautifully wrapped in pink and gold foil. In retrospect, Vivienne would blame the complete debacle on the champagne.

The spring had been lovely; purple crocus and swaths of yellow and cream daffodils along the edge of the duck pond, pale sunlight, and fresh days. All happy reminders of why Vivienne had so looked forward to their return to America. She was surviving at Talbot. Her stomach occasionally ached from the stress, but she felt more competent each day, and the insecurity was slipping away. On top of all that, the publication of Jack's book both in America and the UK was going even better than they'd hoped. He was making a real name for himself.

They'd tucked the champagne away for a special occasion and then, for no reason, decided on a Tuesday evening that it was an excellent time to drink both bottles. Partway into the second bottle, the light conversation they'd been having escalated quickly into something frothy and out of control.

Suddenly Vivienne was screaming about Jack's lack of earning power despite the prestigious awards and fame in the UK, the inequity of their current arrangement in which Vivienne did the lion's share of both earning and housework, Jack's tendency to come and go as he pleased.

Jack yelled back about how he felt nagged and trapped and couldn't possibly write anything under such circumstances and what was she on about, anyway, since she was the one who wanted to come back here in the first place.

Vivienne, who had consumed considerably less of the champagne than her husband, noted the direction things were going and did what she'd thought was a heroic job of wrenching the interaction back on course, avoiding a marital catastrophe.

But, as she was clearing the dishes, enjoying an interlude of muted silence while Jack lay on the sofa, big bare feet dangling over the arm, an open tome (Shakespeare's Plays) on his chest, she suddenly became aware he wasn't turning pages.

"Jack?" No answer. His face was a study in glumness, corners of his mouth down-turned, eyelids heavy. "Jack, what is it?"

He only shook his head at her and went back to pretending to read. He did this. He wanted her to pull it from him, one syllable at a time. Lethargy and a rather oafish indifference at the thought overwhelmed Vivienne. Instead, she slowly finished up the dishes and shut the kitchen light.

As she was stepping over him to pick up the magazine in which two of her poems had been published this month-the room was so small, it required touching one another to pass by the sofa he suddenly asked, "It's about Phyllis isn't it?"

"What?"

"This whole thing is about Phyllis. You not wanting to go back, I mean."

"To England? My not wanting to go back to England?"

This was a talk they'd had days earlier. They'd finished this discussion. No, they weren't going back to England; they'd both agreed. Jack did this sometimes. He made agreements, finished conversations, then re-opened negotiations days or weeks later as if they'd never spoken on the topic before. Finally, he'd outright deny they'd ever made an agreement, or even had the conversation. It made Vivienne feel crazy. Maybe they should start signing contracts, she thought.

"Right," he said.

"First, I never said I didn't want to go back. I said I don't want to go back next year. We talked about it, remember?" She blew out her breath, trying to shake the exhaustion that made her want to shut her eyes and fall asleep, standing right there the way Grampy used to do. "And what do you mean? Your sister? It has nothing to do with Phyllis."

Stop talking, she told herself. This never went well. The more she spoke, the more convoluted things would get, the more tangled knots about money and earning power and everything else. But she couldn't help it. Her mouth kept moving, and words kept flying right out, like dumb little birds.

"Jack, you are the one who called England 'dead.' You said it was 'rotten,' do you remember? You agreed to come. You wanted to come to America." She'd said exactly this a few days ago. And a few days before that. He'd agreed. They'd both agreed. No, England this year. And not next year. Not for a long, long while. Period.

He swung his legs around and sat up, pushing the giant book to the seat cushion. He glowered at her as he stood. His body appeared to expand. The sun had long since gone. The room lit by one lamp, he stood blocking its light, throwing the entire space into darkness. She shuddered, not afraid as much as terribly alone.

"Not this," he said. "Not this America." He flicked a hand to snatch his coat. She rushed to the door. As if you might have stopped him from going? He made a move to get past her, and she matched him.

"You can't leave like this."

"I can. I will. Move out of the way, Vivienne."

She was making it so much worse, but she couldn't stop. It felt good to keep going. "What the hell is your plan, Jack? To just do whatever you please whenever you please? Grow up." Inside, a voice screamed yes, yes, yes, but a more rational part of her knew she was being stupid.

"Right, Viv. Right. Bone idle I am. Is that what you're saying, Vivienne? A do nothing. His wife goes out to earn and support him. I only sit for hours and pretend to write anyway." He'd taken a step closer to her, and she felt suddenly trapped between the door and her husband. She could escape, of course.

"Jack, that's not what I mean. You know that."

"It's what we both mean."

She slid away from the door and turned from him. Her eye landed on the kitchen table, stacked high with a hundred dreary papers on Hawthorne left to read and grade before the week's end. She whirled around. "You know what? You're acting like a spoiled child. You're a genius, and you cannot write? Alright, then don't, but do not whine to me, do not!"

"And what do you do? Crying when your mood is too black to get out of bed when you cannot sleep. Nightmares about the dead, and you expect me to listen, to hold you, to be there."

"Is it so hard? All that is so hard. For a man without a job to do that. And look at all this I—"

She stopped. Took a breath. Nothing she could say would do anything but make all this worse. She swiped at her face, wet now with tears.

His hand was on the doorknob, and he was leaving. She raced forward, grabbing the back of his coat. He turned and pushed at her, and she flew at him, fingers clawed to scratch his neck. He grabbed her hands, and her thumb bent backward painfully. She screamed and lunged at him again. This time connecting with his skin. She drew blood.

"Stop it, Vivienne. Stop it." He had her by both wrists, and she was sobbing now. "You are drunk. Go to bed. Just go to damn bed." He dabbed at his neck; his fingers came away spotted with blood. "Christ," he said and shook his head at her.

She glared at him. "Don't you leave now. You can't leave now."

He scooped his house key from a small dish by the door, stepped outside, and disappeared into the night. When he was gone, Vivienne picked up her glass and flung it at the back of the door. Then she stood watching as the wine dripped down the glossy white wood and made little pools on the floor among the glittering shards of glass.

CHAPTER 36

FURY
June 1958

1

The narrow hallway was stifling and dimly lit, pressing in on Vivienne as she slipped off her coat and navigated along the wall, searching for an open seat. The size of the crowd caught her off guard. She had assumed that a new translation of *Oedipus the King* would hold limited appeal, perhaps drawing a small literary circle, but certainly not attracting so many locals—especially not so many young people. Yet here they were: professors, a smattering of gray-haired wives blending into the shadows, and, notably, a surprising number of young women. Some wore bobby socks, chinos, and oversized button-downs; others, in sparkling cocktail dresses, looked like children caught playing dress-up, their skinny limbs seeming to belong to someone else's wardrobe.

On stage, she saw Jack. The moment he spotted her, his face registered a fleeting shock, maybe even a hint of dismay, before he forced a thin, almost brittle smile. He looked disheveled, his shirt rumpled and his hair unkempt. His attire—a makeshift cloak from a few yards of fabric paired with a second-hand hat awkwardly fashioned into an Elizabethan cap—might have seemed absurd on another man. But on Jack, with his commanding presence, it managed to work. She knew he had bitterly protested the obligation to perform this reading, and yet here he was, embodying the role with that odd charisma that seemed to carry him through everything.

"Why do it then?" Vivienne had asked.

"Something I agreed to a long time ago," Jack had answered, his tone vague and evasive.

He'd kept up a steady stream of complaints through three days of rehearsals and even this evening, right up to the moment before he left for the performance.

"Just tell them you can't do it; say you'll be out of town," Vivienne had suggested.

But he'd brushed off the idea. "I committed, so I'll have to do it," he'd said, as if that settled it.

Vivienne knew better. Commitment and Jack had a notoriously flexible relationship, and this sudden burst of obligation seemed out of character. She suspected there were other motivations at play. Perhaps he was just flattered at being asked.

They were finishing an early dinner before the performance, overcooked meatloaf and undercooked potatoes, when Vivienne suggested, "So, I'll go over with you, and we can make an evening of it. It's been weeks since we've been out." In truth, she rather dreaded the idea. Mid-week, a late night, especially late in the term. She'd have dozens of papers to grade, and this would only put her farther behind. Still, it was true. They'd done very little socializing together recently, and she thought it might do them good. So, it had come as a shock when he'd shut her down.

"No," he'd responded too quickly. "No, no, I mean. It's not necessary. I'll go alone. You'll be tired. After teaching."

She studied his face. His expression was unreadable. "I always go to your readings. It's fine."

"It'll just make me uncomfortable. It'll be awful, and I'd rather you weren't there to hear it."

She picked up her fork and stabbed at the petrified meatloaf. It emitted a bit of a charcoal smell. Not unpleasant. She looked at him. He didn't look up, just chewed intensely.

"Jack? Is something wrong?"

"God, Vivienne. Please." He dropped his fork and pushed his plate away. "It's nothing. Come on."

It took less and less to annoy Jack. But, of course, she'd been irritable herself. The flat seemed to grow smaller, the town's dimensions flattening out, its color fading.

The burden of Vivienne's teaching position was heavier each week. It had been a mistake for her to take on this full-time position. But she reminded herself, a few more days and it would be over.

"Alright. It's fine," she said.

He relaxed. "I'm sorry. I'm just tense."

What did he have to be tense about? His part-time teaching positions? It seemed to come so easily to him. Teaching creative writing to a small group of twenty-year-old girls. He didn't have to prepare at all, and he enjoyed it. He seemed to have plenty of time for his own work, and he'd been publishing well. Jack's fame, if not their pocketbook, was proliferating. Vivienne was terribly proud of him, but it was hard not to think of the other wives. The 'faculty' wives.

Rumors circulated all the time, and sometimes the stories turned out to be true. For example, the writer who'd asked Jack to do the reading was the one who wound up leaving his wife, or rather whose wife sent him packing after an affair was discovered. The story was so ugly Vivienne had found it difficult to believe at first.

The girlfriend (if that's what she was) showed up one night at the family home, hysterical, drunk, refusing to leave. Making many wild accusations about an affair that the writer denied. He'd done the gentlemanly thing and driven the poor delusional girl home, and everyone thought that was the end. Then, three days later, when the writer's twenty-year-old daughter (herself a college student) reported to the wife that the story was true and everyone on campus knew it was true, the writer finally admitted the error of his ways, fell on his knees and begged forgiveness. The wife told him to get the hell out.

The story would have been a nice one except for the outcome. Within eighteen months of the writer's exile from his house, a judge granted the divorce, including an alimony settlement of almost nothing. The writer moved in with his girlfriend. The daughter moved to another state, and the wife, plagued by loneliness, emotional stress, and financial loss, descended into alcoholism and deep depression. In the end, she vanished from the community. There were rumors the writer had her sent away.

Vivienne rushed through grading her papers, then left everything where it was, snatched her coat off the hook, and flew out the door. She walked swiftly up their alley, taking a shortcut through the park and around the duck pond, the heels of her shoes dropping a full inch into the wet spring grass. She exited the garden through a rusty iron gate and crossed downtown. The shops were already shuttered for the night. Only one other soul was about; an older man in a pale cardigan was walking a dog so small it might have been a kitten or a guinea pig, except that it leaped forward and let out a high-pitched bark as Vivienne passed by. She had an urge to kick at it, but restrained herself. Finally, she reached the campus and walked up Xavier Hill, arriving at the small performance hall where Oedipus readied himself at the Oracle.

2

The performance dragged on, the air in the room growing thick and damp, heavy with the mingling scents of perfumes, colognes, sweat, cigarettes, and spilled wine. A few men smoked pipes, and the dense smoke left Vivienne feeling light-headed. The performance itself was stilted, awkwardly paced, and altogether strange—but not in a compelling way. It was hard to tell if the audience even noticed. Only a handful seemed to pay close attention; the rest whispered, drank, or slouched in their seats. A few couples were so physically entangled that Vivienne marveled at their restraint in not going further, right there in public.

Jack knew it was a disaster. Vivienne could see it in the hard lines of his face, the way his mouth tightened as the night wore on. About a third of the way through, he gave up entirely, resigning himself to the failure. His delivery turned flat, mechanical, every line spoken without rhythm or feeling. It irritated Vivienne deeply—how easily he surrendered to frustration, how petulantly he sulked onstage. Maybe this was why he hadn't wanted her to come.

3

Afterward, Jack failed to come out to find her. She waited a long time, shifting from one foot to the other, sweating uncomfortably in her stockings. The space was crowded. She had to turn sideways to allow people to pass by on their way out. At one point, she was trapped between a husky boy wearing a Yale sweater and the girl he'd either picked up or brought along. The girl swayed into the boy's chest, and he struggled to hold her upright. Finally, someone opened the double doors in front of the room. A blast of night air shot through, cold enough to set Vivienne's teeth chattering. The logjam was relieved; people filed out. Still no Jack.

She gave up waiting and made her way behind the stage. A skinny boy with a cigarette stood in the hall. He directed her to a room around the corner. There was Jack and the rest, draped around an array of ruined furniture. Peter Boris was there (Jack's friend from university) and, of course, the professor who'd asked him to read, along with two other women. One, Vivienne knew, was the girlfriend or maybe wife of the cheating professor, but the younger one, Vivienne had never met. She was a skinny girl who looked not over twenty. She sat beside Jack, who slouched with his eyes closed, on a sofa with seat cushions hammock'd almost to the ground.

"Jack?" Vivienne said.

The girl stiffened and moved away from Jack by a few centimeters.

"Hello," he answered.

His eyes half-lidded, he held up the bottle in his hand, more in gesture than offer. He didn't get up. Vivienne had no choice but to sit down beside him, opposite the skinny girl. She felt the humiliation in her cheeks and turned away to hide her face from the group. Fixing her gaze on Jack, she lay a hand on his leg and squeezed lightly. They needed to go. He ignored her. She squeezed harder. His eyes flew open, and he sat up roughly and removed her hand. She stood. They left in silence and spoke not a word all the way home. It was not until they were in bed that he said anything.

"Look, Viv. I'm sorry. It was a terrible night on stage with those lice. You know I hate that. Hate them. I didn't want you there. Awful."

That wasn't true exactly. The hating part. Jack disliked the cheating professor/writer, but he harbored mixed feelings for Peter Boris. They'd been friends for years. Jack liked Peter, loved him. Peter was a writer, but not as gifted as he imagined he was. Jack liked to say that Peter Boris had enough family money to fill in for his lack of talent. Sometimes, Vivienne knew, Jack resented that. Obviously, this was one of those times.

Vivienne's heart lifted. Perhaps that's all it was. Jack's shame at being roped into appearing. But there was the girl. And why then, the look? The shock and then the lousy, shameful, rancid smile? And why did she feel so betrayed?

4

The plan had been for Jack to pick her up immediately after her last class so they could celebrate the end of a long and grueling school year and Vivienne's 'retirement.' They'd both agreed teaching was much too stressful, and the impact on her writing had been devastating. But, as she emerged from the building and squinted into the sunlight, Jack was nowhere to be found. A few students remained, gathered in clumps of two and three, some heading off alone in various directions. Otherwise, the campus was already eerily muted. Vivienne waited a few minutes and then headed off toward the faculty parking lot. Perhaps Jack had fallen asleep in the car and lost track of time.

She found the car and peeked in, but no Jack. Checked her watch. He was now twenty minutes late. The day was warm. A light breeze pushed at the silk scarf she wore and brushed at her hair. It was a lovely day for a walk. Maybe Jack had gone to drop off the library books before picking her up. There was a brick walkway leading from the parking lot to the library. About halfway along, it split in two; the left fork, lined with boxwood and maintained by the college, headed up to the main library and north campus, while the right fork withered to a narrow footpath which cut across the lush grass and led over a low hill and down to Paradise Pond. Thick with flowering trees, secluded and plenty distant from prying eyes, the pond was a well-known hideaway for students exploring the more romantic aspects of undergraduate life.

As Vivienne reached this halfway point, she stopped and took a moment to catch her breath. The day had grown warmer. Her heart thumped, and her bags felt heavy. She wished she'd left her briefcase in the car. She reached up and rubbed at the back of her neck, now sticky with sweat. Her mouth was dry, and her throat scratchy. She'd find a drinking fountain nearer the library. Damn Jack, he should have been there. She rechecked her watch. How could he have missed the time by so much? They'd been planning this; they'd been eager about it for weeks. She'd suffered the entire year of teaching for him. So, he could write, for God's sake. Today was her big 'hurrah!'

Suddenly, she saw him. Or rather, her eyes saw both, but her brain refused to register the information. Instead, she stood frozen, trying to comprehend. It wasn't until the girl—a successful, bosomy, tanned girl with round, dark eyes, and thickish legs that dropped like small tree trunks out of her khaki shorts—made a sort of animal 'wheek!' sound that Vivienne shook herself out of her stupor and took another step towards them. The girl skittered away almost immediately, and Jack did not stop her. What was happening, or rather, what had happened, was clear.

Her husband had just come up the road from Paradise Pond—from that spot at Paradise Pond with a very young woman. And he'd not been simply with a young woman the way one might be with one's mother or with one's best friend. Jack had been with her (leaning in, grinning luridly, gesturing with hands flying a little too closely) the way one would be with a pretty girl who is not one's wife and who one should most assuredly not be with at all. And she, the girl, star-struck, face up-tilted, eyes wide, giggling. Then, the abrupt and shameful change upon seeing Vivienne. The wife. And again, the look on Jack's face. His smile had been fatuous, seeking more than approval. He wanted validation, admiration. He wanted goddamn worship.

Jack was talking, but Vivienne couldn't hear him. The voice in her head was too loud.

They went home, and Jack kept talking. Excuses. Explanations. She's a friend. She's a student. She's an ex-student. She's a friend of an ex-student. I didn't know I'd run into her. I felt obligated to share a glass of wine. They'd brought a bottle along.

"They?"

"Yes, there were two, but one of them left earlier."

Christ, it was even worse than it looked.

Vivienne retreated to the voice in her head. The terrible roaring sound, as all around her, brick by brick, the house she'd so carefully built came tumbling down.

5

They'd fought. Or rather, Vivienne had fought. She'd drawn blood, left claw marks on his face. She'd thrown a glass which ricocheted off the wall, bouncing back to bang her in the forehead, leaving a half-dollar mark, the color of an overripe plum.

"A sham," she'd called him, "full of cheap vanity and foul dishonesty." He'd called her mad, jealous, and turned away. Then came the brutal silence, thickening the air and resting in the bed between them during the night.

The next day, Mother called. Vivienne picked up the phone in the kitchen, leaning against the wall in the cloudy, sticky morning. She studied the dishes and greasy pans which overflowed the sink. She'd barely begun on the laundry leftover from the week before.

"You sound tired, Viv," said Mother.

"Probably because I am tired, Mother."

"Vivienne?" Mother's voice wavered slightly. "What's happened?"

With that, Vivienne's rage exploded, and the story came tumbling out, words spilling over, words as if in a race to escape from her mouth. All about Jack's lousy look when she surprised him at the Oedipus reading, the bosomy girl with the enormous eyes and khaki shorts at the college, Jack's vanity, and the foul lie of their marriage. When she was finished, there was a long silence while Vivienne reeled with thoughts of how she would repair the catastrophic damage she'd just wrought. Shit, shit, shit.

Then, bizarrely, Mother said, slowly, gently, as if she might speak to an extremely young or remarkably stupid child, "Vivienne, isn't it possible you've been under a lot of stress? Teaching full time, keeping house and everything. Do you think you might have overreacted a bit? You know how much Jack loves you."

Vivienne was stunned to silence. Could this be right? She thought. No, a nagging voice in her head reminded her of the truth she'd seen with her eyes. Jack wanted her to feel crazy because it was easier than admitting his own guilt. He wanted her to doubt herself so he wouldn't have to confront his own lies and the terrible betrayal. But did he feel guilty? Vivienne doubted it. Thinking about the way he'd smirked when he'd been with that girl and the way every fight was twisted and left her feeling like she was losing her mind.

Then again, she loved him, and he loved her, didn't he? Of course he did. Mother had just reminded her.

Vivienne watched the water leak from the kitchen faucet. Fat droplets ballooned in slow motion, hanging at the spigot like sailors clinging to the side of a sinking battleship. She squeezed her eyes shut, opened them, then put the phone back on the receiver without saying goodbye. Mother was probably right, she thought as all her rage turned inward, where it alighted on her mind and lay there, unmoving, like a dead black crow.

CHAPTER 37

LORELEI
Fall 1958

1

Mrs. Carol Cahen was in her late thirties, an attractive woman with a shapely figure and frosted blonde hair. When she took off her sunglasses, Vivienne noticed her eyes were heavily made up with bright blue shadow, black liner drawn out to her temples, and false lashes. Mrs. Cahen wore a beautiful, expensive-looking cashmere sweater, and a skirt made of a silky material. However, her stockings and skirt appeared to be worn backward, with the zipper running straight down her belly and the stocking seams running up her shins. Vivienne decided it was best not to mention the fashion faux pas.

"Morning, Mrs. Cahen," said Vivienne, but the woman didn't seem to hear her. Instead, she stood at the desk, her eyes darting around the room. Mrs. Cahen was a regular at the clinic, coming in several times a week to see her psychiatrist. Vivienne wasn't unnerved by her appearance but found her agitated demeanor unusual. She leaned forward.

"Mrs. Cahen? Are you alright?"

"It's them," Mrs. Cahen said.

"Them?"

"Yes, of course. It's them." Her eyes flicked up and to the left. She took a few steps closer to the reception desk, and Vivienne caught the potent smell of an unwashed human body.

"Who is them?" asked Vivienne, following Mrs. Cahen's glance up to the empty corner.

"No," said Mrs. Cahen. "Not them. Them." Her eyes flicked upward again in the same direction. She jerked her chin up and then down.

This time Vivienne kept her gaze still, staring at Mrs. Cahen. She nodded. "I see," she said, although, of course, she saw nothing at all.

Mrs. Cahen nodded and raised her eyebrows. "Do you see? I knew it."

"You knew what, Mrs. Cahen?"

"I've been telling them all, all these men. I've been saying it and saying it."

"You've been saying what?"

Mrs. Cahen rolled her eyes. "I've been telling them who is responsible for this. But you already know." Again, her eyes moved up and to the left. "You know who did this to me?"

Vivienne shook her head, and Mrs. Cahen waved her hands up and down her body as if to show what had been done to her.

"None of them can understand, but you know, don't you? You know why."

"Why?"

Vivienne thought she was probably pushing her luck having an extended conversation with Mrs. Cahen, but curiosity had gotten the better of her.

"Because—" the agitated woman began and then stopped, jerking her head to the right as if listening to someone. Her eyes grew wide. She nodded a few times. Then, after a few moments, she said, "Ok, ok, I know. I won't."

Then she reached out to pat Vivienne's hand. Her small hands were grimy and streaked with dirt. Remnants of coral-colored polish flecked a few of her nails. A pale band of skin ringed her fourth finger. She no longer wore the wedding ring.

The nurse appeared. "Carol Cahen? Hello, Mrs. Cahen, come with me, please."

Mrs. Cahen leaned over the desk, her eyes very focused. She cupped a hand around her mouth and whispered, "That's not my name. I'm not

Carol; I'm Lorelei. Don't tell anyone." Then she straightened up, winked, smiled, and went to join the nurse.

Vivienne watched as the nurse took Mrs. Cahen down the short hall leading to the psychiatrist's office, and they disappeared behind the office door. She resumed typing her report, her thoughts lingering on the unsettling encounter.

2

Although Jack had often asserted that he *would never work for someone else to earn cash to keep alive, to keep working for someone else,* it had been his idea that Vivienne apply for the job at Boston Hospital. Not that Jack expected Vivienne to take on a job either. He didn't care if they ever had any security, financial or otherwise; he hadn't married her expecting he would provide it, nor had he hoped she would. However, he was aware of her rising level of panic over their fragile financial situation. Her $1400 Saxon prize and the little money they were earning with occasional publications left them with no reserves and close to broke almost monthly.

"So, get a job if you can't stand it," he said one evening, not without sympathy in his voice. He understood how emotionally tricky living on the financial edge was for her. He added, "But, Viv, don't do it unless you want to. It's only a suggestion. We'll be fine either way, darling. We'll sort it."

It was that last bit, "we'll sort it," that drove her to apply. Vivienne knew she was not a "we'll sort it" kind of person. The phrase was so fraught with lazy resignation, it lacked even hopefulness. She could not, would not, sit around and wait for things to be magically sorted. So, she'd applied for a job on the psychiatric ward typing up patient transcripts for a group of inpatient psychiatrists. By mid-autumn, she was working half-days typing transcripts on the same ward to which she'd been admitted after her suicide attempt in 1953. That fact went unmentioned, and nobody at the hospital ever became aware, so far as she knew.

The job turned out to be a welcome respite from the unstructured monotony of Vivienne's days. It provided a structured routine that she desperately needed and a sense of purpose that had been lacking. The work itself was interesting and intellectually stimulating, and the endless stream of fascinating patient histories was grist for her creative mill. And, of course, while working as a clerk at Boston Hospital, Vivienne met Mrs. Carol Cahen, aka Lorelei, and it was Lorelei who would help Vivienne see the world in an entirely new light.

CHAPTER 38

RUTHIE
Late Summer 1958

Looking back, it might have been the Anderson interview. Do you know about that? Probably not. Anyway, I think it changed Vivienne. She and Jack moved out to Boston in the summer of 1958, right after she'd completed her teaching contract at Talbot. Right around that time, Lee Anderson took an interest in her. He asked her to record some poems for the Library of Congress, quite an accomplishment for a twenty-five-year-old, relatively unknown poet—especially a woman. Then, just weeks later, she was invited to record for Harvard's Poetry Room, a real kick in the pants since women could not even visit the poetry room in those days. Anyway, in the recorded interviews, Vivienne talked about her own style, her writing philosophy. She was asked serious questions; she was being taken seriously as a writer, as an artist. I think all of that empowered her to separate her work from her marriage.

Jack had these obsessive exercises he made her do and constantly questioned her: "What are you doing? What are you working on?" He gave her conflicting instructions: "Read only Shakespeare, read no Shakespeare, read for an hour straight through, read for three hours but only fifteen minutes at a stretch." But after the Anderson interviews and the Harvard experience, Vivienne started writing on her own and keeping more of her work to herself.

Later that summer, probably in August, one of her best poems was published in The New Yorker. It spanned two glossy pages at the front of the magazine. Vivienne was stunned when she saw it. Don't get me wrong—she knew how good she was, and that this poem was exceptional—but still, The New Yorker!

When I visited her, I was delighted. She looked more like her old self— happy and active. And writing the hell out of everything. She had also applied for a job at the psychiatric hospital, which I only found out about later. That was a curious thing for her to do. And ultimately not a helpful thing. But then, Vivienne always had secrets.

CHAPTER 39

SIREN SONG
October 1958

1

Suicide off the rocks wasn't unusual. People jumped into the sea all the time. Vivienne rather admired cliff jumping to end one's life and thought the frequency of it made sense. But the time of year made this instance unusual. It wasn't summer anymore, but not quite the holiday season either. Who ever heard of killing yourself in October?

If Vivienne hadn't been assigned the responsibility of records disposition for the clinic, she might never have known. Her job was to transport papers of all kinds, from the clinic to various destinations throughout the hospital. One day, she arrived at work to find a patient's chart, a green cardboard folder, on her desk, secured by a thick rubber band with a hand-scrawled note on top: SEND TO RECORDS. Ensuring nobody was around to see what she was doing, Vivienne carefully removed the band and opened the folder.

Vivienne's breath caught in her throat, and she felt bile rise in her mouth. She stared at the word, her mind racing. "Deceased," stamped in red block print across the first page. She whispered the word aloud, as if saying it might somehow make it less real. But the reality of it hit her like a punch to the gut. Her hands trembled as she clutched the folder, and she felt a cold sweat break out on her forehead. The room seemed to spin around her, and for a moment, she thought she might faint.

She took a deep breath, trying to steady herself. The stark finality of the word echoed in her mind. Questions flooded her thoughts—how had this happened? When? Why? The bile in her throat made her gag, and she quickly covered her mouth, swallowing hard to keep it down. The reality of the patient's death, someone she had perhaps seen or interacted with, was overwhelming.

The details noted were brief. Vivienne had not been asked to type this note. Following the patient's date of birth, date of death, and identifying information, there was one sentence:

MRS. CAROL CAHEN, AGE 39, DIAGNOSED WITH NEUROTIC PSYCHOSIS, IS NOW DECEASED, DEATH RULED BY THE CORONER AS SUICIDE, AFTER FALLING FROM A CLIFF AT EGG ROCK.

Vivienne closed the folder with trembling hands and re-secured the rubber band. She sat back in her chair, staring blankly at the desk in front of her. The weight of the discovery pressed heavily on her, and she struggled to compose herself.

She thought about Mrs. Cahen. The last time she'd been at the clinic. Her smile and her wink. The woman had known then what she was going to do. She'd already decided. Something had happened, or she believed something had happened. She'd been betrayed, and she'd made had a plan. Had she almost told Vivienne about it? Maybe.

"That's not my name. I'm not Carol; I'm Lorelei. Don't tell anyone." Carol aspired to be like Heinrich Heine's beautiful maiden who, in despair over her lover's betrayal, threw herself into the Rhine and was transformed into a siren who lured men to their destruction—Lorelei.

Vivienne smiled to herself as it all made sense. Carol Cahen was psychotic, yes, but she'd made a choice, perhaps the better choice. To trade a life of drugs, doctors, and delusions for eternity as a beautiful siren on a rock luring boatmen to destruction. Vivienne recalled the last lines of Heine's one hundred forty-year-old poem:

I fear that the boat and her master
Will slip under the waves before long
And what brought about this disaster?
The Lorelei's siren song.

Vivienne could have asked for more information about Carol Cahen's death. One of the nurses would have told her. She could have asked, but she already knew the entire story, and when she got home, she wrote it down.

2

There was a woman who slept beside her husband every night, dreaming of another world, a watery place she had seen once as a child, where everything she knew did not exist. Each night, as she let down her hair and slipped into her nightgown, she thought the dream might become real. But every morning, she woke up, and things were the same. She had to decide if she could go on, if she could do all the tasks the day ahead required of her. She would glance at her sleeping husband, take a deep breath, and decide to get out of bed.

Until one morning, she opened her eyes and found that looking at her husband wasn't enough to inspire her to get up. Instead, she swam down into the dream's blue water-mist and decided to never come back.

CHAPTER 40

MOTHER
December 1958

Around that time, Vivienne was angry with me. I know I kept on about Jack getting a job, but honestly, I think Viv's rage had more to do with that doctor she was seeing.

Christmas hadn't gone well. It was disappointing for all of us, but I think for Vivienne it was a disaster. She'd wanted something very New England: a roaring fire, lots of family, a huge roast duck, and big snow outside. It was odd because she swore to me she had those memories—white Christmases and all the people and meals before Fritz died—but it's not true. Fritz would never have allowed it. He hated noise, crowds, and especially hated an American display of excess. He considered it vulgar. We had a small tree, a few gifts. Nothing over the top. And the snow? I can't tell you the last time we had an actual white Christmas in Winthrop, but certainly not in Vivienne's first eight years. So, her memory was a complete fantasy. I think for Vivienne, memories were a mishmash of wishes and imagination. Perhaps it's that way for all of us, but for Viv, the intensity was so much greater. She could conjure these stories and convince herself and everyone else they were facts. In retrospect, I think she needed them to be true.

I think she came to Christmas in 1958 with all that in place: her absolute conviction in the reality of her memory, her expectations, and she brought along whatever she'd been brewing up with her analyst, that awful Dr. B.. So, it was a sour mix.

Anyway, they arrived early in the afternoon, she and Jack. They seemed tense, not all that surprising. Jack had developed an obvious distaste for these family events. No doubt he felt the unspoken criticism about his not having regular work and so on. Vivienne was already buzzing, trying to take the focus off Jack. He was morose, muted, withdrawn. Came in with his head down, carrying a few packages, and went straight into the kitchen to make himself a drink. Vivienne was rushing back and forth as if we were having dinner for twelve instead of just Beanie and me besides the two of them. You'd have thought the queen was coming. I remember Vivienne wore her black velvet. She looked lovely. But such a formal dress—not at all suitable for cooking—and Jack in his usual rumpled slacks, although he'd cut and combed his hair and had on a neat shirt. It just struck me as odd, the pair of them together.

We spent the afternoon cooking and chatting. Jack and Beanie had drinks in the living room; I could hear much of the conversation, sounding strained. They never got on particularly well. But we got through it.

At dinner, Vivienne was in constant motion, talking an absolute mile a minute—she was difficult to follow, even for me. She was constantly jumping up to check on something. The kitchen door never stopped swinging; it made this terrible squeaking sound throughout dinner. She was escalating. If she wasn't rushing back and forth, she was spooning food onto Jack's plate as if he were a child. "Oh, try this and have some more of that," she kept repeating. Really awkward. Both Beanie and I noticed Jack's annoyance, but Vivienne seemed oblivious.

Suddenly, about halfway through dessert, as Vivienne was speaking rapidly and attempting to put a second piece of cake on his plate, Jack raised his fist and slammed it down on the table so hard the wine glasses rattled, and Beanie's fork literally shot out of his hand, leaving bits of chocolate frosting all over his new button-down. My son is quite gentle, and such behavior shocked him. Even though he'd seen some of Jack's more aggressive verbal outbursts, he'd seen nothing like that. None of us knew what to do. We just stared at Jack, who stared at Vivienne, who was looking straight down into her plate. Then Jack pulled his napkin out of his lap, placed it carefully on the table, pushed out his chair, and got up. He thanked me for the meal and said he would take a walk. And he left.

It was all so strange. First, the three of us were left there in this extraordinary silence. Then, almost immediately, Vivienne looked at me, shrugged, then got up and cleared the table as if nothing had happened. There's Beanie, mind you, with cake all over his shirt.

So, my son asked me if he should go after Jack, and I told him no. I don't know if that was a mistake, but I thought it might cause a terrible fight. But I guess I was just trying to protect my boy. So, anyway, I sent Beanie into the living room and followed Vivienne into the kitchen, and there she was standing over the sink, not really moving.

"Vivienne," I said. "Viv, what's going on?"

She said nothing. Didn't even turn around, so I tried again.

"Viv, please, I'm so terribly worried about you. What is it?"

When she turned around, I could see she'd disappeared a little. Her eyes were hard, like flint.

"I need you to stop worrying, Mother, just stop. The worry makes everything worse. I'm fine. Jack's fine." Then she looked at me with this coldness. I'd never seen it in Vivienne before. "He's not Daddy, okay? And I am not you. This is not your life, Mother. It's mine."

Her words stung badly, and I felt helpless. Viv was my daughter; we'd been close, or I thought we'd been close, and here she was telling me I was part of the problem. I blame myself now, you know, for everything else that happened. I didn't understand how to reach her then. I didn't understand her pain.

After that, she wouldn't talk about it. It was as if Jack's explosion had given me a glimpse inside their marriage, and Viv couldn't tolerate that. She hadn't wanted me to see it, and she responded by retreating even farther into herself. Deeper into her life with Jack.

We finished clearing the dishes and washed them and tidied up. She wasn't angry, and neither was I, but there was a terrible sadness in the kitchen. We'd carried this thing between us for such a long time, and now it was broken, and it wouldn't be put right again. It felt like we'd put the shattered pieces of this precious thing away in a cupboard, out of sight, and just go on without it.

CHAPTER 41

SESSIONS
5th January 1959

Should I tell you about the holiday?

Would you like to tell me about your holiday?

You know, is it always going to be like this?

Like what, Vivienne?

Like this. These long silences and you waiting for me to sort out what I'm supposed to say?

Is that what you think? That I'm waiting for you to sort something out?

Oh, for God's sake. Of course, you are waiting. What else would you be doing sitting there in your wildly expensive chair with that half-smile as unreadable as a damn cat?

Do you find me unreadable?

No, I don't find you unreadable, Dr. B.. You simply are unreadable, and I am confident it's intentional. They teach you that in psychiatrist school, do they not?

Vivienne?

Yes?

You're frustrated with the boundary between us. It seems more intense today than usual.

I don't even know why I'm here. I should never have come. I'll just go.

You are here, I presume, because you wanted to restart your analysis, and you wanted to do that because you had more to bring to the surface.

Hm. I am not frustrated with boundaries. I've always thought of myself as a person very much in favor of boundaries. I am particularly fond of fences. I also like walls, nice thick ones. Brick or concrete. I don't like gates much.

No, I don't think so.

And what is that supposed to mean?

What do you think it means?

Oh, for God's sake. Forget it. Okay, I'm going to tell you all about my holiday.

CHAPTER 42

DR. B.
January 1959

That January, when she returned to my office for therapy, she didn't appear depressed, but she looked pale and terribly thin, as if she had been ill. I asked her if she'd been sick, and she said she had. She'd been to the doctor, had x-rays, and been on various medications. But despite everything, she wrote quite a lot. And what she'd written, while not the exquisite work of her later years, was nevertheless astonishing and certainly indicative of what was to come.

So, no, not depressed but not happy exactly. But happy wasn't really Vivienne's natural state. She was much too intense for that. I would say her baseline, her most favorable state, was rather like an extraordinarily rare violin, you know, perfectly tuned. Taut, untouchable. Anyway, she wasn't really there either. She was tired, slowed down mentally as well as physically. She'd had terrible dreams. Quite violent. About death and deformity. But mostly, she didn't want to talk about her dreams. She also wouldn't discuss her marriage. She only wanted to talk about her mother. She'd had an epiphany, but not in a good way. At least I didn't think so.

Looking back on it now, I think that was a crossroads for Vivienne. She had her career and Jack on the one hand and her friends and, to some extent, her family (mother, brother, grandparents, and so on) on the other. She was thinking those groups were mutually exclusive. So, the world she was constructing was perilous, and I don't think I saw that at the time. The violent dreams might have been manifestations of her unconscious struggles, but more likely were related to her chaotic relationship with Jack. She was fragile, teetering between creative brilliance and total mental collapse, and I just couldn't see it. I did not have all the facts. But, of course, you know what they say about hindsight. Even psychiatrists don't have crystal balls.

CHAPTER 43

INFAMOUS SUICIDE
Spring 1959

1

Jack and Vivienne walked along the footpath through the cemetery. It was a calm spring day. The sun shone softly, a few clouds hung motionless in the pale blue sky, and the temperature was ideal for a walk. The azaleas were in bloom, their orange, and fuchsia blossoms lining the path. But as they neared the entrance to the last of the three graveyards, the flowers became sparse and then disappeared altogether, as the gravestones crowded more closely together. The graves here were packed, head to foot, so tight that it reminded Vivienne of men sleeping in a poorhouse; there was no room to spread out. It was depressing.

Frederick's marker was a worn, flat stone just beside the path. Small and easy to overlook, it had likely been stepped on or over thousands of times since his burial. Anger swelled in Vivienne's chest as thoughts of her mother surged up. Tears pricked her eyes, and she wiped them away with the heels of her hands. She stooped, pushing aside a few dry weeds, and read the inscription:

Frederick E. Holland: 1885-1940

The letters were chipped and worn, barely visible in the dim light. Beside his grave, someone had left a cheap bouquet of plastic daisies on the neighboring marker. The red dye had faded and streaked, leaving the flowers a splotchy pale pink, the color bleeding into the weedy ground below.

Vivienne felt cheated. Her grief and frustration twisted together. She wanted to dig him up just to prove he was truly dead, to confront the reality lying beneath that neglected stone.

He died like any man. That's what Mother said, twenty years ago. No successful death. Just like any man. And now he lay in this grave, like any man, or what remained of him, anyway. Crowded with the others, six feet of gravel over the top of the grave. And here she was, banging on Daddy's door now for what? Forgiveness? Love? No, that wasn't it. She wasn't here for love, not anymore. But there was something.

Vivienne recalled a day from her childhood, a day when she was six or seven, when she and her father had gone to see the bees. They'd been at the hive for hours. Fritz, absorbed in his work, had forgotten about her entirely, and she had grown bored. Wandering away, she started poking her fingers into various pots and nets, exploring places she'd been explicitly told to avoid. Then, all at once, there was a tremendous crash. Her memory splintered at that point—glass shattering, Fritz's frantic scream, his face looming over her, red and furious. She felt his large hand clamp around her arm, squeezing so hard it hurt. His yelling seemed endless, and eventually, she closed her eyes, exhausted. Then, nothing. Only silence.

"So, what am I supposed to do, Jack? The bastard did this to himself, you know that. Slow suicide by refusing to see a doctor. He had children, for Christ's sake. He didn't care. Or maybe that's why." Her voice wavered. "I loved him, and he did this, and I've wanted him to forgive me all this time. For what? For what?"

Jack didn't reply. He only held her, his presence a steady reassurance. Vivienne knew he understood. They walked on in silence, following the curve of the ocean's edge toward the breakwater and onto the peninsula. She stopped and watched as Jack continued, his figure a dark silhouette against the gray sea, his black trousers and long coat blending with the misty horizon, the waves rolling in all around him.

2

The poet Vivienne had longed to meet stood outside the lecture hall, a cigarette held delicately between her fingers. She was a tall, lean figure, dressed in pale gray trousers and a crisp white button-down blouse. Her short, dark hair was swept back from her face, emphasizing her striking, angular features. Vivienne approached, clutching her book bag to her chest, feeling almost childlike beside this effortlessly elegant woman. Rachel Lee stared back at her, unapologetic and unflinching. She had enormous blue eyes—so pale they were nearly silver—framed by dark, arched eyebrows, full lips, and perfectly proportioned cheekbones.

Vivienne had wavered about attending the seminar. While she greatly admired Richard Larson, especially his latest book of confessional poetry, she wasn't certain she could spare the time. But once she heard that Rachel Lee would be there, her decision was clear. And now, here she was, standing face-to-face with the woman whose work had fascinated her for years.

"Yes?" Rachel said.

"Hello," Vivienne replied.

"I'm Rachel," the woman introduced herself, extending the hand not holding the cigarette. She wore no polish, no rings, no jewelry at all.

"I'm Vivienne," Vivienne responded, awkwardly taking her hand. Rachel's handshake was firm and warm, even with her left hand.

Rachel nodded. "Good, successful. He's a bit of a nut, you know?"

Her eyes were smiling, although her mouth was now hooked around the cigarette. Was this a joke?

"Uh," Vivienne said, feeling stupid.

Rachel laughed, blowing a delicate stream of smoke toward the sky. Even her tobacco smoke seemed beautiful.

"Kidding. I mean, he is a nut, but who cares? Aren't we all?"

Vivienne supposed they were. Lee, Larson, and Vivienne had all been in mental hospitals, all attempted suicide, had been administered shock therapy, and had been diagnosed with this or that terrible psychiatric ailment. Richard Larson's history as a patient at Boston's best mental institutions was nearly legendary. He'd been treated more times than most could count, admitted for bouts of catatonic depression or wild, uncontrollable mania. This, coupled with his family's blue-blood background ("The Larson family business is Harvard"), made for excellent Boston gossip.

"Sure," Vivienne agreed, adding, "I admire your work."

God, she sounded like a child.

"Likewise," Rachel replied. Vivienne was shocked. Had this woman read any of her work? It didn't seem possible. Or maybe?

"Time to go," Rachel said, dropping the cigarette and stubbing it out under the toe of her black ballet flat. As she gathered her bags, Vivienne noted she smelled like eucalyptus and peppermint.

3

Ten students sat around the seminar table. By then, in his early forties, Larson, with graying hair and round spectacles, mainly spoke in shy whispers as he read poetry and spoke, often extemporaneously, to the group. He assigned exercises that the students completed, and sometimes he read aloud. Other times, the students read their work to one another. Rachel, who wrote exquisite poetry, was fearless in her readings. Vivienne, too, read her work and braved the criticism, but she was not as fearless as Rachel. She could not yet pour her confessions into her poems or write with the raw truth she found in Larson's and Lee's work. Instead, she wrote and read in class about myth and nature, and metaphor. Larson could be scathing or lovely, depending on his mood, and most of the time, Vivienne was terrified. Still, she loved the meetings.

Occasionally, there were classes during which almost no literary work happened at all. Instead, Larson sat quietly smoking, staring out the window, speaking, if at all, only to himself, with his words making very little sense. Or, as on one occasion, he came in raging, ranting about the establishment, the formalism of New England poetry, the obscurity of a student's work. "What does this poem mean?" he would ask, shaking the paper. "Someone tell me what it means!"

The worst day, the last day, came at the end of June.

As the first arrivals entered the lecture room, they found Larson slumped at the conference table, chin to chest, hair falling forward over his face, thin hands limp in his lap. At first, it appeared he might be dead—a not unreasonable conclusion given his age, poor health, and previous suicide attempts. One of the women screamed. One of the men gagged and ran out of the room. It was Rachel who quietly approached him and touched his shoulder.

She glanced back at the others and rolled her eyes. "He's not dead, you bunch of babies." She pushed at him a little more firmly. He jerked. "Richard," she said. "Richard, wake up." She leaned down and spoke sharply into his ear, "Richard!"

He startled, legs kicking out, one arm flying up. Rachel had to jump back to avoid being hit.

"Jesus, wha—" he mumbled. "What, what?"

He blinked several times and looked around. Eight faces stared at him: eyes huge. Nobody said a word. Larson straightened himself, looked down at his rumpled clothing, smoothed his shirt, and ran his hands through his hair.

"Ah, right, well, no matter. Sit. Sit down." He made fluttering motions with his hands, showing they should take their seats, but he still looked at them as if they were the ones who had been found sleeping. He looked terrible—skin greenish, lavender circles beneath his eyes. He'd lost weight, which was obvious now without his usual jacket. His collarbones were too pronounced.

Everyone took a seat. A latecomer, a young man with the build of a football player, rushed in, breathless, cheeks healthily pinked by the spring air. He stopped, clearly aware of the tension in the room but having missed the precipitating events. He was confused. Larson held out a hand toward an empty chair. "Have a seat," he said. The young man sat, looking wary, and set his books on the table. Had he done something wrong?

"Well," began Larson, "it's a day. A truly awful day."

Vivienne caught a questioning glance from Rachel. Vivienne shrugged.

Larson sat silently, looking around the table, meeting each gaze with a quizzical and expectant look. Nobody had any idea what to do. Finally, after a while, the professor got up, picked up a sheet of paper folded in half on the table, and moved to the partly open window overlooking Commonwealth Avenue. He pulled a crumpled cigarette pack and lighter from his shirt pocket, tapped one out, put the pack on the sill, lit the cigarette, and laid the lighter back on the sill beside the pack. As he smoked, they all watched, petrified. He planned to fling himself out the window. Outside, the sounds of traffic drifted in. Vivienne wondered if it was possible to survive a fall from this height. Perhaps. But only if one managed not to be hit by a car as well. Then she wondered if they could somehow coordinate a rush on the old man, all at once, swoop in and save him from himself before he jumped. She looked around at her compatriots. Except for the football player and maybe Rachel, they were a pale, somewhat undernourished-looking group, as writers tend to be. It didn't seem likely they could save anybody, much less a suicidal maniac.

They all continued to sit. The day flowed by. Bright sunlight streamed over the transom above Larson's head. It formed a bizarre halo around his thick corona of hair. He sat with one foot on the floor, one knee bent, leg swinging rhythmically, and he smoked and looked out.

"You'll all promise me never to write a single ragged line, or I'll be shamed as a teacher," he said finally, without turning around.

He kept staring out the window. A lock of his hair moved in the breeze. The ash of his cigarette dropped to his pant leg. He didn't notice.

"I've not been able to see any of you much outside of the classroom recently. I've been spending most of my time with my psychiatrist." He spoke as if he were talking to himself, almost mumbling. And again, he did not turn around.

Vivienne decided he was planning to jump. They had to do something. The room smelled like sweat, cigarette smoke, and chalk. Nearly everyone was smoking now. Three of the men were using their shoes as ashtrays.

"Richard?" said Rachel, but she didn't move. It seemed somehow inappropriate, even rude, to move.

Ignoring her, Larson picked up the paper he'd carried over to the window, unfolded it, and slowly read, "I am the queen of all my sins... Once I was beautiful..."

When he was done, he looked up, appearing surprised to find them still there. He nodded once at Rachel, whose stunning poem he had just finished reading, folded the paper, laid it on the sill, stood up, and walked out.

No one moved for another minute, and then, the seminar apparently over, the students dispersed as quietly as if they were leaving a funeral.

That night at her desk, Vivienne recalled Larson's words: "Never to write a single ragged line." She thought about her father's grave, the bleak, flat stone marking it, and her anger at what he'd done. Fearlessly, she wrote: "I lost him once to an infamous suicide..."

When the poem was finished, Vivienne knew she had broken through. After that, she would never again be afraid to reveal herself in her writing.

It would be another week before Vivienne would find out that Richard Larson had driven himself directly from the lecture room to the hospital that day and checked himself in. Larson would remain in the hospital under psychiatric care for nearly three months.

CHAPTER 44

BLUE CREEK
Summer 1959

1

It was Rachel who talked them into Blue Creek, the writer's colony up in upstate New York. She insisted it would be the perfect place for Vivienne to clear her mind of all the domestic nonsense, to shed the burden of trying to be everything to everyone, and to simply write. This advice came from none other than *Rachel Lee*, whose deeply personal, confessional poetry had already gained traction—at least within her literary circle.

Rachel, though, was hardly a picture of stability. She lived apart from her two children, drank excessively, and had, by her own admission, attempted suicide twice. Rachel Lee, the woman whom conservative critics had labeled "an abuser of the English language," was the one urging Vivienne to take the plunge. And to Vivienne, it sounded like a grand idea.

Jack was not so sure.

Vivienne and Rachel had begun meeting weekly for drinks after the Richard Larson seminar. Over those Manhattans, it was Rachel who casually mentioned Richard's commitment to Boston Hospital. Vivienne wasn't exactly shocked by the revelation, but she found it intriguing. Rachel, it turned out, had a knack for knowing things about people—secrets, really—and seemed bound by no particular loyalty.

"I've been around a long time, Vivienne," Rachel said with a knowing smirk.

Vivienne wasn't sure how to interpret this, as Rachel couldn't have been more than thirty, but she nodded and made a mental note to tread carefully when sharing her own secrets.

The Manhattans they drank were marvelous, and Vivienne quickly decided it would be her signature drink. Unfortunately, they were also outrageously expensive, so she limited herself to one, which she sipped with reverence, as though each drop were liquid gold—unless Rachel was buying. When Rachel paid, Vivienne drank as many as her new companion, which was quite a few.

They weren't friends, exactly. Vivienne doubted Rachel had any friends in the conventional sense. They were more like accomplices. They smoked and drank in the middle of the afternoon, cursed freely, and talked about art, death, and the looming specter of the asylum. It all felt strange, almost otherworldly, as if she were meeting a member of another species and discovering, disconcertingly, that she, too, belonged to it. There was comfort in the companionship, even if it wasn't entirely welcome. Perhaps ignorance of this shared darkness might have been preferable, though Vivienne wasn't sure.

Rachel certainly wasn't one to coddle. Hugs and reassurances were foreign to her; instead, she would remark, "You can always kill yourself," with the same indifferent tone someone else might say, "You can always try the salad."

Yet, surprisingly, Vivienne didn't find her depressing. In fact, she found her inspirational. Rachel Lee had managed, thus far, to hold onto herself while producing brilliant, published work. She had a family and children as well. True, she was living apart from them temporarily, but Vivienne was certain that would resolve itself soon. Rachel would make it right. How could she not?

2

At Blue Creek, Vivienne, and Jack lived in separate quarters. For six weeks during the fall of 1959, Jack had a small cabin in the wooded area beyond the main camp, while Vivienne stayed in a large room with a bath at the top of the main house. For six hours each day, they wrote, read, or napped. Their meals were brought to them, and besides writing, enjoying an evening meal, and conversing with the group, they had no responsibilities. It was heaven; Rachel had been right.

After they'd been at the camp for about two weeks, Vivienne felt ill. Vomiting frequently, she felt drained and dizzy at times. When her breasts grew tender, she knew. For the next few weeks, she held on to the secret like a pearl in her pocket. She told no one, not even Jack. The knowledge made her smile at the strangest times—over tea with another member, alone in the forest on a walk, even in the middle of reading aloud to the group.

She decided she would tell Jack when they got back home. Until then, this was for her. She wrote almost nothing during the last weeks at Blue Creek. Instead, she read, napped, walked, and dreamed. For a while, everything was perfect, and it seemed she might very well have it all.

CHAPTER 45

DR. B.
Summer 1959

Vivienne always planned on having children. She once told me it wasn't about when she would have a baby, but that she would have one—that was what mattered. I think that desire was one of the things that drew her to me. By the middle of 1959, I was in my early thirties and already had three children. She admired the idea of balancing a family and a career, "doing it all." What she didn't know, though, was that I wasn't "doing it all" at all. My husband had left and taken the children with him. Two of them barely tolerated me, and the situation was an absolute mess. I might have told her, but in those days, therapists didn't share personal lives with patients—it was all about preserving the transference.

Vivienne, for her part, was searching for role models and connections, especially in literary circles. She found something liberating in her relationships with certain well-known authors like Rachel Lee and Richard Larson. Creatively, she flourished, finding her own voice by 1959. She was well-published and critically accepted, which, for a woman poet back then— dismissively called a "poetess"—was an achievement, even if it didn't come close to the recognition afforded her male counterparts. She challenged social norms in her work, writing about subjects like anger and isolation with startling boldness.

But there was a strangeness to it all. Vivienne had an extraordinary ability to imagine her own truth, to craft her reality as she wanted it to be. Perhaps that's common among gifted artists, but with Vivienne, it was striking. She wanted the world to be a certain way, and she constructed it to fit that vision, filtering out contradictions. I don't think she ever processed how deeply troubled some of her idols were. Rachel Lee, for instance, was a brilliant but devastatingly flawed artist—an alcoholic who failed as a mother and a wife, and ultimately took her own life. Then there was Larson, whom everyone knew struggled with a severe psychotic illness, and who, in those days, also bore the societal burden of being a homosexual, a weight that was unbearably heavy at the time.

Vivienne seemed to idolize these people, aspiring to emulate their creative genius while insisting she could "do it all"—and do it flawlessly. But I doubt she could have named a single woman who had truly done that. I don't think anyone could have. And yet, she held on to the notion as if it were possible, her fierce determination as much a shield as a guiding light.

CHAPTER 46

RUTHIE
November 1959

Was she happy? I think so, though maybe not. It was often hard to tell with Vivienne—she wore so many masks. I knew she was frustrated with herself, but there was a lot going on in her life at the time. It was late 1959. She was pregnant, and they were preparing to leave for England. She kept talking about how they'd had these fourteen months of complete freedom to do anything, yet she hadn't accomplished what she'd hoped for. She believed things would be better in England, where she and Jack would be together all the time.

At first, it made little sense to me. She'd done some remarkable writing that year, met many people, published a fair amount, and all that. They'd even been to Blue Creek. Jack had taken them on a wild writing road trip across America—Texas, Nevada, California—and then back again, a massive loop filled mostly with endless stretches of empty highway. Vivienne described the landscape to me as mostly flat, dusty, and scattered with tumbleweeds, but I think they had fun.

However, when I visited in November, I noticed something different. She spent much of her time making delicate ivory doilies, baking cakes, and generally puttering around the house. It was as if she was trying to balance out too much writing by being the perfect homemaker. There were several of us there: I had come down from New York, where I was writing for the Times; I believe the Baskins were visiting, and Jack had invited one of his editors, an older, rather stiff gentleman. Vivienne seemed anxious around him. She just sat quietly, sipping tea, while Jack did almost all the talking. And you know what? I believe that was the week she was waiting for news on her Saxon grant. It was a critical time for her.

Then, something odd happened. Jack stood up, and one of their sculptor friends poked Jack's belly, saying, "Missing a button, old boy," or something like that. A terrible silence fell over the room as Jack shot a glare at Vivienne and said, "I thought I'd left that for you."

The Vivienne I knew would have exploded at that, maybe even thrown something at him. But instead, she just sat there, her cup frozen halfway to her lips. It was unbearable. I think that's why I recall the details so perfectly, the shock of it.

It wasn't until later that I understood. When Vivienne said she hadn't accomplished what she'd hoped, she wasn't talking about her writing. Here she was, married, pregnant, and at just twenty-seven already published in major literary journals, yet she felt she hadn't achieved enough in her personal life. It was about Jack—she felt she'd disappointed him. So, she was going to England to set things right in her marriage.

My God, she really was determined to have it all—the entire package: marriage, motherhood, and a writing career. It was never something I aspired to; I wasn't strong enough. I just wanted to write. But Vivienne, she was unstoppable. The thing is, none of us imagined she'd end up paying such a high price.

CHAPTER 47

SESSIONS
16th November 1959

I had a dream.

Do you want to tell me about it?

I suppose that's why I brought it up.

Alright.

I think I know who it was.

Who what was?

The squid. Or octopus. Giant squid, I think. It was terrible. The thing sort of had me, you know. All squeezed up in its ghastly tentacles, and I couldn't get away. The strange thing was that I was trying to have a sort of normal conversation with it. I wasn't screaming hysterically the way a person ought to be. I mean, this creature was just sucking the life out of me. I might have at least raised my voice.

What were you saying?

I can't remember exactly. Something like Please go away. I didn't ask for your help. You know, quite polite, but the thing wasn't listening.

How did you feel in the dream?

Well, funny, you ask. I don't remember feeling much of anything until I woke up.

And after you woke up?

It's hard to define, but I believe I was angry.

At whom?

Myself. I felt so stupid for doing nothing.

And what could you have done, Vivienne?

Well, that's why I'm here, Dr. B.. So, you can tell me exactly that.

CHAPTER 48

DR. B
Winter 1959

She came to see me several times that winter before they left. She was pregnant by then. The baby was due in early April. She was lethargic, exhausted, uncomfortable, feeling unwell, but I told her I thought it was more than the pregnancy. I thought she was becoming depressed. She was having strange dreams again, a lot of difficulty sleeping.

She refused to believe she was depressed. She'd convinced herself all she needed was her English husband and her English-born baby and, of course, to live in England. She sort of babbled on about Jack being terrified of disappearing into an invisible American suburban existence, which I found hard to believe since he didn't have a job. Had never had a job.

In our session, I pushed her depression, telling her she might need intensive treatment, which, of course, she refused. I promised her no shock therapy. Still, she refused. I remember she told me her problem was that there were no instructions for her sort of wifeliness. I expect she was right. Vivienne was fighting. Trying to forge a fresh path. She was courageous. Perhaps with a different man, she could have done it. Gently, I asked her once. I asked if she might have married the wrong man. She didn't get angry. She paused for a moment, thought about it and then, calmly shook her head and told me I was mistaken.

We had our last session in December 1959. I remember she was concerned I would worry. She reassured me. They moved back to London a few days later, and I never saw Vivienne in person again.

CHAPTER 49

SESSIONS
10th December 1959

We're all packed, ready to go, I guess. Two more days.

You sound ambivalent.

Do I?

Yes, you do.

I suppose I have the typical cold feet.

What would that feel like? The typical cold feet?

I know what you're doing, Dr. B..

And what's that?

Trying to get me to say I'm making a mistake?

Do you think you are?

No, of course not. This is what we want.

We?

Jack and I, of course. And the baby.

How do you know what the baby wants?

It's a manner of speaking, Dr. B.. It's what's best for the baby. Look, I meant to ask you. I can't sleep. I've not been sleeping, I mean. So, I'm awfully tired. And there's so much to do. So much to do when we get there. Can you give me something? Safe for the baby, of course.

We've discussed this, Vivienne. It's your depression. That's why you are not sleeping. And I've told you what I think we should do. What I think is best for you and the baby.

We are leaving in two days. Did I say that?

Yes, you did.

Will you miss me?

I will.

It's all going to be just fine, Dr. B.. Please don't worry. I'll feel much better once we're moved and settled in a flat and all that. I'm sure. I just need rest. Two more days. Oh, but I said that, didn't I?

PART SIX:1960-1961

CHAPTER 50

COLOSSUS IN LONDON
January 1960

1

They had planned the lunch for weeks. But for Vivienne, it was more than just lunch; she had decided it would be *the* meeting. She arranged every detail: what she would wear and the expression she would maintain when they inevitably rejected her. Her outfit was chosen with care—though options were limited at seven months pregnant and on a tight budget. The blue wool maternity suit fit well enough if she didn't sit for too long. The pale pink scarf and matching gloves, borrowed from her mother before leaving the States, complemented the outfit nicely. The coat was old, but it wouldn't matter since she would take it off as soon as she entered the café. She looked like what she was: a housewife with taste and limited means.

She rehearsed what she would say when they turned her down—or worse, demanded impossible, extensive edits. Everyone in publishing seemed to want impossible edits; she had received countless requests to contort herself into the writer she wasn't. *Your work is too raw. Your verse is too rigid. Too polished or too unfinished. It's too feminine or too harsh for our readers.*

"No," she would say. "I'm not interested in changing the poems. They stand as they are."

No apologies. Not now. She had learned that from Rachel Lee. *Fuck them,* Rachel had said. The baby was due in eight weeks. After that, she would be a mother, a wife, and a writer's wife. Maybe that would be all, and that would be fine.

Distracted by her thoughts, Vivienne pushed open the café door and stepped into the dimly lit interior. She bumped into a thin woman clutching a tiny dog to her chest. After a flurry of awkward apologies, with both women stepping this way and that to get around each other, Vivienne continued, slightly flustered but otherwise undeterred.

2

When Vivienne arrived at the table, the men were already seated. One was middle-aged and heavyset—she had met him twice before. The other, tall and lean with a hawk nose and narrow eyes, was unfamiliar to her. They stood as she approached.

"Vivienne," the older man said, "it's so good to see you. Unfortunately, I didn't get much of a chance to talk with you at the welcome party last month."

He had barely spoken to her at all. Jack, who always dominated conversations at those events, had absorbed most of his attention.

"It's nice to see you again, too, Leland."

Leland Garlington was a senior editor at Forrester & Tunstill, one of England's most prominent publishers of serious literature and poetry. Vivienne wanted them to love her work, and she hated herself for wanting it. It felt like another kind of longing she remembered—another need for approval. She hadn't thought of that until just now, as she shook Leland's sweaty, pudgy hand. She let it go and sat down. He smelled of onions.

Leland introduced the other man as a junior editor and his assistant. Vivienne immediately forgot his name—something with an "F." Fletcher, maybe. It wasn't like her to forget, but she wasn't feeling well. The onion smell, the incident with the skinny, blue-haired dog woman, the dim light— all of it was unsettling. The conversation was light and irrelevant, which annoyed her. At seven months pregnant, she struggled to find a comfortable position in the stiff café chair. The men seemed not to notice.

"So, how are you and Jack settling in?" Leland asked.

Leland, who lived alone in an 18th-century mansion in Chelsea, didn't care how they were settling in. His thoughts had already moved past the question, but she answered anyway.

"Oh, just fine, thank you. We're over on Chalcot Square. It's a bit of a squeeze, but it's near the park. That'll be nice for the baby."

Why was she talking so much? It was a habit when she was nervous. She willed herself to stop.

"Lovely, lovely," he said, absently sipping his tea.

Leland was one of those men who drank tea delicately, with his thumb and middle finger hooked around the handle and his pinky flared. Vivienne watched him in silence. Someone brought biscuits, but she couldn't eat—only partly due to her anxiety. The blue wool maternity suit, which had fit perfectly when she was standing, seemed to have shrunk dramatically once she sat down. Now it felt like a straitjacket—something she was unfortunately familiar with. Breathing was becoming difficult, making eating out of the question.

"Well," Leland said finally, "I expect you'd like to get home sometime today, young lady."

Young lady? She was nearly thirty.

"Both of you," he added, glancing at her stomach and chuckling as if he had said something incredibly witty.

Vivienne, who didn't mind being pregnant—in fact, she rather enjoyed her mountainous abdomen—found no humor in the remark. Instead, she had an overwhelming urge to reach out and pinch Leland's ear, as if he were a naughty little boy.

"Yes, thank you," Vivienne agreed.

"So, we should get on with it," Leland continued.

Here we go, she thought. *The news.*

"As you know from all our correspondence, Vivienne, everyone at Forrester loves your work. Beyond love, really. Your poems are stunning. Original. Fresh. Remarkable in every way."

Leland smiled, and Vivienne noticed he had two bright gold crowns in the back of his mouth. It made her think of the war, which made her sad, and suddenly she wanted to leave the café right away.

Yes, she thought, *blah, blah.* She'd heard this all before. It was usually followed by, *But here's why we can't publish them...* or worse, *do you think you might tone down some of the more brutal aspects?*

"And so, we've spent more time reviewing them," Leland continued.

Could he not just get it over with? She felt like Mary, Queen of Scots, awaiting beheading by multiple blows.

"We've put this together," he said, pulling a leather folio from his briefcase. He opened it and slid a sheet of creamy letterhead across the table. "This is just the preliminary letter outlining our offer. We do hope it's acceptable to you. We at Forrester & Tunstill would very much like to publish your book."

Vivienne stopped breathing for a moment, unsure if she had heard him correctly.

"Vivienne?"

"Oh. Sorry." She took the paper and skimmed the few sentences, then read them again, just to be sure. She felt herself smile. She looked up at both men, unable to stop smiling.

Later that year, Vivienne Holland's first book of poetry would be published to astonishing reviews. It would be the only collection of her poetry she would ever see in print.

CHAPTER 51

CHALCOT SQUARE

Vivienne stood at the tiny sink in their miniature London flat, scrubbing away a bit of marmalade before letting the soapy water run over her new dish. *Her dishes,* she thought. *Her flat. Her family.* A smile tugged at her lips as she glanced outside. From the window, she could see across to Regent's Park, towards the zoo. They could walk to the bird sanctuary or take a quick ride to Charing Cross and Piccadilly from here.

It was three flights up, at least two rooms too small, coal-heated, and showing every day of its hundred years. But to Vivienne, the flat at Chalcot Square was perfect. She and Jack had spent the first weeks after moving in scrubbing, repairing, and painting. They'd sanded the old floors and hauled furniture—borrowed or bought second hand—up the narrow stairwell, squeezing around the corner landings and finally through the doorway. Now, it was a home they both loved—a home for their children.

From here, Vivienne could easily imagine the London home they would have someday big and rambling, with an enormous garden and at least four more babies. For the moment, anything seemed possible.

CHAPTER 52

FAT GOLD WATCH
Spring 1960

1

The baby came in April. He was born at home with the help of a midwife. An unmedicated birth. The pain astounded Vivienne. The void and the utter blackness into which it pulled her. But, as she would be told many times in the months after, she was lucky because the labor had been quick, lasting less than six hours. Vivienne found that argument weak, as if the pain of gouging an eyeball with a hot poker was inconsequential since it took only seconds. Or, more accurately, sawing off a limb over several hours, and so on. She was also stunned by her feelings for the baby. An immense love, the quality of which she'd never experienced.

They named the little girl Agatha, after Jack's maternal grandmother. She was beautiful, with cherubic features, but she was not an easy baby. Agatha was colicky, restless, and needed constant attention. She slept little, fed often, and demanded to be held nearly all day. The toll on Vivienne was immediate and significant. Jack, unable to tolerate the noise, set up a card table just outside the flat's front door to escape the fuss, needing silence to write. That was that. As a result, Vivienne's writing was indefinitely put on hold, as was her sleep.

And yet Jack wanted Vivienne to write. He told her he believed in her talent, insisted she needed time for her own work as well. Through the spring, he occasionally took Agatha in the afternoons, giving Vivienne brief windows to work. But often, she was so exhausted, she simply fell asleep.

After a while, she noticed that childcare seemed to sour Jack's mood, deepening his spells of brooding darkness, so she stopped asking him to help. *It was easier,* she told herself, to spare him the duties. How many fathers, after all, changed nappies or took children to the zoo or the park? Jack did these things, often. He was a loving father, a devoted husband, and a poet finally receiving the acclaim he deserved.

Just that week, they'd been invited to cocktails at Tillotson's, where Jack promised they would meet Auden. Wasn't this everything she could want? They had friends in London now; she'd gone to the ballet with Dee Dee Merwin to see *Antigone*! What more could she possibly need? She had a book of poems underway, and, after all, there would be time for her work later. So much time.

2

The young kingmaker they were calling him. He'd been at The Observer just under five years and had already become so influential that his reviews were more anticipated than those of any other London poetry critic. And today, he was 'stopping by.'

Those were Jack's words this morning, "By the way, Viv, A.C. will be stopping by for tea, and he'd love to see the baby."

Vivienne, exhausted and wobbly after three sleepless nights in a row, stood in the kitchen looking around at the smeary counter, the piles of dirty dishes, and several flecks of grease which had somehow alighted on the ceiling. She shuffled to the icebox and pulled open the door. She closed it again and checked her watch. If the baby remained asleep, she might have enough time to pop down to the shops for milk and biscuits while Jack was still working. He'd be annoyed if he had to watch Agatha, and there was no way Vivienne could simultaneously manage an infant and shopping this morning. Her body ached from fatigue, and she didn't trust her mind to keep track of anything. She might leave the child in the melon pile or mix her up with a sack of potatoes.

She sighed and left to get dressed. There would be no writing today.

3

A.C. was a smallish, dark-haired man with angular features and a little more skin on his face than necessary, giving him the appearance of being ten years older than he was. However, Vivienne had been told he wasn't yet thirty. He wore rumpled woolen trousers, scuffed brown leather shoes, and a turtleneck. He smoked a pipe almost continuously, and his manner was jovial and easy for an Englishman. Jack and the visitor sat together in the living room (or rather in the one-room, which was neither bedroom nor kitchen) and talked while Vivienne served tea and tended to the baby. The conversation ran primarily to Jack's book and his plans for future projects. It was not until A.C. was standing and getting ready to leave that Vivienne mentioned her poetry.

"I wanted to thank you for choosing the two poems you did for the Observer. I liked those two the best." She gave him the titles and watched his face shadow.

"Ah," said the critic. "Yes, I thought they were exquisite poems myself." He squinted at her. Clearly trying to piece things together, A.C. furrowed his brow, then suddenly, his face lit up as realization dawned.

"Oh my," he said. "Vivienne?" She nodded, a small smile tugging at her lips. "Vivienne Welles and Vivienne Holland. You are my Vivienne Holland."

"Yes," she replied with a laugh. "We should probably have clarified that sooner." She glanced quickly over A.C.'s shoulder at Jack, catching his eye.

A.C. shook his head, almost in disbelief. "I apologize. I simply didn't put it together. *You* are Vivienne Holland—my, oh my. I am honored." He stepped back, swung one arm out with theatrical flair, and, with the other, swept a grand bow.

Vivienne couldn't help but laugh. She liked this man. "Thank you," she said, feeling a pang of guilt for the unintended embarrassment. But really, there was no other way it could have unfolded. Despite publishing two of her poems, A.C. had never met her in person and had known her solely as Mrs. Jack Welles.

They lingered in the vestibule, A.C. apologizing a few more times, until the stifling heat in the cramped space became unbearable, and the baby began wailing, cutting their meeting short.

Back inside, Vivienne watched from the window as *The Critic* walked up the street to his car. She kept her gaze on him until he climbed into his little Fiat and drove away. *The kingmaker*, she thought with a smile, feeling a spark of pride.

CHAPTER 53

RUTHIE

Don't get me started on Jack Welles. The entire world has an opinion on the man, don't they? It was in the fall of 1960 that I went to see them. I was in London on an assignment. I hadn't seen Viv since she'd had the baby.

As soon as I arrived at their flat, Vivienne was pulling me into the kitchen. She was telling me how famous he is. "He's a lion," she said. Or maybe it was, "He sees himself as a lion." But, anyway, I remember she said, "I'm his wife, and you have no idea how famous he is here in England, and, well, it's my job to help him." It was like she was trying to convince herself. Or maybe she was just embarrassed and trying to convince me. I don't know.

She was holding the baby on her hip and had this ridiculously enormous wooden spoon in her hand—I swear I'd never seen a spoon that big—and she had her back to me, stirring whatever was in the pot. I remember she'd done her hair in a very complicated sort of bun, but it was coming loose from the steam in the kitchen. Tendrils of hair were sticking to her neck. I kept thinking she'd hate that if she knew about it. I was watching her, and he was out there chatting and drinking brandy, and I wasn't saying anything. You know, later, years later, after it all happened, I kicked myself about that night. Why didn't I set her straight? Why didn't I knock some sense into her? But now, I guess I understand twenty-eight-year-old me a little better.

It wasn't so unusual, what she was doing. All the literary men we knew thought themselves lions on both sides of the Atlantic, and the famous ones were insufferable. And she was right; Jack was getting recognized, at least in our little world. Of course, one of London's most prominent publishers had accepted Viv's book—a manuscript many of us found far superior to anything her husband had completed.

But it was 1960, and we were all capable of this weird doublethink. If Vivienne wanted to believe in a utopian marriage, if she wanted a husband and baby along with her career, then she'd made a sort of Faustian deal. She'd agreed to be a baby minder, milk-cow, secretary, cook, laundress, housekeeper, and whatever else. If she seemed terribly brittle for the effort, well, that was her own doing. I remember feeling relieved to escape the flat that night. Jack walked me out to my car, and I asked him if he thought Vivienne was alright. Was she getting enough rest and so on?

"What? She's fine." I had offended him, as if I'd queried him about something deeply personal, like her toilet habits. I dropped it. I decided that, as tightly wound as Vivienne seemed, she was doing the impossible, like she'd promised she would: having it all. So, she must be happy, right?

I told Jack to thank Vivienne again, and he smiled in the way people do without their eyes. Then, he closed the car door for me, and before I had the key in the ignition, he just disappeared, and I was sitting there alone, staring into the empty glow of the streetlight.

CHAPTER 54

A YORKSHIRE CHRISTMAS
December 1960

1

They arrived at the Welles family home in Yorkshire three days before Christmas. The moors stretched out before them, a skeletal, unwelcoming landscape as desolate as a graveyard. Vivienne shivered as she stepped out of the car, her boots crunching on the icy ground. Jack's uncle, sent to collect them from the station, laughed heartily as he wrestled their bags from the car's boot.

"Aye," he chuckled, "ye've forgotten the cold, have ye? Grown a bit feckin' tender?"

Vivienne, who hadn't seen Uncle Walt since she and Jack left for America in 1957, suddenly remembered why she disliked him. He was a selfish, tight-fisted bully, a man who had built a modest fortune in textiles during the Depression by exploiting local men and women struggling to make ends meet—yet he shared none of it with his extended family. Walt had an unyielding knack for making people feel small, as though belittling them was as natural as breathing.

"Sure," she said, not bothering to meet his eye. "I suppose."

The Welles house itself was peculiar. It was a flat-fronted, two-story structure made of smoke-blackened brick, with three upstairs windows (two square, one rectangular) and two downstairs, flanking a plain white door directly in the center. It looked like a child's simple drawing of a house: two-dimensional, all squares within squares, with a neat little chimney poking out of its low-angled roof. Smoke curled from the chimney, its smell thick in the cold, still air. Most peculiar of all was how the house seemed to loom over the narrow, treeless street at the end of a row, flat on two sides, giving it the look of a blocky, bald head. Standing too close, it looked as though the house might suddenly yawn open and swallow one whole.

The houses up the street were all attached by shared walls, their facades occasionally broken up by the personal touches of neighbors—a bush, a trellis, or an old bench topped with clay pots, likely brimming with bright geraniums or sweet alyssum in the summer. In contrast, Mr. and Mrs. Welles had left their home's threshold completely bare, as if decorating was an unnecessary frivolity. The crumbling cracked brick of their doorway stood plainly visible, unembellished.

Walt and Jack carried the bags inside, and Vivienne followed, holding the baby and the car keys. She allowed herself a fleeting thought of escaping, but then the noise from inside hit her, raucous and unavoidable. Dishes clattered, iron pots banged, and Jack's mother was hollering instructions to Mr. Welles, who mostly appeared to ignore her.

The house Vivienne had grown up in—at least until Daddy died—had been quiet, almost church-like. Fritz Holland had despised what he called "disruption," although his definition of disruption shifted often. On some days, it was the sound of children running through the house, laughing and squealing. On other days, especially after he grew ill, "disruption" could mean something as simple as a murmur or even a whisper. On those days, speaking to her mother was done in hushed tones, and any child would quickly be sent outside to wait. And they would wait for what felt like forever.

But this house, Jack's house, was not that. Mrs. Welles let out a delighted cheer when she saw them come in. She rushed forward to snatch the baby, apparently unaware of Agatha's protest. Poor Agatha had to endure Mrs. Welles smashing thick wet lips all over her face, neck, and the top of her head. After fifteen seconds of shocked silence, the baby flailed, arched her back, and finally screamed until, worried she might fling herself onto the floor, Vivienne rescued her.

"Well, well, let me look at ya then," said the older woman, holding Vivienne at arm's length by both shoulders. "Too thin, of course." She glanced at Jack. "And you as well."

Mrs. Welles was strong. A big-boned woman. She was not as tall as Vivienne, but her wrists, calves, ankles, and jaw gave her a masculine appearance. If she'd been a man, she'd have been handsome. Jack looked an awful lot like her. She was ruddy-complected, although not worn looking the way Vivienne's own mother was. She kept her hair very short and wore no makeup, except for lopsided lipstick. Except for a thin gold wedding band, she wore no jewelry. Standing very close like this, Vivienne thought her mother-in-law smelled like clean laundry and strong soap.

2

For dinner, they ate rabbit stew, which Vivienne could barely stomach. She might have done better with it had she not known its ingredients—or at least had she not known the poor creature had been caught, killed, skinned, and disemboweled that very morning. The whole messy nightmare was apparently considered appropriate mealtime discussion.

"Aye, the feckin' little bugger had me for a minute. Nearly chewed his own feckin' leg off, he did. But he didn't get away, did he now?"

That was from Walt as he laughed and shoved a forkful of the little bugger into his mouth. Vivienne poked at the stew with her fork but tried to put as little as possible into her mouth. No one seemed to notice.

There was a lot of focus on neighborhood gossip: Mrs. Heberdon's sciatica behaving badly, both the Ranier twins getting married, that girl over on the estate pregnant again, and so on. Vivienne thought there was an awful lot of interest in the goings-on of women. She glanced at Jack, already on his second helping, eating enthusiastically. He was nodding along with his mother, but Vivienne knew he wasn't listening.

About an hour into the meal, when Mrs. Welles was well into her third glass of wine and telling a story that had something to do with Mrs. So-and-so's recent weight loss, which was followed by an enormous weight gain, which was then followed by a terrible bout of something absolutely godawful that she contracted from starving herself in the first place—cow. Mr. Welles appeared to fall asleep in his chair, his head bobbing forward, his eyes not closed but not quite open for some time, suddenly fluttered shut entirely, and he let out a gargantuan snorty snore.

"Ed!" said Mrs. Welles sharply.

His head popped up. "Yes?" Amazing. He was instantly awake.

"Please."

3

It was the shoes. Vivienne would think about them in the months afterward. Sleek, black boots with a very low heel, pointed toes, and a ridiculously bright gold zipper up the back. They were what screamed, "I've just arrived back from Paris, and I want everyone to know." Vivienne hated them and wanted them right away, and she hated Phyllis for owning them. But, in retrospect, she couldn't help thinking that if Phyllis had not worn the boots, perhaps the tension would not have escalated, and the whole dreadful evening might have been avoided.

Phyllis, all her life, would describe Christmas 1960 as the holiday of true colors, implying it was the holiday during which Vivienne Holland finally showed the family who she really was. Jack, for his part, would never mention the events of that Christmas at all—not even years later, after everything had happened, lopsidedly defending the choice of his sister as manager of Vivienne's estate.

4

Vivienne and her sister-in-law, Phyllis, had met in person only a handful of times, though they'd maintained a cordial, if somewhat formal, correspondence by mail. Both were bright, articulate women with literary leanings, and Vivienne found Phyllis's letters engaging—filled with news of Europe, bits of gossip, and sharp literary insights. But face-to-face, their interactions always seemed tinged with a subtle hostility, a quiet resentment that neither could fully suppress. Vivienne suspected jealousy simmered on both sides. Phyllis led a glamorous, single life in Paris, working as an executive assistant for a renowned literary magazine, mingling with famous figures. But Vivienne had a husband and a child—things Phyllis would never have. And then, of course, there was Jack.

Once, Jack's mother had casually mentioned that he and Phyllis had shared a bed until he was nearly seven. The remark was so startling that it shut down the conversation, leaving an uncomfortable silence over the rest of the visit. It was never spoken of again, yet never forgotten. Jack refused to discuss it but had admitted to Vivienne that Phyllis had been more like a mother to him, especially during the bleak years of the war, and even more so after Rowdy's death. Without her, he said, he wouldn't have survived. So Vivienne did her best to make peace. Jack's relationship with Phyllis was essential to him, and Vivienne hoped that this Christmas would offer a chance to bridge their differences.

Phyllis arrived in Yorkshire the day after Jack and Vivienne. She was as stunning as ever—sleek and slim in tall boots and a fashionable black silk pantsuit, her short hair dyed a striking holiday red, shimmering in the winter light. Bold gold earrings dangled against her neck, and she carried a scent of exotic spice. Next to her, Vivienne felt dowdy and colorless.

"Oh, Vivienne, you look so different," Phyllis remarked upon seeing her in the sitting room. "I've heard motherhood changes your hair color. I wondered if that was true."

Vivienne, holding Agatha, was painfully conscious of her once-platinum hair, now faded to a dull shade of brown. She twisted a dry strand between her fingers, swallowing back the sting of sudden tears.

"Yes, I suppose. I don't know."

To Vivienne's surprise, Phyllis suddenly stepped forward and threw her arms around both her and Agatha. Vivienne was too shocked to hug back.

Lately, Vivienne had been struggling with bouts of nausea and suspected there was more to it than the rich country fare. She'd resolved to keep her pregnancy a secret from Jack until they were back in London, preferring to share the news in private. She wasn't entirely sure how Jack would react. They'd wanted more children, but hadn't agreed on the timing, and their finances were a lingering concern. Yet Vivienne was proud of herself for handling the Welles family with composure. She tuned out Mrs. Welles's endless chatter and ignored Phyllis's tendency to talk to or around her, as though Vivienne were an inconveniently large and unattractive piece of furniture. Phyllis seemed uninterested in forming a sisterly bond, but Vivienne managed to remain polite.

On Christmas Eve Day, a brief warm spell arrived, prompting Jack and Vivienne to escape the house for a rare walk together. The trees stood as blackened silhouettes against the silver-gray hills, and the air was thick with the scent of pine. Yorkshire lacked the vivid brightness of New England, but it offered something timeless, something ancient and mysterious. They walked slowly, their pace unhurried, looking out over the rolling hills toward a bank of fog that hung low over the bog. The only sound was the steady crunch of their boots on the gravel path.

"It's lovely," Vivienne murmured, leaning her head on Jack's shoulder. She felt the comforting warmth of his hand sliding into hers.

5

The peaceful feeling Vivienne had experienced on the moor dissipated the moment they entered the house. Phyllis and Mrs. Welles had had a row over some issue with Christmas Eve supper. The kitchen was a narrow, darkened space with a window at one end. It had an awful tendency to clog with greasy smoke as soon as the oven was lit. And it smelled, almost all the time, of leaking gas.

The women squeezed in sardine-style, elbowing one another for space and control. Now, Phyllis and Mrs. Welles were crashing into one another, struggling over exactly how to season a goat—goat being one more culinary adventure Vivienne might have done without.

"Phil, out, out, out! My kitchen, this is my kitchen," Mrs. Welles was trying to say, but her voice sounded weak and childish.

"Mum, I would go, but you have no idea what you're doing. Just look at this. We cannot possibly eat this. At least I won't eat it like this. Christ. I'll do it all over again."

She was leaning over the pot, her face inches from its hot edge. Vivienne had a momentary vision of leaping forward and slamming her sister-in-law's lovely white skin into the stew, her coming up with bits of goat meat in her radish-red hair, floury brown gravy running down her silly Parisian clothes.

Instead, Vivienne turned to find Agatha, who was fast asleep in her playpen.

The argument continued for some time—mostly Phyllis criticizing her mother, Jack trying without success to calm things down, and finally Mrs. Welles collapsing into a heap of martyr's tears and going to bed, where she remained for some time.

Strangely, the total fiasco seemed forgotten by dinnertime. Jack explained that's "just how things are" and "nobody makes too much of Phyllis." Apparently, at middle age (after all, she was in her thirties), Phyllis could act like a spoiled brat, and nobody did anything about it.

Jack agreed they would forgo Boxing Day and leave straight away on Christmas morning. It was too hard on Vivienne. Agatha was behaving strangely, spitting her food, screaming uncontrollably. Vivienne had only to make it through one more meal. "Be positive," she reminded herself. These were Jack's people, and she loved Jack; therefore, Vivienne would do her best to love his people.

6

"Phyllis, I wish you'd just lay off." The words came out of Vivienne's mouth so suddenly that she surprised herself. She froze, forkful of cake halfway to her lips, staring down at her plate, chocolate crumbs catching her eye as she considered bolting from the room. *What had she done?* But no. She'd started this; she might as well go all the way. Vivienne took a breath, set her fork on the edge of her plate, and looked up, straight into Phyllis's eyes.

"You are, undoubtedly, the most critical, the most judgmental person I've ever met, and I want you to leave Jack be."

That wasn't entirely true. Her father had probably been worse. She remembered the enormous red Xs he would scrawl on his students' papers, and the countless times she'd tried to earn his approval with dances, lists of scientific terms, anything she thought might please him. But Daddy was gone, so her statement stood. Vivienne pressed on.

"You never stop, Phyllis. You're constantly criticizing everyone—your mother, writers, your so-called friends."

It was true enough. Phyllis was a competent but not particularly talented writer herself, yet in her letters, she always had a fresh store of critical opinions to share.

"And now you have the audacity to attack Jack for saying what he thinks about writers you've never even read."

This was the spark. Over supper, Jack had aired his disdain for certain American and French poets, and Phyllis, apparently tired of his diatribe, had finally told him to stop, calling him "narrow-minded, overly critical, and judgmental." That was when Vivienne had burst out, telling her to "lay off."

For a moment, the table froze. Mr. Welles looked down into his lap, pursing his lips, and Mrs. Welles sat staring at Vivienne, slack-jawed and watery-eyed. Vivienne dared not look at Jack. Finally, Phyllis set down her wineglass, drew in a sharp breath through her nose, and glared at her.

"Bitch," Phyllis said, the word landing like a small explosion over the table, shocking everyone into silence.

Then she went on. "You're a nasty, selfish bitch, *Miss Holland.*"

The choice of her maiden name, and the patronizing "Miss," hit Vivienne harder than the insult itself.

"You act as if our house, *my* house, is your palace, and you're the queen, free to do whatever you want. Who do you think you are? You eat everything in the house, sit around expecting to be waited on. You're a bitch. An immature, selfish woman trying to come between Jack and me."

Phyllis pushed her chair back but didn't stand. Instead, she raised her voice, nearly shouting, "You are nothing but a spoiled, selfish *bitch.*"

Vivienne felt her throat swell as tears threatened, and she hated herself for showing weakness. She looked to Jack, then to his mother, and back to him again, but no one came to her defense. Jack remained rigid, silent. She wanted desperately to leave the table, to escape this humiliation, but she found herself saying, "Go ahead, Phyllis, go on then," half-daring her to continue.

Phyllis did. Her words piled on like hot lava—*bully, greedy, insensitive, bitch, bitch, bitch.*

"You know," Phyllis said, with an almost sinister satisfaction, "yesterday on the bus, Jack and I ran into some people. Everyone thought Jack had a new redheaded wife."

Even Mrs. Welles seemed flushed with embarrassment, but Jack remained still, his mouth set in a hard line, as if he were simply waiting for the storm to pass. Phyllis ranted until she'd worn herself out, then abruptly ran from the room, leaving a trail of anger behind her.

Eventually, Mr. Welles wandered off in search of brandy, and Mrs. Welles slumped in her chair, babbling as Jack tried, awkwardly, to comfort her. The scene was so bizarre it calmed Vivienne, grounding her in a surreal sense of detachment, as if she were merely watching the debacle unfold from afar. She rose, retrieved her coat and scarf, and left the house without any destination in mind.

An hour later, Uncle Walt—who had thankfully missed the entire scene—and Jack found her strolling along the moonlit countryside. Jack was gentle, apologetic, and suggested it might be wise for her to avoid Phyllis until after her wedding. Vivienne couldn't help herself and asked if marriage would somehow transform women into more reasonable, congenial human beings. Did domestic life act like a lobotomy, smoothing out the rough edges?

The following day, as the sun rose over the river, Vivienne and Jack would leave Tawton, both silently deciding that Phyllis would no longer serve as their daughter's godmother, an honor they intended to pass to Ruthie Hampton. But the decision would never make it onto paper. Jack would maintain his close bond with Phyllis throughout his life, but Vivienne would never see her sister-in-law again.

CHAPTER 55

PARLIAMENT HILL FIELDS
February 1961

1

"Look, I'm not sayin what happened between the two of 'em was right. Hittin a woman is never okay. He shouldn't have done it. But obviously, all I'm sayin is that it was 1961. Times were different. Men did that sort of thing back then. Chaps, I mean. Smacking yer wife because she got a bit bonkers was acceptable. Even expected. You can't blame a bloke for that. Not after the fact. That's all I'm sayin."—Uncle Walt.

2

On the telephone, there is a woman's low, husky voice. Her accent is Irish. She sounds seductive and much too young. "Senior Head of Schools at the BBC," the voice says, calling for Jack Welles, interested in having him come for lunch to discuss his project. Vivienne hands the phone over and bounces the baby on her hip while Jack makes the appointment and confirms plans. "Yes, that's good, that's very good. I'm sure they'll love it. Yes, yes." 1961 was Jack's year. Everyone agreed.

3

The meeting went long. The Poet arrived home an hour late. The BBC executive, an exhaustingly dull woman named Myrina, who talked more than she listened, had kept him until he insisted he needed to get home so his wife could get to her job. When he arrived at the flat, Vivienne sat at the kitchen table, which was covered in sheets of typed manuscript. Beside her, near her thigh, was a wastebasket, full almost to overflowing with shreds of paper. She stood quickly as The Poet entered, dropped a last bit of writing, pushed back her chair, and waited, her arms folded across her chest.

His breath caught when he understood what she'd done. Then came the rage.

"For fuck's sake, what have you done, Vivienne? What in the hell have you done?" Before he'd taken a step, she lunged, attempting to drive her fists into his chest. He grabbed her wrists, shoved her out of the way, and moved toward the piles of paper. He was howling at her. "What is this? What in the hell is this?"

On the table and in the basket lay strips of his manuscripts and recent poems on the floor—crumpled, torn, shredded into bits, some no wider than a half inch. Ruined, disarranged, beyond recovery.

"How dare you ask me that question. How dare you." Vivienne shouted, her face red and swollen. "You are nothing but a cheating-lying-duplicitous-coward-bastard." She ran the insults together into one continuous string. "Do you think I don't know where you've been? Do you think I'm stupid? Do you think I don't know what you were doing with that slut?"

He ignored her and began snatching at the bits of paper.

"Where is the rest? Vivienne, what did you do with the rest of my manuscript?"

She lunged for the table and grabbed the remaining pages—the ones she'd left intact—and backed away from him. She began tearing at the pages in her hands and frantically tossing the remnants about like confetti.

"Stop!" he screamed, rushing toward her. "Are you mad? Stop it."

A stupid question, he thought. But, of course, she was mad. Bloody loony at that.

She did not stop. Instead, she dodged around him, continuing to tear at the paper. "What will you do, Jack?" she taunted. "Hit me? Go ahead. You've done it before. Is that the answer when you've been out fucking someone?"

"You're crazy, Vivienne. You've lost it."

What was she saying? Hit her? He had not hit her. Fritz had hit her. Vivienne told him. More than once. Perhaps her mother had even hit her. He and Vivienne had had a few physical incidents. He'd pushed her, and that he had immediately regretted. But hit her? No, not that.

Vivienne was screaming. "How dare you. You're an empty shell, an ignorant louse, nothing—not the man I thought I married. I should have done this a long time ago. Bastard, bastard, bastard."

Jack was sure she did not know what she was saying or what she was doing—shredding pages, screaming, howling, crying uncontrollably. Her chest heaving with sobs, she looked as if she could hardly breathe. He tried yelling at her to stop, but that only made her worse.

Finally, desperate, he slapped her across the left cheek. The blow sent her reeling backward. She hit the wall shoulder first and slid down until she sat on the floor, no longer holding anything in her hands. He hadn't meant to strike her. He felt immediately sick inside. She stared at him, unblinking, unable to move or speak. He moved toward her, but she flailed her arms at him, so he backed away and began retrieving torn pages instead.

"Jesus, Viv, what were you thinking? What were you thinking?"

"You slapped me," she breathed.

He looked at her. She wasn't bleeding. She was okay. "I'm sorry, I'm really sorry. You wouldn't stop," he said. "You just wouldn't stop."

In the silence, they heard Agatha making gurgling sounds in the bedroom, beginning to wake up. It was a miracle she had not been awake through the entire fight, or if she had, she'd gone back to sleep. Vivienne pushed herself to a standing position and plodded down the hall to see to the baby. As he watched her walk away, it occurred to him he could have just told her the truth. The BBC executive had been a gray-haired, heavyset, middle-aged woman old enough to be The Poet's mother. And yet, he'd chosen not to do that. Instead, he'd let his wife's imagination fly.

4

The Poet dreams of the sea and Irish mermaids. In the dream, he weds a green-haired merrow and, to keep her, he steals her magical red cap. Without it, she can no longer travel from deep water to dry land and back again. "No matter what," she tells him, but then she turns and runs from him. He chases her until he is tired and must stop to rest. When he looks down, he finds he hasn't moved at all.

5

Two days later, the blood came in a sudden gush, soaking the bedsheets and badly frightening Jack, who rushed to call the doctor.

"It happens this way sometimes," said the doctor.

Vivienne, wrapped in a cocoon of smooth white hospital sheets, lay basking in an opiate cloud. She was entirely focused on the marvelous coolness of crisp cotton against the backs of her hands and the tops of her feet. She wished, for the moment, that the doctor, who seemed like a nice man, would go away. But he continued talking without turning to look in her direction. He was pretending to fiddle with something in his bag. Vivienne knew he was pretending—he'd been standing like that for a long, long time. Possibly hours. What was he saying? She tried to focus.

"Usually, this sort of natural termination is a blessing," said the doctor.

Right, that's what he was saying. She was lucky. Once again, Vivienne was fortunate.

The doctor continued, "In the end, perhaps we will never know why."

The pregnancy had been a surprise, anyway, making itself known as it did just before Christmas. Vivienne had continued to feel unwell, tired, and nauseous into January, and, as expected, the doctor confirmed the news. The baby was due in summer. They'd been happy, she and Jack. Hadn't they been happy? Another baby so soon after the first? Vivienne had been worried, and Jack had been lukewarm at best. Now, there were no feelings in the antiseptic hospital room with its artificial silver-white light. There were, in fact, laws against feelings—written on the walls here and there in ink Vivienne was sure was invisible. She was numb beneath the frozen sheet. A mummy. And what was the doctor saying? Natural termination? Maybe they would never know why. What about the fight? The slap? Vivienne's body slamming against the wall. She'd felt it then. Just two days before. They wouldn't talk about that. Nobody would talk about all that.

Vivienne stared up at the medical man, a small man with tiny eyes and a broad face, peculiar in its flatness. She wanted to ask him if his mother might have thought it a blessing had he been naturally terminated some months before his actual birth. But she said nothing. He seemed like a nice man. Or had she already said that out loud?

The man kept talking. "Possibly, there was something wrong with the fetus, you know."

The fetus. The baby. Her baby. Her summer baby. She'd already chosen names.

"You'll be fine, Mrs. Welles. Absolutely fine."

Now he looked at her, smiling. His teeth were a neat line of slightly yellowed pearls between thin lips in the weird face. She decided it was a doctor's face—or at least the sort of face that could only belong to a doctor or perhaps a biology teacher. Certainly not a salesman or businessman.

"Some rest, and you'll be completely fine and ready to try again in no time. You were quite fortunate. There's no infection, no damage. So, you should feel quite hopeful."

She nodded. "Yes," Vivienne said agreeably, although she felt nothing. Only some kind of conspicuous absence. "Thank you, doctor." She watched him close his bag. He would be gone in a moment, and she could go back to thinking about her knuckles and her toes. "Nobody can tell?" she blurted.

He turned back to her. "I'm sorry?"

"What's lacking," she said. "They won't know?"

She wasn't making sense. She didn't know how to explain it to this probably very nice doctor.

"Oh, oh, I see," he said. But she knew he did not see. He thought she wanted reassurance. Comfort. He reached for her hand, took it in his own. "No, no, dear. Nothing to worry about. No one will ever be able to tell. It'll be as if all of this never happened at all."

After the doctor left, Vivienne pulled the stiff white sheet up over her face, closed her eyes, and waited for sleep.

CHAPTER 56

THE MERWIN'S ATTIC
Spring 1961

1

A late spring day in 1961 found Vivienne in the attic study she and Jack were borrowing from the Merwin's. Vivienne claimed the mornings, seven days a week, while Jack took the afternoons, and the freedom was intoxicating. Free from domestic duties for three or four hours daily, for the first time since marriage, she was writing with the ease and speed she'd always imagined. Her novel, long neglected, was finally taking shape, and she'd written to her mother that it was "going like gangbusters."

It was the story she'd started ten years earlier—the tale of a college girl who moves to New York, only to be disillusioned and ultimately suffer a breakdown. Yes, it was slightly autobiographical, but Vivienne believed in using what she had, and she had *this*: GO TO NEW YORK-HAVE A NERVOUS BREAKDOWN-TRY TO KILL YOURSELF BY HIDING UNDER THE HOUSE. The creative paralysis she'd felt for a decade had evaporated, replaced by a torrent of words flowing onto the page. By mid-spring, she had published two of her best poems in major UK literary magazines, and by May's first week, she received news that Knopf would publish her debut poetry collection in America.

Her mornings passed in blissful isolation at an old wooden table, glossy from years of use, strewn with pages edited in red marker, and a wastebasket stuffed with crumpled drafts. The remains of a half-eaten peach sat on a china saucer, its juice pooling beneath it, while an empty teacup with a few minty grounds in the bottom sat to the side. Her long hair, twisted into braids, would occasionally brush against the pages until she'd shove them out of the way, slightly annoyed. A neat stack of manuscript pages rose steadily at her elbow, a tangible marker of her progress.

On this particular morning, she was so engrossed that nothing broke her concentration. Only when the sun shone white-hot through the dormer windows and a deep ache settled into her neck did she glance at her watch—nearly one o'clock. She'd lost track of time entirely. Hastily gathering her papers and pencils into her bag, she double-checked to ensure she hadn't left anything behind. She couldn't risk leaving her manuscripts in someone else's home. Hat and gloves in hand, she headed downstairs, leaving the heavy Olivetti typewriter behind.

The Merwins' townhouse sat on an upscale street, not far from the considerably less glamorous flat she and Jack were renting. It was a short walk home, but she knew Jack would be irritated by her lateness. He had been more than fair, agreeing to watch the baby in the mornings so she could write. Her mother had even been impressed by his devotion—certainly, her father would have never considered such an arrangement.

Vivienne pushed the door open, jamming it against the wall and yanking the old key from the lock. She stopped for a moment, listening. Voices and laughter echoed down the hallway. Jack and another man were deep in conversation, evidently enjoying themselves. As she continued down the hall, she heard Jack telling some humorous story about Agatha. He adored their daughter and never tired of recounting tales of her intelligence, beauty, and charm. While this always pleased Vivienne, the presence of an unexpected guest added an unwelcome layer of complication to her day.

"Ah, Vivienne," a voice boomed as she entered the tiny parlor. Lucas Baskin, an enormous bear of a man, stood and opened his arms wide. Almost instinctively, Vivienne stepped forward, allowing herself to be enveloped in his hug.

"It's so good to see you, my dear."

"And you, Luke," she replied, though she struggled slightly to break free from his embrace, her face pressed uncomfortably against the velvet lapel of his rumpled dinner jacket. *A velvet dinner jacket?* she thought. Luke was always eccentric to the point of the absurd—a sculptor and American, known for his monumental and often grotesque works featuring bosomy beasts and strange, half-dragon women. His theatricality was irritating, but Vivienne tolerated it, understanding that life as a large-scale sculptor in America must be an exhausting challenge, especially for a man with Luke's flamboyant tendencies.

"I thought you were arriving next week?" she asked, keeping her voice polite. "Weren't there deadlines?"

Jack intervened, his tone cautionary. "Ah, Viv, Luke's business in Cambridge didn't take as long as expected, so he took the train down to London. He called last night, but I must've forgotten to mention it."

Vivienne felt a red-hot irritation rising, but she forced a smile. "Oh, so when did you leave Boston?" she asked, more to buy time than out of interest. Her mind raced, cataloging everything that would need doing— meals, sleeping arrangements, clean linens. The flat was in disarray, and she hadn't planned for a guest. Did they even have enough food for supper?

"Just last Tuesday," Luke replied with his usual cheer. "I'll have more time to spend with you both, and of course, this little cutie," he added, gesturing toward Agatha, who sat beside Jack, contentedly tugging on his shirt collar with one hand and munching on a sugary biscuit with the other. The biscuit was nearly gone, and whatever hadn't made it into her mouth was efficiently ground into both her pinafore and the sofa cushions. Two tumblers and a half-empty bottle of scotch sat on the table, clearly part of the visit's festivities.

Vivienne resisted the urge to ask how long he planned to stay, knowing it was out of the question. Luke was one of Jack's dearest friends, one of the few Americans Jack loved. Luke had introduced Jack around Boston, helping him make connections. Despite the inconvenience, Vivienne resolved to be gracious. The poor man had lost his wife a few years prior, and he looked thinner, more disheveled than she remembered. She'd take on the burden of playing the host, putting her writing and life on hold—for Jack, for Luke, and for the baby.

"How are your boys, Luke?" she asked, recalling that his twin sons must now be in their twenties.

"Oh, you know, they had a rough time after their mother..." He trailed off before adding, "But now they're grown." He held a hand over his head to illustrate their height. "Both at Harvard now. Scientists! Don't ask me how that happened." He chuckled.

Vivienne forced a smile. "It's good to see you, Luke. Let me go change and get things started."

The baby needed a bath, she'd have to shop, and she'd need to make a more elaborate dinner for their guest. Turning to Jack, she whispered, "Would you mind moving the crib into the kitchen? I'll let her nap there so Luke can have the sofa."

Jack looked at her, clueless. It was astonishing how two grown men could while away half a day in conversation without sparing a thought for food or accommodations.

"The kitchen?" he echoed, as though it were an outlandish suggestion.

"Yes," she replied, suppressing a sigh. "Where did you plan for Luke to sleep? Our bed? I assume he'll take the sofa, which leaves no room for the crib in our bedroom. The kitchen is the only place left, and we can't subject Luke to her midnight cries." Sarcasm crept into her voice despite her efforts to keep it at bay.

Jack finally nodded. "Right. Okay, we'll do it when we get back. We're off to see the sights this afternoon."

Vivienne bit her tongue, longing to ask the question she'd sworn she wouldn't: *When will you be leaving, Luke?*

2

While they were out, Vivienne cleaned the flat, bathed the baby, washed up the breakfast dishes, and ran to the shops to buy meat, potatoes, wine, and supplies to make dessert. After snack time, she bathed the baby again and then worked on dinner; she cooked pork loin, twice-baked potatoes, green beans, and custard. She'd hoped to squeeze in an hour of reading, but by the time the men got back (having had "a lovely time slowly perusing the Tate and particularly enjoying the German Expressionists"), she was too exhausted to do more than set the table, serve the food, wash the dishes, and fall into bed as soon as she got the baby to sleep.

In the morning, Jack kissed her and thanked her for the beautiful meal. Then he got up with the baby and left her to sleep a few precious extra hours. He's a man, Vivienne thought drowsily, her arms and legs aching and heavy as lead logs. A successful man. A special man, and she was a fortunate woman.

3

Luke stayed for ten days, a blur of unmade beds, dirty laundry, greasy pots, complicated meals, and trips to the shops for tea, milk, meat, and pie. Curiously, Luke, who had been married to an intelligent, modern woman, had less inclination to pick up after himself than the baby, who could not toilet herself and had only recently learned to walk.

4

By April 20th, Luke's tenth day in London, news of the disaster in Cuba reached England. Vivienne sat, staring at newspaper photographs. In one, a pair of combat boots stood beside the savagely burned remains of a sleeping bunk. The boots were untouched except for a light coating of ash. In another, a ragged family with their faces in their hands, the caption read:

"FAMILY OF EXECUTED MAN CLAIMS CASTRO DENIED PLEAS."

The Bay of Pigs, an inexcusable tragedy, laid squarely at the feet of a government—her government, her president. "There is no hiding this. I am the executive of the government." But they were hiding. Something. Everything. Vivienne felt like sliding out of her American identity, slipping it off like rotten skin, but neither was she English. The class-ruled society, the oppressive existence of royalty, and all that it implied. It seemed to Vivienne that someone ought to march straight up to the Palace and give the Queen a smack, stop all that curtsying, and shock everyone out of the silly fantasy of the Divine Right, and so on.

Vivienne was sitting on the bed, papers spread out before her, busily contemplating all of this—the wrongness of events in Cuba, her general sense of being a woman in exile, the irrelevance of almost everything except perhaps her daughter—when Jack called from the kitchen. His timing could be astonishingly lousy. Vivienne folded up the paper and stood slowly, her lower back aching with fatigue.

They were seated at the kitchen table, drinking coffee and waiting patiently for breakfast, which Vivienne guessed they thought would arrive on magic floating trays, cooked by invisible kitchen fairies. They looked up as she entered, both giving her big, open grins. Agatha sat happily in her highchair, gnawing on what looked suspiciously like the stem of Luke's pipe. A closer look revealed it was, in fact, not the pipe, but just a wad of pipe cleaners. Vivienne snatched them away.

"Jack!" she shrieked, holding them up.

"Oh, yeah," he said. "But they're clean; Luke said so."

The baby had already wailed. Vivienne rolled her eyes at him and moved to the sink to start whatever it was she was supposed to start. She stopped. In that instant, Vivienne knew exactly how she must look to them, the men. She saw her mother—pale, gaunt, resigned. So diminished, she'd been hardly a flicker of light. The world was so huge and loud around her, she'd become the barest breath in a hurricane.

"Viv?" Jack was saying. "Viv, are you alright?"

She ignored him, plucked Agatha out of her chair, and strode out of the room. She didn't stop until she reached the hall, where she'd left her pocketbook and keys. She picked them up and walked out the door.

5

Vivienne returned an hour later to find Luke and Jack standing in the sunlight on the sidewalk, waiting for Luke's cab to arrive. Both were leaning against the building, smoking. Luke wore the velvet dinner jacket, now stained down the right sleeve from where he had dipped it into the fondue at dinner on Tuesday night, and Jack stood with one hand shoved into his pocket. They looked sheepish, like naughty teenagers. Both dropped their eyes as she approached. She was confident they didn't know why she'd been so angry. "Apologize first," she'd heard Luke say once. "Ask questions later."

The goodbyes were awkward. Vivienne held the baby and allowed Luke to peck dryly at her cheek. She felt the sandpaper scratch of his unshaven skin against her face and had to repress the urge to pull away. He smelled of sweat, old gin, and cigarettes.

Vivienne left the men on the sidewalk to wait for Luke's cab—the cab that would give her back her freedom. She'd start right away this morning. She'd go to the Merwins', run to the attic. To hell with everything. She'd leave Agatha with Jack and spend the rest of the day writing, writing, writing!

She took the stairs, quickly at first, then slower. At the top, she thought, no. First, she'd send a letter to Luke. An apology. Her behavior had been horrific. Unladylike. Ungracious. How could she? And Jack's best friend at that. It wouldn't do.

Inside, she put the baby in her playpen and went to the window, looking down on the street. The black cab pulled up. She watched Luke drop his cigarette to the ground and stub it out with his toe. Then the men shook hands and embraced. A moment later, the cab was pulling away. Jack stood with his hands in his pockets, watching until it disappeared around the corner.

I'll write Luke, Vivienne thought. Immediately. Tell him how sorry I am. That will set things right. She looked around the kitchen. First the dishes, then the letter. Poor Jack will need to get to the Merwins'. He has written nothing in days. I'll get back there tomorrow.

In the kitchen, she pulled a fresh apron from the drawer under the sink, neatly stacked and folded. She wrapped it around her waist and tied it in the back. She began stacking the dirty dishes beside the sink. She felt lighter now—a loosening of the crushing weight of guilt.

CHAPTER 57

UNDER A DRUMMING HATCH
Summer 1961

1

The house was not a house. It was a ship, a ruin, a haunt. It was an ark washed up hundreds, perhaps thousands, of miles across a blackened, stormy sea, now come to rest on this broad green pasture. No one was home unless one counted the woodworms and black beetles that had claimed it. Held together now by fog and stones, it smelled of sheep, earth, and moss. Still, its beauty was undeniable.

"What do you think?"

Vivienne hesitated, searching for the words. "It's remarkable, Jack. I've never seen one like it; I can certainly say that."

"Exactly," he said, without taking his eyes off the ruined building. "Come see the inside. I know you'll love it." He took her hand and pulled her toward the front door.

Stuart, the estate agent, was a squat, prematurely balding young man, only twenty-five, and he was nervous and fidgety. He wore rumpled brown slacks and a cheap wool jacket that Vivienne suspected was probably his best. He looked a bit in over his head, as if someone, perhaps his mother, had sent him along on this sales mission against his own better judgment. Vivienne wanted to reassure him. They were all deeply in over their heads.

"Springhill House," Stuart told them, "had been the home of a Duke and Lady, although not for many years."

"The place has fallen a bit," he added by way of explanation. "Needs some looking after."

Stuart smiled; his teeth were large and unusually straight, but the color of butter. Still, he was eager, and Vivienne liked him. Increasingly, she appreciated Springhill House as well. Besides its aristocratic history, the three-hundred-year-old house had nine rooms, a servant's cottage, and a lovely, thatched roof. There were three walled acres with cherry and apple trees, raspberry and blackberry bushes, and dozens of enormous elm trees. The River Taw ran directly through the property, and she could imagine Jack fishing every day. Never mind the ruin, the overgrowth, the smell of mold—they could manage.

Suddenly, she felt Jack's hand in her own, firm and gentle. She looked at him and nodded. Springhill House would be their home—their children's home. The monumental fact of its isolated location was, at that moment, utterly irrelevant, and, like most of the other decisions they made together, in a moment of careless and impulsive passion, they agreed.

"Yes," said Jack to the estate agent. "Yes, we will buy this house."

Vivienne and Jack scraped together money from friends, family, and savings, and borrowed what they did not have, and bought the house that was not really a house. In the summer of 1961, Springhill became both the first and last house in which the Welles family would ever live.

2

It made perfect sense to sublet the London flat to the couple from Cambridge. They knew Wyatt Clark and his wife, after all—or at least Jack knew the husband, a Canadian poet, from the Cambridge group, and they had met his lovely wife, the German girl. That's how Vivienne thought of her: The German Girl. They got on well with the pair, and the two seemed like reserved, responsible people. They had no children, and the husband, despite being a poet, had a steady income as an instructor at a local boys' school.

Still, they should have seen the truth as it was written in the stars. Astrology, tarot cards, the Ouija—it should have been blazing there in the

Two of Pentacles or the High Priestess. Later, Vivienne and Jack would both wonder how they could have missed it so entirely. But not then, in the golden summer of 1961, with a gorgeous baby girl and Springhill House on the horizon, and all their choices wrapped like gifts in the gossamer glimmer of youthful optimism and hope.

3

Jack and Vivienne moved their few belongings and their baby down to the enormous house in Devon, where they spent days busily unpacking in the summer heat. Meanwhile, the Canadian poet and the German girl—who was actually half-Jewish and had been raised in Israel—moved into their flat on Chalcot Square. The German girl sent Vivienne a housewarming gift: a large decorative piece she'd purchased on a trip abroad the previous year. It was a wooden snake that Vivienne placed carefully on the new (ancient) mantle. It would be many months before a visitor would point out that the carving's vicious face bore a disturbing resemblance to Nachash from the Garden of Eden.

After unpacking, they spent much of the first month at war with the gardens, hacking back aggressive vines, yanking out weeds with taproots as long as a man's leg, and turning over thick, wet English soil. Much of the work that remained—removing dead trees, rotten stumps, clearing the orchard—would have to be left to hired help, meaning postponement until funds were available to pay for it. For now, Vivienne was thrilled with the results they'd achieved. That summer, the gardens exploded with beetroot and cucumber, white roses and pink peonies, some plants likely older than Vivienne, twisted together until one was nearly indistinguishable from the other.

She and Jack each had their studies now, and Vivienne's overlooked the vegetable gardens. An elm tree just outside the window provided birdsong in the morning and lovely shade from the glaring summer sun in the afternoon. Vivienne and Jack had painstakingly sanded and painted the old hardwood floors, and she'd laid a warm and brightly colored rug across her study. She'd added flowers, a few prints, and lots of books on shelves Jack made from found lumber and bricks. Looking around, Vivienne declared it perfect. Her novel was nearly finished, and she could not imagine a better place to bring it to closure. It was good, this book—Vivienne knew it. All year she'd been gaining confidence: four more poems in *The New Yorker* and glowing praise for the one about the mussels.

Her mother was due to arrive in August. Life was good, but still, Vivienne felt an undercurrent of irritation that intensified as her mother's arrival drew near. There had always been tension between her mother and Jack—a strain Vivienne had assumed would settle as the marriage steadied itself. The problem was that things still seemed a bit wobbly. Perhaps all marriages were wobbly. There ought to be a course for girls, a course in wobbliness. Uncertain, unstable, unsure—that is the status quo. So, get used to it, ladies. You will never feel surefooted again, not one time after puberty, not once.

Jack felt no wobble, however. Life looked rosy to him—rosy and steady. Praise was coming from all directions. He had publications in *The Atlantic*, *Harper's*, *Vogue*, and *The New Yorker*; he recorded short programs for the BBC and *The Sunday Times*. Jack had even been offered a lucrative teaching position at the University of Washington, which they'd both agreed to decline. But now Vivienne wondered if that had been a mistake. Poverty, as it turned out, was not trivial, and Vivienne was not unaffected by it, no matter how indifferent Jack claimed to be. Moreover, Springhill House had no heat, and the hard, dusty wood floors made the cold particularly bitter—intolerably bitter.

In those months, Vivienne continued to write but was also feeling overwhelmed by housework and childcare. Increasingly, Jack stayed overnight in London whenever he recorded for the BBC, which only escalated the tension and grew the silence between them like rot.

CHAPTER 58

THE CRITIC

I think it began with that ill-fated trip to France in the summer of 1961. If I'm honest, I blame myself for what happened. Jack and Vivienne looked up to me. I had been supporting them for some time, writing about their work, promoting them, and both were thriving. Vivienne's first book of poems was due out the following month, and though she'd kept it a secret, she'd even finished her novel. And Jack—well, everything seemed to be going brilliantly for him. They listened to my advice, trusted me, and I was the one who invited them to visit the Duchess at her villa in the south of France.

In fairness, I truly thought it would help. Jack was miserable. He'd been confiding in me, and likely others, that he felt "confined" in the marriage. That was his word: confined. Even in Devon, he was restless and spoke of feeling like a "prisoner." It didn't bode well. Vivienne, meanwhile, had taken a darker turn in her writing. Her poetry was slipping into new, starker themes, more visceral and revealing. She wrote about love running off like a horse, about feeling caged. The work was brilliant, suggesting the depth of what she would produce in the fall of 1962, but it was clear she was struggling.

That summer, she was suffering—though few noticed. I saw it. Perhaps Jack did, too, had he been looking. But things had already begun to unravel, and I only realized too late that my attempt to help might only hasten the inevitable.

Anyway, France. Vivienne was miserable and awful to be around. I understood. She had no tolerance for jealousy. When confronted with it, she pulled inward, isolated herself, and disappeared into her poetry. I'd seen it many times at social events, awards ceremonies, and parties. Jack was an egoist.

He was very handsome, and he responded to women regardless of the presence of his wife. He thrived on the attention. In Bordeaux, the Duchess fascinated him, as she did most men. She was beautiful, intelligent, and complicated. She spoke five languages and had traveled all over the world. She'd been brought up to entertain. She told remarkable stories. On a few nights, Jack, and the Duchess stayed up long after the others had gone to bed, talking, drinking, smoking, and what have you. It would have annoyed any wife. Without access to her study, her papers, her typewriter, or her privacy, Vivienne became sullen and then enraged. She was lazy around the house, rude to the hosts, refused to come to dinner, and, once, she disappeared in the night. Jack found her outside in the garden wearing only a thin nightgown and no shoe.

In the end, Jack made multiple apologies for her behavior and cut the vacation short. As far as I know, neither of them ever spoke of that trip again— not to anyone else and not to one another. I'm not an expert on marriage, but it seems to me they ought to have talked. Don't you think?

CHAPTER 59

DR. B.

By mid-1961, Vivienne had moved to Springhill House in Devon, far southwest of London. It was isolated, a quiet countryside retreat where she hoped to settle into family life with Jack and Agatha. Around that time, she wrote to me—perhaps her second or third letter of the year. The first ones had been light, mostly updates on Agatha, who was, as Vivienne put it, "growing like a weed," and had developed a fascination with bugs and crawlies. A fitting interest, wouldn't you say, for someone who later became such a unique artist?

Then, in that summer letter, Vivienne's tone shifted. She reached out for advice on handling her mother and hinted at her new pregnancy. She wanted me to be her psychiatrist, by correspondence, if you can imagine. I had to remind her that I could be her friend, but not her doctor. Reflecting now, maybe it was an error to offer either.

Vivienne wrote that she was pleased about the baby, due in January, yet I sensed an underlying worry. They'd just moved, had no real routine, and Devon's isolation might have weighed on her. And, as understanding as a husband might be, there was a limit in those days to what even the best men would do around the house. If a man were truly exceptional, he might dry a dish or change a nappy occasionally—and Jack, I believe, did. But Vivienne was still adjusting to full-time motherhood. And the memory of her miscarriage hadn't faded; it lingered, a quiet sadness she rarely voiced.

And then, of course, there was the German girl, an unsettling presence that found its way into Vivienne's poetry. If you've read those poems, you'd understand her concern.

There's something else from those letters that has stuck with me. Vivienne wrote that she'd taken up beekeeping. Not a trivial hobby—it's an all-consuming endeavor. She'd ordered these enormous bee boxes, like miniature coffins, each humming with activity. Beekeepers dress in full suits with netting, gloves, and veils—there's almost a ritual to it, a kind of cultish fascination among them. At first, I thought it was an eccentric interest, but then, that was Vivienne. She never gravitated to the ordinary. And, of course, her father had been a beekeeper. Apiculture, they call it—the art of managing honeybees.

Looking back, I see now that the bees were more than just bees to Vivienne. They were threads of her father's influence, and in returning to them, she was perhaps reconnecting with him. I assumed she'd moved past Fritz and the trauma he'd left her with, but her poetry told a different story. She was writing the "barbed wire poems" then—harsh, entangled works that now seem to hold a kind of self-protective ferocity. I thought her anger was just a poetic device. But for Vivienne, the art and the pain were one and the same.

CHAPTER 60

WINGS OF GLASS
Fall 1961

Vivienne felt naked. She had the strange and sudden desire to pull the scarf she wore over her face and hide the way she had as a child. Her lips were too fat, her face swollen to the size of a melon, her neck hideous, her calves thick, and they were all staring at her, were they not? The rector, the former teacher, the man who ran the tobacco shop in the village, the one whose name she could never recall. She knew these people—her neighbors. Some of them were friends. But they were all alien to her now. They were pulling on visors, black netted hoods, and all at once, they became invisible, or at least indiscernible, one from the other.

The beekeepers of their little village got together every week during the season. They wanted her here; she reminded herself. Learning of Vivienne's interest in bees, they'd summoned her. Why use that word? *Summon.* That's how it felt. *Where is your box, Vivienne?* They'd asked the month before. *You must have your box and manage your own hive.* She hadn't known. She'd stood around idly, stupidly, and watched one man, the rector, handle his hive bare-handed the way her father had done, moving back and forth between the honeycombs, wax yellow and sticky. Bees everywhere. *Transition,* the man said. *A new queen,* he said. Vivienne asked about the old queen. Nobody said a thing. Vivienne imagined the dying queen, ravaged by the hive, no longer able to raise her glassy wings in flight.

CHAPTER 61

BLACKSTONE
Winter 1961

1

Vivienne strolled along the outer edge of their property, surveying the frozen fields. Beneath the heavy gray sky, dirty woolen sheep with yellow teeth and slits for eyes stood among the heather. She turned onto a narrow path that led to the village, her boots crunching on the ice. The morning's chill bit through her coat, but she hardly noticed; she'd been restless in the mornings, leaving the house while Jack and the baby slept, as if walking could work out the dark tangle inside her. It was early, barely dawn. The only light came from the houses in the town below. The quick descent of winter in Devon always took her by surprise, left her breathless and uneasy. She took in a deep breath, feeling the sting of the wind on her face, letting it shock her awake.

Jack, meanwhile, seemed immune to it all, the bleakness, the gray, the cold. For him, winter felt crisp and full of possibility, and she didn't begrudge him that—only envied it, that buoyancy, how he never seemed affected, let alone troubled. She caught herself smiling, remembering how he'd bounced around the house last night, singing Christmas carols and carrying on like a child. But then, it made sense; praise was pouring in for him, from both sides of the Atlantic. He seemed stronger, happier, every accolade adding fuel to his spirit. She'd tried to match his cheer, but the truth gnawed at her: they'd depleted their savings to buy this house, and every penny left was slipping through their fingers, going into endless repairs. Wasn't he worried at all? Didn't it keep him up, the way it did her? She shook her head, trying to shake loose the bitterness. No—Jack helped, didn't he? The man changed nappies, for God's sake. It would be cruel to ask for more.

But by early December, she was seven months pregnant, sleeping poorly, consumed with worry over the state of their marriage. She could feel the anger flaring up inside her, igniting over the smallest things. She hated the way she'd been picking fights, only to curse herself afterward, feeling like some nagging, tiresome wife. She knew it was driving him away. He stayed in London so often now, and she could feel him slipping further away with every night he was gone. She could feel it—the silence between them, spreading like rot.

2

They'd expected her brother Beanie for Christmas, and she'd been counting on it, on having someone from her own family with her in this isolation. But when he canceled the trip in November, disappointment hit her with a force she hadn't expected. She'd pleaded with him to come anyway, but she knew he couldn't. On what money? He'd sent his apologies; he felt terrible about it. And she tried to understand, but how was she supposed to get through this? Did he know how lonely she was, how desperately she needed family, her American family?

The weather turned as if to mirror her mood. The sky hardened, gray and pitiless; the wind grew bitter. Every morning felt colder than the last, and she found herself pacing the house at night, listening to the wind clawing at the windows, feeling the familiar darkness settle within her. She tried not to let it overtake her, tried to distract herself by reading essays from *The Nation*, obsessing over the state of the world. She'd been writing letters to Ruthie and her mother, pouring out her anxieties—the military build-up, the rise of corporate power, medals being given to former German officers. The world felt like it was tilting into chaos. Was it even right to be bringing children into a world like this?

3

One evening, Jack had come up with a suggestion. "What do you think about inviting the neighbors for Christmas?" he'd asked, as if it were the most natural thing in the world.

Her immediate reaction was to say no. Christmas meant work—cooking, cleaning, putting on a show. Every fiber of her wanted to walk off into the moor, to disappear into the fog rather than host a holiday. But poor Jack. He was trying. "Why not?" she'd replied, forcing a smile. "That's a good idea." She could try. She could at least try.

So, they'd invited Barbara and Daniel Campion. It seemed right, after all. They were kind neighbors, the closest to them, though "close" was a relative term in the Devon countryside. Vivienne recalled how the Campions had come by in the summer, introducing themselves, bringing a basket of fruit, offering to help with any chores they might need. Vivienne liked them. Barbara was a retired schoolteacher, intelligent and funny, and had taken a liking to Agatha, offering to babysit so Vivienne could write or rest. How many times had Barbara stepped in and given her the relief she so desperately needed? Vivienne found herself wishing she could talk to Barbara, to open up, just a little. But she held back. That wasn't the kind of friendship they had.

One morning, just before Christmas, Jack had turned to her with a sleepy smile. "I had a dream," he said. "You'd won a prize."

"A prize?" she asked, breaking the yolk of an egg into the frying pan.

"Yes. Twenty-five pounds," he replied, laughing. "And we were over the moon, as if twenty-five quid could fix everything."

She laughed softly, turning the egg in the pan, but the words lingered. As if it would fix anything. How often had she caught herself thinking the same, that if only some miracle would happen—just enough money to lift them out of the shadows a little, just a little relief from the weight of it all.

Later that day, the post arrived, and with it, a letter addressed to her. She opened it, and for a moment, her breath caught: she'd won the Saxton Grant, a sum of two thousand twenty-eight American dollars. She read it again, stunned. Two thousand dollars. Real money. She laughed, clutching the letter, and found herself dancing around the living room with Jack, their minds racing with plans. A new thatch on the roof, rugs to warm the house, a trip to Spain—the possibilities spilled out in breathless chatter until they were both laughing hysterically.

In the end, they invested in a few rugs, three additional electric heaters for the coldest rooms, and tucked the rest into savings. The relief was palpable, a warm weight in her chest. Maybe things would be all right after all. With the grant and the baby's impending birth, some of the tension eased, and Vivienne found herself actually looking forward to Christmas.

She threw herself into preparations: she decorated the tree, arranged stacks of wrapped presents, baked fruit bread, cakes, and pies. She dyed her hair strawberry blonde and finished knitting the scarf she'd started six months ago—a Christmas gift for Jack. She wanted things to feel bright, festive, like a real home.

On Christmas Day, they had breakfast together, just the three of them: black pudding, poached eggs, soldiers. Jack took Agatha in his arms and showed her the decorations, making her giggle, and for the first time in months, Vivienne felt a warm glimmer of happiness. She watched Jack finish sanding and polishing the cradle he'd made for the new baby, admiring his focus, his patience, and felt a rush of affection for him that nearly brought tears to her eyes. They spent the afternoon with the Campions, who'd come for a big American-style Christmas dinner. Turkey, sweet potatoes, Brussels sprouts, gravy, apple pie—it was more food than she'd made in a year, but it was worth it, she thought, seeing their smiles.

She found herself saying, more than once, that this would be the first of many Christmases in the house, imagining them celebrating every year at Springhill House, surrounded by friends and family. She meant it, believed it. The house was perfect for Christmas; she could see it in her mind's eye— a place where warmth and laughter filled every corner.

It was December 25, 1961, and Vivienne could almost believe that this was her home, that this happiness was hers to keep. But, somewhere in her heart, she felt the faintest echo of doubt. This would be her only Christmas here, her only Christmas in the grand house in Devon.

PART SEVEN: 1962

CHAPTER 62

BLESS THE CHILD
January 1962

Their son arrived in January 1962, born at home with the help of a midwife. The birth was wildly painful but, mercifully, uneventful. Jack, who had tried to reduce Vivienne's discomfort with hypnosis, stayed by her side throughout the process—something uncommon for fathers at the time—though, in truth, he was mostly useless. She'd squeeze his hand in agony, and he'd whisper words meant to calm her, but they slipped past her like mist. His presence was both comforting and a reminder of how alone she truly was in the intensity of this moment.

The boy was spectacularly beautiful, and Vivienne felt herself fall in love the instant his slippery, squalling body was placed, hot and wet, against her chest. The midwife whisked him away a moment later to check, clean, and wrap him. She returned him quickly, his tiny face and curled fists poking out of a blanket, and Vivienne held him close, in awe of this fierce, delicate creature now in her arms.

Jack leaned in, slipping his arm around her shoulders, looking at his son with an expression that was equal parts curiosity and wariness. Dawn was breaking, the first soft light of morning spilling through the east-facing windows, casting a warm glow over father and baby. Vivienne studied them, noticing the resemblance immediately—the boy was all Jack.

"Hold him," she said, handing the baby to Jack. He took him awkwardly, his hands tentative, as though he'd never held a baby before.

"You won't break him. It's not been so long since your daughter was this size," she said, smiling.

"How soon they change," Jack murmured, his eyes tracing the tiny features. He looked almost hesitant.

"He looks exactly like you," Vivienne said, watching his expression closely.

Jack chuckled. "Ah, you mean I look like a wrinkly old man who's just lost a pub fight?"

She laughed, but the sound felt hollow, a little forced. Jack's expression softened as he looked more intently at the boy, as though trying to unlock some mystery in his little face.

"Yes, maybe he looks like me," Jack conceded, "but he's got a lot more kindness in him."

Vivienne blinked, feeling a flicker of confusion. Jack must have seen it; he gave a half-shrug, as if he hadn't meant to say it aloud. "I mean more...ah, I don't know what I mean. He's perfect, though." He looked down at the baby one last time, then handed him back to her, as if the warmth of the newborn was something he couldn't quite bear. "I'd better go over to the Campions and collect our little girl. She'll be awake soon, if she's not already, bugging the shite outta them."

Vivienne nodded, feeling a pang of worry as he turned to leave. She could almost feel the distance between Jack and the baby, something she'd sensed even during the pregnancy. He hadn't connected with this child, not the way he had with their daughter, and she wondered if he ever would. Would he favor Agatha? Or would this son simply take time to find his way into Jack's heart? She hoped it was only a matter of time. But right now, exhaustion pulled at her, muffling her worries.

She lay back for a while as the midwife changed the bedding, then propped herself up on fresh pillows, holding her son as she fed him. The warmth and weight of his tiny body pressed against her calmed her, a fierce tenderness blossoming with each passing second. She closed her eyes, burying her nose in his fine baby hair, inhaling his sweet, milky scent, feeling her heart slow as his nearness seemed to soothe her completely. When he finished feeding, she brought her fingers close to his lips, feeling the delicate warmth of his moth-breaths against her skin.

Finally, she handed him over to the midwife, who gently laid him in the bassinet beside the bed. Vivienne settled back, feeling the quiet pull of sleep wash over her as she watched her son, now tucked up snugly, and let her eyelids grow heavy.

CHAPTER 63

BARBARA CAMPION

We became friends quickly after they moved to Devon, and by January 1962, we were close. I think Vivienne was desperate. If they'd been in London, she'd have looked right past me, but as it was, she had little choice. I suspect that in her mind, it was me, Barbara Campion, or the "stump warts." You know that's what she called them? So awful—she'd have never said it to their faces, of course. Vivienne was much too kind for that. But look, the village women were older than Vivienne, older than me even, and I was past forty. And these women, they could be hard—very judgmental, rigid in their ways. They were hard on her. She dressed peculiarly: colorful skirts, bright stockings, and this lovely long braid down her back, which at one point she dyed an odd cherry color. These women were from traditional English country backgrounds—most born in the early twentieth century. Vivienne was a creature from another planet.

It was after she had the little boy that she started trying. She was lonely, wanted to fit into the community. Probably Vivienne imagined they'd be staying a long time. Anyway, she'd invite them for tea, and I'm sure they'd have long talks about their ailments and distant relatives and what have you. Vivienne once told me they'd speak a lot about wallpaper. I don't know if she was serious. Probably. It wasn't until I told her why I never attended that she gave up trying with most of them.

"Why is it I never see you at any of their to-do's?" she asked me. Although, I think she was primarily interested in why I didn't feel obligated to socialize with them. It was so typical that she would ask me that question, of course, and not ask my husband, who was as socially idle as I was. He certainly could have

been involved in the community if he'd had an interest, but there was no pressure on him to do so. He was a man, and it was assumed he had more important things to do. Anyway, I just told Vivienne the truth. We'd moved to Tawton nearly a decade earlier, and it had taken the community about five minutes to discover I was a divorcée. On that basis alone, I'd been excluded. I didn't protest because I found them all to be awful bores, but it was dreadfully unfair on principle. Poor Vivienne. She was horrified. She wanted to take up my cause immediately. You know, march into one of those stupid meetings, guns blazing. Can you imagine anything worse? I finally convinced her to leave it alone. After all, it made no sense to fight for my right to do something I had no interest in doing in the first place.

I think Vivienne Holland was a confused person with a generous heart. Brilliant, charming, and so funny, but confused. And she needed a good deal more than Tawton could offer. Me? I was happy with my garden, my cats, my books, and my silly husband. But Vivienne needed London. Intellectual people with whom she could talk, debate, explore. She also required a certain amount of privacy and anonymity, and oddly, a city gives you more of that than a small village. I don't believe she should ever have come. By early spring, people discovered her husband was famous, and they were prying. Dropping by the house, interrupting Vivienne's life, making her writing life impossible. And Jack—he loved the attention. He just ate it up. That turned out to be a whole different sort of disaster. So, no, in answer to your original question, they shouldn't have come.

CHAPTER 64

UNDER THE LABURNUM TREE
Spring 1962

1

"Brigitte Bardot and, of course, Lolita; I absolutely love Lolita."

The girl's voice was so eager, each name of her favorite female stars popping from her lips like little explosive soap bubbles. Vivienne wondered if now might be the time to tell her that *Lolita* was fictional, while Bardot was, mostly, an actual person. Or was it the other way around? Before she could decide, the girl started up again.

"But there are so many others. I only wish I could trim my shape to look like one of them," Lucy said, running her hand over the smooth curve of her flawless teenage hip.

"What could be wrong with your shape?" Jack's tone was casual, but his words struck Vivienne as spectacularly stupid. She shot him a look.

Vivienne had been sitting in the kitchen, savoring her coffee, feeding the baby, and looking forward to her precious hours alone in the study. The baby was three months old now, and she and Jack were finally settling back into their pre-baby schedule: three uninterrupted hours each morning for Vivienne and the afternoons for Jack. It had only worked out a half-dozen times so far, but Vivienne was optimistic. Jack was trying—or at least he had been. But now, with this girl showing up mid-morning, Vivienne's disappointment soured her mood. *Why couldn't Jack just send her away? Or better yet, not open the door?* He never did. He seemed thrilled each time, always ready with coffee or tea and a chat.

The girl was sixteen-year-old Lucy Tarin, the pretty but not particularly bright daughter of Harold and Liza Tarin, owners of the village's only grocery store. One day, Lucy had simply appeared at Springhill House's doorstep, as if summoned by Jack's restlessness. She claimed to be on "break" from her boarding school, but as the weeks passed, Vivienne suspected Lucy might never go back. She seemed far more interested in Jack than in her education. Smitten and possibly a little in love, she clung to his every word. *Oh my gosh, I've never met writers before,* she had gushed upon first meeting them. *I thought maybe I could be a writer. Would you like to read some of my work?* Mostly, though, her interest was squarely in Jack.

Jack's fame was growing. Some in the village knew of him, and Lucy's parents, considering themselves more cultured than their neighbors, likely saw an opportunity to cozy up to the Welles family. Although Jack disagreed, Vivienne suspected the idea to "stop by" had first come from Lucy's mother. Initially, Lucy came by to sample books Jack recommended, to have him read her writing, or simply for the excuse to linger.

When Lucy finally returned to school, Jack continued corresponding with her, supposedly to help with her studies. He critiqued her clumsy English papers, recommended more books, and suggested films he thought might "expand her horizons." When she returned to Tawton for spring break, Lucy appeared at Springhill House wearing an elegant pastel skirt and low heels, her hair perfectly coiffed. She looked older than sixteen, lovely and tall.

And now here she was again. And Jack seemed in no hurry to get her out or end this invasion of their privacy. If anything, he encouraged it. Vivienne tried to focus on spooning mashed peaches into the baby's mouth, but blocking out their conversation was impossible.

"You know, I saw that film, the one by the Fellini guy," Lucy was saying, her tone casual. "It was terribly strange. I didn't get much from it, so I got bored."

"La Strada," said Jack, nodding along. "Yes, you're right. So much hype around that one, but it can be a bit dull. You're absolutely right."

Vivienne shot Jack a glare. *The one by the Fellini guy?* Jack adored that film. She'd lost count of how many times they'd watched it together. *Liar.*

Groveling, stupid liar, she thought, and for what? The girl babbled on, oblivious to Vivienne's irritation. Finally, Vivienne stood, handed the baby to Jack, and forced a polite tone.

"I need to start work. Your daughter will be up soon, so please keep an ear out."

She imagined Lucy running home to her parents, eager to report that Mrs. Welles was a thoroughly rude and dreadful hostess. No doubt, the entire village would be lamenting by noon over poor Mr. Welles being "saddled with such a witch of a wife." *Sod it,* she thought, *I need to work.* She'd make it up later—bring them all baskets of Eccles cakes. God knew they all loved their baked goods.

2

The following month, things got worse. The girl visited so frequently that Vivienne began turning her away at the door. Her excuses evolved from the pathetic—the baby is sick, the house is a mess—to the more creative. We've had plague exposure, or the baby has been bitten in the face by a crow. Vivienne quite liked that last one; nobody wants to see a baby with a crow bite on its face. Jack was horrified. Vivienne claimed desperation.

Word was getting around: the Welles family was unneighborly.

"We must correct this," said Jack. "It's a small village; people will not forgive easily."

Vivienne stared at him. This was a different husband. Where was the one she'd left in New England? The one who thought people who cared about social etiquette were fools, slaves to the rules of a middle-class hell.

"This is different," he said. "We have children to think about."

Why did Vivienne feel it was about something more?

3

In late April, ostensibly to "smooth things over," Jack left the children at home and went round for tea at the girl's house with her family. Vivienne refused to attend. "Better to be unneighborly than a hypocrite," she said. She could imagine very few activities less palatable than an afternoon trapped in the garden with Lucy and her ridiculous parents. It didn't escape Vivienne's notice that as recently as six months earlier, she might have loved a social outing with Jack. Any social outing. Something was changing. Deteriorating. Tolerance, patience, motivation, optimism, and attitude.

It had started after the baby was born. A sort of withering. Different from the darkness of depression. Not the weight she'd experienced in the past. This was more like a gradual fading from existence. A dehydration process. It was like lying down, strapped to a bed, and being hooked up to a bunch of reverse intravenous tubes, forced to watch as the essence of you was slowly sucked away, not fast, but in one direction. She was deflating, and the worst part was suspecting it was supposed to be like this. She'd been a child, a teenager, a young woman, a lover, a wife, a mother. Maybe that was it. The world was done with her. She'd birthed the babies and even birthed Jack's career. They didn't need her. Well, that wasn't exactly true. The baby required her a little longer, at least until he was done breastfeeding. But then what? Like an old queen bee. Like wings of glass. Done. Time to go.

She stood, pushing away the morbid thoughts, and began gathering up the breakfast dishes. The children would wake from their naps soon, and she'd take them out for a walk. She wasn't depressed. This was stupid. Wasteful. Indulgent. She was at risk of becoming one of those nasty old bitches nobody aspired to be around. Maybe she would bake a cake this afternoon, a cream cake.

4

Jack was late returning from tea. The afternoon became evening, and the evening stretched into night. Around eight, Vivienne opened the front door and looked down the path, peering into the dark, not really expecting to see anything. But there he was. There they were, Jack and this teenager, under the laburnum tree. The outline of their bodies in the moonlight. Jack pontificating, the girl's attention rapt, her face tilted up towards his. Vivienne felt her body clench. She'd seen this before.

The chemistry between her husband and this child was undeniable.

Vivienne was barefoot, holding the baby on her hip, and wearing what might have been her oldest and grimiest housedress. She stepped outside and onto the narrow porch. Jack glanced up, and Lucy followed his gaze. Vivienne marched toward them, ignoring the pain as bits of bark and sharp pebbles ground into the soles of her feet. Lucy's eyes widened as she mumbled something about coming inside to listen to Vivienne's German records. Vivienne glared at both of them, then turned sharply and headed back into the house. A moment later, she returned with the records.

5

In the dream, The Poet is home in Yorkshire or somewhere that looks very much like home. He is standing on a hill overlooking his village below. He has come here hoping to re-experience the wonder and excitement he remembers from his boyhood. He waits a long time, but nothing comes. Instead, the sky is dull and pale, the colors of the moor appear muted and vague. What he recalled as a carpet of brilliant purple flowers now appears as only dusty weeds. He is bored, his heart and mind are numb. He feels only hopelessness.

Suddenly, the sky darkens. And an icy rain begins. The water stings his face, like needles, and he is quickly soaked. The Poet blinks, struggling to clear his vision. In the distance, he sees something. A figure, not a man. A creature, half-winged but running. It comes for him at tremendous speed. Racing upwards from the valley below. In an instant, it is closer; a griffin, a chimera — he cannot tell. It is monstrous, coming straight at him, head down, gnashing its teeth. It means to attack. He looks around frantically for a place to hide. He runs faster and faster, his heart pounding wildly in his chest. He can hear it, the terrible beat of its wings slap of its hooved feet in the mud, gaining on him. Finally, terrified, he leaps without looking over the edge of the cliff.

The creature races past, and he is safe, caught on a ridge a few feet below.

After a few minutes, he catches his breath and climbs slowly back to the road. The monster is gone, the rain stops, and the view returns to what it was when he first arrived. He and sees that he is completely uninjured. The Poet sighs as the terrible boredom engulfs him once again.

CHAPTER 65

BARBARA CAMPION

It must have been late that spring in 1962—the tension between them was palpable. There were times they barely looked at each other, especially after Vivienne put a stop to the whole thing with the teenager. You know Jack went right on, don't you? I remember once he'd brought this young woman back from a reading in London and put her up in their guest room. Swedish, I think. She might have been a fan or maybe a photographer. I honestly cannot imagine why Vivienne put up with that. Daniel and I left that evening just shocked, trying to sort out what in the world Jack had been thinking. But, of course, that was the beginning of the end of everything.

I will say, there was a time around Easter when things seemed better. Springhill House was just gorgeous. Old as anything, falling apart really, but stunning. Rolling and lush. Quite a bit less dreary than old London. Vivienne loved the sunshine, and Springhill House always had daffodils exploding across the property. There were thousands of blossoms, and Vivienne set about cutting them to sell by the dozen at the grocer's market. Daniel was over there all the time. He and Vivienne must have cut hundreds of flowers. He helped her wrap them and ready them for the market. The two of them had such a time together. Vivienne really appreciated Daniel—as a father, you know.

She was doing other domestic things: painting tiny Germanic flowers and hearts all over the furniture and doorways. Sometimes, she would even spend hours or days cooking these enormous meals, veal cutlets and stewed potatoes. All English, of course. Although she was an American girl, she grew her own vegetables. She would clean and cook and have everything lovely, and the babies—darling, but so much work. The little one was always with the runny nose. Vivienne was consumed with doing it all perfectly. It was all too much, and it alienated many people.

Still, she'd been asked to do the BBC, so I imagined money was less of an issue. I had a few conversations with her that first week of May, and she seemed genuinely happy, maybe for the first time since I'd met her.

But then, I didn't know her all that well, did I? I wish I'd paid better attention. But it was right around then that my husband, Daniel, became ill. It was swift, very unexpected, and I was distracted, I suppose you could say. Completely distracted.

CHAPTER 66

DREAMERS
Spring 1962

1

They were late. The Canadian poet and his wife—the couple to whom Vivienne and Jack had sublet the Primrose flat. And the so-called "German girl" wasn't a girl at all. She was older than Vivienne, and she had a name: Bertina. On the phone, she had introduced herself as Bertina Gutman Clark. Vivienne found it strange—she'd used her maiden name. Vivienne had accidentally dialed her at work, at the ad agency in London. "Bertina Gutman Clark, can I help you?" she'd answered, and Vivienne had been stunned. Most women worked as assistants to the men in executive roles, but this one apparently had enough clout to answer her own phone.

And now, Bertina and the Canadian poet were very late. Vivienne had invited them down to Springhill House for the weekend, and lunch had already come and gone. The babies were hungry and cranky, and Vivienne tried to keep the chaos at bay. Agatha was busily pulling a garden wagon across the house, and Vivienne watched as thin, reddish-brown streaks appeared on the living room floor. Hours ago, she'd abandoned the debate over wagons staying outside; her daughter, not quite three, had already mastered a way with words that left Vivienne at a disadvantage. So instead, she bent down to wipe the floor for what felt like the hundredth time.

Five minutes after she cleaned the floor, the baby squished a mushy banana into his hair, and Vivienne, still maintaining an outward calm, wiped it out with a washcloth. Moments later, a milk jug slipped from her hands, shattering on the floor, sending a river of milk shooting across the kitchen like a burst dam. Still, she did not lose her temper. But when Jack finally came in from his walk down the road to "see if they might be stuck" and tossed his wet rain slicker onto the sitting room sofa, Vivienne reached her breaking point.

"Where in the bloody hell are they?" she said, the words coming out louder and sharper than she'd intended, stopping the entire family in their tracks. "Sorry," she added quickly, forcing a smile. "I'm just getting a little annoyed, is all."

"They'll be here," Jack replied with calm assurance, heading into the kitchen.

Vivienne watched his slicker sit there stubbornly, soaking water into the upholstery of their only piece of furniture and clenched her fists.

2

Vivienne was passing her daughter the last biscuit when she heard Jack open the front door. The man's voice, the Canadian, sounded just as she remembered it: nondescript, middle-toned, dull. But the woman's voice— each time Vivienne heard it, the rich resonance and perfectly posh English accent took her by surprise. She sounded like a jeweler from Kensington. Vivienne listened as they settled into the front room and glanced around the kitchen in dismay: spilled tea, milk, biscuit crumbs, and two rumpled children who looked nothing like the tidy little angels they'd been that morning. If only the guests had been on time!

She quickly went to work, tidying up her children and smoothing her hair. A quick glance at her reflection in the toaster, and she slipped off her apron. Taking a steadying breath, she stepped into the front room to face her visitors.

3

Bertina was taller than Vivienne remembered. She wore dark slacks and a silky orange blouse, both fitted perfectly. And she was beautiful—

stunningly, painfully beautiful. Had she changed? Or had Vivienne simply been too distracted by her own fortunes a year ago to see it? Had she been too focused on the move, the baby, and the pressures of this strange life in Devon to notice that the woman before her was a vision?

It was the most beautiful face Vivienne had ever seen: delicate jaw, full lips, high, solid cheekbones, and those almond-shaped eyes, an impossible shade of deep blue. She'd lined them in black kohl, which only made their color more intense, and wore long gold earrings that caught the light when she moved. Babylonian, thought Vivienne. Some goddess of myth, complete with a commanding presence and a glint of humor in her gaze. How did some people have the time, the energy, the natural elegance to move through life as if they were just ... born for it?

Vivienne tucked a stray lock behind her ear, suddenly, acutely aware of her own body's heaviness. It was impossible not to compare. She felt unwieldy, weighed down. Four months postpartum, she was still carrying what felt like an enormous amount of pregnancy weight. Her clothes didn't fit—still stained, faded, ill-sized. Her breasts ached, her hair was a mousy mess, her nails ragged. She felt cow-heavy, ungraceful, her whole self pressing into the earth like an anchor. She glanced down at her own clothes, wrinkled and faded, and thought, *Useless as a dead whale.* Her life was spilling out into milk-stained fabrics and unkempt hair while Bertina stood there, radiating, exuding poise and perfection.

Was it terrible, how much she wished for that—to be seen, admired, even envied? Was it wrong to want to be that light, rather than just a shadow behind the children, behind Jack? What she wouldn't give to slip away for just one hour and feel a sense of herself again, to go somewhere anonymous, somewhere she could just be Vivienne. Had she been like this once? Hadn't she been vibrant, too, in the life they'd left behind? Here she felt like an accessory to her own life, a ghost.

Bertina stepped forward and kissed Vivienne's cheek. She smelled faintly of lemon and cinnamon spice, the kind of scent someone chose with care. Then Bertina kissed Jack. As she did, her hair fell across them both in a perfect, drifting curtain, momentarily hiding them from the world. Vivienne felt her chest tighten as she watched them, transfixed.

4

The babies napped while the adults sat in the garden, drinking wine and eating vegetable pie. Bertina was speaking, but Vivienne was struggling to follow the conversation. Something about marketing. Bertina worked in marketing, but what she "really wanted to do was be a writer." Oh, for God's sake, was there anyone who aspired to be anything besides a writer? How many times had she and Jack laughed over this very sentiment? Yet here was Jack, furrowing his brow, nodding with what looked like genuine interest, even offering to "give a look" and read some of her work. *Hell's bells,* thought Vivienne.

"Your accent," said Vivienne finally. "It's not foreign."

The others stared at her. She had completely lost track of the conversation and thrown out the words impulsively. She had a habit of living inside her head, expecting others to be in there too. Judging from the looks on their faces, her comment was out of place. She pressed on.

"What I mean is that it's English."

"My accent?" asked Bertina, her tone smooth and polite, showing absolutely no sign of offense. Perfectly posh English manners.

Vivienne decided she was already too deep to back out. "I thought you said you were born in Berlin?"

"Oh, yes." Bertina set her glass down, and Vivienne noticed her nails were unpolished but filed into a lovely oval shape. *No dishwashing or nappy-changing for this one.*

"I was born in Berlin, yes. But we left when I was eight."

Vivienne could do the math. She knew what was coming before Bertina spoke.

"The war, of course." Then, meeting Vivienne's eyes, she added, "The Nazis."

"Oh my." Vivienne's hand flew to her mouth. "That must have been terrifying. And for a child..." She paused, then added, "My father was German," regretting it instantly. "Where did you go? Your family, I mean?"

"Oh, first Italy. And then Israel. I grew up in Israel."

"Your English is so—" Vivienne stopped herself, nearly saying "posh." Her American directness was a hard habit to break. Bertina smiled.

"Oh, yes. It surprises people all the time that I'm not from London. My mother insisted I go to an English girls' school. Private. I never fit in, but I did learn to speak well."

Hard to believe that Beautiful Bertina Gutman never fit in, thought Vivienne. Other girls would have twisted themselves into pretzels to fit in around her.

"And the rest of your family?" Vivienne asked.

"Viv," Jack said, a little too sharply, placing a hand on her arm. She pulled away.

Bertina shook her head, her beautiful eyes glistening. "My father was Jewish. His family was in Russia. We never saw them again."

Vivienne was silent. What could she say?

"So, you said your father was German?" Bertina prompted gently.

"I'm sorry," Vivienne replied, reaching for the wine bottle between them. She poured some into Bertina's glass.

"It was a terrible war, tragic," Jack added, stating the obvious in that way he did when he was nervous.

"Yes, Bertina's family suffered from both sides, really," her husband added. It was almost startling to hear his voice; he spoke so little.

The conversation drifted to lighter topics, and once again, Vivienne lost track. Instead, she focused on studying Bertina. Her beauty was undeniable, but it was something else, something more elusive. Bertina had a way with men—a subtle shift in posture, a tilt of her head that inflated the significance of whatever a man was saying. Suddenly, he was Winston Churchill addressing the House of Commons in 1940: *We shall fight on the beaches,* and so on. Jack was especially susceptible.

It didn't matter. In two days, they'd be gone, back to the flat in London, and Jack would be buried in his books and poems again. No trouble at all, this German-Italian-Israeli-Jewish woman. There was nothing here, Vivienne told herself, jabbing her fork into the crust of her vegetable pie like a dagger.

5

"Tangiers?" Vivienne asked. "I didn't know you'd spent time there."

It was Saturday morning, and the two couples were out on the moor, ostensibly shooting blackbirds with air rifles. But, as it turned out, only Jack and the Canadian were shooting; Vivienne had no taste for the killing, and Bertina claimed she hadn't shot a gun since they'd lived in Tangiers.

"Oh yes. Two years, while Wyatt was working on his dissertation." Bertina tipped her head toward her husband, then rolled her eyes.

The expression startled Vivienne. Did she not like her husband, or perhaps she found him ridiculous?

"It was dreary," Bertina added.

"Really? I've heard such wonderful things," said Vivienne.

She'd known only one friend who'd lived there, and the best things she'd heard were that a wife and mother who wanted to write could afford to hire people to do the cooking, cleaning, and childcare. Otherwise, she'd heard, the weather was dreadful, the people indifferent, and the streets dangerous.

"Oh no, no. It's lonely and hot. Terribly hot, all the time. But I got through it," said Bertina.

Vivienne noted that Bertina had said "I got through it," not "we got through it."

The hunt wasn't going well, at least not for the Canadian. He hadn't managed to get off a single shot, and Vivienne could see his frustration mounting. Jack continued shooting in silence, probably just as well, since if he spoke, he was more likely to tease and cajole than support. Jack could be merciless in these situations. To Vivienne, the whole thing was vile: Let's go out, murder some birds, and harass the poor bloke who isn't very good at it. Then we'll carry the bleeding, feathery mess home for our wives to cook into something inedible, and we'll get drunk. The activities men labeled "fun" never failed to surprise her.

It continued for perhaps another hour until finally, a bird went down, its wings flapping awkwardly as it fell into a far field. Both men ran toward it and, upon reaching it, stopped, looking down at the bird's body. Vivienne and Bertina stood back, watching in silence. A breeze picked up, rustling the trees. Otherwise, there was no sound as they waited.

"It's still alive," said Vivienne.

"What?" Bertina asked.

"They're just standing there. That means the poor creature is still alive. I hate this."

"Oh god."

The Canadian suddenly picked up the rook, holding it high over his head. For a few moments, he did nothing, just stood there with the bird dangling, its wings grotesquely spread against the pale blue sky. Then, without warning, he brought it down, smashing it against an enormous boulder beside him and Jack. Blood sprayed, and black feathers and bits of bone exploded into the air. Jack leaped back, almost stumbling to get out of the way. Bertina screamed, her hands covering her face. Then, astonishingly, the gentle, soft-spoken Canadian poet raised the bird—what was left of it— and once again smashed it against the rock. Over and over, he slammed it, grunting, sweating, blood splattering his clothes, his hair, his face. Still, he didn't stop. Bertina dropped to her knees, screaming, tears streaming down her face. The smell of blood filled the air, and Vivienne thought she might be sick. Jack stood frozen, watching. The Canadian didn't stop until the bird was reduced to just a few feathers and the feet he'd been gripping. It was a dreadful sight. When he finally stopped, he tore off his filthy shirt, used it to wipe his hands and face, left it by the stone, and trudged back to join the women.

They drove back to Springhill House in silence.

The Canadian was muted at dinner, although Vivienne noticed he drank steadily, more than he had the day before. They had a fine meal of pot roast and potatoes, and no one spoke of eating blackbird. The conversation was light and entertaining—Bertina telling stories from her travels, Jack regaling them with humorous tales of life in North Tawton. They discussed poets and poetry, listened to music, and skillfully avoided the bizarre events of the afternoon. Vivienne climbed the stairs to bed early, leaving the others to chat late into the night.

6

"I had a dream," said Bertina over coffee and biscuits. "A giant fish, it was. A pike, I believe you call it. Nothing specific, but you were there, Jack. You and the pike."

Vivienne looked up from feeding the baby. Had she heard correctly? A pike? Did Jack remember they'd left a framed print of his poem *Pike* hanging on the wall at the London flat? Bertina had seen it. Vivienne glanced at Jack, who seemed so overwhelmed by the flattery, he'd either forgotten or, more likely, wasn't bothered.

"Lovely, just lovely," he said.

Christ, thought Vivienne. He was mesmerized, gone stupid with infatuation. Jack would take this dream—or the report of it—as a mystical sign. His new muse had come to him in the form of this beautiful, manipulative woman.

7

Women were creatures conjured by men to be cooks, housekeepers, secretaries, nursemaids, milkmaids, incubators, whores, and, if they were lucky, mystical muses.

8

Vivienne found them in the kitchen—a linoleum-and-laminate cliché. Turned towards one another, her husband and the German. The German's gold bangle bracelets were clinking against the rough skin of his forearm, her thick forelock falling into her face, and she didn't bother to brush it away. *Her many-blooded beauty, the dreamer in her,* he would write later. Her eyes were weeping streams of glitter onto his chest, just above his heart. Vivienne saw it so clearly. Then, an instant later, it was gone. Just two adults, utterly platonic, standing in the kitchen chopping onions for lunch and talking about her escape from Berlin as a child.

And Vivienne, lingering behind the door's edge—she'd only come in to get more wine but found herself unable to tear away from the scene, from listening. They were only talking.

Just then, Agatha came bouncing in from the garden. "Mummy?" she asked. "Mummy, alright?"

Vivienne looked down at her small daughter. She nodded, taking the child's soft hand and cupping it in hers. "Yes, yes, sweetheart. Mummy is alright."

CHAPTER 67

RABBIT CATCHER
Summer 1962

1

The dream is about a married man driving home. Although he might also have been leaving home. Either way, it is a stone black night, impossible to see two feet ahead or around the car in any direction. The man thinks this is what he has always feared most: being buried alive. The man is anxious, short of breath, beginning to panic. Suddenly, there is an ominous thump beneath the wheels of his car. He slows down and stops, gets out, and walks back. In the taillights, he can see he's run over a hare. Its blood and insides are spread all about across the macadam. It is dead, no doubt. He feels not disgusted, nor is he aggrieved or remorseful. Instead, he is refreshed, renewed, and re-energized. His breath comes lightly and easily. He gets back into his car and he senses a new clarity and direction in his life. He drives on.

2

When Jack finished telling her about the dream in which the man runs over a hare, he took a casual sip of his coffee and asked, "What do you think?"

"Think?" Vivienne replied without turning around.

She was at the sink, washing up an oatmeal bowl. What she thought was that he shouldn't have told her about his dream with the hare.

"Yes, what do you think of the dream? What do you make of it?"

"Hm, well, I suppose it's about a man who enjoys running over animals."

Jack laughed. It was the lighthearted laugh she hadn't heard in weeks, maybe months. It felt out of place.

"Perhaps," he said.

Had he forgotten? Once, very much in love, he'd told her the hare was her totem. That afternoon, while the children napped, she went up to her study and, on the back of a slip of Talbot College memo paper, scratched out a few lines for a new poem:

Tight wires between us ... the constriction killing me as well.

3

Vivienne read the letter twice, satisfied only when she'd confirmed there was nothing more to it—just a simple thank-you note and a sweet, thoughtful gift. Enclosed in the large envelope was a needlepoint kit, the exact one from Harrods that Vivienne had mentioned wanting, and Bertina had even offered in the letter to exchange the thread colors if Vivienne didn't like her choices.

The letter itself was chatty and superficial, including instructions for needlepoint but nothing at all about the awkward end to their weekend, with Vivienne nearly screaming for everyone to leave. Her behavior had mortified Jack. It had felt like France all over again. Had she been too hasty? Had she imagined the moment in the kitchen? She'd been exhausted, wracked with jealousy, and had only vaguely mentioned it to Jack. After the couple left, she felt ridiculous about the whole thing. Naturally, Jack might find Bertina attractive—the whole world seemed to be in love with her— but so what? Finding someone beautiful didn't mean he was planning to sleep with her. But then, there had been Wyatt's strange behavior with the rook. Was it something a powerless, jealous husband might do? Vivienne pushed the thought away.

She slipped the letter into a drawer—something about it made her feel guilty—but kept the needlepoint kit, working on the pattern throughout the summer.

The garden flourished with primrose and rhubarb, attracting pheasants, hummingbirds, and butterflies. The nearby River Taw came alive with kingfishers, and its deep, clear pools filled with trout. Then, finally, the bee boxes arrived, and Vivienne donned her white straw hat with a black nylon veil, joining the other Devon beekeepers and tending to a new hive of her own. The sunshine nourished Vivienne, and her spirits lifted. She forced herself not to think about the terrible weekend in May. Instead, she wrote a bit and spent much of her time outdoors with the children, visited with neighbors, and for a while, life seemed to steady itself.

CHAPTER 68

AMONG THE NARCISSI
Summer 1962

1

Daniel Campion died in June. Barbara called Vivienne and Jack just after dawn.

He lay crumpled like a small child between the sheets, surrounded by a ridiculous heap of pillows, as if comfort still mattered. Someone had bound his jaw and propped an enormous book under his chin to hold his head in place. His eyes were slightly open, exposing a clotted, milky substance—not at all eye-like—and his face had sunken, giving the impression it was continuing to fall inward, a sort of slow-motion collapse. It struck Vivienne that, in a few moments, there might be nothing left but a nose and a few stubbly gray hairs. She felt ill looking at him.

Daniel had been afflicted with some vague illness, but Vivienne and Jack hadn't known it was this serious. Barbara, always the optimist, had mentioned only that he was "taking a few tests." Now, standing over him, Vivienne thought, *He'd apparently failed the tests.*

He'd died suddenly in the night. Heart failure. Or a heart attack or some such issue with his heart. Barbara was not hysterical; she wasn't even crying, though her eyes were rimmed red. She sat quietly in the kitchen, sipping tea and staring into space. The doctor had come, the undertaker had been called. There was nothing to do but wait.

"He's been sick," Barbara kept repeating. Daniel had wanted no one to know. He was a private person. He wanted to keep things private. Her hands, wrapped tightly around her mug, were red and chafed to the point of peeling. She'd lost weight. Vivienne tried to remember how long it had been since she'd seen Barbara. How long had they been suffering alone? Guilt twisted in her gut.

"I'm so sorry, Barbara. I'm so very sorry."

2

A day later, Daniel's body had been moved to the living room, where they'd placed the coffin—a box stained to look like walnut but clearly made of something cheaper. Brassy handles were affixed to the sides, and a small plaque bore his name and date of death. The lid was propped open, and a veil covered the body. Barbara lifted the veil to expose her husband's face. It had been powdered but was still yellow; the eyes were glued shut, and the cheeks had sunken into a hollow, lifeless gauntness. Vivienne glanced, then quickly looked away.

The funeral was a dismal affair. There was no hearse, just a cart to haul the body to the burial site. The procession passed a field of dried narcissi, only a few gray stalks left from early spring. Vivienne recalled those mornings with Daniel at Springhill House, clipping blossoms and wrapping them in brown paper. When was that? February? March? Was he ill even then?

At the gravesite, only a handful of mourners gathered: Barbara, Vivienne, Jack, a few villagers, two of Daniel's former students who had traveled from London, and the minister. That was it. Across the cemetery was a school, where rows of young children sat outdoors eating lunch. As the minister spoke, a few children glanced over at the funeral attendees, curious but indifferent.

Afterward, the mourners walked home in the harsh, feverish light of the afternoon.

CHAPTER 69

CHLOROPHYLL
Summer 1962

1

The Poet hurried along the alley, checking addresses as he passed. He'd assumed the weather would be cooler here in the city, though the assumption had no basis. It was much hotter, and sweat now poured down his back, soaking the underarms of his dress shirt—the one his wife had insisted he wear. "Nobody at the BBC will find your old farm shirt acceptable, Jack. You need to change." God, how he felt confined by those expectations. By the time he got back to the recording room, everyone, including Vivienne, would know he'd been outdoors, wandering some distance on foot during his lunch break. *Sod it,* he thought. He needed to see her. He absolutely had to see her.

He and Vivienne had ridden the train from Devon to London in silence. Jack reviewed his notes for the recording, while Vivienne pretended to read a tattered copy of *Macbeth,* her gaze drifting to the blur of the English landscape—the rolling green fields, vast stretches of seawater, rocky coastline. He knew she found this part of England striking, like something out of *Wuthering Heights,* but today she seemed miserable. It didn't matter that she'd recently beceived praise from A.C., who'd accepted all three of her poetry submissions, calling them "very fine," with one, written from the perspective of an old tree, singled out as "superb." Such praise from *The Critic* was rare, and Vivienne knew it. But lately, nothing seemed to satisfy her. She'd been in a black mood all year—irritable, suspicious, sleepless, and, worst of all, unpredictable. She was exhausted, and he couldn't do it anymore. He'd given up, and the space between them, once filled with conversation, had turned into a vacuum, harboring something monstrous that neither of them dared touch. For a long time, The Poet had thought he was the one dying. Then came the weekend in May. Then came Bertina.

And now he had to see her.

Suddenly, he stopped. He'd found it. The squat gray building, nicely trimmed but unimpressive, sat on a small street just a mile from the recording studio. He ran up the steps and pushed open the doors, greeted by a blast of artificially cooled air that hit his face, making him pause to savor the unexpected relief. Behind the counter sat two prim-looking Englishwomen, busy on the phones. One held up a finger, signaling for him to wait. So he waited. And waited longer. Finally, she hung up and looked at him, a certain disapproval in her expression.

"I've come to see Bertina Clark," he said.

The girl studied him, then clarified, "You mean Bertina Rudman Clark?"

"Yes," he replied, suddenly very aware of how hot, wet, and smelly he felt.

"Your name?"

He gave it, and she instructed him to have a seat.

The Poet sank into a very narrow, uncomfortable chair, one of four pushed up against the wall. To fit, he had to sit rigidly upright with his legs stretched straight out in front of him. He felt like a trapped animal—killed, stuffed, and mounted—completely out of his natural habitat.

The girl returned. "She says she can't see you now, but you can leave a message." She handed him a notepad and a heavy silver pen.

On the top sheet, he wrote, *I've come to see you despite all marriages,* read it back to himself, then tore off the page, folded it in half, then quarters, and handed it back unsigned.

He was back at the BBC before anyone knew he had gone.

2

Three days later, an envelope arrived at Springhill House, The Poet intercepting it before his wife. Inside, there was a single blade of grass.

Grasping it gently between thumb and forefinger, he pressed it to his lips. It smelled as if it had been soaked in her perfume.

3

Two weeks later, The Poet took the German Girl to 112 Sidney Street. He slipped the old key into the even older lock, jiggling it until it clicked into place. The heavy door swung open with a low creak, and an odor, damp and sweet like rotting flowers, greeted them as they stepped inside. The shades were drawn against the summer light, and when he raised them, she put her hands up to her eyes, shielding them from the glare. He noticed she'd removed her wedding band. It was the first time.

"Oh my," she murmured, her voice throaty and soft.

"Uh oh," he said, turning toward her.

The space flooded with sunlight now. Dust motes danced in the beams, and the worn spots in the old rug nearly showed through to the wooden floor slats. Yet, the flat on Sidney Street was one of those uniquely old English spaces, untouched by modern conversions into multiple bedsits; its walls, ceilings, and windowpanes were original to the house. It remained architecturally intact, just as some nineteenth-century designer had intended—to capture the light, the air, the pulse of London.

"What does that mean?" he asked, moving closer.

"It's beautiful. I mean, it's gorgeous."

"It's not mine, of course."

He'd already explained, so why was he explaining again? Because none of this was his—not the flat, not the city, not the woman.

"A mate's flat."

"I know," she said. "But it's ours for tonight, right?"

She moved toward him, and then she was kissing him. She was kissing him, not the other way around. That's how he would remember it later, when the sting of guilt became too much to bear.

4

When it was over, and they lay together, sweating and spent, his arm loosely draped over her shoulders, her hair spilling across his chest in a dark sweep,

The Poet closed his eyes, letting his mind drift. He was caught somewhere between the unfamiliar scent of this strange, beautiful woman and the woody, familiar warmth of his own life, and for a moment, he wasn't sure where he belonged.

What am I doing? The question lingered, rising up and making him wince. He glanced at her—she looked serene, at ease in a way he envied. *So unlike Vivienne,* he thought, feeling a familiar stab of guilt twist inside him. His mind turned to Vivienne: her restlessness, her dark eyes that seemed, lately, to see right through him. And here he was, betraying her, choosing silence over honesty, distance over connection. He hadn't been sure what he wanted, but now...he felt this, too, wasn't it. He shifted, his mind unable to settle.

He'd been here once before. Years earlier, he'd smuggled his young wife up these same stairs, into this very flat. *Was that really me? Was I that man—the one who loved her completely, who looked at her with wonder and admiration?* He could almost see it again, that night in flashes, both of them lying close, holding up their rings to admire those cheap, oversized things slipping around their fingers. They'd laughed, eyes meeting with a depth and excitement he'd taken for granted. She'd chattered endlessly, her excitement so pure, so infectious. He could hear her voice, her accent—so American, so brash and new.

In the early morning light, he had marveled at her—his new wife, his new life, his new America. *Where had all that gone? How had he let it slip away?*

He glanced at Bertina, at the softness of her profile, her eyelids closed, her features peaceful. She looked like someone who could remain forever untouched, undemanding. But the thought settled uneasily, weighing down the quiet.

CHAPTER 70

DR. B.
Summer 1962

Vivienne wrote to me about his behavior changes. She said it had been going on for much of the summer. She wanted to believe Jack was having a nervous breakdown. He'd been getting up terribly early, staying up late, and rushing to check the mail. But he was full of energy, talking about writing plays and winning a Nobel Prize (for what, I don't know—certainly not physics). Yet, he wasn't accomplishing much. According to Vivienne, he was saying awful things. For instance, he'd tell her he'd been "asleep for the entire marriage" and even referred to the new baby as a "usurper."

One might have thought Vivienne was exaggerating, but she was extraordinarily pragmatic, especially for an artist. She spoke plainly—nothing flowery or excessive—and I don't believe she ever exaggerated. If anything, she was prone to minimize, to cover for him.

I think it became clearer to Vivienne in July that Jack was unfaithful, though she wasn't sure it was just one specific woman. She suspected he had dalliances whenever he was in London. When she confronted him, Jack denied it, assuring her he loved her and loved the children. Vivienne did what many women do; she wanted to believe him, despite his behavior. Remember, this was 1962. She was financially dependent, had two very young children, and it was England. And, for whatever reason, she loved him.

But then, an episode convinced her he was involved with one woman in particular. It involved a book—a beautiful, leather-bound edition of Shakespeare's love sonnets. Red leather, specifically, which had particular significance for Vivienne. It was a small gift sent to Jack by mail, but Vivienne intercepted it. It was sent anonymously, clearly meaningful, and unmistakably from a woman. Vivienne thought she knew who had sent it, and that she simply could not tolerate. What doubled the humiliation was her mother's presence. Vivienne's mother had come to Devon to visit for a few weeks and help with the children. It was a terrible time for her to be there, witnessing the unraveling of the marriage.

According to Vivienne, this woman Jack was involved with was practically evil incarnate. She'd been unfaithful to her third husband with her second, attacked her first husband with a knife—many wild and terrible things. Vivienne was experiencing nausea, shortness of breath, and difficulty sleeping—classic symptoms of neurotic anxiety. I was very concerned. She began writing letters in which she expressed a sense of powerlessness. She kept saying she was married to Jack for life and couldn't tolerate the humiliation, the lying, the hypocrisy. She believed she was trapped and, not surprisingly, I detected a vein of paranoia around that time. She struggled to differentiate delusion from reality.

Understand, paranoia is not the same as exaggeration. As I said, Vivienne was a pragmatist to the end.

CHAPTER 71

TELEPHONE
Summer 1962

1

It was barely daylight when the phone rang. Jack hated phones. Vivienne's job was to catch the calls, particularly at odd hours, since the phone was in the hall at the bottom of the stairs, a space neither here nor there—a spot reserved for unwelcome interruptions.

"Hello," Vivienne said. Silence. "Hello?" she repeated, a more insistent tone in her voice. She looked up to see Mother coming down the stairs, holding the baby, her face etched with concern. "Who is this?" Vivienne asked.

A voice—low and indistinct, almost as if it were a woman's, trying to sound like a man—answered, "Can Mr. Welles take a call from London?"

"Mr. Welles?" Vivienne repeated, instantly alert. This was someone they didn't know. Or didn't know well.

"And who may I say is calling?" Her palm grew moist around the heavy receiver.

"The party does not wish to say," droned the voice.

Vivienne glanced at Mother, whose face had gone pale. She turned toward the stairs and called for Jack, but he was already halfway down, practically leaping two risers at a time. He snatched the receiver from her hand.

A woman's voice, thick and unmistakable, seemed to seep out of the phone and into the air around them. Vivienne heard it. They all heard it.

"Can I see you? I need to see you," the woman said.

Jack muttered something inaudible and quickly hung up.

Vivienne's heart lurched, and she clamped her lips shut to stop herself from retching. Then, in a sudden motion, she seized the phone cord with both hands and yanked it from the wall, tearing off a generous chunk of forest-green paint and plaster along with it.

"Oh, fuck," she muttered, stomping toward the kitchen. Her mind flashed to the thought of a knife, a large one, to cut him to pieces—but the urge (if not the idea) passed quickly. She couldn't let the children see that mess. *She'd kill him in his sleep. Quietly. Later.*

Instead, she turned and headed up the stairs to their bedroom.

2

They stayed awake all night, Jack refusing to tell the truth, insisting there was nothing to the call. Nothing to her fears. Nothing at all. He swore he hadn't touched another woman since they'd been married.

"Besides, why would she call here? She knows I don't answer the phone," he said, as if that settled everything.

Then, near dawn, Vivienne told him to get out. Just get the hell out. In the morning, Jack promised the children he'd be right back. He'd be home soon, he said. Then he took the train to London.

Liar.

3

In the late afternoon, Vivienne lit a fire in the vegetable garden behind the house. She fed the flames with stacks of papers culled from Jack's study: half-written poems, partial manuscripts, notes, letters. She burned his work. She burned her latest novel. She burned and burned and burned. And still, it wasn't enough.

As evening deepened, Vivienne stood before the flames on bare feet. No, that wasn't right. She was wearing those ruined sandals—the ones they'd bought together in Spain. How long ago had Spain been? Benidorm. The trip had been perfect, hadn't it? The cottage by the sea, the old woman and her son, pitchers of ice water so cold Vivienne had to sip it slowly to avoid the sharp sting in her head.

But wait, she was misremembering. There'd been no electricity, no running water. Heat so thick they couldn't sleep, and Jack complaining relentlessly about having no space to write, to think. To think! He'd been irritable, angry. They'd had a terrible row the second day. Over what? His black moods had come as a surprise to her then. He'd stormed off for hours, leaving her to worry, pacing that small cottage, wondering alone. More memories surfaced. The butchering at the bullfight. The bewildered bull, the picador, all the blood. Vivienne had hated it; she'd wanted to leave, but Jack had insisted they stay. And yet, they'd been in love then, painfully, hopelessly in love. The kind of love that left gooseflesh, that made eating impossible without the other nearby. The symphony in a woman's mind convincing her that by his glance, he might tilt the world. *Stupid, stupid.*

Vivienne stared into the flames as they licked and nipped at her feet; she hopped back just far enough, feeling the sting on her toe, her thigh, her cheek. Mother came outside. Thank God Vivienne had had the sense to leave the babies inside.

"Vivienne!" Mother's voice came from the other side of the pyre—yes, that's what it was, a funeral pyre. "What are you doing? What is this?" Her voice rising to a shriek.

"It's a fire, Mother. What do you think?"

The sky had darkened, and sparks leapt forth into the night like darting bats. Ash floated down around her like hot snowflakes. Vivienne fixed her eyes on the flames, their biting edges, ignoring Mother as she approached, calling, wailing. "Why would you do this?"

Then Vivienne saw it. A bit of stationery unfurling on the edge of the ruins, the cream paper browning to black. She kicked at it with her sandal, barely feeling the flames against her skin. She bent to read the letters still visible on the half-burned scrap: the whore's name, still clear. *Whore, whore, whore.* Vivienne laughed. It was funny—the thought of him scrambling to hide the evidence, missing this one. Ridiculous man. Small man. Liar.

Vivienne snatched the bit of stationery from the flames and pressed it cool between her palms, then looked up into the night sky, into the empty, doorless face of the moon, and laughed and laughed and laughed.

CHAPTER 72

THE CRITIC

Jack arrived at my flat that summer of 1962 in quite a state. It was sweltering outside, and at first, I thought he'd just been overwhelmed by the heat. He was sweating, disheveled, his hair in wild disarray, but this wasn't just a typical bout of anger or frustration. I'd seen him lose his temper a few times before, but nothing like this. He seemed almost deconstructed—frantically euphoric. To my surprise, he'd brought champagne, and not the cheap kind, either— genuine, costly champagne. He announced that he wanted to celebrate his birthday, which was ludicrous because his birthday was months away.

"Vivienne's ruined the telephone," he blurted out the second I opened the door. "In a fit of jealousy, she just ripped the cords from the wall and told me to get the hell out, so I got the hell out!"

He was talking nonstop, hardly pausing for breath, pouring out a torrent of thoughts as he came inside. The words spilled over each other as he ranted about his life, his future, all the things he wanted to do, needed to do and write. He kept circling back to the same refrain: his newfound freedom, the open road ahead of him. He seemed exhilarated, almost dazed by the possibilities he saw for himself now that he'd broken free.

I knew what he was after, of course. His infatuation with Bertina Rudman had been clear for some time. Most of us in London knew about it. Bertina hadn't been discreet. That wasn't her style. She'd shown people notes and letters Jack sent her, and so on. She was remarkably insensitive, or perhaps her intent was to make the relationship public. Her husband suffered terribly. I believe he attempted suicide at one point. An overdose is what I recall. Sleeping pills, maybe. But that was later in the fall.

Bertina and her husband had been staying at mine for a few days that July. They'd been with me while some repairs were being done at their flat. But they were gone by the time Jack arrived. I tried telling him that, but he was in such a state. He stomped around my flat, looking for her, repeatedly asking where she was. He couldn't have cared less if her husband was present. It took him a few minutes to accept that Bertina wasn't in my flat, and then he set to drinking and ranting, pacing back and forth across my parlor like a madman.

"I've come awake," he said. I remember that phrase specifically because he repeated it several times. "I'll live where I like, do what I want, write without interruption, choose my friends and see them when I like. No more censorship. Vivienne confining my every inclination." Something to that effect. It was alarming, really, especially as I'd become such friends with Vivienne. I'd published a lot of her work and grown to respect her enormously. And here he was telling me she was so awful, and he'd spent years repressing his desires and curtailing his existence for her.

"And Vivienne?" I asked him when I could get a word in.

"She's a tough one. She'll be fine. Just fine. She'll have the house, the children. Her writing." I asked him about his children, and he said something like, "The baby, he's still odd to me. I don't really know him. I do worry about the girl. I'll have to make arrangements to see her."

In the end, I asked him if he intended to leave his family. I couldn't believe the Jack Welles that I knew would really do that. But he immediately settled down, looked straight at me, and told me he'd already left. I suppose he had.

At that point, the question of his physically returning to Springhill House was probably moot. In his mind, in his heart, he was gone. So, it was all terribly sad. But of course, I didn't know the extent of it.

CHAPTER 73

LEBEN
August 1962

The horse was a rich chestnut, gentle and steady, with enormous black eyes and a deep mahogany mane. She was young but mature, her long, sinewy muscles quivering and bright with sweat after a hard ride. Her name was Leben, and Vivienne had chosen her from among several others at the ranch. Twice a week, Vivienne took lessons, feeling herself grow stronger, more confident, more alive with each ride. With the rhythm of the horse's gait, she felt she could fly. She was the arrow. She was Godiva.

CHAPTER 74

DR. B.

Vivienne and I exchanged letters in those weeks after Jack left. She even thought of flying back to America to see me in person, but she simply couldn't afford it. I refused to treat her by post, but honestly, she was a friend, so the letters continued.

For a while, I thought she was doing better. She'd settled in at Devon without Jack. She'd found a new part-time housekeeper, and her mother had returned to America. Vivienne was, of course, writing. The galleys for her novel arrived shortly after that disastrous phone call—from Jack's lover. She had also taken up riding, something she'd always wanted to do, and found an almost spiritual satisfaction in it.

Still, she was in a great deal of pain. For Vivienne, though, I think it was the sexual betrayal that crushed her most of all.

Back then, sex just wasn't a topic of conversation. Not for women. It simply wasn't. But with me, she was very open, and I suspect I was the only person she spoke to about it. Vivienne saw herself as sexually evolved, very unlike other women—aggressive, highly charged, even experimental. For that time, she was unusual, and she liked that about herself. I think Jack's abandonment for another woman, particularly an exquisite and childless woman, and so soon after the birth of Nicolas, shattered her. She felt wretched, worthless, and ashamed for wanting him back so badly. But Vivienne had tremendous energy, and she poured it into her work, her children, her home, and that horse. She knew she was talented, brilliantly imaginative, and hilarious. So, reading her letters, I naturally thought she was gaining traction in her individuality. Making space for her own life.

What I didn't understand, what I couldn't know without seeing her in person, was that, despite everything, she remained delusionally committed to reconciliation. I don't think she ever truly planned on living a life without Jack Welles. One must remember, Vivienne was a writer—a genius in that way. She could portray herself as anyone she wanted in her letters. And, of course, this is exactly why we do not treat patients by post.

CHAPTER 75

LIES AND SMILES
August 1962

1

The Poet blamed himself. It was his endless deference to others, he thought. Always giving in, tending to their needs, and letting go of his own desperation. In letters to his sister Phyllis, The Poet swallowed his pride and began asking for money. As much as it pained him, he saw no other way. Cash, he specified, deposited directly into an account in his name. For no nefarious purpose, of course—just the smallest bit of freedom any man of passion and ambition needs to breathe. "Please, Phyllis," he wrote. "I must move a bit; I cannot do anything here in London without money." He asked her to send only what she could afford, nothing more.

Vivienne, he complained, had grown to be just like her mother, a woman he could barely tolerate. "I blame myself," he wrote, "for the monster I have cultivated."

He should have ended things that day at Talbot, he told her, when he'd come up the path with the young college girl. A simple chat, perfectly innocent—conversation and some wine. But he'd been late, and Vivienne had been in a frenzy, enraged. He'd tolerated it, even humored her outrage. The Poet confided to his sister that he'd always tried to appease Vivienne, no matter how outrageous her demands. Her jealousy, her possessiveness. All those times she'd flown into fits. He had allowed it. "No more," he wrote. "It's been a monstrous life. And for all of it, I blame myself."

The Poet was careful to avoid any mention of the German beauty he'd recently fallen in love with. There would be time for that later, and besides, she was still married—not yet willing to commit, still living with her third husband. But The Poet was certain she loved him; she said as much all the time.

In his letters, he explained that his stars had shifted, with Leo now in the Ascendant, which he believed accounted for his new perspective on life and marriage. Cracks had existed in the union for years, he confided to his sister. They'd been good for each other once, he and Vivienne—for a few years, maybe. But Springhill House had become more prison than home. He hadn't written anything substantial in years, except during Vivienne's brief hospitalization after the miscarriage. But now, he was coming back to himself. *The Poet.*

Ultimately, he decided, it all came down to the inevitable clash between the rigid demands of domestic life and the irregularities his artistic soul required to thrive. Nothing to be done about it. Nothing at all.

2

There he stood in the living room without even the decency to look remorseful or the slightest bit sheepish. His hair was ragged, clothes rumpled, mouth slightly agape. Vivienne couldn't help thinking he looked like an overgrown, stupid child. She wanted to snap her fingers in his face. *"Hello? Hello? Anyone in there?"* Instead, she only shook her head and shrugged.

Agatha's entrance broke the silence.

"Daddeeeee!" she shrieked, running to him.

Jack had been gone nearly a month, and Agatha was bursting out of her shoes with excitement. Jack bent to scoop her up, planting kisses on her face, accepting her hugs and frantic squeals. Vivienne felt queasy watching them. Her eyes lingered on the way Jack's hand smoothed the back of Agatha's head, his fingers running through her silky hair. *He has no right,* she thought, a bitter pang rising in her chest. She hoped the baby would remain asleep.

Jack hadn't even bothered to phone ahead to let them know he'd be arriving. He'd simply shown up after barely a word in weeks. He'd been "staying in London with friends," he'd said. And now here he was. Vivienne knew he'd run out of money. Their joint bank account was nearly empty, and he had no access to the account she kept in America, so, of course, he was back.

"Tea?" she asked him coolly.

"Yes, please," he said, still holding the euphoric little girl in his arms.

3

They all had tea and chocolate biscuits, and when the baby woke up, they sat together in the kitchen as if there was nothing unusual about the afternoon. Afterward, Jack played blocks with the children while Vivienne washed up, using a fork to scrape bits of chocolate off the dishes, hard enough to leave scratches on two of the plates. She wanted Jack gone. Or he had to stay. They'd talk about it later, she supposed. Or maybe they wouldn't.

Discovering the identity of Jack's lover had been like shock therapy. Despite the initial, excruciating pain, a strange sense of clarity—and even exhilaration—had followed. It was as if something had reset in her brain, rewiring her from the inside. At first, she'd felt as if she and the children had been cast out of Eden, with nowhere to go and nothing left to do but lie down and give up. But, after a week in bed, Vivienne had seen a way forward. She'd started writing again, worked on the galleys for her novel, hired a new nanny, lined up her supports (Barbara Campion, Ruthie, her mother, other women in the village), and began looking for a doctor. An English doctor this time because she knew Dr. B. was right—she couldn't have a psychiatrist halfway across the world. In the meantime, though, Dr. B. had been willing to correspond. Vivienne had written half a dozen letters, receiving nearly as many in return: "Get a separation. Get a divorce. See a lawyer." She'd felt stronger with each passing day, building her path toward legal separation and divorce.

But now he was back. And as Vivienne stood at the sink, scraping dishes and listening to her husband laugh with the children, she felt all the power she'd worked so hard to accumulate drain from her body as quickly as water from an open vein.

4

That night, Vivienne asked him, "Why? Why did you do it?"

His answer came swift and plain. Unapologetic. "You, Vivienne. I did it because of you."

Everything inside her turned ice cold. For a moment, she thought she might pass out from the pain of it. She closed her eyes, gritted her teeth, and, after a few seconds, opened her eyes again. "Me?"

"I did it because you wanted to put me in prison, and I cannot live that way. I aspire to be here. I love you and the children. No one else. Alright. But please, don't do that to me. Don't confine me. Don't be my jailor."

Suddenly, with a sharp pang of disappointment, Vivienne realized he had misunderstood. Jack thought she was asking why he'd left. But that wasn't right. That wasn't her question at all.

5

Two days after Jack's return, Vivienne finally gave in to the sickness and weight loss that had been threatening to overtake her for weeks. "It's pneumonia," said the doctor. Her fever climbed to one hundred and three, and she fell into a state of exhaustion that made further debate or decision-making about her marriage impossible. For a time, she allowed herself simply to float.

Jack was unexpectedly helpful. He brought her beet soup and sliced oranges, cared for the children, and let her sleep. In a week, she began to recover. In two, life returned to routine. But it wasn't exactly normal. Everything felt strangely artificial, as if they were living on a movie set: every wall propped by support beams, furniture half-built, children borrowed temporarily, reciting their lines, dressed in costumes. If she said nothing, if she did nothing, they could go on like this: eating breakfast, writing a little, doing housework, playing with the children, cooking supper, sleeping. They had not made love, nor had they discussed recent events. They could continue this way indefinitely, except that with each day, each moment, she felt it becoming harder to breathe, as though the air in the house was slowly being drawn out.

She was doing what she'd sworn she wouldn't: giving Jack a home to retreat to, a respite from his London adventures. She was a mother, cook, laundress, childminder, housekeeper, even gardener and handyman now. Jack came and went as he pleased—to London for meetings, readings, "appointments," often staying overnight. He never admitted to meeting other women, but to Vivienne, it was glaringly obvious. And it was the obviousness that made it so humiliating. If she dared confront him, he'd reassure her, gently. He loved only her, he loved the children, the family. He would do nothing to jeopardize that. His meetings and readings were simply work.

If she didn't press him, he didn't get angry. At least not immediately. Vivienne knew she needed to do something. Tell him to leave. Ask him to stay. Demand an explanation. But every day, her resolve weakened. And so they went along, one day rolling seamlessly into the next, until it became a life Vivienne had never intended to live.

CHAPTER 76

THE LIGHT OF TEN THOUSAND DESIRES
August 1962

1

Jack told her to take the train back to Springhill House. Vivienne nodded agreeably—and then she took the car instead. He'd left the hotel on foot, walking into Mayfair, claiming he was meeting friends for lunch. He was lying. Bertina worked in Mayfair. Vivienne imagined Jack returning to the hotel, fresh from seeing his lover, only to find the old Traveler gone. He'd be livid. Probably curse at the concierge.

Then again, she wondered if perhaps taking the car had been Jack's intent all along. Later, she was certain of it. After all, he must have known she'd do exactly what she did.

The trip to London had been intended as a treat, or so it seemed. One of Vivienne's benefactors, unaware of their recent marital troubles, had invited them both for dinner and an overnight stay at one of the city's most posh hotels. Vivienne was genuinely surprised—and pleased—when Jack readily agreed.

Dinner was lovely. The wine flowed, the conversation was light and enjoyable, and Jack was almost his old self: full of humor and compliments. "Did you know Vivienne's new book had an excellent review in *The New York Times*? Vivienne's been writing some remarkable poetry—very intense."

Vivienne felt confused, elated, hopeful. After dinner, they retired to their suite. They made love for the first time in months, and the sex was slow and gentle. Jack caressed her cheek, kissed her neck and breasts and stomach—things he hadn't done in so long. It was a relief to feel his touch, his weight, his rough skin against hers. Vivienne slept well in the big, soft bed and awoke feeling euphoric. Perhaps she'd been wrong about everything. The fatigue and depression after the baby's birth, the stress—maybe she had just needed to let his affair run its course, as friends had suggested. Jack was back now, and that was what mattered. They could start fresh, even better than before. She pressed her face into his pillow. It smelled of him—ink, smoke, and sweat.

She lay under the creamy sheets, waiting for him to emerge from the shower. The picture window overlooked Mayfair and the West End. It was a gorgeous blue day, and from her comfortable spot, she could see the edge of the park and the National Gallery. She'd forgotten how much she adored this city—the people, the food, the art. They'd be back someday, she thought happily. There was plenty of time.

Jack stepped out of the bathroom, his hair still wet but already dressed in trousers, buttoning up a crisp white shirt.

"Hello?" she said, confused. "You've dressed already?"

"Yeah, I thought I'd go into town and have a drink with a few friends." He kept buttoning, then turned to the bureau mirror, smoothing his hair.

"Friends?"

"Yeah, friends." His tone was too casual, and he didn't look at her.

A wave of sickness came over her.

"Oh, alright, well, I can dress quickly." She forced her tone to stay light.

He turned. His face was tense, though his words were kind. "No, no, it's fine. You rest and then just take the next train back on your own. I'll meet you later in Devon."

That was the death knell. There was nothing to say. She clenched her jaw tight to keep the words from spilling out. *You bastard, you lying fucking bastard.* And all the rest. It would do no good. He knew she knew. That was enough.

Hastily, he sat down in the chair farthest from the bed, in the corner, put on his shoes, jumped up, grabbed his jacket, kissed her forehead, and was gone

2

Once Vivienne was in the car, driving the long road back down to Devon and Springhill House, she began to have second thoughts. The train might have been the wiser choice. The isolation and time to think were working against her, and her panic grew with each mile. For something like the next twenty years, she would be raising two children on her own, without Jack, without anyone, in relative isolation, four hours from London, in a centuries-old house that was nearly a ruin—and probably without the funds to support any reasonable life. Terror snaked through her, coiling tightly inside.

By the time she reached the outskirts of Devon, she felt completely overwhelmed. She'd never write again; there'd be no time, no energy. She'd never be an adequate mother on her own. Her own mother had barely managed, and she'd had support from Grammy and Grampy. And there it was—the dreadful thought that she was turning into her own mother. Her breath came faster, her heartbeat thundered, her hands grew clammy on the wheel. She forced herself to focus on the road. The skies had darkened, and thunder rumbled in the distance. She heard it once, twice, then a third time, so close it shook the floorboards beneath her feet. She pressed down on the accelerator, needing to beat the rain and get home before the panic overwhelmed her. "Deep breaths," she told herself, "just take deep breaths." But even as she said it, she knew it wouldn't work. *Why didn't you pull over? You could've pulled over anytime.*

Her vision narrowed, tunneling in from the edges. She squinted, but it didn't improve. Her heart thudded wildly against her ribs as she pushed harder on the accelerator. *You're close now. Just get there.* Darkness descended, and the rain began. *Go faster. Drive!* Reckless, she knew it. She'd driven this road enough to remember the sharp curves near the end, the way the car could skid on wet ground. She knew, and she didn't care.

She didn't stop. She pressed her foot all the way down on the pedal. Then, suddenly, it felt as though the road flew out from beneath her wheels—not the car leaving the road, but the road leaving her. That's how

Vivienne would remember it. And she was in the air, suspended in the thick, dark sky—then there was nothing.

3

There had been an accident. The hospital called, asking for both of us, my husband and me. Obviously, they didn't know Daniel had passed away. Some people found it strange that Vivienne had listed us, Barbara and Daniel Campion, as her next of kin, but you understand—she had no one else. I mean, she had friends, but no one close. Her mother was in America, her brother somewhere abroad, and her husband...well, I'm sure she'd removed him sometime earlier. Anyway, I drove down, terrified. I thought she was dead.

Vivienne had some stitches, ugly bruises, and two badly sprained wrists, but nothing was broken. Remarkably, since the car was completely totaled. It had flown off the road, turned over twice in a ditch, and somehow landed upright. She'd been driving much too fast in a storm, with poor visibility. The doctor was suspicious, as was I. Vivienne knew those roads, and she'd had that car for a while. She was a good driver. I don't think there was much doubt she'd done it intentionally, though she denied it to the end. Claimed it was an accident.

Only once did she say something odd to me. It was a week after she'd come home from the hospital. She'd lost a lot of weight and was still doped up on painkillers. Her thinking was unclear; she was swinging between an almost euphoric state—agitated, refusing to sleep—and days where she wouldn't get out of bed. That day, she blurted out that he'd wanted her dead. I asked who, and she said, "Jack, of course." I think Vivienne believed it. She claimed that was why he'd "made her take the car," which, of course, made no sense since he'd asked her to take the train. Anyway, that's what she said: Jack wanted her dead.

After all that, I couldn't understand why she agreed to go to Ireland with him, but she did. And so, of course, that would be the end.

4

It was in the fall, after the crash, that The Poet was finally able to see. He had been constrained for months, years, centuries. Marriage—the awful, intimate intrusion of marriage. But now, in the light, with all his ten thousand desires in full bloom, he was insatiable.

He would travel the world, live where he wanted, live as he wanted. He would learn Italian, French. German. He would write for long, uninterrupted stretches. Make love, make friends. See whom he wanted, wherever and whenever he pleased.

5

In the dream, The Poet walked in sunlight after a storm. The path was boggy, and he had to step carefully to avoid deep trenches and puddles. Everywhere, there was the smell of grassy fields and wet wool. After a while, The Poet came upon a young boy holding a dead fox cub.

"A quid," said the child. "You can 'ave 'im, one quid."

The Poet shook his head. What did he need with a dead fox cub? And besides, his family would not appreciate the blood and fur and mess of a thing like that. The Poet walked on ten paces, and suddenly, he stopped and turned around. The child remained where he'd been, watching The Poet with dark eyes, big as moons.

"Yeah," said The Poet. "Give 'im here. I'll buy 'im, yer fox. I will."

CHAPTER 77

GREEN STARS
September 1962

1

In the end, they both agreed: It was fame that did them in.

2

Ireland was Jack's idea. At least, that's the way Vivienne remembered it later. After the accident, there had been a fog of pain and medication, a cycle of insomnia, agitation, and sedation that left her confused and more depressed, but still, she was sure it was Jack who'd suggested Ireland.

"We'll find you a place in Ireland," he'd said. "A house for you and the children, and a nanny so you'll have time to write. Somewhere by the sea. You love the sea."

Later, he denied ever saying it, just as he'd denied promising her a winter house in Spain: "A home big enough for a live-in housekeeper so that you'll have time to write," he'd said. "I'll come and visit the children," he'd promised. But always, he'd disappear again.

After the accident, Jack had changed. He'd hardened. Even in his more open, jovial moments, he was inaccessible, distant. He came and went from Springhill House as he pleased, vanishing for hours or days without warning. When he was around, he drank, smoked, swore, and said terrible things to her, often in front of the children. He called her a hag, a burden, a jailor.

"In a world of beautiful women, I married a hag," he said. "This is a prison," he said. "You are an institution."

He had surpassed irresponsible and selfish; he had become cruel. If she dared to question him, he became violent, raging and terrifying the children. By late August, money was becoming a critical issue. Vivienne's Saxton grant funds were nearly gone. Jack, after a summer of withdrawing from their joint cash, had opened a separate account. Whatever he earned from the BBC and book sales no longer came into their shared account. By September, Vivienne had less than two hundred pounds. She had to let the part-time nanny go and no longer had the means to pursue legal avenues of separation and divorce.

Jack's fame in England now eclipsed hers, and as a woman, regardless of talent or critical acclaim, Vivienne wielded no real clout in artistic circles. Without money or the social and professional connections that came from being Jack Welles' wife, she feared her literary career could be cut short. She had hoped—or perhaps only fantasized—that the courts would compel Jack to support her enough to continue writing without him. Instead, looking at their joint bank balance in September felt like a blow to the gut. Isolated at Springhill House, alone with her children, overwhelmed with household duties, and financially desperate, the black pit of depression loomed again.

So she agreed. What choice did she have? When Jack offered to buy her a house in Ireland, a place by the sea, a home for her children, what choice did she have? So, in mid-September, they passed through Galway, headed toward the wilds of Connemara.

3

The village of Cleegan sits on the edge of Connemara, a place of raw beauty, where gentle hills roll before dropping knife-sharp over blackened cliffs into the sea. Vivienne loved the muted simplicity of the village with its white cottages, cobblestone streets, and friendly locals. She and Jack stayed in a farmhouse belonging to Brandon O'Malley, a friend and fellow poet. The house was so near the sea that salt crusted the wood floor, and the roar of the waves could drown out conversation.

Vivienne and Jack spoke little during their stay, even when they took walks together along the cliff. The stiff wind blew through them as if they were hollow, and when they spoke, it was as if to the birds, never once looking at each other. There was nothing to say. They didn't make love.

"It's difficult," Vivienne confided to Brandon one evening. "Jack lies. All the time, he lies, and I'm losing patience with it."

They'd been drinking whiskey in the small sitting room, a fire crackling in the stone fireplace. Jack had left for a walk in one of his moods, and sometimes those walks stretched on for hours. Vivienne was a little drunk, and she knew she should stop talking, but Brandon's quiet, warm silence invited her to go on. She confided more than she'd intended, admitting that friends had encouraged her to seek separation or divorce. The marriage was destroying her, and yet she felt she couldn't let go. Their union, she said, was too complete. She wouldn't be whole without Jack, nor he without her.

"Vivienne," said Brandon when she'd finished, "might it be possible that you're applying some outdated, puritanical beliefs to your marriage? Might it be that you and Jack are...above that? Artists. Highly intelligent. Creatives?"

She blinked at him. "So, you're saying we're far too evolved to stay faithful?"

Brandon, who, as far as Vivienne knew, had only relationships with young men barely out of college, grinned.

"I suppose, I mean, perhaps Jack needs the freedom to move about. Maybe the marriage could work if he has that?"

Vivienne stifled a bitter laugh. *What about my needs?* she thought. *Am I to remain in Devon, playing housekeeper, cook, property caretaker, laundress, parent, milkmaid, and so on? Then Jack returns to use me as his personal punching bag?* Vivienne shook her head. Brandon, kind as he was, couldn't understand. He was, after all, still a man.

"You're probably right, Brandon," she said.

She swirled the amber liquid in her glass, then took a sip, feeling the whiskey burn down her throat. She held the glass between her palms and let her gaze drift to the window. In the moonlight, she could see the jagged cliffs and, glistening in the distance, the dark, roiling sea.

4

The sound of Jack rifling through his overnight bag at the foot of the bed awakened Vivienne. She sat up, clutching the quilt to her chin in the frozen gray.

"What are you doing?"

He glanced at her briefly, then went back to rummaging. "Hunting," he said. "Thought I'd shoot some grouse this morning. I'll be back this afternoon."

She squinted, trying to study his face in the faint dawn light. His cheeks were deeply creased from sleep, and shadows loomed under his eyes. Vivienne got to her knees on the bed and moved toward him.

"Jack," she whispered. He didn't look at her. "Jack," she repeated, reaching to wrap her arms around his neck. He flinched, stepping back. A sickness shot through her as she realized she'd misread the moment.

"Sorry," he said. "I'm sorry, Vivienne. I didn't sleep well. I just need a moment on my own. I'll be back, alright?" She nodded numbly. He zipped the small bag, slung it over his shoulder, kissed her forehead, and walked out.

Vivienne rose from bed and wandered to the kitchen. She made tea and sat by the window. The dawn stars in Connemara were not the blue she knew from Devon; they were green—a pale, silvery green that reminded her of mermaids and filled her with melancholy. *The green stars of Ireland,* she would remember them for the rest of her life. She sat there for a long time, watching as night softened into day, and the stars faded. The green stars of Ireland, stolen away in the light.

5

In the afternoon, Vivienne waited with Brandon. Wrapped in wool blankets, they stood on the bluff as the sky grew dark, the sea churned, and night fell. Yet still, her husband did not return.

All night, Vivienne waited, but Jack did not come back.

The following day, she sat at the rough-hewn table, sipping tea from a China cup so delicate that the sunlight passed through it as if it were made of paper. Vivienne thought she'd like to smash the teacup against the table's surface just to see how thin the shards might be. Instead, she thanked Brandon when he served her a lovely Irish breakfast, then sat staring at her plate as the yellow egg yolk sickly ran into the caramel syrupy spread of the baked beans. She poked her fork into the sausage, picked it up, and pushed the meat into the egg-bean mess, squishing it around until the whole thing looked a bit like roadkill. Finally, Brandon laid a hand gently on her forearm.

"You don't have to eat it, Vivienne. It's alright."

"Thank you, Brandon," Vivienne said, setting the fork down. Then she got up, went to the loo, and vomited a thin stream of clear bile that burned her throat like fire.

6

Two days later, Brandon drove Vivienne to the station alone. She would take the train to London and then to Devon, where she would collect the children. She had wanted to stay in Cleegan longer, but it wasn't possible, Brandon told her. An unaccompanied woman staying in his house would be unacceptable. The village would talk. The church would talk. Everyone would talk. It wasn't done—not in Ireland, not in 1962.

7

A telegram was waiting at Springhill House. Jack had returned from Ireland but would be staying on in London for a few more weeks. That was it—no explanation, no warmth. Vivienne let the telegram slip from her hands, and it remained there on the hall floor until Jack finally returned, deeply tanned, unshaven, and visibly exhausted, five days later.

He told her he'd been in Spain, that he'd spent a week by the ocean. Vivienne knew he'd been with *her*. He'd met this woman on the coast, basking in the Mediterranean sun, swimming in warm waters. She could see it all so vividly that it felt like a scene unfolding in her own memory.

Once Jack fell into a heavy sleep, Vivienne gathered his belongings and threw them out the second-story windows, where they landed in unruly heaps among the roses—his clothes, his books, his papers, spilling into the garden.

She opened the door to his study and found him sprawled across the worn velvet sofa he'd picked up second-hand, his long frame too big for the piece, knees dangling awkwardly over one arm, one arm flung out, the other folded across his chest. He looked like a vanquished knight, a vision of collapse. *She hated him.*

She thought back to his arrival the night before, to his words, still fresh in her mind.

"You look tired, cross, angry," he'd said.

She'd stared at him, letting the words settle before replying, "And that's surprising to you, Jack?"

He'd poured himself a drink, irritation flashing in his eyes. "Can't a man even have a drink? What sort of wife have I married?"

It was as if he'd returned only to reinforce his misery, to reaffirm that his life with her at Springhill House was intolerable. Vivienne watched in silence as he ranted, obviously already drunk. The man before her wasn't the man she'd loved. He wasn't even someone she *liked.*

Vivienne felt an unfamiliar calm as she kicked him lightly in the side with her gardening boot.

"Wake up. It's time to go now." The words tasted refreshing, like a sip of ice-cold lemon seltzer on a scorching day.

Jack stirred, squinting against the light. A foul odor rose from him: stale wine, unwashed hair, and the unmistakable scent of infidelity.

"What? What are you on about? Time to go where?"

"The next train to London comes round at half nine. I'll drive you. You'll have to find someone to collect you on the other end." She felt a thick lump form in her throat, but she pressed forward. "I don't want you back. Never."

Her chest tightened as if a weight were pressing down, making it hard to breathe. But she didn't cry; she'd promised herself she wouldn't.

"What?" He sat up, groggy, rubbing a hand over his mouth and chin. He looked up at her with one eye still shut. "You are not making sense."

She turned away, feeling her anger drain away, replaced by a profound, haunting grief. She felt like a woman in a photograph, frozen in time, already ten years dead.

CHAPTER 78

RUTHIE

I saw her in October 1962, early in the month. I was in London for an article and took the train down to spend a few nights at Springhill House. It was just after she'd kicked him out. Vivienne said he'd been sleeping with everyone in London. Not just every woman—everyone. Of course, I thought it was terrific, her throwing him out like that. But she wasn't well. She laughed too hard when she told me about his escapades. She'd lost so much weight, and then she cried quite a lot, too. I should have seen it, but I didn't. To be honest, I was probably less concerned about Vivienne that fall than at any other time since we were children. I thought she was strong, decisive. A little angry, but full of plans. The house was a ruin but beautiful, and her garden and bees—oh God, all those bees. And, of course, she was writing like a demon. Very little ever stopped Vivienne from writing.

The work was quite dark, but I'm sure you know that.

We baked sponge cake, drank some wine, and took turns rocking the baby. He was a dear little boy. Very quiet, more beautiful than most babies. Such blue, blue eyes. I worried about the little girl, though. She wandered around the house looking lost. Vivienne tried, she really did. She'd pick her up and sing, but it felt forced. I don't think Agatha wanted much to do with Viv after Jack left. She'd wriggle free and ask about Daddy constantly. She was high-strung, and Vivienne made plenty of excuses for her. But honestly, how would I know? I had no children, and I was only there for a couple of days.

But like I said, overall, I thought they were doing alright. Vivienne was edgy, sarcastic, tightly wound, but that was normal for her. She was also authentic and brilliant. She slept little and was always full of energy, but she was on an incredible creative run. The poems poured out of her.

In the years since, so much has been made of that time in her life. For God's sake, entire reams have been written about October 1962. Writers, critics, biographers who never knew Vivienne Holland like to say it was all about her father, or about Jack. From the way they write it, you'd think Vivienne's artistic voice suddenly sprang into existence that autumn and that somehow the world should credit those men. But that's not how I saw it. Not how I saw it at all.

CHAPTER 79

FANGS
Fall 1962

1

Vivienne neatly penciled "To Chemist for pills" into her calendar, her handwriting precise and square. Below it, she wrote "Call Dr. H," but quickly scratched it out. Dr. H., her kindly but somewhat inept general doctor, wouldn't be needed this time—just the pills. The real problem was sleep. Or rather, the lack of it. Insomnia had tightened its hold on her, worsening each night.

She'd been glad to have Ruthie visit. It had been refreshing, listening to stories about Ruthie's life—no husband, no children, no home to tie her down. They'd stayed up late, baking, drinking, and talking until the early hours. But now Ruthie was gone, and the loneliness that followed was sharper than Vivienne had expected. Since her friend's departure, sleep had become more elusive. On the rare occasions she drifted off, she'd wake abruptly, sometimes gasping, the remnants of nightmares clinging to her like a shroud.

In her dreams, she saw hideous creatures, grotesque and misshapen, and giant machines that hummed and crackled with electricity, designed for torment. She'd wake in a panic, her body trembling, her screams echoing in the darkness. But the terror didn't always fade with the morning light. Once, she thought she'd heard voices—muffled and indistinct, as if doctors were conversing just out of earshot. They seemed to be discussing her, though she couldn't make out the words. The voices seemed to come from the room below her, but when she crept downstairs, turning on every light along the way, she found nothing but silence. No one was there.

After that, Vivienne began checking each room in Springhill House every night before bed, peering into closets, behind doors, under furniture—just to be sure. Soon, she started inspecting the house each morning, too, repeating the ritual in the cold light of day, trying to convince herself that everything was still under control. But each time, the shadows in the corners seemed to grow darker, the silence heavier, and the feeling that something was terribly wrong only deepened.

2

The atmosphere in Devon was dank and dark, matching Vivienne's state of mind and pulling her downward. Her brain felt mushy and unwashed, her body heavy and haggard despite the weight loss. She avoided mirrors, yet her reflection haunted her everywhere: in the toaster, the car's boot, the baby's bathwater—silver and exact, cruel in its honesty. The thickness of her features, the bluntness of her nose.

At Barbara Campion's suggestion, Vivienne began using the early morning hours to write. By eight, the children would be awake, and the rest of the day would be given over to chores and childcare. But in the gray-blue silence before dawn, she could think and write without interruption. She'd been averaging at least one poem a day, and they were good. She'd finally found the words to write about Daddy, although the way the poem had evolved to include Jack surprised her. Or maybe "surprised" wasn't quite right—*bewildered* was closer. How much of it had she known from the start? Back in Cambridge? All of it? None?

The lack of sleep and continued weight loss were catching up with her, and her moods were shifting, her sensitivity intensifying. She felt less in control of her emotions, or perhaps it was simply more exhausting to keep them in check. It seemed so much easier to give in—to scream, to cry, to laugh uncontrollably. Vivienne recalled the baboons at the London Zoo, staring directly into the eyes of anyone who cared to look. Most people were too busy snapping photos or tossing bits of contraband into the enclosure, but Vivienne had looked. She could see it in their eyes—the baboons knew how stupid the people were, and they hated every single one of them. Vivienne didn't blame them. She could sense the animals waiting for any opportunity to do something awful. And when one couldn't stand it anymore, he or she would howl, bare fangs, race around, leap at the watchers, or throw excrement. Increasingly, Vivienne felt like those baboons.

She had resisted hiring an agency girl until one of Mother's friends visited and, alarmed by the state of the house and Vivienne's weight loss, felt compelled to report it back to America. This frightened Mother into immediately arranging for "a girl to come in for a few hours a day, and I will not take no for an answer." Vivienne wasn't sure where the funds were coming from.

Vivienne sat in the kitchen, spooning mashed apple into the baby's mouth as he reached for her hair with his tiny fists. The agency girl had taken Agatha outdoors, where they were splashing in puddles left over from last night's rain. The child giggled and bounded into view through the half-open kitchen door, pretending to be a swashbuckling pirate on a mission to vanquish her sitter. Agatha could be such a demanding and fickle child at times, but at others, she was so delightfully full of cheeky imagination. She was doing better, Vivienne thought; perhaps she would forget him, her father. Possibly that was for the best.

3

Winter was coming. These would be frigid, daunting months alone with the children, months during which Vivienne would need to care for seventy fruit trees, the bees, the house, do the muck hauling, the coal scooping, and the snow shoveling. Jack would be no help. They were on their own. Her little family's survival depended entirely on her ability to carry on. And carry on, she would.

4

Recalling the disastrous result of her last drive between London and Devon, Vivienne opted this time to take an early train and arrived in the city just after ten. It was a beautiful fall day, nothing like the gloomy, drizzly weather she'd left at Springhill House. The sky was a brilliant azure with a few soft puffs of cloud; the trees were draped in crimson, ochre, and gold, and the air was crisp and cold. The walk to her solicitor's office in the West End left her breathless and eager. Vivienne knew what she wanted and, for the first time in a long time, felt confident she'd get it.

The solicitor's office was in a grand, pre-war building, one of the few of its kind to survive both world wars. Reaching the steps, Vivienne paused, looking up at the stone facade and readying herself. She unbuttoned her coat, reached in, and tugged at the waistline of her skirt, twisting it back into place. Her clothes were all too big. She'd continued to lose weight, possibly as much as twenty pounds since Ireland. She was far too thin to be healthy, and she'd used makeup to mask her gaunt look and the dark bruising beneath her eyes. Ultimately, it was a hopeless task, and she'd given up, deciding that this man, this solicitor she'd never met, was meant to be on her side anyway. *So sod it,* she'd told herself. But standing here now, she felt miserably self-conscious.

5

The mahogany desk was so polished, Vivienne could see her reflection as she leaned forward to take the man's hand when he offered it. The solicitor was a slight man, elegantly dressed, with crisply dark brown hair and startlingly blue eyes. She judged him to be somewhere past fifty, although the dye job made it difficult to tell for sure. She liked his looks. The referral had come from Barbara Campion, who had a friend in London who had a brother-in-law who was this man. The whole thing felt awkward, with the reduced fees and the connection. Vivienne suspected the solicitor was also taking the case for the notoriety—if not hers, then certainly Jack's. His fame only seemed to grow with the separation, the alleged affairs, and now, the impending divorce. London's gossip columns couldn't get enough of the handsome poet's increasingly scandalous love life.

On the desk lay a folder—thin, gray cardboard, containing only a few sheets of paper. The solicitor did not open it. Instead, he began by explaining he'd reviewed all the background information, including Vivienne's legal and financial situation. He folded his small hands atop the folder and looked at her with an expression that bordered on pity.

"Alright," she said. "Just tell me my options. I'd prefer the information straight."

"Well," he replied, shifting a little in his seat. The hair at the top of his head moved not quite in sync with the rest of him. *Not a dye job,* she realized. *A wig.* "You don't have many options. Divorce laws in England are unambiguous—there's no room for negotiation. So long as she doesn't work, a wife is entitled to one-third of her husband's income. No more."

Vivienne's breath caught in her throat, sharp and cold.

Before she could protest, the man raised a hand to stop her, adding, "That's regardless of what she contributed to the marriage, or whether a wife believes she helped build his career."

There was an emphasis on the word "believes." *Whether a wife believes she helped build his career.* Vivienne kept her eyes fixed on his desk. There was a small glass paperweight shaped like an egg, its interior filled with delicate, suspended snowflakes that would never fall. It was, perhaps, the saddest paperweight she'd ever seen. She focused on breathing. One breath. Then another. She felt as if she might need to remind her heart to beat. One, two, three.

"One-third?" Vivienne finally asked, her voice almost a whisper, her gaze still fixed on the frozen paperweight.

"Yes, I'm afraid so."

An absurd thought crossed her mind—to take the paperweight, shove it into her handbag, and carry it home, where she'd sit in her garden, watching the hummingbirds flit among the gladiolas. Then, when she couldn't stand it anymore, she'd smash it on the paving stones and free every last snowflake, one by one.

"But it was me. It was all me."

The solicitor looked away, silent.

"Yes, I'm sorry," he said again. "And that's for everything—the house, the children, your spousal support."

Vivienne felt an urge to laugh, but she stopped herself. "You're not kidding, by any chance? This isn't a joke?" She forced a weak smile.

The lawyer paused, and then, cautiously, he continued. "There are two other options, but neither is particularly good."

She nodded, the answer already in her mind. "I could stay married."

"Yes. Your legal and financial position is much stronger if you remain Mrs. Jack Welles; I'm sorry to say it."

"No," she said firmly.

The lawyer gave a nod, opening the folder at last. "Everything I've said is based on what the courts would decide, unless, of course, you can convince him otherwise."

"Convince him?" She shook her head. "You mean *beg* him?"

The solicitor said nothing, only looked down at his papers.

"And my own income?" she asked, already expecting more bad news.

"Anything you earn reduces what the courts would award you." He glanced down, shuffling papers. "Based on my calculations, given your likely earnings, you may receive nothing from his income at all."

Vivienne leaned forward, picking up a lemon drop from a small candy bowl opposite the frozen snowflake paperweight. She glanced at him.

"Please," he said, and she popped the sweet into her mouth. "Under the circumstances, I'd advise you to talk with your husband. In my experience, most men don't want to abandon their families entirely. They'll work something out—provide what you and the children need."

"Yes, thank you." Vivienne nodded, wondering if he could see into her thoughts, just as she could read the thoughts of the baboons in London.

"I'm sure there's no need to worry, Mrs. Welles."

"I'm sure," she replied, biting down hard, cracking the lemon drop into pieces. Sour juice coated the inside of her mouth, running like acid down the back of her throat.

CHAPTER 80

STUPID HAPPY AMONG THE HOLLY
November 1962

1

The Critic's flat was in one of those London neighborhoods popular with artists and writers—up and coming, but more coming than up. Vivienne splurged on a cab; after the disastrous meeting with her solicitor, she wasn't in the mood to battle the Tube. Arriving, she banged on his door until he appeared barefoot, wearing a pair of corduroy shorts and a long-sleeved green sweater with tobacco burns at the cuffs.

"Vivienne?" he asked, blinking in surprise.

"Where is he?"

"Where is who?" She stared at him unblinking. "Oh, Jack. He's not here."

Vivienne pushed past him into the apartment, her head swinging around on her neck like a boom in a storm.

"He is here, A.C. I know it, or at least he's been here."

"Sure, he was here, but not for long. I couldn't stand it. Hey, would you like a drink? You look a bit rough."

"Thank you for that. You look marvelous yourself, A.C." She nodded toward his clothes, then pointed at his hair, which hung long and greasy.

He touched the top of his head. "Well, if I'd known I had lady visitors, I'd have shaved."

"Hm." She threw off her coat, stepped out of her shoes, and plopped onto the woven rug. "Drink?"

"Yes, coming up. Make yourself comfortable." He moved toward his makeshift bar—a tiny dining table covered in bottles of liquor and a small army of mismatched glasses. The loft was sparsely furnished but well-stocked. He poured her a double whiskey and brought it over to where she lay sprawled on the floor, then sat down beside her.

"So, what's happened?" he asked. "I mean, what else has happened?"

Turning her head, she gave him a look out of one eye. "Bastard, he's a lying, cheating, whoring bastard, A.C., and he's deserted us."

The Critic found himself unable to argue in defense of his friend. He'd been shocked by the breakup—so certain, naively perhaps, that Vivienne and Jack were that rare thing: a blending of intellectual, sexual, and emotional forces. Somehow, he'd thought that Jack's affairs (and there had been more than one) were superficial, dalliances that could be weathered. But now he saw the destructive force of them and the wreck they'd made of Vivienne, a woman he admired greatly. Over the years, he'd come to respect her writing more than he'd ever valued Jack's. Vivienne's work had an intensity and raw force he'd never encountered in a female poet—or even a male one, for that matter. Yeats, perhaps. Or Thomas.

He took a long sip of his drink and set it down. "He's with her," he said finally.

"I know. I already know, but thank you." Her words were flat, and then she finished her whiskey and pushed the glass toward him. He refilled it and brought it back. As she drank, she told him about her solicitor—the grossly unfair English divorce laws, the helplessness she felt trying to sue Jack if he refused to support her, the humiliation of begging for money, and her absolute refusal to do so.

Suddenly, she sat up, pushed her hair out of her eyes, and gave him a radiant smile. Her eyes were too bright, he thought, and it wasn't just the booze. For the first time, he saw how unwell she was. Her bluish veins showed through translucent skin, and her collarbones were sharp as blades.

"I want to read you some of my recent work. I brought it along, but it's written for the ear, not the eye. You must hear it."

Her words were tumbling out quickly now. She picked up her bag, dumped it onto the floor, and scattered its contents—wallet, coins, lipstick, scraps of paper, cigarettes (he hadn't realized she'd started smoking), two lighters, and several crumpled pages of poetry. It was all so unlike her. She was usually meticulous, a master of neatness and order.

"Here, here," she said, shuffling the papers. "Listen."

And he listened. For hours, they sat before the studio's only source of heat as Vivienne read the most magnificent poems he'd heard to date. Some of them were among the best he'd ever encountered, period. Vivienne remained perfectly composed, even cheerful; nothing in her manner suggested she was reading poems filled with relentless and unapologetic imagery: the Holocaust, suicide, nuclear annihilation, total personal destruction.

It was extraordinary, he thought. And tragic.

2

Later that evening, The Critic accompanied Vivienne to a cocktail party for Faber. The London literary scene had missed her. Her recent publications and the positive critical reception of her book in England—despite her struggles to find an American publisher—had elevated her to minor celebrity status in these circles. People wanted to see her, to be near her, and she seemed to thrive in the charged atmosphere. Yet he worried. Her rapid speech, high-pitched laughter, and some of the off-color stories she was telling were unlike her. She was drinking too much, standing too close to some of the men. The married men.

Afterward, The Critic accompanied Vivienne back to her hotel. In the cab, she smoked and chattered breathlessly, nearly euphoric.

"I've made up my mind, A.C. It's not Devon, not Ireland, and certainly not Spain. No, no, no, not Spain at all. I mean, just look around! It's London, of course. I'll come back to London, and everything will be wonderful, won't it? We'll have salons and soirées, art galleries, people, and the children will have an excellent school and friends. Yes, yes, of course. I don't know why I didn't see it before!"

As the cab pulled to the curb, he gently touched her arm.

"Vivienne, I've been meaning to ask. I should have earlier. You seem—"

He didn't finish before she'd pushed open the door and was stepping out.

"I'm perfectly alright, especially now. I'm a famous writer, A.C., didn't you know that?" She flashed a grin. "A brilliant, famous writer."

He started to follow, sliding over on the seat, but she held up her hand, her long, ringless fingers ghostly white in the moonlight.

"No. I'm fine now. I'm on the train in the morning. I'll send word when I'm settled in London, and we'll have tea. I've solved it all, A.C. Thank you, thank you!"

She smiled again, but this time there was a strange coolness in her face. Then she straightened, turned sharply, and disappeared into the night.

CHAPTER 81

BARBARA CAMPION

We were concerned. Thanksgiving '62 was nearly upon us, and Vivienne seemed oblivious—a sharp departure from her usual self. She was scattered, erratic, and unfocused. Springhill House felt cold and disheveled, lacking its usual warmth. She hadn't washed her hair, and she spoke in a continuous stream, story after story, each one intensely personal and spilling out without pause. She kept saying it was all "experience." "Grist for the writer," she'd explain, as if her pain and turmoil were just fuel for some grand, positive arc she imagined for herself.

She was determined to take the children and leave, and no one could dissuade her. She made everything sound lighthearted, even humorous, but her laughter—strangely hollow—left us uneasy.

CHAPTER 82

DR. B.

Did you know the American publisher had rejected her novel? Yes, the one that later became an American classic. The rejection came in December, before she left Springhill House to move back to London. Nobody knew about it at the time—that's how Vivienne handled things. I suppose she might have told Jack if they'd still been together, but as it was, she faced the blowback on her own. I saw the publisher's letter years later, and it was curt—insulting, if you ask me. But Vivienne didn't let it stop her. She sent the manuscript off to Harper with incredible courage, though perhaps to a fault. She sacrificed so much for her work.

I knew she was becoming unwell throughout the fall of '62. I'd refused to be her psychiatrist—me in America, her in England—but I wanted to remain her friend. She was struggling badly, highly unstable, very driven at times, manic even. Meanwhile, Jack was living in London without a stable address—a peculiar move for a man with children. He'd become a kind of adolescent, hiding out.

Money was a huge worry. Jack told her to "economize," which was absurd given his own lifestyle. She shared some of the details with me, including his suggestion to "eat less roast." Vivienne had even written to Jack's mother, hoping she might encourage Jack to reconsider his family obligations. Jack agreed to send a minimal amount—enough for food and perhaps the light bill. But then she received a response from his mother that devastated her, telling her to count her blessings and stop bothering Jack. It was yet another rejection.

And there were the letters Jack left behind at Springhill—love letters he'd written to this woman, Gutman. Vivienne found them while packing up the house. Jack had written about the woman's "ivory body," their lovemaking, and his relief at "hacking the leach from his ring finger." For Vivienne, reading those words was deeply painful and humiliating.

She fell ill several times with the flu and, eventually, pneumonia. She called Jack for help, and he may have come once or twice, but at a cost. Vivienne overheard Jack speaking with their family doctor, Dr. H., a well-meaning but old-fashioned man. They joked in a way that hinted her illness was "neurotic." While that might seem ridiculous now, it left Vivienne with a gnawing fear: if she asked for help, Jack might use her illness against her, even to take custody of the children. In her letters, she insisted she was "quite sane," just furious at the situation.

A few months after the separation, she began feeling trapped, a sensation that escalated, possibly toward delusion. She imagined Jack and his lover entwined together, blocking every path forward. Most friends had gone along with Jack rather than staying with her, which except for her loyal women friends, was true. Her mother, Lorah, wanted her to return to America, but the relationship was fraught. Lorah's letters came with a stream of unsolicited advice on everything from mothering to writing to marriage. Lorah wasn't a monster, but her high expectations weighed on Vivienne, so she pulled away.

As I was thousands of miles away, I didn't know the full extent of Vivienne's struggles until later. I didn't even know about her most disturbing poetry from that period, filled with images of violence, darkness, illness, and death. Looking back, I wish I had known more. But I also wonder if it would have changed anything. Vivienne was no victim—she was a strong, talented woman living with a terrible illness in a harsh situation. She may have already written her story, penned her own tragedy.

CHAPTER 83

THE BEES ARE FLYING
December 1962

1

Vivienne stepped outside into the dazzling December day. The pewter bangles on her wrist glinted like diamonds in the sunlight, and she reveled in the sharp, rhythmic click of her new leather pumps as she strode onto the sidewalk. She slipped the key (her new key) into her bag and turned briefly to read the little plaque beside the front door: *YEATS LIVED HERE*. Incredible. Securing a flat in London had been challenging enough, but discovering *this* one felt nothing short of miraculous.

She'd found it after a grueling day of touring small, dark London rentals that, despite being in crumbling buildings in bleak neighborhoods, were all out of her price range. Then, by chance, she'd taken a walk down Primrose Hill toward the park and spotted the little blue sign along with a hand-marked notice: *FLATS TO LET*.

Vivienne had gone straight to a phone booth to call the estate agent, agreeing to take it immediately upon seeing the space. The agent, however, initially refused to rent to a single woman, forcing Vivienne to involve Jack for his signature and assurance that they were married. Finally, after Vivienne paid a year's rent in advance, the contract was approved. Today, she'd met with the estate agent and had been given the key at last.

2

Vivienne decided they would move immediately, throwing what they could into cardboard boxes. They'd come back for the rest after the cold snap, she figured. But for now, what mattered was reaching London before Christmas. It seemed suddenly urgent—being in London, being among people, *your* people. *Your friends*, she thought. *They'll come to you and love you. They'll all be there.* That's what she believed. Her poetry would finally gain recognition, and the children would attend good schools, be surrounded by fine art and good books. All would be well. *Move, move, move.* And it was a bonus that Jack, already living in London, would see the children more often.

She pushed the move even though Jack was unavailable, and Barbara Campion was out of town and couldn't help. Fortunately, the agency girl agreed to stay on a few extra days. With movers hired cheaply through a neighbor, Vivienne and the agency girl packed while alternating shifts to watch and feed the children. Finally, they closed Springhill House for the winter, leaving whatever remained in the orchards to rot. Vivienne sealed the house, and without looking back, started the car and drove away. It was December 9, 1962. She would never see Springhill House again.

CHAPTER 84

THE AGENCY GIRL

I told the missus; I told her I says, I have to go, but she just wernt havin it. She begged me, and I felt so sorry for her finally, I says I'd stay until after they moved to London. She wanted to go right then, to London, I mean. There she was, up all night. Loony she was. No sleep at all, packin' them boxes, and there we were on our way in the freezing fog, barely able to see past the front end of the car. Her talkin a mile a minute and me, not a word in and her full of ideas and plans and me fit to be, with worry for them babies and meself. Not sure we'd all survive the trip.

And she was tellin stories. Everything big, you know? Hundreds of this and thousands of that. Like she was on somethin. Pills, that's what I thought. My cousin Vincent, he takes them pills, makes him all jumpy like that, and if I hadn't a known better, Ida said she was on them jump-up pills. And she was talking about magic, too. Thinking it was magic, she found that flat in London when I already knew she went over there on purpose. I think she forgot she told me she had a plan to do it.

An you shoulda seen the place. The flat, I mean. A right wreck it was. And no phone, no electricity. Them boys she hired were there movin things round by candlelight into the evening. Right pissed off they was, an all them stairs too. She wanted the second-floor flat, she says, but I'm telling you, with two babies and all them steps. She were off her trolley, Mrs. Welles were. All of them decisions she was makin.

You know I told Mrs. Welles it was me own personal reasons, me leavin, but really, I resigned me post because she weren't well. I couldn't handle it and a course I had me own mother sayin Mrs. Welles was mad as a March hare, and I better leg it out of there before she did me in with a hatchet. Course me Ma was only jokin' but...I feel terrible about it now after what happened. And in the flat too, with them little ones right there. Gives me shivers to think. But how was I to know? I was only nineteen, just a child meself at the time.

CHAPTER 85

GULLIVER
December 1962

1

The flat was spacious, with three bedrooms, a light-filled living room, and a narrow galley kitchen. The children would have the largest upstairs bedroom overlooking the street, and a tiny room beside it—just big enough for a twin bed—would go to an au pair once Vivienne found one. Downstairs was another bedroom with floor-to-ceiling windows overlooking the neighbor's garden, with its sycamore trees, and beyond that, a maze of London rooftops. She'd use this room as both bedroom and study, decorating it in cool blues and grays. She planned to write to Mother, calling it her "blue period." Jack had disliked blue, preferring the warm reds, golds, and autumnal tones of Springhill House. This flat was hers, alone.

Budgeting would be tight, but that was manageable. Vivienne was an excellent accounts manager; she'd been doing it for years. Still, a twinge of resentment surfaced as she thought of the money Jack's manuscripts were now bringing in, and how little of it he was passing along for her and the children. *No matter,* she told herself. *This is your life now. Your London life.*

2

Vivienne ran a gloved hand over her hair, feeling satisfied with the fresh, contemporary pageboy cut and the soft bangs she'd chosen. They suited her, and she thought A.C. would like it. They'd been meeting most afternoons when she could manage a few hours away. Over wine and poetry readings, their meetings sometimes turned intimate, but she wasn't sure where it all was leading. Still, his brilliance, his insight, and his unflagging support—and, she had to admit, his reputation as one of London's most influential critics—made him compelling. Did she love him? Not like Jack. But since spending time with A.C., her perspective had shifted. The air felt crisper, her boots had a surer step on the ice, and even her tea seemed to taste different.

She wore her camel-hair coat, a blue tweed skirt, and the new pumps she'd splurged on with her last BBC check. A touch of cherry red on her lips and nails gave her a polished look, even if she was a bit pale and thin. It had been ages since she'd bought herself anything new—Jack had always said clothes were trivial. But it felt good to look good, to feel out in the world. *Maybe,* she thought, *divorce will suit me.*

No one in the marriage had said the word "divorce," though others had whispered it. Jack's fame had only grown, along with rumors and prying questions. Journalists, persistent as they were merciless, crowded her path. "Mrs. Welles is your marriage over?" they'd ask. "What about Jack's involvement with another woman?" She'd steady her face, keep her fingers unclenched, and answer as her solicitor advised. *Certainly not,* she'd say, keeping her voice smooth and unruffled. "We are working things out." A delicate smile, a polite nod, and a quick exit.

Aside from the occasional gossip and stares, her first weeks back in London had gone well enough. With the children, the new flat to set up, and her editing work, she barely had a moment for her poetry or her novel. This was supposed to be her oasis after the isolation of Devon, yet she was drowning in a never-ending list of tasks. But today was for A.C., and she planned to invite him to spend Christmas with her and the children. He'd enjoy it, she felt sure—he didn't have family plans for the holiday, and she couldn't bear the thought of another solitary occasion, like her October birthday. Then, it had been Ireland, then those terrible weeks of illness and loneliness in Devon.

She tilted the rearview mirror to check her lipstick, dabbing carefully at the corners of her mouth. *No,* she thought, *she would not spend Christmas alone with the children.* Opening her handbag, she took out a small tin box. Inside were the pills Dr. H. had prescribed, tiny "pep pills" to be taken twice daily, though she hadn't always followed his instructions precisely. She tipped one onto her tongue, swallowed it, and tucked the tin back into her bag, feeling its reassuring snap. When the bitter taste faded, she stepped out of the car, smoothed her skirt, and set off toward A.C.'s flat.

CHAPTER 86

WINTER TREES
December 1962

1

In the early morning quiet, Vivienne sat at her desk, meticulously picking apart the envelope, her fingers tracing the return address. She'd read the letter more than once. The novel would not be published in America. Two rejections. No remaining options. And this particular rejection felt like a final blow, coming just after the British reviews. The reception had been primarily positive, but unremarkably so—praise for her "dry wit" and "convincing narrative," with one reviewer calling the novel a "considerable achievement." *The Listener* had "strongly recommended" it, though the review was buried among others and unlikely to push her toward bestseller status.

For Vivienne, the risks she'd taken to write this story—the decision to fictionalize friends and family to tell the tale of her breakdown—suddenly felt misguided. She had been prepared for backlash, even from her own mother, but now there was only this: rejection, and not enough of the success she'd hoped for to justify the cost. She picked up the creamy stationery and read the curt response once more:

"...as a reader, I found the protagonist's illness and her subsequent suicide attempt unrealistic and overblown. As a result, the novel never worked for me."

The female editors doubted the main character's plunge into madness. Nothing traumatic, they noted, had occurred to make a young woman's breakdown believable. No girl, they insisted, would reach such despair over something so trivial as an encounter with the big city. Surely, she'd have been ecstatic at the opportunity. Perhaps a little anxious, but driven to madness? Certainly not.

Vivienne folded the letter carefully along its creases, sliding it back into the envelope. Outside, the fog hung low, impenetrable, as though wrapped around the morning itself. In the distance, red rooftops descended into the white mist, the sky above a blank slate, starless, like water. She felt her bones grow still, her mind empty, hollowed out. Inside, there was nothing, nothing, nothing.

2

He hadn't come. Not really. A.C.'s casual drop-by for a drink had hardly been the warm acceptance of her Christmas invitation she'd imagined. Instead, Vivienne and the children had spent Christmas with the Boltons— a polite, respectable family she barely knew. Of course, it was Barbara Campion who had arranged it all, reaching out to her contacts in London to ensure Vivienne had a place to go. *"Please come, do bring the children,"* they'd said, warm and well-meaning. But it all felt so empty.

The Boltons: nice, nice people, with a beautiful house and a calm, lovely family. She remembered their faces only faintly, polite smiles and soft laughter. But she did remember the trees. She could still see them—an entire row of broad, ancient trunks at the edge of the Boltons' garden, sprawling branches etched stark against the fog, each one dark as ink. She had sat in the Boltons' sitting room, watching those trees through the frosted window, envying their silent strength, their stillness.

Why can't I be like that? she thought, as she watched Jillian Bolton hover, refilling her teacup, speaking kindly, nodding at all the right times. *Look at them,* she thought, her eyes moving to the trees again. The trees endured. They didn't care about the bitter cold or the mud. They stayed rooted, graceful and upright.

But here she was, smiling thinly at strangers, pretending to be "fine." Pretending the children were "fine." She'd put on her nicest dress, touched up her lipstick, and braided Agatha's hair with a ribbon, but everything felt like a lie. She had hoped so desperately for a day filled with warmth, with A.C.'s laughter and her children's joy, with a sense of togetherness—a sense of home.

Instead, she'd found herself looking at those trees, something bitter gnawing at her. She took another cup of tea and waited, her mind drifting into that cold fog, feeling, more than ever, like the branches of those trees—stretched too thin, too vulnerable, reaching for a ground that would never hold.

3

The Critic

Look, she was difficult by then. She became grating, desperate, a burden. She was the subject of so much gossip it was impossible to have her around without a tremendous amount of drama. Still, I was publishing her work and reviewing it well. Not because she was a friend, but because I believed in her genius. Still, those last days, she was just out of control. Nobody wanted anything to do with her. We all just sort of turned away. Not just me. She was so awful to be around by then. And, I'll admit it, the whole of London, indeed all of England, I don't know the entire world, was patriarchal. There wasn't a place for a single woman. Since then, I've been told maybe two in a thousand marriages ended in divorce at that time in the UK. And something like ninety-eight percent of households were headed by men. I mean, there was literally nothing for a woman alone with two children. It didn't matter if she was financially independent, and Vivienne didn't even have that. I know she felt like a failure without a man. Feminism hadn't touched her, as far as I know. She was proud, brilliant, but not liberated.

Anyway, I went by on Christmas Eve, mostly because I felt terrible about how everything happened. So, I stayed a few minutes. One drink. And then I left. After that, I never saw Vivienne again.

PART EIGHT: 1963

CHAPTER 87

RUTHIE

In January, she'd cut her finger with a cooking knife. It became infected and swollen; it smelled god-awful, and I swear she barely noticed. It was early January, and she was in such a state. Her mood was up, but not quite. She was running around, constantly doing, doing, doing, but accomplishing nothing. That's how I knew something was off. She spoke insanely fast and non-stop. She was making plans that no longer made any sense. And she'd come down with a terrible flu over the holiday. All three of them were sick. She was confused. One minute, she was planning to wait out Jack's affair—as so many men in those London circles were having affairs, almost like it was normal, taking advantage—but the next minute, she was too angry. She was either going to divorce him or kill him. She despised him, loved him, blamed him, then didn't blame him. She was all over the place.

I think she might've had something going with that critic. Not exactly a love affair, although Vivienne did like powerful men. It might have been a love affair—I don't know. But look, Vivienne needed connections; she had to make a living. Back then, a woman had only one way into those ridiculous men's clubs. And I think that asshole took advantage of her vulnerability. I'm not saying Vivienne was a victim, but she was in a terrible state. Anyway, A.C. rejected her—not precisely rejected, just ended whatever it was they'd been doing. He met someone else, fell in love. That fast. And it all happened just before Christmas, a holiday that had always been important to Vivienne. Another blow she didn't need. And didn't deserve.

I'll never forgive myself for leaving London in January. I was sent to America near the end of the month. I wasn't there, and then the damned phone situation. Vivienne was alone. She had her mother in America, who sent money when she could and lots of letters. There was a woman friend of hers back in Devon, but I think most of her social circle dried up as Vivienne deteriorated and her behavior became troubling. Then there was that American psychiatrist she'd gotten involved with. That should never have happened.

Anyway, as I was saying, that infected finger was horrible. So, I forced her to go over to A & E and let a doctor look at it. At the time, I thought Vivienne was lucky they didn't amputate. Just before I left the city, I remember telling her it was her own fault she'd end up with another awful scar. But, of course, I was wrong. I wish so badly I'd had a chance to see that scar.

CHAPTER 88

SHEEP IN FOG
January 1963

1

January brought a dramatic change in the weather. What began as gray skies and heavy clouds soon turned into relentless sleet and ice. Snow followed, falling so heavily that the children's wellies were swallowed by drifts that rose to their chests. The cold intensified, plunging to depths not seen in England for over a century. Fountains froze in mid-flow, power outages became widespread, pipes burst, railcars were entombed in snow, and the River Thames solidified into a thick sheet of ice where people skated as if it were a winter festival.

At the Fitzroy flat, the lights went out before the heat—something Vivienne had to be thankful for. Cold, compared to darkness, was undoubtedly the greater evil.

With their pipes frozen, Vivienne grappled with intermittent water supply issues. No clean drinking water, no hot baths. When the ceiling leaked, the landlord's explanation—"It's an old building; the roof wasn't built for snow"—felt woefully inadequate to Vivienne's American sensibilities. However, he stopped by with a gadget of some sort, measuring this and that. After a cup of tea, he measured again and finally reassured Vivienne that there was "no risk of total collapse." She stared at him as if he were speaking a foreign language, wondering how this information was supposed to help her wet and freezing family. When he remained silent, she simply nodded, thanked him, and offered him a biscuit to go with his second cup of tea. She didn't suppose that arguing, screaming, or berating the silly man would make much difference anyway. Besides, he was a friendly chap, and she was tired.

For mysterious reasons, the flat lost power every day, and with the power cut came the loss of heat. Even when the small electric heaters were working, the temperature remained frigid; the children spent their days wrapped in layers of clothing and blankets, while Vivienne typed with gloves that had small holes cut in the fingertips. Her hands turned blue. Without power, they often stayed in bed together, wrapped up and waiting for the click and buzz that signaled the heaters were running again. Her downstairs neighbor, a professor at a London college, reminded her to cook with gas and to use hot water bottles and tea to keep warm.

2

Before the New Year, Jack had been stopping by every few days to see the children. It was too cold to take them out, so he visited the flat. Vivienne found it difficult to see him. She wanted him gone. She wanted him to stay. A part of her died each time he left; every time she watched him return to his lover, she knew.

Jack spent most of his time with Agatha, barely acknowledging the baby, who craved his attention during the visits. The baby crawled all over Jack, reaching for his face, calling for his "Dada." Jack didn't seem to like him— didn't seem to like his son, Vivienne concluded. She could see it in his face, read it in his eyes. Perhaps he detested all of them, although he complained about their daughter.

"She's regressing," Jack said. "Don't you think?"

"So, what does that even mean?" Vivienne asked.

"It means," Jack said, "that she won't talk. Instead, she's wetting the bed, throwing tantrums. She's going backward."

"Well," Vivienne replied, "why do you think that's happening?"

"I don't know," he answered, as if he truly didn't.

Vivienne had nothing to say in response. Or rather, she had everything to say, but she clamped a hand over her lips to keep herself from speaking.

Then there was the terrible night after dinner at Gautier's. Jack had agreed to meet her to discuss the details of their separation—childcare, household issues. But she'd had too much to drink. She'd been drunk, lost control. In the street afterward, she'd practically thrown herself at him, begging, pleading with him to come back, to love her. "Anything," she'd said. "I'll take anything." She'd been so, so drunk. Desperate. Terrified of the future. Petrified of the voices in the night. She hadn't told him about that, managing to restrain herself because she knew what he would do. What he *could* do to her if he found out.

After that, Jack came to the flat only once more. Vivienne had tried to keep quiet, afraid those same pathetic words would slip from her mouth again like greasy stones. But in the end, it hadn't mattered.

Jack hadn't been back in over a week. The days blurred, one into the next. The effort required to get the children dressed and out to buy food was overwhelming. They hadn't been able to get a phone installed in the flat. A two-month wait for phone service in London was not unusual. So, Vivienne had to bundle the children and herself and make the three-block trek in the frigid weather through snowdrifts to the nearest telephone box to call the doctor, or Jack, or anyone else.

One particularly icy afternoon, as she returned from the phone box, her downstairs neighbor handed her a milk bottle, remarking cheerfully, "Well, at least the milkman delivered today!"

Vivienne stared at him. What a wonder, she thought, that a country capable of producing a Shakespeare could also exist for over a millennium and yield a population with such remarkably meager expectations. Apparently, one could cheerfully freeze to death in a leaky flat if one had a bottle of milk.

"Yes, you're right, Mr. Teasdale, at least we've got our milk." She took the milk, gave him the broadest grin she could muster, and turned with the children toward the stairs.

3

His son's birthday. He'd forgotten. He'd been out all day, busy. The Poet had become adept at making excuses, though none of them were any good. By the time he remembered that today was his baby's first birthday, it was no longer today. It was past midnight and too late to do anything about it. There was no phone in the Fitzroy flat yet; Vivienne hadn't been able to arrange it for some reason. So, he couldn't even call. Walking in this weather was out of the question. Coldest winter in London in—what did they say? A hundred years? A hundred fifty. Even the cabs had shut down.

In all honesty, he hadn't been ready to see Vivienne just yet, anyway. The last few visits had been unpleasant. Worse than unpleasant. They shouldn't have had dinner alone together, not even to discuss the "business" of their marriage, as Vivienne had suggested. The Poet thought it went alright— until the end. He hadn't realized how drunk she'd been. In retrospect, she seemed more than drunk. Drugged, possibly, or some combination. He'd seen her take two little pills during the meal, and she'd refused to explain, only saying they were prescribed by Dr. H, so they were "alright."

Afterward, they'd walked toward Vivienne's flat but stopped first in front of DeeDee's. That had been his mistake—allowing Vivienne to poke and prod into his private life. *Are you staying with her? Are you in love with DeeDee now? When are you getting to your place? Where is Bertina?* He'd refused to indulge her, thinking his silence would settle her down. But Vivienne only escalated until they were circling each other in the dark street—her screaming, him yelling, her sobbing—until she collapsed into his arms, and he took her upstairs into the empty flat. DeeDee wasn't there, of course. There was no affair with her; she wasn't even in London at the time.

The Poet had hoped the emotional flood might end with sleep, but Vivienne kept on. The grief was so immense, beyond her ability to control it. The neighbors were pounding on the ceiling for peace. All night it went on, drowning them, killing them both.

And so, he'd been a coward and avoided her since, which meant he hadn't seen the children. That was ten days ago. He'd go round tomorrow, he told himself. Tomorrow.

4

In the dream, a woman riding a white stallion has lost the reins and stirrups. As the horse gallops through the streets, her arms cling tightly around its powerful neck. She bounces helplessly, like a small child, and The Poet feels certain she will slide to her death on the hard macadam below. Then, suddenly, he becomes the horse. A brick wall appears, and he jumps it; the woman slides off, rolling beneath his hooves, and he stumbles over her body. On purpose, he thinks. She caused him to trip with intention. But as he slows his stride and turns to look back, he sees that the woman is dead.

CHAPTER 89

DR. B

It was 1963; the letter was dated January 31, but I received it the day before. Clearly, the date held significance for her. It wasn't a long letter—much shorter than usual. Everything she wrote indicated a sort of magnification in her perceptions. The depression, hopelessness, and self-recrimination had all become insurmountable. She saw herself as a failure at everything—studying, motherhood, writing, marriage. Her mood was terribly grim, and she described a kind of paralysis; she found it torturous to dress herself and the children, to cook, plan meals, and so on. But she was fighting, trying to pull herself out of it.

There was one ray of hope: she was about to start work with a female psychiatrist, which I found encouraging. Also, her mother and family doctor had arranged for a part-time au pair. I think they'd had terrible trouble finding someone reliable, so it was a relief when they finally secured this German girl. I'm certain Vivienne should have been hospitalized, but she refused. She wouldn't have wanted to leave the children, and, as everyone knows by now, she was petrified of hospitals. In any case, the decision was not mine to make.

CHAPTER 90

GETTING THERE
January 1963

The flu returned, sweeping through the household and leaving everyone with a relentless cough and high fever. For Vivienne, things grew worse: she developed chilblains—an affliction straight out of a Dickens novel—causing agonizing pain in her hands. Who would have thought such an ailment existed in the twentieth century? Dr. H stopped by, prescribing codeine for the cough, tonics for appetite, and refilling her sleeping medicine and pep pills. Noticing her weight loss—nearly thirty pounds—he frowned, remarking on her thinness. Vivienne glanced at her housedress, now hanging from her hips like a flour sack, and didn't deny it. She admitted to Dr. H that money was tight; she and the children had been surviving on little more than potatoes.

Alarmed, Dr. H insisted she eat properly or face hospitalization. Vivienne promised to try, but Dr. H still sent a visiting nurse. When her fever soared a few days later, he ordered x-rays, and the diagnosis came back as double pneumonia.

Hospitalization was out of the question, Vivienne insisted. She accepted bed rest at home with the nurse's help, relying on stronger medicine, and slowly the household began to stabilize. Vivienne and the children gradually improved, though her spirits didn't lift as easily.

The winter freeze in London dragged on, money worries loomed larger, and the BBC had recently rejected most of her latest poems, dismissing them as "too emotionally charged." The rejection stung, deepening her gloom and leaving her feeling unmoored.

As her physical strength returned, she began writing again. She sent letters seeking advice from other women writers; she wrote beautiful and intelligent reviews for poetry anthologies that did not include her work. She wrote poems. She wrote by candlelight, her fingers frozen, her health still fragile, her appetite suppressed, her cough requiring codeine to keep it under control. At night, she swallowed sleeping pills to hammer her brain into unconsciousness, and pep pills to wake up in the morning. She drank flu tonics and cough medicine for her pneumonia and tried to eat when she could. Dr. H visited often, and each time, with as much diplomacy as possible, he suggested she consider "going away for a rest at the hospital."

No, Vivienne always replied. *I'll never go back.*

And she never would. Hospitals, after all, had hanging men.

PART NINE: FEBRUARY 1963

CHAPTER 91

BALLOONS
4 February 1963

1

The baby has a wandering eye. There's a name for it, but Vivienne can't remember. They will need to get it fixed, but not today. Today, he holds a blue shred of a balloon in his chubby fist. Delighted, he giggles and looks up at her from his spot on the carpet. These balloons have been around for a few weeks—Jack brought them for the children as a gift, and they've been slow to deflate. Agatha lost interest quickly, but the baby remains fascinated. Like round animals, the balloons float about, rubbing against each other and the furniture. He delights in snatching one and chewing on it until, with a mighty snap, it pops, leaving him holding a piece of rubber in his palm. Strangely, he is unfazed by the noise, while Agatha, Vivienne's bold child, runs to hide. For a moment, Vivienne worries that the baby might be deaf.

She claps her hands together and calls his name. He looks up, and she feels relieved. He is not deaf. He is perfect. Both children are perfect.

Jack stopped by yesterday, without presents. They had lunch—meatloaf, which she'd managed to make only with supreme effort. The conversation remained civil, though Vivienne broke down and wept several times. Jack held her, wrapping his arms around both Vivienne and Agatha while they all cried.

"I've been calling everyone Vivienne lately," Jack said.

Her heart jumped. "What? What did you say?"

"It's hard for me too, Viv. All of this. I wish it could be different."

What the hell was he talking about? Why wasn't it different if he wished it to be? She murmured something about love into his shoulder, but he didn't hear her.

"I can't come back," he said. "Not to the same thing. It would kill me."

It all had to do with Vivienne's center of gravity, Jack said—her dependence on him, her need for him. He would be a prisoner again. He already felt it was happening, seeing her as much as he was. Perhaps he needed to leave London, he said. *For her,* he said. Agatha heard this and understood.

When Jack left, he took all his happiness and independence with him. Agatha immediately asked when her daddy would visit again.

2

While the children nap, Vivienne sits down to write several letters. She's been behind on her correspondence for weeks. First, she writes to her mother, who sent a check and a note a few days ago. Vivienne wishes her mother would stop sending money she can barely afford to give; it only deepens Vivienne's guilt and sense of obligation. She tries to make the letter chatty and upbeat but feels irritated by her mother's suggestion to send Agatha to America to "reduce the load." Vivienne writes that the idea is preposterous. Given the emotional upheaval the child has already endured, sending her off alone, thousands of miles from home, would undoubtedly do terrible damage.

Next, she writes to the priest at Assumption College with whom she has been corresponding, thanking him for his recent counsel regarding certain theological aspects of her poetry. She also suggests he read Yeats.

She makes tea, takes the cup, and sits beside her babies, watching them sleep—Agatha in her little toddler bed and the baby in his crib. The long winter has prevented much airing out, and their bedroom is filled with their scents. She inhales the familiar smells of milky baby and biscuit, and Agatha's strawberry shampoo. She reaches through the crib's bars and lays a hand on the baby's back, feeling the slow, rhythmic rise and fall of his breath.

Vivienne has allowed the balloons to float around in the children's bedroom, and just now, a yellow giraffe hovers near Agatha's little bed. Vivienne leans toward it, carefully grasping it between two fingers. It might be a giraffe or possibly a long-necked dog. It's one of those twisted animal shapes someone in the park made in exchange for a few coins. Some of the limbs have lost a bit of air, leaving it looking somewhat crippled. Agatha loves this one. She's partial to animals—anything with fur, scales, or whatever. She's like her father in that way, Vivienne thinks. So much like her father.

Vivienne releases the little dog-giraffe and stands. There's work to do. She returns to her desk and sits down to begin a long letter to Dr. B. in America.

It will be her last.

CHAPTER 92

GIGOLO
5 February 1963

1

The radio play is about a man who runs over a hare. Vivienne stumbles across it by accident, turning the dial through the channels as she washes dishes after the children are in bed. It's strange because she never forgets the times and dates for Jack's BBC readings, and this one is something she's never heard before. Had she forgotten it was going to be broadcast? Or could Jack have chosen not to tell her? No, not likely. Even in their bitterest moments, Jack's ego has always gotten the better of him. A BBC event like this—he would have announced it to the world, and he especially would have wanted Vivienne to know. She must have forgotten. How awful. Her mind must really be going.

It's a play, and not a very good one. The manuscript is a disaster— misogynistic, full of empty promises, overblown phrasing, and symbolism heavy enough to crush a skull.

The protagonist, named Finn, is on his way to visit one of his mates but is distracted by thoughts of his impending wedding, confused about what to do. He's madly in love with another woman—his wild, willful, and beautiful mistress.

Lost in these thoughts, Finn feels an awful bump beneath the wheels of his car. When he stops and gets out, he finds he has run over a hare. It lies dead on the road. Confused and fearful, he takes a blanket from the boot, wraps the creature in it, and takes it along.

"It might be an omen," he tells his friend when he arrives. "The hare, I mean. But does it mean I should cancel my impending marriage? Forsake the chaste woman whom I admire but for whom I feel no passion, and instead marry my mistress—a viper who sucks my blood but to whom I am bound by heart and soul?" He pleads with his mate for guidance. "Who should I choose? Or should I cast off both and find another—a new goddess of neither extreme, one of balance and perfection, a nurturer, a beauty, a giving and devoted lover for all time?"

2

Dr. H. had come around early in the morning. He'd asked Vivienne if she'd noticed any "changes" since starting the new antidepressant he'd given her. Vivienne told him no, but that had been a lie. What she'd noticed was a burning sensation inside her head. It wasn't happiness, but it felt good—a pleasant hatred. She also didn't tell Dr. H. what she'd realized: that hate, in small doses, was annoying, even painful, but in enormous proportions, it became something else—a dubious luxury, like too much chocolate, whiskey, or sex. Every night now, hate flapped out of her brain like a bat, leaving love in its shadow to wither and die. Vivienne enjoyed rolling the words "I hate you" around in her mouth as if the letters were little cubes of sugar.

Still, she knew Dr. H. would disapprove, so instead of telling him the truth, she said, "I think perhaps I need a higher dose."

Dr. H., a very amiable doctor, agreed. He also refilled her bottles of cough medicine and pep pills, for which Vivienne thanked him and assured him she would use only as prescribed.

3

The combination of medicines and tonics makes it easier for her to tolerate listening to Jack's dreadful play.

Vivienne finishes the dishes and makes herself a cup of tea. They've had heat and running water for a solid week now, and she silently gives thanks for both as she wraps her hands around the warm mug. The flat is still unbearably cold, but at least the children's room stays above freezing with the help of electric heaters. She curls up on the sofa beneath a blanket and continues to listen.

The play drags on. The protagonist, the hare-smasher, whines for some time until, finally, his mate slaps him across the face and then plies him with drink. They sit on a bench overlooking the wilds of northern England, slowly becoming inebriated.

"Your trouble," says the friend after quite a lot of dull, extraneous dialogue, "is that you know what to do; you just need to go right ahead and do it."

At last, the pathetic protagonist jumps up from the bench, yelling, "I'll do it. I know what to do." With that, the two men return to the house, and, feeling unreasonably jubilant, they cook the hare and eat the creature for dinner in a great celebratory relief at having "solved" the problem.

Everyone hears it, Vivienne thinks. Everyone knows. Bertina is the viper. The new woman in Jack's life (there is always a new woman in Jack's life) is the goddess, and she, Vivienne, is the chaste and unloved wife—represented, of course, by the now-dead and consumed hare. And everyone, at least everyone who knows them, will know without a doubt that Jack intended for Vivienne to hear the whole awful mess.

Humiliated, heartbroken, and frantic with rage, Vivienne takes two extra pills and falls asleep on the couch.

CHAPTER 93

A DIFFERENT GOD
6 February 1963

On Wednesday, Jack stops by while the children are napping. He's heard something from Bertina, who heard it from someone at her agency, who got it somewhere else: Vivienne has been spreading lies. Telling people she was abandoned the previous fall, left penniless in Devon with the children. She's been going around London saying Jack abused her, that he'd been vile all winter. A monster, he is. Such lies!

When he arrives, he's livid, purple in the face, waving his arms about, using that big booming voice he loves so much. Vivienne shushes him as he steps inside. He falls silent when she warns that she'll kill him if he wakes the babies. From across the room, she can smell him—the sweat stink of him. He isn't bathing enough, she thinks. His hair is dirty.

"Vile all winter?" she says. "Not vile all winter, Jack. You've been vile all year. No, scratch that. You've been vile all marriage. Try that one. Or perhaps all your life. It's fundamental to you."

Does she mean that? She does. *I hate you; I hate you.*

He shoves a letter from his solicitor at her—a cease and desist—but she refuses to take it, pressing her hands into her skirt pockets. The letter flutters to the floor.

"Stop, Vivienne," he hisses. "Stop this immediately. I've sent you thousands of pounds. Hundreds every month. Treated you too well. That's the problem—my inability to say no. My acquiescence. You need a god, a father replacement. Not me. Not me."

"Who is the liar, Jack?" says Vivienne. "You've given us nothing, or next to nothing. How could you send money when you spend all you have on your whores?" She smiles and repeats the phrase, "Your whores." She likes the way the words hang in the air between them.

He bends to retrieve the letter, smooths the paper, and sets it down on the table beside the sofa.

"You need help, Vivienne. You don't know what you're saying. Spreading rumors, lies, damaging me in public—that hurts you and the children. Just stop. And you know I've helped as much as I can right now. You're not well. You know that."

He takes a long, shuddering breath before continuing. "And there is gossip about you as well. I hate to hear it."

Vivienne stiffens, bracing herself for his words.

"You're becoming desperate, burdensome to our friends, Viv. They don't want you around."

She takes several steps backward, finally folding herself onto the sofa. She studies her husband. He's not lying, and he's not wrong, except when he says, "our friends." She supposes he doesn't realize that those people are only his friends now.

"Right, right," is all she can say.

He sighs, softens. "Oh god, I'm sorry, Viv."

She interrupts him. "What are you going to do with that?" Vivienne jerks her chin at the letter. "Sue me?" She laughs. "Go ahead. Take the cutlery. Or maybe the wall clock—it's worth at least fifty pence. You are an idiot, Jack. You've damaged yourself. Do you think I am the only one who knows what you do? What you've done? Adultery, abandonment. Your children cry for you. Agatha wakes in the night screaming for her Daddy. And what do you do? Come and go as you please. Torturing all of us so you can fuck your whores, Jack."

That lovely word again. Vivienne makes a mental note to use it more often: *whore. Whores. Whoring.*

"Do you think I care if people like Walt Merwin, AC, Baskin, and your friends at Faber think I'm difficult? Fuck them. I wrote a few letters. Asking for help—reviews, publication, whatever. It's a man's world, Jack. You know that. I can't get anywhere without contacts. And without you, I've lost all my credibility. For what? For nothing." She takes a few breaths, forcing herself to calm down. "You've taken everything, and here I am practically next door to you, watching as you flaunt it in my face." She pauses, considering, then continues. "And that broadcast, that awful, awful play. What could you have been thinking?"

He looks at her, his brow furrowed. He's not angry, but confused.

"Viv? What are you talking about? What broadcast? What play?"

"The hare, Finn, and the smashed hare and the..." Her voice catches on a sob. She can barely continue. "They eat the hare."

She looks at him. His eyes are blank. He doesn't know. He honestly does not know what she's talking about. But then, suddenly, he does. "Shit."

"You thought that was my play, Viv? Oh my god. You heard Russell Park's broadcast last night, and you thought that was about us?"

"Of course you did. But, of course, you thought it was about you. The hare, the goddess, the chaste woman."

It occurs to Vivienne that he might be lying. Maybe he wrote the play and gave it to Russ Parks to produce. Jack and Russ were close friends, after all. With his connections, Jack could easily have made it happen. But why? Why would he want that? The answer comes lightning fast—publicity. Money and publicity. How many people tuned in to hear that trash? Thousands? Tens of thousands?

She steps back from him.

"No," she says. "No, I didn't mean that. I mean, yes, I thought so for a moment. But not really."

What was she saying? She was making no sense. Jack would report this to Dr. H. They would section her. She was acting crazy, paranoid. *Get it together, Vivienne. Get it together.* She wanted to ask him who the new woman was. Who was he seeing besides Bertina? Who was the goddess in the play? But she couldn't ask. He would say she was wrong, accuse her of being psychotic. It had happened before.

Suddenly, Jack changes. His shoulders slump, and he hangs his head. He might even be crying. This is the thing that hurts her—the thing he does, shifting gears, confusing her.

He falls onto the couch beside her, and she can feel the heat of his body. He's so sorry about the play. Of course, he didn't write it—it wasn't his play, and it had nothing to do with them or their marriage at all. But he's sorry she thought it did. She's right, he tells her. He doesn't deserve her. Doesn't deserve the family. He'll get out of the way if it will help her. He'll leave London. Perhaps leave England altogether. He might move north.

"Move?" Vivienne thinks. "Is that what he just said?" She sits away from him.

"With Bertina?" she asks, though she tells herself she shouldn't. When he doesn't answer, she explodes. Now she's screaming at him. "You were together over Christmas," she cries. "You and Bertina, I know it. You and your whore. While I sat alone with the children. Your children. Freezing and sick!"

Vivienne cannot calm down. Her breath is coming too hard, a sob is lodged in her throat. She's made a terrible mistake to show him even this bit of vulnerability. Her voice is brittle, her face flushed and swollen. Jack moves in to hold her, wrapping his arms around her.

"No, no, love," he whispers. "It wasn't like that."

He's lying. Vivienne knows he's lying, but she lets herself lean into him. Her cheek on the rough wool of his sweater, she closes her eyes and lets him rock her. She doesn't have the strength to push him away. Instead, she watches as the words spill from her mouth, beyond her control, each one dropping in twisting turns, doing their damage.

"Can we leave together? Get out of London with the babies, all of us? Can we try again? Please. Please."

"I don't know," he tells her. "I don't know."

More lies on top of lies.

She is wounding herself. The words catch in her like hooks, fighting for breath.

"But promise me," she says. "At least promise me we'll sit together next summer under the laburnum tree. Promise me."

"Yes, yes, yes," Jack tells her. "I promise." He drops the word to the floor, and Vivienne hungrily laps it up. But they both know she needs a different sort of god—one who could hold her in his bare hands while she burns through to the bone, while she quiets.

CHAPTER 94

PARALYTIC
7 February 1963

1

Vivienne paces the frozen floors of the flat, muttering to herself. There is no word for it—a woman alone with children. Not a widow. Not a divorcée. Just a woman who once had a husband and is now without a man. Unemployed, without prospects, rejected, alone, and frantic.

It is half-past five in the morning on Thursday, and she hasn't slept. She hasn't bathed in two days, and she is barefoot despite the cold, still wearing the clothes she had on when Jack came over. She cannot stop obsessing about this word that really should exist.

"Think," she says to herself, slamming her palm against the side of her head. "What could it be?"

She's scoured her thesaurus but has found no vocabulary to reflect a woman's status as both mother and abandoned wife. The term "abandoned mother" fails, blurring the identity of the actual abandoner. The mother could have been left by Santa Claus, for all that title implies. "Single mother" exonerates the father completely. No, Vivienne believes there ought to be another word—something akin to "widow" that implies the spouse's role in the complete fiasco.

The sleeping pills aren't working. Near dawn, Vivienne feels like she sees God—or it might be indigestion. She isn't sure. Either way, she leaves the children sleeping, goes out to the phone box, and calls Jack. She's never left the children before, but this time it feels essential. She's compelled to tell him her thoughts. He answers, despite the early hour.

"You must leave London," she says. "Within the fortnight. You must. I can no longer stand it. Promise me," she says, her lips pressed against the receiver, breathing in the stench of old cigarettes and other people's stale breath.

"I can't leave just now, Vivienne. I'm broke. Where would I go?" She knows he is lying; he'd said just recently he would go. Her anger flares.

"You must go! Now, just leave, leave!"

He promises he will, but then takes it back, saying he doesn't know how he can make it happen. This is how it always goes with Jack—back and forth, up and down, the truth elusive. Finally, when she no longer remembers why she came to call him, Vivienne hangs up. Her fingers are blue inside her mittens, her face stiff with ice.

2

Later in the morning, Dr. H. arrives, bringing more antidepressants, codeine, and sleeping pills. He expresses concern over the state of the flat. "The baby's playpen is filthy," he says.

"Yes, but we don't use it," Vivienne replies. She no longer puts the baby in there, though she hadn't noticed how disheveled it had become until the doctor pointed it out. "It is a bit shabby, isn't it?" she adds, thinking this might bolster her credibility as a mother.

"You don't use it?"

"I mean, not for the baby. It's just storage for toys now." She glances at it again. It's stained with food and urine. No toys in sight—she's made a misstep. Vivienne feels a bit confused. She's usually a fastidious person. Has she had guests? Messy ones? Maybe she's forgotten. She'll check the calendar after the doctor leaves. If so, she'll certainly never invite them back. The flat probably smells terrible, but she has no way of knowing. All her senses are dulled, numb. Except for pain. Is that a sense?

"Hm, I see," says Dr. H., his tone friendly, not judgmental. "Vivienne, I'm concerned." He looks directly at her, and she tries to hold his gaze, choosing an innocent, blinking expression. Maybe he won't notice she's terrified.

Which part is he worried about? she wonders. The messy flat? The crib? The mountainous piles of laundry? The children? Or is it her mind? Her soul? She wonders if he can see inside her brain, as if her skull is made of glass. Can he see everything breaking apart in there? She feels an urge to grab a towel or baby blanket and throw it over her head to block his view, to stop anyone from looking in. There has always been safety in darkness. Suddenly, a memory surfaces.

A long time ago, her head beneath an oversized cloth napkin.

"Don't worry about us, Doctor. We'll be alright. Especially with you stopping by every day," Vivienne says, managing a smile.

Dr. H. doesn't want to leave. He would feel much better if he could simply lock Vivienne up in an enormous brick building with tiny little rooms. Instead, he gently suggests she go to the hospital for "appropriate treatment." He also says he "isn't at all sure it's a good idea to wait until your appointment with the woman psychiatrist on Monday."

"That is five days away!"

If only Vivienne would agree, poor Dr. H. might be able to eat his supper tonight without gastritis and maybe even sleep. Worry clings to him like a heavy shawl, and Vivienne feels sorry for him. She assures him she'll be fine and hopes he enjoys his supper without any tummy troubles; she really does like him very much.

He gives up trying to convince her, laying a hand on her arm as they stand by the door. He makes her promise to take the medicines, get rest, and let the nanny do the work she's being paid to do.

Vivienne agrees to everything. She doesn't tell him that the nanny, a boy-crazy Belgian teenager, has already quit.

CHAPTER 95

KINDNESS
8 February 1963

1

Jack is outside Vivienne's Fitzroy flat, pounding on the door. "Vivienne, open the door, open the fucking door."

She waits a long time before opening it. Jack stares at her. She's dressed in her cleanup clothes: dungarees and one of his old work shirts over a black turtleneck sweater. Her hair is scraped back in a red bandana. She wears thick white socks, no shoes. Barefaced and so thin that when she caught sight of herself in the bathroom mirror this morning, she looked like a seriously unwell teenager.

Without a word, she turns and walks back inside, leaving the door open for him.

"Vivienne!" he's shouting now. "What the hell is this?"

He waves the letter in the air as if it's made of kryptonite. She ignores him, picking up the mop she was using when he arrived and resuming her mopping.

"Don't yell," she breathes. "I've got things to do. I need to finish cleaning before I go."

"Stop it." He snatches the mop from her hands. "Tell me what this is."

She stands still, looking at him. "It's a letter. I only mailed it today. I thought you'd get it tomorrow, after we'd gone."

This is true. Damn the London post. Usually unreliable, yet today, in the middle of a freeze, they deliver it within hours—much too efficient.

Jack reads the letter aloud: "Goodbye, my love. I'm ending everything. We're going away. Love, Vivienne."

He looks up at her. "So, what does this mean? What the hell does this mean?"

She says nothing, takes the note from him, walks to the stove, turns on the gas, ignites the flame, and sets the paper on fire. The edge glows orange, then red. A thin stream of smoke curls from one corner, and half the page is alight. She drops it into the sink. It strikes her as a shame that she's reached the age of thirty without appreciating the glee of watching things burn.

"Vivienne," he says. "Look at me. What is going on?"

"It means, Jack, I'm ending things with you. With us. And the children and I are going on a trip, Jack, that's all. For the weekend."

She gestures to the suitcase by the front door. He sees it, and she hears him exhale. He's calming down. She thinks she can almost hear the slowing bub-thrub, bub-thrub of his heart. Then, oddly, it occurs to her that it might slow to a stop. She's not sure if that's a good thought or a bad one. She makes a mental note to consider it later.

"Where are the children?"

"Jillian took them for the afternoon so I could prepare."

"Jillian?"

"Jillian Bolton. You don't know her. She's Barbara's friend."

Jack wants to protest her leaving the children with people they barely know, but Vivienne sees him stop himself. It would be unwise to question her parenting. Those who live in glass houses and so on.

"Alright," he says instead.

"The Boltons have been supportive, especially with the children. Now you need to go."

Jack glances around. The flat is in order today, though it smells peculiar. Vivienne knows it still harbors the odor—rotting fruit and old biscuits. She'd been unable to eliminate all of it. He likely senses the forced calm in her demeanor, too.

"I'll see the children next week, then?" he asks.

She says nothing, only picks up the mop and pushes it across the floor. It's then she realizes she's been mopping the same section of linoleum for the past hour. She glances at Jack from the corner of her eye. He hasn't noticed.

"Alright, then, Vivienne, I'll go. But I'll stop by later, just to check you're alright. Please take care."

Vivienne watches him go and thinks he means it. Jack means to come back, but he won't.

2

The Boltons' home feels unfamiliar. Jillian's face looks different, but Vivienne knows it must be Jillian because her husband is here, and Vivienne remembers him for some reason. He seems less changed.

Jillian is talking, "You're so thin, dear. Wouldn't you like something to eat? How about a rest? You look tired. I think you need rest." She's making pea soup, chiding her husband, sending her older children out, ordering everyone about. But she smells wrong—bitter and noxious. The place feels cold, and their faces are filled with mysterious, unreadable expressions. It's like being onstage in a play Vivienne half-remembers but can't quite place.

But Vivienne will stay. She promised Dr. H., whose Friday morning assessment—"your condition has sharply deteriorated"—left her little choice. He could section her, legally forcing her into the hospital if she didn't follow orders.

Yes, she'd told him. She would spend the weekend with friends. And yes, she'd agreed to see the new psychiatrist first thing Monday.

Jillian sits down in a hideous overstuffed chair across from Vivienne. Vivienne, knees drawn to her chin, sits in an identical chair, except someone had the sense to cover its dreadful gladiola pattern with a gray afghan. Vivienne wonders why she hadn't noticed before that everything in the Bolton home was *too much*: spaces crowded with chintzy florals, poofy pillows, and ornate furniture. Even the smells compete: thick lemon and warm cherry wood. Why does everything have to be *something*? Too many, too much, too loud. *This house could make a person crazy*, Vivienne thinks, and laughs.

Jillian brings tea again, setting it on the table beside Vivienne.

"That one," Jillian points to the cup in Vivienne's hand, "has gone cold." She pauses, adding, "I'm just so worried about you."

Vivienne lets her gaze drift around the room, then out the picture window. The winter trees are still there, but they look different. She tries to count them, but the scene is vague, the trees like hollow staffs set into crumbling whiteness. She might blink, and they'd disappear.

"He still loves me, and if it weren't for that barren bitch—that Munich whore—our family would never have fallen apart."

Vivienne hears herself speaking with a British accent. It sounds nice. She continues.

"And now what is it? Now I must watch while they live the high life. Here and there they go, and I'm tied to poverty. Her, with her big blue eyes and lovely face and a hundred abortions. Did you know that about her? It's all true, of course." She's raving again. "Where did I put my pills?"

"Drink your tea, Vivienne," says Jillian. "God, you look terrible. How many of those pills have you taken?"

Vivienne ignores the question. She's on a roll.

"And you know who else I despise? My sister-in-law. Phyllis. An awful name, don't you think? Phyllis, philanderer, phillumenist—that's a person who collects matchbooks. Did you know that? And philistine—that's her, a hypocrite. Thinks she's an artist, but she's nothing of the sort." Vivienne pauses to take a breath. "I suppose there's philanthropic and philharmonic, but—" she waves her hand dismissively. "Very strange. She doesn't have children either, but I don't think it's for the same reasons. I think she's in love with Jack. Disgusting, I know, but true. They slept in the same bed, until some awful age. Jack's mother told me—way beyond appropriate." Vivienne sees Jillian's eyebrow raise. She's hit a nerve. "The mother. I hate her too. It's fair, though. They hate me. Most people do, but they're rarely honest about it. They won't go around telling you how much they dislike you. Imagine if people were completely honest all the time." This strikes Vivienne as hilarious, and she can't stifle a laugh.

"That's not true, Vivienne. A lot of people adore you."

Vivienne looks at Jillian, then around the cluttered, overheated room.

"What would a person even do with all those matchbook covers, Jillian? Some phillumenists only keep the labels, those tiny bits of paper scraped off the top of the matchbox. What would you do with all of that? Build something? A tiny colorful teepee, perhaps?" She smiles. "It's a lovely word, though. Phil-lu-men-ist. Don't you think?"

Vivienne stops. Her lips feel strange, swollen and slow, as if they're not keeping up with her thoughts. She has the urge to move her lips with her fingers but knows this won't help her credibility. Instead, she sits on her hands. Jillian raises her eyebrows.

"Vivienne, how many of those pills have you been taking?"

"Pills?" Vivienne asks, vaguely. "Do you mean my pep pills? They're for sleep."

"Why would you have something peppy for sleep?"

Vivienne shrugs. "That's what Dr. H calls them. I've no idea. But I'm fine, really." She coughs. "Oh, besides, pep is good for a girl." She repeats the word. "Pep. Pep. Peppy." She drops the accent; "peppy" is better in American.

"You're not fine. You're sick. Your children are sick, too. They have fevers and runny noses. What does Dr. H think about that?"

Vivienne doesn't like Jillian's tone. In fact, she's beginning to suspect this person who doesn't smell like Jillian might not be Jillian at all.

"Leave Dr. H alone. He's a wonderful doctor. He's doing his best. But we've all been sick all winter." She pauses. "Or all my life, maybe. I've been sick all my life, did you know that? I learned that in 1953. That's ten years ago now. All my life."

Her words tumble out faster than she can organize them, and Vivienne is aware she might sound a little mad. She bites her tongue, literally, to stop the flow.

"I don't want to argue with you, darling. But you're exhausted. You have awful gray circles under your eyes, and you don't look well at all. So go upstairs and rest, alright?"

Vivienne thinks that's a good idea. She goes upstairs and lies down on the bed, but she can't sleep. Instead, she stares at the ceiling, thinking terrible thoughts about the future. She doesn't imagine the distant future, as people often do when they can't sleep. Instead, she obsesses over the very near future—the less-than-two-days-away future. Dr. H. has planned for a live-in nurse to care for the children. He's arranged for a psychiatrist to evaluate Vivienne at the London Psychiatric Institution, not at his private office.

She knew what Dr. H. meant by all of that. He was sugar-coating the truth. If she didn't go voluntarily, he would section her on Monday. Back to the loony bin. Back to the hangman.

CHAPTER 96

TOTEM
9 February 1963

1

It's Jillian's husband who says it first.

"She's leaving him. That's what I heard. Finally leaving that Canadian husband of hers. What I can't understand is why the man tolerated her behavior all this time."

Jillian flings out a leg and kicks him under the breakfast table, but it's too late.

Vivienne pushes her chair back, stumbles down the hall, and makes it to the bathroom just in time to throw up.

2

In the afternoon, they go to the zoo. They take all the children, including Jillian's teenagers. It's a brisk, beautiful day—the first in a long time—and they bring a picnic to eat on the hill overlooking the zoo. Jillian brings red wine, and Vivienne drinks several glasses, although she vaguely recalls Dr. H. warning her against mixing red wine with her new antidepressant. She's been coughing and taking the flu tonic Dr. H gave her, and she doubled her dose of sleeping pills the previous night. This left her groggy this morning, prompting her to increase the pep pills. Jillian—this new, watchful Jillian— gives Vivienne that strange, slightly suspicious look a few times, and

Vivienne reminds herself to keep quiet. Talking too much is apparently a bad idea when trying to mask one's fractured mental state.

For a few hours, Vivienne feels blissfully numb, forgetting why she's been so worried. *Divorce,* she thinks. *Divorce is the only answer.* Staying married to a lying, cheating, whoring cad is out of the question. So, get on with it. She feels proud of herself for solving the problem and spends the rest of the afternoon floating through the world on the back of a unicorn.

Vivienne is certain her friends remain unaware of her chemical assistance through the afternoon. But when it's time to leave, she finds that walking while talking is challenging. She stumbles on her way to the car, and the cat, as they say, is out of the bag.

Back at the Boltons, Vivienne sleeps deep into the night. When she wakes, it's still dark, and a thousand-pound weight sits on her chest. She can hear the voices of her executioners reverberating through the walls, and the grim terror of what is coming crashes down around her.

CHAPTER 97

CONTUSION
10 February 1963

1

"Viv, what are you doing? You've been up all night. We could hear you. Calling him. Repeatedly."

It's Jillian. She's standing in the guest room, wearing a pink silk, Japanese-style kimono nightgown with enormous blue lotus blossoms. She's holding yet another cup of tea, this one in a bright yellow mug—and giving Vivienne that look again. Vivienne thinks Jillian is far too colorful for this hour of the morning.

"What does it look like I'm doing? I must go." She resumes shoving the few pieces of clothing she brought into her suitcase.

"Vivienne, please. You're not well."

Vivienne thinks that if one more person tells her she's not well, she will kill them. She will stick the nearest sharp object straight into their eye. That goes for Jillian if she repeats the words. Vivienne glances around for something sharp.

"Just leave me alone; I need to get home. I have washing to do. Things to do for Agatha."

Jillian wisely doesn't repeat, "You are not well." Instead, she says, "Okay, okay. We'll drive you, but maybe you should leave the children here, Viv. Also, this calling Jack at all hours—don't you think you should stop all that?"

Vivienne whirls on her. "First, no, my children are not staying here, and second, Jack is going to marry that bitch. *Your husband said it!* She's free to get married now. What do you expect me to do?"

Vivienne squeezes her eyes shut, as if she can somehow push the words back into her mouth. She needs to stay quiet. It might have been better to stick a pencil into Jillian's eye. There are three pencils on the desk right next to her.

As expected, Jillian starts up. "Viv, we just think...."

Vivienne isn't listening. She is packing and leaving. First, though, she'll need to find all her medicines. She's missed a few pills already this morning.

2

At the flat, there's another letter from Mother, offering help, offering money she doesn't have, begging Vivienne to return to America. Mother doesn't understand—there is nothing in America. Things would be worse there. She knows no one. No one in the literary world. She would be that thing with no name—a woman with children and no man. Not even a career. Vivienne will write back later. Right now, she's too tired.

3

Vivienne's body feels thick and slow, as if she's moving through a giant tub of molasses. She feeds the children mashed potatoes, soft pasta, and carrots from the containers Jillian sent home with them. She'll have to figure out getting more food later. But right now, her head hurts. Every movement requires herculean effort. She lies on the floor while the baby plays with blocks, and Agatha scribbles on the wall with a red crayon.

After lunch, Dr. H stops by. He studies her. Vivienne can see what he sees—her weird, vacant distress, her sickness looking back at him. What is there for him to do but what he's preparing to do?

"I understand," Vivienne says.

"I'm glad," he replies. "You will be safe," he adds. "I promise. The nurse will take care of the children, and it's an excellent hospital."

"I know," she says.

"I'm glad," he repeats.

Dr. H checks her pill and tonic supply. Vivienne shows him she's run out of the pep pills, but Dr. H says that's alright because he wants her to sleep more, so he doesn't give her any more. He tells her he'll be back tomorrow morning.

4

Jack appears beneath the streetlights like an apparition. His outline is blurred, but his voice is unmistakable.

"Viv, please," he says. There's no pleading in his tone—only a simmering rage. "It's the middle of the night; you got me here; what is it?"

Shivering in the cold, Vivienne stands outside her flat. In a dome of plum sky, the moon is a pale disc, casting an eerie glow. She feels a jolt of fear as she studies him, uncertain if she had, in fact, invited him here. His refusal to come inside only adds to her agitation.

She narrows her eyes, trying to make sure he's real. His coat bunches and strains at the underarms and side seams, his pale hands hidden behind his back. In this light, he could be wearing a straitjacket. The thought makes her smile, but the movement on her face is imperceptible to him.

"This is ridiculous, all these hysterics. I won't have it, not again," Jack says.

Vivienne thinks, yes, he's real.

He turns, as if to leave, and finally, she makes her mouth move. "I want you to give me back what you took."

She senses, rather than sees, him tense up.

"For God's sake, Vivienne, what are you talking about?"

"My life, Jack. You took everything. How can you not see it?"

She's on the verge of losing control, her throat tight with unspoken words that feel like rocks lodged inside.

"You're doing it again, Vivienne—acting crazy, trying to punish me," he says, taking a step toward her. His face glows beneath the gaslights, but his voice softens. "Look, you need rest. I can see how tired you are. Dr. H. called me. He says you're not sleeping. Go on in; I'll come round tomorrow. How's that?"

There are icy tears on her cheeks, though she doesn't feel the cold. "Just tell me something, Jack," she says.

He sighs. "What is it, Vivienne?"

"Was I wrong?"

"About what?"

"All of it."

He hesitates for a long time. Then, turning away, Vivienne catches a faint whiff of *her*—the unmistakable scent lingering on him. She can't stop herself. "Was I ever wrong? All those times you said I was."

He heads down the step, striding toward his car, and finally glances back. "No, Vivienne. You were never wrong."

Her boots crack against the iced pavement as she heads back up to the flat. Though temperatures are rising in London, the city remains coated in ice, with hills of snow everywhere. Silence wraps around her, broken only by a faint whirring that might be a distant car. A hazy mist hovers over Primrose Hill, and Vivienne feels a peculiar, settled calm.

She lets the heavy outer door swing shut behind her before making her way upstairs to her sleeping children. There is much to accomplish before morning.

CHAPTER 98

EDGE
11 February 1963

1

Technically, it's early morning, but not nearly close enough to daylight to excuse what Vivienne is about to do. She feels terribly rude as she knocks on her downstairs neighbor's door.

She waits, then knocks again. Vivienne and the Professor have seen each other hundreds of times, but now, standing at the door in his pajamas, he looks older than she'd thought. Gray hair sticking up around his face, knobby feet shoved into threadbare slippers. Behind him, she notices his apartment is full of neat stacks of books—dozens, maybe hundreds. She wonders if she's looked at him before without really seeing him.

"I'm sorry, I'm very sorry. Do you have any stamps?"

"What?" He's visibly irritated, looking at her as if she's lost her mind.

"Postage. Any postage stamps?"

"Vivienne, do you know what time it is?"

She jumps a little at the sound of her name. He says it kindly. "Not really, no. I'm so sorry to bother you, but it's an emergency."

"A postage stamp emergency?"

It sounds ridiculous when he says it that way. But in her mind, the plan had seemed entirely plausible. She scrambles to salvage the situation.

"Yes, well, I have some letters that absolutely must go out with the morning post, and I just discovered I'm out of stamps. It'll be a disaster if I don't get them out. Do you see?"

His expression shows that he does *not* see and, in fact, suspects she's slightly unhinged, but he steps back to let her in. Suddenly, Vivienne realizes he isn't surprised at all. He's thought she was unwell for a long time.

"Yes, alright. Come in."

She declines, staying at the door while he retrieves the stamps.

"I must pay you," she says, fishing in her coat pocket for change.

"Later," he says, trying to close the door.

"No, no," she insists. "I wouldn't feel right." She pushes the money into his hand. He looks confused, now a little more concerned, but he accepts the coins. "And—can I ask what time you go to work?"

He shrugs, apparently giving up on making sense of her motives. "Uh," he stammers, running a hand through his thinning hair, "I'm up at eight and usually out before nine."

"Thank you so much. Goodnight." She turns quickly before he can say anything more or reach out to stop her.

Behind her, he calls out, a bit unsure, "Well, goodnight, Vivienne."

2

Vivienne's mind is clear light. She is moving with the same frustrating sluggishness, but her physical body is no longer relevant. There is only the quickly vanishing space of her mind and the one thought within it. She has one thing to do. She's done it before. It is an art, like everything else. She does it exceptionally well.

She is an Olympic diver, toes curled around the edge of the board, heels up, arms up, back arched, ready to fly.

3

Water in a rushing river suddenly becomes a narrow creek and then a tiny eddy. The droplets are forced to wait their turn as the banks narrow and the bottom comes up to meet the surface, pocked and bobbled by smoothed pebbles, twigs, and leaves. Rivulets now, barely moving at all.

She watches her feet as they step lightly across the squares of kitchen flooring. One... two... three.

She hasn't slept. Not last night and not the one before that. Not for a hundred nights. She doesn't sleep anymore. Her body has turned to a husk—dry and without needs, except for one last request.

4

Vivienne sees to the children first. She has left the letter to America in the post—Beanie and his lovely new wife will receive it in time to handle things. To take care of the children. Now, she fills small cups with milk and places them near the cots, careful not to wake them. She allows herself one lingering glance but does not kiss them. That part is done. It is time to let go.

She cracks open all the windows in the room, worrying for a moment that it might get too cold. *But it won't be long,* she decides. Stepping out, she shuts the door. In the short hallway, there's a roll of silver tape and a stack of rags. Vivienne stuffs the rags into the doorjamb and the space beneath the door, then runs tape all around to secure the cloth. The work is tiring, and the ache in her shoulders surprises her. Stepping back, she inspects her work. She is satisfied; the gas won't reach the babies, at least not for some time. Just enough time.

5

It is morning now and bright in the tiny kitchen. Sunlight bounces off the chrome surface of the toaster, and she blinks and shields her eyes. Timing is important. The babies are still asleep, but not for much longer. The new nurse will arrive within a few hours, and the downstairs neighbor will be awake for work and hear them if they cry. This must be finished before they wake up, but not so soon that they are left alone long enough to be afraid.

It takes less time to secure the kitchen after she's had practice in the children's room. The silver tape rolls easily between her fingers, and the rags fit together effortlessly around the doors and windows. *I could do this for a living*, she thinks, smiling at the irony.

When it's done, Vivienne removes her sweater and drops it to the floor. However, she does not remove her shoes to expose her bare feet. These are good shoes. They have come so far with her. Someone might like the shoes and, if she's wearing them, they'll be easily found. So, yes, she'll wear the shoes.

She turns the oven knobs full up but does not light the pilot, then pulls open the heavy steel door. It makes the familiar creaking sound, and she thinks suddenly of roast. She'll be a roast. That's funny, but of course, not true since there will be no heat. Perhaps others would not find it funny.

Your sense of humor can be so macabre, Vivienne. Can't you write about lighter things? The blood jet of poetry is hushed now. Yeats comes to her mind, flowing easy as water through an empty pipe.

And you would murmur tender words…though you have the will of wild birds.

She kneels, her housedress shifts up around her thighs, and the vinyl tiles are chilly and terribly hard beneath her knees. *If men were cooks, kitchens would have carpets.* She places two carefully folded dishtowels inside the oven's surface. Why experience the discomfort of metal racking on one's face as one dies? She turns her unlined face to the left, towards morning, and presses her cheek into the softness of the towel. She closes her eyes and inhales the fumes into her lungs.

One…two…three.

CHAPTER 99

Ruthie Hampton

I was there that day. I'm not entirely sure who called me—maybe the police. It just happened I'd arrived in London a few hours earlier. The small flat was crowded with police officers and a few of Viv's friends. Barbara Campion was there, along with Vivienne's new friend, Jillian something-or-other, and her husband. A few others I didn't recognize. People mumbled to one another, whispering as they do in a museum or a cemetery.

I stood at the threshold, my heart pounding, trying to make sense of the tragedy. Viv, my dearest friend, was gone, and the weight of her absence was suffocating.

When I arrived, they had already taken Viv's body away. Despite the crowd, the flat felt hollow, devoid of her vibrant energy. I wandered through the rooms, each step echoing with memories.

The kitchen was cordoned off with police tape. Someone told me it happened in there, but I already knew. She'd gassed herself—that's what they were saying. Such a horrible thing to say, even if it was true. In the coming days, I would say it and write it more times than I could count. In my journal, poems, and letters, and in the telegrams, I would send to friends. "Vivienne gassed herself on Monday morning." I was never good at finding words of comfort.

Then he arrived, The Poet. They found him at 112 Sidney Street. He had gone there with his new lover to escape Vivienne's calls. Bertina gave the police his number, and a special inspector called him with the news.

He burst through the front door, his face flushed and breathless, as if he had run the entire way. He was always larger than life, but now he seemed even more imposing, like the center of a storm that had uprooted our lives. I don't know what compelled me, but I confronted him, my voice shaking with anger and grief.

"Where the hell were you?" I demanded, my words sharp and accusatory. He stared at me, his eyes wide, filled with a pain that mirrored my own. It was as if I had slapped him—the shock and hurt etched across his face.

Later, I would learn that he had gone to the Merwin's after receiving the news. He'd wanted to see the children, he said, to break the news to them in person. They were both alright, their faces a little swollen from hours of early morning crying, he said, but otherwise too young to understand what had happened and physically unharmed.

A pang of guilt twisted in my stomach. Maybe I should have done that. Maybe, in my grief, I had been too quick to judge. But in that moment, all I felt was rage and betrayal.

Seeking solace, I wandered upstairs to Viv's study and stepped inside, closing the door behind me. Her scent lingered there, despite the open windows—sweet, like apples and talc. Vivienne had hung floor-length drapes at the south-facing windows, blue velvet, very dramatic. They were pulled back to allow the sunlight to stream in. Viv had always loved the theatrical effect of big draperies. It was odd for a woman with such a clean, well-edited aesthetic. The walls were painted a sharp white in contrast. She'd hung one painting—a cubist-style rendering of two women seated in a garden. The wood floors were polished and bare.

The room, I could tell, was a sanctuary, filled with her books, notes, and smelling of her favorite candles. I traced my fingers along the spines of her books, lingering over titles that spoke of dreams and adventures we had often discussed.

On her desk, I found a diary, its pages filled with her thoughts and feelings. As I read, tears streamed down my face. She had been struggling, and I had been too blind to see it. In her last entries, she spoke of a darkness that had engulfed her, a pain that she could no longer bear.

Viv was more than just a friend; she was a force of nature, a brilliant mind with a gift for words that touched the deepest corners of the soul. As I sat in her study, surrounded by the remnants of her creativity, I was struck by the *profound greatness of her writing. Each piece of paper, each notebook, was a testament to her genius, filled with stories and thoughts that were uniquely hers.*

I was looking for something, although I wasn't sure what.

But then, there it was. Just beside a small vase that held a cluster of dying purple pansies, I found a stack of unfastened pages, neatly squared. This was the work of Vivienne's last months—the howling, terrible, beautiful truth. On the first sheet, across the middle in simple font, she had typed the words:

FABULOUS BEASTS: A Love Story.

I picked up the stack and sank into Vivienne's chair. I ran one finger across the first page and then carefully peeled it back. Like the layers of an onion, the pages came away, layer by layer. I read of Cambridge and Swedish hair and a red bandana and Spain, a cottage on the beach, a wide wooden table, fevers, birth, and azaleas in a cemetery. I closed my eyes and saw a blue flannel suit and a thousand daffodils. I saw her at 112 Sidney Street on her wedding night, her smile wide, a fine line scar beneath her eye. I saw her at work in this study, head bent over this old green typewriter, small fingers flying like tiny ferocious birds. And in the silence that grew around me until it was as deep and still as the waters of Loch Morar, I heard her. I heard Vivienne Holland, and I knew.

Jack would never be able to give this work the grace and attention it deserved.

Viv's writing was her way of making sense of the world, of grappling with her own demons. It was a lifeline, a means of expressing the inexpressible, of finding meaning in the chaos. Her words were her legacy, a gift to the world that would endure long after she was gone.

As I closed the manuscript, I felt a deep sense of loss but also profound gratitude for having known Viv. Her writing reflected her soul, a soul that was beautiful, flawed, and endlessly fascinating.

Viv's greatness lay not just in her talent but in her ability to touch the lives of those around her, to inspire and to move. Her words were a beacon, a reminder of the power of storytelling and the enduring strength of the human spirit. I packed up that last journal and the manuscript and took them with me. I would wait for the right time and the right person and turn them over only then. And as I left her study, I carried with me the knowledge that Viv's light would never truly fade, for it lived on forever in every word she had written.

PART TEN

Morning Song
1939

In 1939, Vivienne Holland is six years old, down at the sea wall alone for the first time. Last night's storm was big and brutal, but it's left the day still and bright, with sunbeams—white as lightning—hitting the beach and dazzling her eyes. Best of all, it's kept the adults busy cleaning up broken furniture, downed trees, and piles of junk blown in from the sea, leaving no one to notice as she snuck away.

She's climbed down the wall and walks carefully across the sand, feeling the warm powder nuzzle between her toes. She pauses now and then to examine a broken mussel shell, a tuft of kelp, or a piece of smooth sea glass, placing each back where she found it.

Finally, she reaches the water's edge. Grammy doesn't know she's here—not yet—and the thrill of that secret bubbles inside her, mixed with a hint of fear. Her time here is limited, which only makes it sweeter. For now, she is the Sea Queen, ruling over everything she sees and beyond: as steadfast as the seawall, boundless as the ocean, utterly invincible. She smiles and wades ankle-deep into the turquoise water, letting the gentle waves splash against the hem of her dress. Soon, she'll be too wet to deny what she's done, but she doesn't care. A tiny wave rolls toward her, soaking her dress to the waist, then another and another. She takes one more step until the water is up to her thighs. She closes her eyes, lifts her arms to the sky, and raises her face to the brilliant light.

A larger wave rolls toward her, but she doesn't see it. Grinning, her heart swells as she licks the salty sea spray from her lips, utterly free.

The End

About the Author

WA Schwartz is a psychiatrist and novelist, raised in the US and the UK. She studied literature at UC Davis and novel writing at Stanford and was a ballet dancer until entering med school. Earning an M.D., she specializes in helping women with severe psychiatric illness, depression, and a history of childhood and adult betrayal trauma. When not helping patients or writing, she travels extensively and enjoys yoga, long daily walks, and the roses and tomatoes in her garden. She loves to sew and quilt but hates to cook, something, thankfully, her husband does well. She has three grown children and lives in Northern California with her English lab, Scarlett.

"An intelligent, fast-paced thriller with well-drawn sympathetic, flawed characters and authentic southern Louisiana atmosphere. A great read-into-late night novel."
—Martha, Goodreads Reviewer
EDEN
W.A. SCHWARTZ

Note from W.A. Schwartz

Word-of-mouth is crucial for any author to succeed. If you enjoyed *Fabulous Beasts*, please leave a review online—anywhere you are able. Even if it's just a sentence or two. It would make all the difference and would be very much appreciated.

Thanks!
W.A. Schwartz

We hope you enjoyed reading this title from:

www.blackrosewriting.com

Subscribe to our mailing list – *The Rosevine* – and receive **FREE** books, daily deals, and stay current with news about upcoming releases and our hottest authors.
Scan the QR code below to sign up.

Already a subscriber? Please accept a sincere thank you for being a fan of Black Rose Writing authors.

View other Black Rose Writing titles at
www.blackrosewriting.com/books and use promo code
PRINT to receive a **20% discount** when purchasing.